UNDEAD WORLDS 2

A POST-APOCALYPTIC ZOMBIE ANTHOLOGY

THE REANIMATED WRITERS   RYAN COLLEY
JUSTIN ROBINSON   VALERIE LIOUDIS
JESSICA GOMEZ   JOSHUA C. CHADD
R.L. BLALOCK   R.J. SPEARS   GRIVANTE
LC CHAMPLIN   ARTHUR MONGELLI
DIA COLE   ALATHIA PARIS MORGAN
RICH RESTUCCI   JAVAN BONDS
EE ISHERWOOD

Cover Design By
CHRISTIAN BENTULAN

CONTENTS

INTRODUCTION

Welcome back to Undead Worlds!

If you're new, here's what Undead Worlds is all about. Undead Worlds is the flagship publication of The Reanimated Writers and it features brand new short stories from each author's zombie-filled universe. It gives you a chance to check out what they are all about and decide if you want to read more of their work.

In Undead Worlds 2 we have a mix of new and returning authors. Some of our returning authors have continued their stories from Undead Worlds 1 and others have completely new tales to share. This year we have a great mix and believe there is something in here for every zompoc lover to enjoy!

If you missed out on Undead Worlds 1, you can now grab it for free at your favorite ebook retailer here!

We want to give a special thank you to a trio of individuals who were the winning bidders in our Kill-Starter Fan Auction. These folks donated big money to help us fund this project and we are very grateful! So grateful in fact, that we killed them all, in some cases multiple times! Be on the lookout for their names throughout Undead Words 2 as they die gruesome deaths!

Thank you to

Douglas Kay-Fraser

Neal Smead

&

Jacinda Yotti

Lastly, if you enjoy zombie stories, you may want to come join the companion group on Facebook to hangout with the authors and fellow fans, you can find us at

https://www.facebook.com/groups/reanimatedwriters/

or on the web at www.reanimatedwriters.com

Kevin M. Penelerick
Reanimated Writers Founder

1
———

LA PETITE MORT

BY RYAN COLLEY

La Petite Mort. That is the name of the restaurant that exists at the end of times. *My* restaurant. It's French for "The Little Death", modern use describing the sensation of an orgasm. Beautiful and deadly. I felt it was an appropriate name for my restaurant. After all, how else would you describe making well-known cuisine at the end of the world?

I wasn't an amazing chef, not even before the dead started walking. I wasn't even a good chef, but I knew how to use an oven and what seasoning worked well with which food. I knew how to season meat, and that is all I felt I needed to know. Meat, I believe, is the cornerstone of any decent meal. However, the patrons of my failing pre-apocalypse restaurant didn't see it that way. They wanted vegetarian options, or even *vegan* options. Well, now that people are living among the dead, they don't get much choice when it comes to their dietary wants and needs. They are thankful for meat, tasty meat – nice cuts of meat. Not that meat is so freely available during the end times, not to the everyday survivor anyway. But, if you're like me, you know how to get it. And that is how I succeeded as a chef in the new world, my dream finally realized. When the dead started to walk, eliminating most of the life on the planet, not many industries survived – and even fewer people who knew how to operate those industries lived. A lot of professions became redundant. This all benefitted me of course, as the restaurant industry was one that became non-existent. Celebrity chefs died. Michelin Star restaurants disappeared. Even readymade dinners went away. So, someone as mediocre at cooking as myself no longer had any competition. I thrived. Don't get me wrong, I'm not saying my cooking got better during the end of the world – although I definitely got more creative – but my customers didn't exactly have a myriad of choice either. When there are very few options out there for people to choose from, you make a name for yourself.

I remember the first time I cooked for someone during the apocalypse – not as a restaurant owner but it was definitely a preface for it. I had been out scavenging, trying to find something to make myself a decent meal. I had found some roadkill – amazingly still a thing in the post-apocalypse. It wasn't a lot, but a couple squirrels were more than enough to satiate my hunger. On the way back I was forced to take an alternate route. My normal path seemed a lot more active with the undead than usual, and a quick journey back wasn't worth the level of risk. As I was not familiar with my new path, I took my time returning to ensure I was careful. I looked for paths that I could take if I needed to make a quick escape or detour from the living or undead, both were just as much a threat as the other. Being hyperaware of my surroundings, I noticed a rosemary bush growing on a bit of public greenspace – or it would have been public greenspace if that was still a thing. I took several sprigs from it and made a mental note of where the bush was – herbs were hard to come by and a living herb in the city was like gold dust. If the cuttings I took didn't grow when I planted them, I would always have the original bush.

I wasn't one for taking risks; I always tried to be careful when I left the safety of my home. I avoided the undead and the living alike – I wasn't much of a fighter and had only survived through cunning. However, on that day, the stars aligned in a peculiar way. Maybe it was the scent of the roadkill, or maybe I had gotten lax with my own safety when I spotted the herb. Regardless of the reason, a lone zombie wandered out from one of the many destitute buildings that I had strayed to close too. It wasn't a particularly fresh zombie, so it couldn't move very quickly. Nonetheless, the decrepit husk made its way towards me. You couldn't avoid the undead in the new world, but spotting them before they saw me was key to my survival. On that occasion, the zombie had seen me first. I should have smelled it immediately, but I was too busy rolling the herb between my fingers and inhaling the aroma. The ghoul was nearly on me by the time I'd realised what was happening, but I couldn't move. I mentally and physically couldn't run. People always say you have a "flight or fight" response to danger. They never mention the third "F", which a lot more people do, and it's exactly what I did. I just ... froze. I just stopped in my tracks and stared, mouth agape and trembling. I didn't know what to do! Shockingly, considering I had survived for so long, I hadn't needed to kill one of the undead before. Hell, I hadn't killed anything before. Not even an animal. It was the reason I never served lobster in my restaurant! I just couldn't bring myself to kill.

The zombie continued to shuffle towards me. Hand outstretched and its own mouth a hungry maw on its ragged and grey face. Its clothes hung from it, misshapen, filthy and torn. The zombie was almost beyond recognition as having once been male or female – the tell-tale sign being the bra that hung from its shoulder. A ripped breast was exposed, and that only held on due to a few slivers of vein and stretched flesh, supported and resting on the loose bra. Its belly was swollen, distended and full of flesh that would never be digested. It would only be a matter of time before the lining of its stomach was pushed beyond its limits and tore, depositing the malodorous gore onto the ground – would the zombie move on, or see it as a new meal and feast again? That, or it would be forced through the entire digestive tract by the consumption of more muscle and tissue, exiting the same way all human waste did. At least, that's what I hoped had caused the distension. The alternative was an unborn child that had never been given a chance in the world. A stillborn forever resting in the body of unlife that carried it. The zombie still made heavy, uncoordinated steps towards me. Its body swayed and moved to some unheard and macabre song that all the undead seemed to hear – the call of the flesh. *My flesh.* It came, as if I was the one who sung the siren song and her rotten form was the lustful sailor being pulled to its doom. I was as good as dead – I didn't have the mental or physical fortitude to save myself. I had given in to my fate, unwillingly but resigned nonetheless.

Then someone appeared, as if they had answered my silent and fearful prayers. He seemed to materialise from the shadows, as if he had stepped out of the wall like some sort of ethereal being entering our world. How long had he been there? Had he been watching me the entire time? Did he mean me harm? In that moment, none of it mattered. Whether I died by the hand of the undead or the man, I was just happy that I may have had a few moments extra of life.

The stranger wore dark clothes, stained with cruor. From a sheath on his belt, he produced a large kitchen knife. He moved quickly and silently, each step methodically executed. The zombie didn't even see him coming. He stalked the creature, closing in swiftly. He was no more than an arm's reach away from the undead woman when he placed a hand gently on her shoulder, holding the creature steadfast. Before it had chance to react, his other hand thrust the knife into the base of its skull and through its neck. It didn't burst through the throat as I expected, but the zombie collapsed heavily in a heap on the ground. I stared in shock as the man casually wiped his knife off on his trousers. My eyes fell to the zombie on the floor, its own eyes watching me back and mouth forming a snarling motion. At first I thought it was going through its death throes, a repeated motion as dying electrical impulses scattered along its nervous system. That was before I realised its eyes were moving back and forth between the mysterious man and myself. It was still cognisant! I stared with morbid curiosity – I had never had a chance to observe one of the undead so closely – but that didn't last long. The man raised his foot and slammed the heel onto the head. He did this again, and again, and again – until the eyes no longer moved and the rest of the head was pulp. I just stared at the man, dumbfounded as he began walking towards me.

"Th-thank you!" I stammered out. The hulking figure continued in my direction. I couldn't help but think I would die in that moment.

"No problem," he replied gruffly and simply, sheathing his knife and continuing by me. And that was it. I didn't die. He didn't even make an attempt on my life. All the fear and anxiety dissipated and I felt like I owed him.

"Let me cook for you!" I exploded suddenly. He stopped

midstride and my heart leapt into my throat. *Why did I say that?* Then there was a long pause that hung in the air like the fetid stink emanating from the corpse on the ground.

"Ok," he finally said. He then turned to face me, waiting for me to lead the way, and I did.

I lead the man back to where I had been living – an old restaurant. Not my pre-apocalypse restaurant, but it had been someone's. I disarmed the trap that I always set up before leaving, being careful to obscure my technique to the man – in case he chose to come back and kill me later, as opposed to killing me then and there. I showed him through the door and shut it behind us. We were in a corridor entrenched with shadow – it had been a staff entrance once upon a time. My hand reached out and found a flashlight I had hung from the wall – it was an instinctive action. I unhooked it, clicking it on and waiting for the light to flicker to life. Once it was fully illuminated, I guided our way through the darkness and into the kitchen. There were many clean, stainless steel sinks and ovens. The pots and pans hung meticulously and not a single one was out of place. Cutlery and utensils polished and in their appropriate location. Of course, they weren't clean when I found my way into the kitchen originally. Rotten food and stagnant water was everywhere. Meals that had once been mid-creation and in the process of being cooked. Dead and undead in the kitchen. Broken glass on every surface. Well, it just needed some love and care! After I guided the undead out and lost them in the streets, I made my way back to the kitchen and moved the corpses outside. It wasn't an easy task, they were heavy and cumbersome and I couldn't decide where to leave them either. Once all corpses, walking and stationary, had been removed I had to focus on cleaning the kitchen. Luckily, the power and water was still operational at that point, so it wasn't an issue. Loading up dishwashers over and over again while scrubbing the surfaces using a healthy dose of elbow grease got the place up to my standard. It was an impressive feat and only took a few days – I happily hide away from the madness on the streets. The real irony was that the moment the kitchen was spotless, the power went out and the water soon followed. I had spent so long making everything pristine, that I didn't even get chance to use it. To say I was disappointed was an understatement. I had to eat everything cold and uncooked. Not long after, I found a generator and the fuel needed to operate it. I hooked it up to the duel plug-in hob I found at a travel store and used that to prepare my own food going forward. So much beautiful equipment around me and I couldn't use any of it. It was the chef equivalent of riding a bicycle around a racetrack designed for a Lamborghini, but it was where I would live. Sometime later I would find a much bigger and better generator to operate more of the kitchen. I could have found a hundred other places to call my home and survive. Places with more secure doors and windows. Somewhere with fewer problems. Less undead and less bodies to move. However, I felt drawn to that kitchen. It felt safe. It needed my love and care. It felt like home, so home is what I made it.

I told my companion to sit down and then I attempted to skin the squirrels. After all, I had promised my saviour a meal. I hacked away at one of the tiny creatures, cutting through the fleshy sinew attaching skin to meat. The body slid around, gore making the surface slippery and an almost impossible task. More often than not, I left most of the meat attached to the fur that I was trying to separate it from. The entire time, the man watched me intently and unspeaking. It was unnerving, but it pushed me to focus on the squirrel even more. I did this for several agonising minutes until I had finally finished the first one. I sighed and pushed the poorly skinned squirrel to one side. I moved the second one in front of me to begin the process all over again. In one swift motion, the man stood up and was next to me, one hand on the unskinned squirrel and the other on the knife I was using.

"Like this," he said, softly this time. He then took the squirrel and chose another knife from my selection. The one he selected was longer but narrow than the one I was using – a filleting knife. He then began slicing away at the body, quickly and smoothly – nothing like the hacking motion I had done. In what felt like mere seconds, the second body was neatly skinned. He nodded at his handi-work and then sat down again. I smiled and went back to work.

I cut portions off the squirrel and into serving size pieces. The next step was preparing something I had found in one of my previous scavenges – buttermilk. Admittedly it was powdered buttermilk and just needed the addition of water, but nonetheless I mixed it up. I added powdered garlic, paprika and cayenne pepper. It was dried herbs and spice, and out of jars. It wouldn't compare to anything fresh, but it would do the job. I added the squirrel bits to my concoction. I left it to soak while I added salt, pepper and flour to a Ziploc bag. I drained the squirrel in a colander before placing it into the bag and then I shook it until the squirrel was sufficiently coated. I heated up my skillet, put in a couple of teaspoons of vegetable oil and dropped in the prepared squirrel bits. I fried the rodent meat, flipping it with tongs, until it was golden brown. I placed the thor-oughly seasoned squirrel onto, what was obviously, the good plates. A sprig of parsley for decoration and then placed in front of my guest, who had remained silent and motionless the entire time. He didn't move and just stared at me. I put out some clean cutlery. He still didn't move. He just continued to watch me, unblinking. I sat down anyway, I had worked hard on the meal in front of me and I wanted to enjoy it. I began eating and, when I swallowed my first mouthful, he began to eat also. I suppose you couldn't trust strangers to cook you a non-poisoned meal in the post-apocalyptic world.

The entire time I ate, I watched the man eat his share. Not because I was being cautious, but because I wanted to see if he had got the same explosion of flavour that I did. The very quiet man, the same man who appeared reserved and didn't display emotion, smiled and looked up at me.

"Beautiful," he stated simply, and he was right. It was. Then he asked an equally beautiful question, "Are you a chef?"

"Yes, yes I am," I said and beamed – the recognition warmed me to my core.

"People would pay for food like this," he said, devouring another piece.

"Well, it's a shame money isn't any good anymore," I said dejectedly and continued to eat.

"Trade still exists," he replied simply, finishing the rest of his meal. He then looked at me and repeated, "People would pay for food like this."

With that, he got up and started to leave. I, on the other hand, was deep in thought regarding his statements. Trade? Pay for food? Not for the first time that day, I had a thought extremely unlike me pass through my mind.

As he was walking into the darkened corridor to leave, I called after him and asked, "Do you want to be my sous chef?"

He stopped walking away for the second time that day and said, "Ok."

And that was how I got my second-in-command. The guy who would do my dirty work. Skinning anything that was needed. Cutting and filleting the meat into appropriately sized portions to cook. Any preparation I needed, he did it for me. He even helped me come up with a menu for the post-apocalypse – testing every meal and giving suggestions. With his help, I could focus on what I well and truly wanted to do, making meals for people to enjoy. The apocalypse just made the business side of things easier. The only issue was getting meat and, let's face it, everyone wanted meat. You could roast or sauté vegetables all day long, but customers would always want meat. Getting it wasn't an issue, animals still existed, but getting large quantities would always be difficult. That is when someone came to me with a business opportunity.

A man approached me during the early days of my post-apocalyptic restaurant, back when I didn't have many customers and I certainly didn't have any regulars. He had an offer. He was a hunter, and had been one pre-apocalypse. His idea was simple. He would provide me the various meats from whatever he hunted. All he wanted in return was a hot meal when he made deliveries, and bullets matching whatever calibre weapon he was using. I wanted to consider his proposal before answering, but I could not see any answer other than "yes" – it would be beneficial for all! Others may have developed trade in the apocalypse, but we had developed an economy based on supply and demand. People traded all sorts of things for one of our meals. Bullets. Herbs and spices. Fresh vegetables. Tins of food. Everything they provided us just furthered our ability to produce cuisine. Those items would either go into producing more food, or providing our hunter with bullets to provide us with meat, both of which meant producing better quality meals. Rinse and repeat. Business was booming, and word of mouth meant a hell of a lot more when the human population had nothing to talk about other than a restaurant that had appeared at the end of the world. It was amazing.

And it was amazing for such a long time. Business was sustainable. Until one day it wasn't. Like any business venture, there is the risk of growing too big too fast. Supply and demand become an issue. Either you maintain what you're doing and have to turn away customers and trade. Or, you make a change, and continue to grow. These changes can make or break a business. I made amazing meals. Hot meals. Unique recipes with meat in it. Yet, I wanted to grow. So, I told my business partner to bring me any meat he found – not just what he had hunted but *anything*. As long as I was providing my customers with meat, it shouldn't matter if the quality degraded a small amount. So what if the meat was found on a roadside, or it wasn't so fresh at times, or that I unofficially encouraged him to steal it? Or that it occasionally had a tattoo or piercing on it. No one would know. Meat is meat after all, so why did it matter what or who it came from? My dream was realised. My restaurant at the end of times. The Little Death. *La Petite Mort.*

ABOUT RYAN COLLEY

I always enjoyed reading fictional worlds, but creating my own was always my passion. My Year 8 English teacher told me I should pursue writing after a short story I had written for a school project. I don't know where my love of zombies come from, but it just happened, and now it is my life.

Things changed and life moved on, but even while I was graduating from my Bachelors and Masters in Psychology, I still wrote stories and I still loved doing it. Writing is my passion, and everything else I do is a means for me to carry on with that passion.

I'm also prepared to move to a secure location at a zombie's notice ...

a

THE LAST DAY

BY JUSTIN ROBINSON

Every twenty years or so, the city had to bleed. That was the unspoken explanation, danced around on the front page and the evening news. Los Angeles swelled with hate and fear, and when it couldn't hold any more, the city's veins opened. It had started in the same place it always had, in the raw wound of South Central. That it would stay there too, eventually cauterized by more brutality, was also unspoken.

Ricky comforted himself that the violence wasn't going to get any closer. He was far away in Glendale, north of the rioting with Downtown in between. He watched it unfold on the news, saw it in the helicopters buzzing through greasy columns of smoke like steel dragonflies, smelled it in the charred winds. Adults mumbled reassuring platitudes that this was no different than the Zoot Suit or Watts Riots, but something deep in the persistent tangle of Ricky's guts, told him that this time was different.

He insisted on going to school that Thursday. It was the only place he would feel safe. Not the whole day, but for one hour at least. One hour when he wouldn't feel all twisted up in burning knots. One hour where he wouldn't hear his blood frantically buzzing in his ears. It was all thanks to Mr. Novak. Maybe if Ricky had a dad at home, he wouldn't need to see Mr. Novak, but the world was built on maybes.

Ricky changed his clothes in the locker room that always smelled like an old sponge, throwing his jeans and *Purple Rain* t-shirt into the locker and donning the black and red gym clothes marked with the happy dynamite stick mascot of Glendale High. His Converse All-Stars squeaked on the hardwood floor as he joined the rest of his gym class, lining up in alphabetical order, Ricky finding his spot right between Ethan Roark and Pablo Robles. The room echoed with the nervous murmurs of people who had been walking on razors the entire week. Ricky, not wanting to see his own fear echoed in the eyes of another, looked up at the walls of the gym, where the school's championship banners, accumulated over eighty-four years, now hung.

The bell gave its screeching call, one that had been running claws over Ricky's nerves the whole day, but here, in this place, it didn't bother him. The reason for that came stalking into the gym. Mr. Novak looked like he was halfway between a fire hydrant and a pit bull. Dressed in his usual gym coach uniform of black shorts, a red polo shirt, with a whistle bouncing against his broad chest and a clipboard clutched in one meaty hand, Mr. Novak could have been ridiculous. He was a short man too, with most of the seniors and even some juniors and sophomores able to look down on the pink dome of his bald head. But Mr. Novak was a stern throwback to another time. He could be mean, and even cruel, but he was always fair, making the rare times when he softened, even slightly, all the more special. Mr. Novak was as white as it was possible to be without being a literal ghost, but when Ricky pictured what a father looked like, the word itself personified, it was Mr. Novak.

"All right, ladies," he said. "Be quiet and when you hear your name, say 'here,' got it?" It was the same thing every time, and the comforting cadence of Mr. Novak's voice already settled the butterflies in Ricky's stomach. The rioting was far away, and would remain that way. It wouldn't dare disrupt Mr. Novak's class.

He waited until he heard "Robellada," pronounced wrong, and called back "Here!"

Mr. Novak split the class into groups and gave each one a basketball. Soon the room was echoing with the squeak and rumble of pickup games. Action stopped only with the shrilling of Mr. Novak's whistle, and a barked admonishment of someone's last name. Ricky forgot the fires consuming the city for a short while.

The door swung open about halfway through the period. Its sound was consumed in the din of the gym, only the bright sunlight calling attention to it. A human silhouette stumbled in. Ricky thought the man had to be drunk. Ricky knew what drunks moved like; back when his father still lived with them, he'd seen the old man stagger in, swerve through the apartment into Ricky's mom's room, followed by the persistent squeak of bedsprings and the occasional clap of a slapped face. It took an experienced drunk to move the way this man was moving now, in a continuing forward fall. The door swung shut behind the figure, the blinding light once again locked out, along with the world. The drunk's features resolved in the artificial light of the gym.

Only he wasn't a drunk. He was hurt, badly. Bleeding from half a dozen wounds. Crimson wept from a shredded cheek. His collar was soaked nearly black from a ragged laceration on his neck. His clothes looked chewed, flowers of blood blossoming at every hurt.

"Sir?" Mr. Novak said.

The man didn't react, instead staring at the gathered boys with milky eyes.

Mr. Novak stepped closer, and then paused, cursing under his breath. "Sir, if you want to have a seat... Brennan! Go to my office and call 911!"

Chris Brennan was still, staring at the injured man.

"Brennan, clean the wax out of your ears and call!"

Chris sprinted for the office. The motion drew the injured man's attention like a dog tracking the lime green bolt of a tennis ball. He lurched after Chris, but soon found a group of recoiling boys in his way.

"Sir," Mr. Novak said, gesturing to the side of the gym where the bleachers extended from the wall, "why don't you have a seat over there while we get you some help?"

The injured man ignored Mr. Novak. He had keyed in on Doug Kay-Fraser, watching him with those white-sheathed eyes. Chapped lips skinned blunt incisors in a parody of a grin. The injured man made a sound in his throat, deep, somewhere between the rattle of a cough and the purr of a cat. Then he lunged.

Doug screamed. It wasn't close to the manly bellow that the other high schoolers would have fantasized in their darkest dreams would be their reaction to sudden violence. No, it was the high pitched yelp of a child. Of a boy who learned that monsters were real and they were coming for him. The injured man went right for Doug's neck, the teeth tearing into the boy's throat. Doug's scream went wet and red after that, and he fell beneath the injured man.

Everyone was frozen. Everyone except Mr. Novak. "Fraser!" the gym teacher shouted, his short legs covering the distance between them in seconds. He grabbed the injured man by the shoulders and hauled him off the student, casting him bodily away. The injured man stumbled, fell, and slid over the polished hardwood, leaving a streak of gore as he went.

Doug Kay-Fraser gurgled. Blood, nearly black, bubbled with his breath, pooling in the ragged place where his adam's apple had been. His skin was ghastly white, his quivering hands fluttering upward, but not quite meeting his throat. His eyes were wide, seeing nothing.

Mr. Novak cursed again. That was nothing unusual. Mr. Novak cursed sometimes even though he was a teacher and wasn't supposed to. It showed the students that they were in a club with their teacher, one that had its own quiet shibboleths.

Mr. Novak dropped to his knees next to Doug, putting his hands on the boy's throat. "Fraser, I want you to look at me. Look at me. You're not going anywhere, you understand me? You're gonna be just fine." Mr. Novak was nearly barking orders at the boy, but it wasn't doing any good. Ricky could tell Doug was dying, and Doug knew it too. Knew it in the terrified emptiness of his eyes. Doug Kay-Fraser, who had peed in his pants in the second grade on a field trip to the Griffith Observatory. Doug Kay-Fraser, who told everyone he had touched Amanda Rosenberg's boobs after the homecoming dance. Doug Kay-Fraser, who sang Duran Duran songs under his breath without knowing he was doing it.

Dying.

Mr. Novak saw it too, whispering "Fuck." Then, louder: "C'mon, Fraser. You're a tough son of a bitch. I know it." Fraser might have been a tough son of a bitch, but no one survived long without a throat.

Their attention had been locked on the teacher and the hurt boy, no one saw the injured man getting up. It wasn't until Tony Carias screamed that everyone noticed. The injured man was over Tony's shoulder, holding him like an aggressive boyfriend, tearing meaty chunks from the boy's neck with his teeth and slobbering them down. Before anyone could react, a sheet of crimson ran down Tony's shirt like an awful waterfall. The student's struggles were already feeble, his cries swallowed by the injured man's eating.

Mr. Novak leapt to his feet and charged like a bull, pulling Tony out of the injured man's grasp. The boy took two shuddering steps before collapsing on the hardwood. The injured man stumbled back, but quickly recovered and lurched forward. This time Mr. Novak caught him by the back of the head, and powerfully hurled him into the bleachers. The injured man's skull made an echoing crack as it ran into the wooden seats. It should have been enough to daze anyone, especially a man who looked half dead as it was. But no, he was already struggling to get up.

"Somebody, put some pressure on Tony's wounds," Mr. Novak said, settling into a wrestler's crouch. Then, to the injured man. "Listen, you son of a bitch, I don't know what's wrong with you, but you're gonna cut the shit right now or I'm gonna make you sorry you walked into my class."

The injured man lunged at Mr. Novak, but the gym teacher was too fast. He gripped the man's arm and neck, wrenching both until sickening pops echoed through the gym. The injured man snapped like a mad dog, desperately trying to get his teeth around meat. Mr. Novak's impassive face made Ricky think of a picture he'd seen of the statues on Easter Island. Mr. Novak was merely *doing* without thought of why. His body was reacting, turning him into the protector Ricky always knew Mr. Novak to be. Pure instinct keeping his students safe. He hauled the injured man to the side of the court, and then brutally slammed him headfirst into the wall.

This time the crack was of the man's skull splitting in two. He kept moving, though, teeth kept snapping. Mr. Novak didn't stop either, pulling the injured man back and slamming again and again, until the head came apart like a melting ice cream cake. Only then did the man stop moving, his headless body collapsing beneath the hideous jellylike stain on the wall.

Mr. Novak, red to the elbows and stippled in ruby, turned to the class, sucking air. "Men..." then he moved again.

Ricky jumped, his brain catching up to what he was seeing. Doug Kay-Fraser was sitting up, his eyes glassy and faded. Mr. Novak caught him fast. Doug was snapping just like the other man had been, desperately trying to bite his teacher. Mr. Novak gave Doug the same fate, his headless body thumping to the wood next to the man's. Someone wretched, and the gym filled with the stench of recycled breakfast, boiling underneath the coppery tang of gore.

"Is Carias dead?" Mr. Novak barked. When no one responded, he barked again, "Is Carias dead?"

Joshua Wong nodded, eyes wide. Mr. Novak picked up the body. It started to struggle by the time he hauled it to the wall, but soon, after several more sickening cracks, it was still.

"Mr. Novak?" It was Chris Brennan, looking almost as pale as Doug had been. "911 is busy."

"Busy?"

Chris nodded. "What's going on?" The syllables were childlike and broken.

"I don't know," he said, then jogged to the doorway. Mr.

Novak's movements had only the hint of hesitation. He didn't want to know, but he had to. For his kids. Ricky found himself running next to Mr. Novak, unwilling to be farther away from safety. The meaty stench of blood came off Mr. Novak in a miasma. He paused at the door, and glanced at Ricky. "Robellada," he said with a hint of approval that made Ricky glow. "Stay back."

Mr. Novak nudged the door of the gym open. From their vantage, they could see all the way across the asphalt yard and to Colorado Street beyond. It was horrifying. Men and women, sporting similar wounds to what had covered the injured man, staggered everywhere. They moved like wolves in slow motion, cornering and attacking screaming people, falling into masses of wet screams and tangled limbs. The riot had come to Glendale, but it was worse than Ricky could have imagined. This was nothing less than the end of the world, happening all around him.

"Holy shit," Mr. Novak said. One of the injured people – no, they were worse than merely injured, they were dead – turned to the door. One of his eyes were gone, teeth marks running from brow to cheekbone. The dead man grinned, and began to lurch toward them. Mr. Novak slammed the door and threw the locks.

"Fulgencio! Lock the other doors, now!"

Jaime Fulgencio ran to obey, just as something hammered into the door Mr. Novak locked. A scrabbling sound, like claws, pawed at the other side. It was the dead man. Clawing to be let in like a hungry dog.

"Mr. Novak," Ricky whispered. "What's happening?"

"I don't know. Come with me." Mr. Novak led Ricky into the back, past the lockers and his office, to a metal grated door. He unlocked it with a heavy ring of keys, throwing the door wide. Equipment waited on metal shelving, arranged by sport. Mr. Novak picked up the half dozen aluminum bats that waited on a rack by one wall, handing one to Ricky. "You know what to do with this?"

Ricky nodded. "If one of those things comes in, I make him sorry he did."

"That's what I like to hear." Ricky preened as the two of them entered the gym. Mr. Novak passed four other bats to his favorites, and Ricky was pleased to see that he didn't ask Ricky to surrender the bat he'd gotten. He was validated. He took up a position by Mr. Novak's shoulder. He was ready to do whatever the teacher needed of him.

A hand went up. It belonged to Jesus Reyes. "Mr. Novak? What's going on?"

"The riot," he said. "It's here."

Ricky nodded, only it wasn't a riot. Ricky knew it better after what he had seen through that door, but they all knew it was something worse. Something Biblical and horrible. It was the last day anything would ever make sense. A single look at the three headless corpses by the side of the gym told that story. The awful scrabbling sound on the other side of the door spoke almost as eloquently.

"What are we going to do?" Jesus asked.

Ricky didn't have to ask, because he already knew. Mr. Novak was going to figure out something to get them all out of here safely. Mr. Novak wouldn't let anything bad happen to them. Somehow, he would figure it out. Ricky's faith was ironclad and forged in blood. He waited for the words to come out of his trusted teacher's mouth, the plan that would save them all and make everything okay.

Mr. Novak watched his students, his eyes narrowed, his mouth working silently. When the teacher finally spoke, after an eternity of staring at his class, Ricky felt himself falling apart.

"I have to go," Mr. Novak whispered. Then, louder, "I have to go."

The class started murmuring to each other, speculating what Mr. Novak meant by his declaration. Finally, Chris Brennan said, with the pathetic hope Ricky felt too, "Going to get help?"

Mr. Novak swallowed, and for the first time, he looked at the floor. "I'm sorry, men. I have to go. My wife, she's... I have to go. I have to get to her." He walked to the door quickly, unable to look anywhere else.

Ricky ran after him. "Mr. Novak, what are you doing?"

"I'm sorry, son. I have a family."

"So do I."

Ricky chased Mr. Novak's eyes, but they darted away.

"I'm sorry," the teacher whispered. He unlocked the door, then stopped. "Lock this behind me. Don't let those things in."

"Mr. Novak, please. Don't go. We need you."

But Mr. Novak didn't say anything. He merely flinched once as the words burrowed into him like ticks. He was fleeing, not just the situation, but Ricky's need. He was abandoning them to the horror.

Mr. Novak threw the door open and a dead man staggered inward. The gym teacher hit a home run against the dead man's skull, battering him out the door. Then Mr. Novak ran into the sunlight, among the awful animate corpses. Dead people eclipsed the short man quickly, converging around the door to get at the terrified meals within. With a broken sob, Ricky slammed the door and threw the lock. The clawing sound started up immediately, echoing hollowly through the gym.

Ricky's limbs trembled, filling with cold fire. He kept seeing Mr. Novak running. Fleeing. *Abandoning.* He had known hatred before, for his own father. But not like this. His father had been weak and a drunk, but leaving had been the best thing he'd ever done. Mr. Novak was so much worse. He had been stronger than anything. Someone who couldn't break. And then he had. Leaving his class to die.

As the scratching multiplied at the door, rebounding off the walls all around, a piece of Ricky Robellada snapped like a rubber band, never again to be fixed.

ABOUT JUSTIN ROBINSON

Much like film noir, Justin Robinson was born and raised in Los Angeles. He splits his time between editing comic books, writing prose, and wondering what that disgusting smell is. Degrees in Anthropology and History prepared him for unemployment, but an obsession with horror fiction and a laundry list of phobias provided a more attractive option. He is the author of more than 10 novels in a variety of genres including detective, humor, urban fantasy, and horror. Most of them are pretty good.

Justin is the co-host of Tread Perilously a weekly "worst of television podcast (featured on Fanbase Press).

COOKIE JARS AND BLUE BIRDS
BY VALERIE LIOUDIS

Avery

The cookie jar rattled in my backpack as I tried to sneak down the alleyway. Somewhere along the way, I had picked up a companion. Rayna followed close behind me, hoping not to alert the dead that we were in the area. When the outbreak happened, I was holed up in my childhood home alone. I struggled with anxiety before the monsters came to life. The constant moaning and running caused me to latch onto something I could control. That was when the hoarding began.

The cookie jar was the last piece that still existed from my original hoard. Late one night, trapped by my piles, a fire broke out and swept through my home. Alone, and panicked, I dug through the piles of useless treasures and was able to pull the cookie jar out as I escaped the fiery prison. All the control I had managed to accumulate was gone in a flash. The only thing that kept me from lying down and giving up right there was that glass cookie jar. It was the first piece I ever found, and with it I could start all over again.

I was determined not to confine myself into a home filled to the brim with piles of items that could turn into an avalanche and bury me alive. But the pull was still there. I still needed to bring order to the chaos. The best solution I could think of was a traveling home. It took time for me to find a suitable camper. It needed to be small. I could drive, but I was no truck driver, and the roads weren't clear, so maneuverability was key. I spent a week sleeping in the office of my town's thrift store trying to scope out the perfect ride, and when I finally found one that worked, it was as if the stars had aligned to leave it there for me.

I tapped on the windows of the busted-up Winnebago. Silence. Scanning the area, I made sure it was clear to make a little more noise. Once I was sure I was alone, I banged as hard as I could on the door. If there were dead inside, I wanted to know. My life depended on my thoroughness. Nothing. I pulled at the handle and expected it to be locked. Nothing was this easy anymore.

I pulled a bit harder than I should have and the door flung out at me, along with the putrid smell of death. Not the zombie rotting kind of death, but the completely dead and rotting away peacefully kind of death. Oddly, there was a difference. It was hard to explain, but the zombies had their own distinct stink, and what hit me in the face wasn't it. I pulled a bandana up around my nose. When you get hit with the smell of death all the time, you come prepared.

On the floor in the main living area was a middle-aged woman with a gaping hole in her head. In her arms was a small and equally dead toy dog of some sorts. It was hard to pin down the breed with that much decay. Thank god animals didn't carry the zombie disease. Her kind of dog scared me more than the idea of zombie bears or lions. Just imagine a pack of the ankle biters attacking you without warning. There would be no way to fend them off, and you're more likely to stumble on them.

In the driver's seat sat what I could only assume was her husband. He had a self-inflicted gunshot wound. The longer you spend wandering around in a world full of broken snapshots, the easier it becomes to imagine a back story for each scene in front of you. Karen and Jim tried to run from the zombie threat in their trusty camper. Little Fluffy was a yappy little monster who was never trained to behave because Karen treated him like a person and not a dog.

"Sheesh, Karen. If you could have just given Jim more of your love, and not flaunted your obvious favoritism of Fluffy here, maybe you would still be on the run from the monsters together." I said as I pulled Karen out into the street.

Lucky for me, Karen had a death grip around Fluffy, so I wouldn't have to drag them out separately. Jim on the other hand, was going to give me a bit of trouble. He was wedged in the seat, and death makes the body bloat. He was most likely a portly man before death, but now he looked like that girl from the chocolate movie who ate the forbidden candy. Except he wasn't purple or blue. Pop culture used to matter, but it was almost impossible to remember those details anymore.

"Geez, Jim. You should have laid off the cheeseburgers. Or, maybe you could have shot yourself over near Karen. Nobody ever thinks of the person who has to clean all this up."

It was becoming commonplace that I would talk to myself. I wasn't sure if that was a bad sign or not. It wasn't like Jim or Karen were going to jump up and start rattling off some good old fashioned small talk about the weather or the state of politics. Once the bodies were resting nicely in the summer sun, the urge to pull them a thousand feet away from the camper became a thought that I was going to have to push to the back of my mind if I was ever going to get my new rolling palace cleaned up and ready to go.

Step one would have to be airing the thing out. I didn't know how long Jim and Karen had been closed up in what essentially was an easy bake people oven, but it was going to take a few days to get their smell out. Once I got the tiny side windows and screen door moving some of the death cloud out of the camper, I could breathe again, but only because we were all a bit nose blind these days.

I prayed to a god that I hope was still listening and made my way back to the driver's seat. A sunbeam shone down from the heavens and a choir of angels sang Hallelujah in my head. Dangling from the ignition was a lucky rabbit's foot attached to the key for the camper. Thank god for small miracles. I was resourceful, but I wasn't hot wire a camper resourceful. Turning the key, I was afraid that even with all the pieces falling in place that the camper wouldn't start, but it did.

"Thanks, Jim!" I yelled out glad that he was still in earshot.

I rolled down the front two windows and popped out the ones that looked like wings. A rush of cool air blew onto my face, and I finally sat down to rest in my new home. After fifteen or so minutes, the smell overtook me again, and I accepted that I would be leaving to find some extremely strong cleaning products. I popped the keys out and danced my happy dance out the camper door.

"Thanks, guys. I'll be back tomorrow to take care of the mess you left behind. The more I think about it Jim, it would have been kinder if you would have taken care of business out here. I'll forgive you, though, if you forgive me for taking off with your ride in the next few days."

The entire walk back to the thrift shop, I felt like I was being followed. I had taken residence in the upstairs office after my house burned, and while those kinds of shops had a mix of junk in them prior to the outbreak, my nesting had brought double the contents there for safekeeping while I hunted down a suitable long-term solution to my living situation. I could use the front door to get in, but I had become accustomed to climbing up the tree at the corner of the store onto the roof, and in through the office window.

Rituals helped me feel in control. The world outside was dying but hiding in my worn brown chair each evening as I listened to nineties music on loop made me feel safe. Climbing in the window was the way I went in the first time, so it would be the way I went in every time. I pulled myself up, and as I was closing the window a squirrel snuck in at the last moment. Startled, I froze. He bounced around the room off of each piece of furniture, finally landing on the desk and grabbing the granola bar I had waiting on the desk for me when I got back.

He snatched it up and bolted out the window again. He was gone before I could even react. It had been so long since I had seen another living creature that I wasn't sure I actually saw it happen. I slowly shut the window the rest of the way, this time locking it. I was pretty sure that squirrels couldn't open closed windows, but I didn't want to chance it. It was the first night in a long time that my rituals were unable to make me calm enough to fall asleep. So, I spent most of the evening tossing and turning before finally succumbing to darkness.

In the morning, my tiny friend was waiting patiently at

the window for me. I opened my eyes and saw a small head popping up and down through the glass pane. I was a pretty cautious person, but it seemed safe enough to see what the little guy wanted. I popped the lock and slid the window open, and as soon as there was enough space for him he squeezed right in. This time he skipped all of the other furniture and headed over to the desk where he had found the granola bar the night before.

"Sorry, little dude. I didn't think to leave you out a morning snack. Wait right here, and I will grab you something from my stash."

I knew it was stupid to waste what little food I had, but loneliness will make you do weird things. My tiny friend wasn't about to be left behind in the stuffy office. As I opened the door to head downstairs, after knocking three times of course, he climbed up my leg across my shirt and onto my shoulder. We made our way through the store together, with him jumping off of me and onto the piles I had collected, then back on my shoulder.

"You're a curious little guy, huh?"

I moved the pile of empty boxes that hid the closet filled with food. I figured if anyone ever broke in, they would see all of my other piles and assume there was just more useless junk over in the corner. I was pretty good at collecting, and even with food being scarce, I had a decent sized pile for one. I loaded up my backpack with a few days' worth of food and the box of granola bars. The plan was to load the office with a bit of food, pack enough for my trip out to clean the camper today, and let the squirrel have a granola bar every time he shows up at my window. It might be nice to have a companion.

I hadn't noticed that he had crawled down my shirt to one of the shelves and was feasting on a bag of stale, and probably moldy, chips. "Dude! I'm not sure those are okay to eat." I said as I stared at him.

Who was I to take the food away from him? That shelf was all questionable food that I had no intention of eating until I had no other choice. He had been taking care of himself this whole time, I would have to trust that he was capable of knowing what food was good and which wasn't.

"Alright, bud. Let's go. I have some work to do today."

I didn't think that squirrels knew English, but he climbed right up on my shoulder as I shut the door and reset the boxes. I should have been more concerned with the fact that a woodland creature was acting more like a human than animal. But for some reason it seemed as normal as anything else in this new reality. I had witnessed the dead rise and walk among us, men with chainsaws corralled and beheaded monsters, and now squirrels could understand people. Seems normal enough to me.

We made our way up into the office, and that was where we parted ways. As soon as I handed him the treat, he was off out the window and out of my sight. I hoped he would be back, but only because he gave me the boost of interaction without the need to figure out the pitfalls I normally fall into trying to relate to other human beings. I had a mission anyway and needed to find industrial strength cleaning supplies to clean the mess Jim had made dispatching Karen, Fluffy, and himself.

A group of burly guys in trucks had cleared the area near the thrift store, including the supermarket a half a block away. While they were still in town, I made no moves towards the store. That particular group of men, while useful in destroying hordes of zombies, were not the group I would want to run with, not if I wanted to stay safe and happy. Once they pulled on towards their next destination, I did a careful pass through the store, and was happy to see that no dead had found their way back in.

It took a full day of work, but I was able to shore up all the windows and doors. There wasn't much left in the non-perishable food section, it was looted long ago when there were still enough survivors to raid a store. The perishables were long spoiled and kept away most sane people with working noses that may still be hanging around in the shadows. But on a day like today, when I needed something that hadn't been a high priority when the outbreak first began, it was the first place I would try.

I still did my signature triple knock and was happily greeted with silence. With a store of this size, though, I walked up and down the walls I had in place checking to see if there were any breeches to my defenses. It was weird, but I could swear that I was still being watched. Paranoia might be setting in. God knows that my mind wasn't healthy before this all began, and the high level of stress I had been running at was eventually going to break me. Hopefully later, and not sooner.

The shelves slid over easily. In all reality most zombies were creatures who hunted by opportunity and ease. If there was something in their way, and they didn't think there was a meal behind it, they ignored it. So, the walls didn't have to be strong, just complete. The smell dropped me to my knees. I had forgot to pull my bandana up over my face and pulling it up before I hurled seemed like a bad idea. So, yet again, I let my hard-scavenged breakfast come up, and then tried to move on without chastising myself too hard.

I pulled the vapor rub out of my pocket and uncapped it, praying that there would be a small bit still in the bottom of the little blue jar. One or two dabs was enough to cut the smell, and I could think straight again. The nice part about staying in your hometown was knowing the floorplans of the buildings you frequented when electricity still lit every aisle and corner. You didn't have to waste time wandering around praying that you would find the item you needed.

In my hand I held the weirdest and yet most useful find I had at the thrift store. Flashlights were a necessity but needed batteries. Not my trusty shaker flashlight. I stood there flailing my arm around for a few minutes and built up enough juice to light my way through the whole cleaning supply run. It wasn't the brightest, but damn it was convenient. I grabbed one of the carts that had been abandoned in the aisle and made my way to the back. It took less than five minutes and I was out the front door with everything I would need over the next few days.

I pulled up with my haul and Jim and Karen were waiting patiently for my return. It was awful nice of them not to get up and start attacking people. You never knew about the dead these days. They just didn't seem to have the good sense to stay dead.

"Don't you worry, Jim. I will get her all shined up and ready for the road. You won't have to be embarrassed by old Bessie anymore. All she really needs is a bit of lemon scented love."

The bandana went up before I entered the camper. I really didn't need to lose any more calories to the pavement. The apocalypse was a hell of a diet. Problem was, I had a tiny frame to begin with, so losing mass wasn't really the healthiest option for me. As I was spraying the blood-soaked carpet for the third time, I was joined by a familiar face.

"Little dude! What are you doing here?" he may understand English but thank god he wasn't talking to me yet. "Alright, now is as good of a time as any to eat lunch. Let's take it outside, though. The camper is going to need a few more days before we can eat in here."

I pulled down the fire escape ladder on the old brick building next to the camper. The metal grating right outside the second story window was hardly big enough for one person, but the squirrel and I fit just fine. From high above, I could eat and scan the area for any threats, maybe let my guard down a bit. Or maybe not, we didn't want to get crazy.

"Does this make us friends now?" I pondered out loud. "I didn't really have a ton of friends before." I trailed off with that last bit. "I might have liked to, but people were always hard for me to deal with. They never live up to your expectations, or worse, they do. I think the only person who ever really got me was my grandmother, and she knew enough to not try too hard."

The squirrel was a really good listener, but I couldn't say the same for his conversation skills. In all honesty, he seemed less concerned with me, and more with what I had in my backpack. "Fine, no deep conversations, little dude. It isn't worth dragging up the past anyway. It, like the dead, should be at rest."

I pulled out a granola bar and placed it in front of him. He just sat there on his hind legs staring at my bag. "Subtle. If you want a little variety all you have to do is ask." I said as I laughed at the idea.

If he started speaking to me, I was sending him away. I didn't care how lonely I was, I was not going to encourage the development of another neurosis. I tossed him a few beans from the can I was digging into, and he popped them into his cheeks. Then he ran up my shirt, circled my neck a few times, sniffed my ear, and then ran back off. That must have been some kind of squirrel thank you, because he grabbed the granola bar and took off after that.

"Maybe, I talk too much," I said, half insulted.

The next few days consisted of the same routine. I would wake up to his face in the window, and I would give him a treat for appearing. Then like clockwork he would show up at the camper when the sun hit the middle of the sky. He did the same weird little exit routine and would take off. He let me pet him once, but only for a second. It looked like he forgot himself.

One moment, I'm stroking his soft fur, and the next, he is frantically scanning the area below us like he lost something. I didn't try that move again. Anxiety was easy to spot when you spent a lifetime fighting it. I didn't like it when people would intentionally poke at my buttons, and I wasn't about to do that to someone else. Even if that someone else was covered in fur.

It took a few days longer than I expected to get Karen's mess up out of the camper. I wasted a few days scrubbing the same portion of carpet until I finally realized there wasn't a cleaner powerful enough in this new world that would make that smell go away. So, I ripped it up and threw an area rug down that had been sitting in the thrift store. I swear that place was a gold mine for that weird thing you suddenly needed.

"Well, Jim, that is the last bit right there. Now Bessie is ready to hit the road. All, I have to do is fill her up with all my goodies, and we are going to have to part ways. Don't cry, Karen. I know we have grown close over these last few days, but you had to have known that it wouldn't last forever. This friendship was like a candle burning. It was hot and full of life, but now it has run out of fuel. We are just going in different directions." I snorted at that last bit. It reminded me of the cheesy soap operas I used to watch with my mom. Break ups were always so melodramatic on daytime tv.

As I made my way into the thrift store, I heard things being rattled around downstairs. I was so close to leaving, and now my entire stash was in danger again. If it was a zombie, I would have to find a way to lure it out into a more open area. I knew there would be no way for me to fight and win in the piles of treasures downstairs. If it was humans, things could be even worse. Humans can think, and for the most part were much larger and more powerful than I was.

My heart was racing as I made my way silently down the steps. I peeked over the railing towards the front of the store and saw no one. Something fell and crashed to the ground on the floor in the direction of my food stash. My heart sank. Food was the only thing that I wouldn't be able to replace easily. My first hoard taught me a lesson. It could all burn to the ground, and as long as you had the important things, you could start again.

I rushed down the hall with my axe held high above my head and was startled by the team that was raiding my closet. "Little dude, what the Hell!" I yelled.

A small girl, maybe nine or ten years old, turned and screamed. The squirrel ran down from her shirt and up mine. He tugged at the cuff of my sleeve on my arm that was holding the axe. "Oh. My bad!" I fumbled with my words as I lowered the weapon.

I looked down at my furry friend with hurt in my eyes. He was stealing from me. I thought an animal would be different. My back slid down the wall as I crumpled up on the floor. Things had been going so well lately, but now this kind of betrayal shook me to the core. Now, who was being melodramatic?

"You're weird," she finally spoke.

"Excuse me. I would think that if you go around stealing other people's food that you probably shouldn't insult them, too. It seems like bad manners to me. Plus, I'm not weird, I'm sad."

"Not that," she said as she sat on the floor and offered me one of my own waters. "You talk to dead people. That's weird."

"Have you been watching me? Of course, you have. You were following me around with this little spy of yours," I said, motioning towards the squirrel. "How did you train him anyway?"

"I dunno. I found him when he was a baby, and he just does stuff. Back then my parents were with us. Dad said I couldn't get another dog. Said they eat too much and would be too loud. I found this guy and hid him in my pocket for a month before they figured out I had him. Now he is with me all the time. Dad wanted to name him Slappy. Said that was the name of a squirrel on a cartoon he used to watch. I said that was dumb and named him Frank. He looks like a Frank, right?"

And I thought I talked too much. "Sure kid." I knew better than to ask her where her parents were since she used the past tense when she brought them up. We were all orphans at this point, no matter what our age was. "You here to just steal my stuff, or are you two sticking around?" I asked not really sure how I felt about them staying or leaving.

"We could stick around. You're weird, but not dangerous. That's if you want us to." She scratched Frank's head as he tucked himself into her shirt pocket.

"Well, I can't have you shopping in my pantry and not paying off your debt. We are going to be busy for the next few days. I'm not staying here much longer, and you can decide if you want to come along for the ride after we spend some time together. You might decide my kind of weird is annoying," I said as I grabbed dinner for the three of us.

"I'm thirteen. Weird and annoying are kinda my thing," she said.

"Thirteen! Damn, you're small!" I blurted out, covering my mouth as I realized I just cursed at a kid.

"You're not too big yourself. Don't worry though, I can keep up. Small isn't always bad. We taking the camper out of town once you put your supplies in it?" She asked.

"How do you know about my camper? Oh, geez! I knew someone was following me. I thought it was just Frank. I should have known a squirrel wouldn't have set off my creeper sense."

"Yeah, small works when you're following someone. The smaller you're the better. I was the hide and seek champion of my elementary school before all this happened." She was obviously proud of herself.

We spent the next few hours doing the small talk thing while we ate and set up an extra bed for her to bunk in the office with me. The two of them had been sleeping in random cars since she lost her parents. Frank had kept her nourished by running the same con he had run on me. Rayna followed behind him, but never revealed herself. She would work out the schedule people kept, and then raid their food when she was sure they wouldn't be around. She had gotten sloppy with me because she didn't fear me.

I probably should have been angrier that they were planning on robbing me blind, but she was just trying to stay alive, and it was nice to have someone to talk to. Sometimes things just work out the way they were supposed to all along. The extra set of hands made loading up the camper that much easier, and while we were at work, Frank stood lookout on the top of our new rolling palace. His head scanned back and forth all day as he sat upright on his hind legs.

"So, he just acts that way with no training?" I stood in the doorway looking up at our tiny centurion.

"Yeah, weird, right?" She replied, arms overloaded with the last bit of gear from the office.

Turns out the camper was a perfect fit for the three of us. Rayna was small enough to use the bunk above the driver's head. Something that had just been storage when Jim and Karen were using Bessie. My stuff went to the back where the only bedroom was located. As we moved our things in, I tried to curb the voice telling me to bring all of my items. The living were more important than the inanimate. My area was overflowing, but the common space was clean. It was the best I could do.

Frank had a cabinet fit for a squirrel king. Rayna had taken one day off from helping me load up the camper to scavenge around for pint sized pieces of furniture to put in the overhead compartment that was closest to her bed. I knew for the most part that it would be wasted time, since he never left her side, but it was nice to see her act like a kid, even if it was only for a moment in time. What she ended up creating was a squirrel sized studio apartment, with a couch, bed, and desk. I guess even squirrels needed a place to sit and write out their thoughts.

The last thing I needed to put into the camper was my cookie jar. I was in the thrift store with Rayna doing one last sweep when we heard Frank squeaking frantically outside. I ran to the window and looked down into what should have been an empty parking lot. There was a small group running across the blacktop with a horde of the undead following behind them. They were not going fast enough to get away. Both of the men were limping, and the woman was trying to hold one of them up enough for them to keep moving.

"Leave me, Ann. You have to leave me, and Doug!" he said. "We are all going to die!"

"No, Stan! If you guys die, I die. I can't do this alone! If you want me to live, you're just going to have to move faster. Let's go!" She pulled him along, as their companion limped behind them but the horde was getting closer.

"We have to help them!" Rayna tugged at my shirt.

I was frozen. I didn't know those people. What if they weren't safe to be around? I already took in a girl and her pet. Wasn't that enough?

"Avery!" She was dragging me across the room.

"Rayna, think! We don't know them! You and I are really small, and don't have much to defend ourselves. What if it is a trick?"

"How could it be a trick? They're going to die! They're hurt!" She pleaded. "I'm going to get them in the camper!" She said as she took off.

"Damn it! Fine!" I shouted, pushing past her as we hit the back door. "Let me go first."

The cookie jar rattled in my backpack as I tried to sneak down the alleyway. Rayna followed close behind me, hoping not to alert the dead that we were in the area. We needed to get to the group, and somehow use our tiny bodies to each lift a full-grown man into the camper a hundred feet away. Sure, easy peasy. Somewhere along the line, my small grasp on controlling the chaos around me had been severed. As I turned the corner, the sight of the trio and the horde chasing them set off an anxiety attack.

"Rayna, we need to go. There are too many of them, and they're too close to them. I can't do this. We need to leave." I staggered towards the camper and not the commotion.

"Coward!" She yelled after me. "Leave without me then. I'm going to save them." Frank ran across the parking lot and up to her shoulder. The two of them were going to take on a sea of zombies themselves.

My head was swimming from a lack of oxygen. Each gasp brought in less and less lifegiving air. I was going to die right there in the parking lot without getting to the camper. I was going to die, and it would have all been for nothing. *Count backwards from ten.* I could hear my mother's voice trying to calm me. *Deep slow breaths. Feel the ground beneath you, solid and strong.*

I could think straight again. In front of me was one of the shopping carts we had used to get all of our supplies into the camper. It was a metal chariot waiting to be used to save us all. I gripped the handle and took off towards Stan and his busted leg. Rayna was already there trying to get Doug to move faster with no luck. Without a word, I shoved Stan into the cart headfirst and whipped back around towards the camper.

He screamed in pain with each bump and pot hole we hit. There was no time to adjust him for comfort. Rayna gave up on Doug and grabbed Ann's hand. The two of them chased behind me to the camper. I slammed the cart into the side of our home and knocked it over on its side. Stan toppled out onto the pavement screaming obscenities at me. Behind us Doug was overrun by the horde. His screams overpowered Stan's profanities, and I used that opportunity to get this mess back on track.

"Get in if you want to live!" I shouted back.

Rayna pulled the door behind her, and with a turn of the key, we were suddenly a party of five on a road trip to an unknown destination. "Avery," Rayna tried to apologize from the rear.

"Don't!" I huffed not ready to discuss what just

happened. "Don't anyone talk. Rayna shore up the openings."

"Where's Doug?" Ann cried out as we got ready to pull away. "We can't leave without him. He is all alone. No one should be alone."

God, I wish I was.

The camper was a bit flimsy for my taste, so I had rigged up a mixture of chain link and plywood covers that could be secured from the inside. *Backwards from ten,* I thought as I turned the key. The engine growled to life. Plowing through the dead was easier than I had expected. As long as I advanced slowly, they were just bumps in the road and then a red smear under my tires. Frank had snuck his way onto my shoulder. I guess he was self-appointed as co-pilot.

"Well, little dude, I blame you for all of this. It's a good thing you're cute," I said as I broke off a small piece of granola bar and handed it to him, then flicked the bluebird charm hanging from the rearview mirror.

ABOUT VALERIE LIOUDIS

Valerie Lioudis is an author who writes both novels and short stories in several genres, but her main focus is horror. The New Jersey native penned The Many Afterlives of John Robert Thompson, her debut solo novel, in 2017. Along with her husband Kristopher, she had already published book one in the Aftershock Zombie Series in 2014. She loves the art of writing a short story and has been published in 10 anthologies, most notably Undead Worlds. The Reanimated Writers, a group of indie zombie fiction authors, created a best-selling anthology that featured 22 undead worlds. Valerie spearheaded the project, along with several other endeavors including the Reanimated Rumble with this online community. She hangs out in The Reanimated Writers Facebook Group, and will talk to just about anyone, so join and say hello! If you are looking for her books, they are available on Amazon. If you type Valerie Lioudis, you will find her. She is the only one!

4

INCEPTION

BY JESSICA GOMEZ

My eyes pinch close as a blinding light strips my vision. There's a pregnant pause before chaos ensues, engulfing me, while screaming reverberates through the air. My heart pounds against my ribcage, understanding that everything has changed in this one instant. I gather enough courage to open my eyes and look around.

My mother is no longer standing to my left, but slumped lifelessly on the ground, her shopping bags clutched in her hands. The scenery is hazy, with a white film blanketing our surroundings, as if a nightmare has highjacked my reality. Emotions intrude, slamming against me from multiple directions, relaying fear, confusion, and undeniable panic.

"What the hell?" The words tumble from my lips as shock roots me in place. Almost every person around us has dropped to the ground in contorted piles, their lives suddenly snuffed out. There are few people left standing, some twitching at awkward angles, while others sob and scream. My own terror acts as a glass of ice water thrown in my face. Squatting down to my mom's motionless form, I shake her. "Mom! Are you okay? Mom!"

There's no reply. I have the presence of mind to check her pulse. Nothing. She's gone.

A sob escapes when I lay my head against her chest. I squeeze my eyes shut as my pain tears through me. The little voice in my head is screaming at me to move; this situation's not safe. The Flash dropped these people within seconds of its appearance, surrounding me with dead bodies.

After a couple of minutes, I collect myself and sit back on my haunches. Startled, a yelp escapes me when a growling man dashes by, inches from knocking me over. He beelines for a young girl who's hysterical and crying for her sister to wake up. He slams into her from the side, dragging her to the ground before she's aware enough to fight back. He sinks his teeth into her fleshy neck and tears a chunk free. The wet rip of skin is unforgettable. Her shout for help is smothered by the blood she's choking on, and then she goes silent. The man remains huddled over her body, ripping meat from her bones, enjoying his gory meal.

I gasp loudly, attracting the attention of the infected. He snaps his head in my direction, a piece of bloody flesh slapping his cheek. I shrink back from his demonic appearance. Only minutes after the flash in the sky, people turned grotesque—true living zombies. The creature continues to chew, crawling over the girl like a spider, heading in my direction.

My inner voice is pleading for me to move, to run, to do *something*. Anything besides staring like a crazy person, but fear has claimed my mobility. Its features are clearer the closer it creeps, spotlighting its disfigurements. Its face is sickly and covered in pustules. The skin is rubbery, stretching heavily, as if melting off the bone.

Adrenaline pumps through my veins, preparing me for

flight, when movement behind the infected draws my attention. A middle-aged man looks in my direction as he runs at full speed down the back corridor, hoping to find refuge. The infected senses him too, and dashes off toward his new prey, leaving me seconds away from pissing myself.

What the hell is wrong with him? I look down at my mother, her face soft and serene, peaceful in her passing. Nothing like the zombie human I'd encountered moments earlier. Glancing around at the other fallen, they all resemble normal humans, sleeping, but with their eyes wide open.

"Duck!" The word is roared out, and the next thing I see is a machete flying straight toward me.

I scream and duck, listening to the warning, my body finally unlocking itself.

A wet whack hits my eardrums, the sickening crunch of bone and tendon snapping apart. Another whack, and the head of an infected hangs from its spine, an upside-down vision of our apocalyptic world. An infected had crept up behind me, and this guy came out of nowhere to cut it down.

"Let's go. There'll be more." The man holds out his hand, expecting me to grab hold. He's covered in blood, plastering his blond hair to his forehead, but his caramel-colored eyes are soft and frantic, like mine.

I reach out and place our palms together, wanting to trust him. Honestly, he's the best chance I've got.

Without words, we run through the mall, my mother left far behind. Everywhere we turn, there are dead bodies that litter the ground, their lives left back in time. I quickly learn that there are two different levels of infection, both resulting in decomposition of their bodies. One's fast and brutal, attacking anything living. The other is slow and confused, unlikely to engage. We're on the ground floor of the mall, allowing us to exit quicker, while those left on the third floor are still desperate to get out.

The air hits my face, and it's as if a veil is lifted. Outside is worse than inside, as death stares us in the face from every direction. Cars are crashed together, alarms are blaring, and screams pierce the air. The man holding on to me doesn't allow me to help, even though there are cries begging for assistance.

He reaches into his pocket, pulls out a key, and unlocks a small blue car. "Get in." He opens the driver's side door and pushes me inside, climbing in after. He starts the car and whips out of the parking lot, driving like a bat out of hell. "We've got to get out of the city," he declares.

My mom was my only family. Now that she's gone, I see no point in deviating from his plan. The city isn't a safe place to remain. With the machete resting between his legs, he maneuvers through the cars, trying to miss all the bodies, but not all are avoidable. We keep our eyes straight ahead, as our car bounces over them like speed bumps. Living people are sparse, and the ones we see are running for their lives, as the infected sense them and give chase. The apocalyptic world around us resembles nothing of the normality of its past, plunging us into chaos seconds after the Flash.

My chest is near bursting with anxiety and heartache for those we've lost and the ones trying to get us to stop, pleading and waving their arms in the air. "Should we—" I begin to mumble, but the man cuts me off.

"No. Look closely. Some of them are infected. We have no way of knowing who's sick and who's not." He glances my way for a second, before returning his eyes to the road.

I nod instead of answering, my shock washing over my body again. *How on Earth is he this calm?* My tranquil demeanor belies the internal battle raging inside of me to stop and help, to break down and cry, but all I can do is sit still in the front seat of a fleeing car.

The destruction passing by my window is unfathomable. Who would have thought that everything we knew would be gone in the blink of an eye? No one thought to plan a future when one no longer exists. Cars are piled together, making the roads impassable, leaving us to drive off-road during our journey of escape.

We're several miles outside of the decrepit city, the sun setting at our backs, before the aftermath catches up to me. I begin to sob uncontrollably, hiccups breaking up my tears intermittently, mourning my mom.

The man driving glances at me again, fear more prominent on his face now than before when he chopped the infected down. The simple reaction causes me to switch from sobbing to laughing uncontrollably. Again, the man looks at me, probably wondering if he saved a crazy person and brought her along for the ride.

"I'm not crazy, I promise." I wipe the tears from my face, attempting to collect myself.

He chuckles. "That's good to know. I'd be worried if you didn't have a reaction to what just happened. I'm Darren, by the way."

"Hi, Darren." I sniffle, wiping snot across the back of my hand. "I'm Mya."

"It's pointless to drive around without a destination. I'm almost out of gas too. I didn't get a chance to fill up before I hit the mall. Can you think of anywhere we can go? My place is downtown in an apartment complex. Probably not the smartest stop," he reasons.

"My grandma gave us her house after she passed away

about a month ago. It's on the outskirts of town, and it's been empty since then." I have no idea of its condition.

"Sounds like it's the best option for now. What's the address?" He turns the car down a side road that leads back to town, toward my grandma's house.

As he drives, I check my pockets. After the Flash, and the attack by the infected, I apparently dropped my purse, and my phone. "Do you have a phone?"

He leans to the side and pulls out his cell, tossing it to me. "Who you calling?"

"A couple friends. My mom was with me back there." I don't elaborate. Not a subject I want to relive yet. Instead, I busy myself with calls that go unanswered. No matter how many times I try each number, there's no answer. Clicking the dimmer on the side of the phone, I cradle it in my lap.

"No answer?" Darren questions.

"No," I whisper. "Is there anyone you want me to call for you?"

His fists tighten on the steering wheel. "No."

I decide not to pry, as my mind wanders to the light in the sky. "What do you think happened? You saw the light, right?"

"Yeah, but I have no idea what it was or why everyone dropped where they were standing. Others turned...insane, or became sick. Then there's you and me, and there's nothing wrong with us. Are we going to suddenly turn into one of those monsters?" We lock eyes, realizing for the first time that his question can become reality.

"I sure hope not. I don't want to live like that. They don't seem to be able to control themselves. They're extremely sick."

"They're not sick. There's no cure coming for this one. We're not getting any response through the cell, and all the cars are crashed on the side of the road. We're starting from scratch. Let's get to the house, keep watch, and gauge our situation."

We arrive a short while later. Grandma's neighborhood is sparse, holding only three other houses, separated by at least fifty yards. The lights are on at the house next door and the one across the street. The third house sits dark, and as blacked-out as Grandma's.

"Pull in the driveway, it leads under the carport. Dim the lights so we don't draw attention."

He pulls in smoothly and as quietly as he can, shutting the engine down. We wait, barely breathing. The anticipation is digging at my anxiety, causing my hands to shake. There're less people out this way, but they could still be infected.

"I think we're good. What's the best way to get in?"

"There's a side door over there." I point to the side of the house, only twenty yards from us. "A key should be under the mat. Like I said, I haven't been here in a long time, so I'm hoping it's still there."

We exit the car, quietly latching the doors behind us, as the insects of the night echo their calls. We tiptoe toward the house, staying in the shadows and out of the moonlight. Yard debris is piled high next to the door, covering the mat from view. We sift through the crunchy pile of leaves and tumbleweeds, the noise amplified by the calm of the night.

Darren bends down to flip the mat and find the key. Its right where I remember it being. He clicks the screen door open, the springs creaking, signaling our location again. I don't bother to tell him to shush, as he's well aware of the consequences.

A flash of movement catches my eye, snapping my head in that direction. The night is motionless, making me wonder if I'm seeing things. Darren clicks the lock open and turns the handle, and that's when I realize nature's no longer singing a tune.

"Get inside...something's coming." My heart is pounding, sensing danger. I push Darren inside, into the living room, just as the pounding of feet rush in our direction. I slam the door closed and lock the handle again.

"Shit. Is it one of them?" Darren pulls me back against the wall.

"I don't know. I didn't get a good look, but if they're not infected, they didn't say anything." If the person's looking for shelter, you'd think they'd announce themselves.

We wait a few minutes before Darren slowly steps forward to look out the window in the door. He's about a foot away when a face appears, obscured by the lacy curtain. We both jump and shout, pinpointing our location to the intruder.

"Hello?" A voice I recognize comes through the door. It's Mrs. Yotti from next door. I used to watch her do Muay Thai in her yard when I stayed at my grandma's house.

I step next to Darren. "It's Jacinda Yotti." I reach to unlock the door, when Darren grabs my arm, stopping me. I glare up at him. "I know her. She's okay." I reach for the lock again, but I'm stopped a second time.

"She sounds funny," Darren says.

"How the hell do you know she sounds funny? You've never met her." I reach a third time, and again, I'm intercepted.

I open my mouth to protest, when Jacinda speaks again. "Is that you, Mya? I'm glad I caught you," she giggles. "You wouldn't happen to have a cup of sugar? Your Grandma said to stop by anytime." Her words confuse me. She was at Grandma's funeral.

Instead of opening the door, I flick the curtain to the side, and scream.

Jacinda's distorted and blistered-covered face stares wildly back at us. There's no recognition, even through she spoke my name moments earlier. The skin below her sockets is drooping, as if melting off, highlighting the frantic search of her yellow eyes. Focusing on us, her smile stretches, blood covering her lips and teeth. "Hello, dear."

"Back away from the door." Darren grabs my elbow.

Confused, I resist for a second, until the first attack hits the door. I stumble back against the wall, startled by the commotion. Remembering my grandma's love of an evening fire, I rush to the left and grab the fireplace tool set. Watching her stir the fire at night, shoots a memory straight through me. *Mya, darling, if you're ever in a pickle, these fire pokers will work perfect as a weapon.* She was always giving me "life's learning lessons" as she called them.

"Where the hell are you going?" Darren mock whispers.

"Here, take this." I toss him the poker and keep the shovel for myself. Jacinda's still banging against the door, but not breaking through the window. Her speech is off, slurred, and a little confused. She's not thinking logically, or she would have broken the window and gained entrance within moments.

"We need to do something about this, or she's going to draw attention to us." Darren speaks the truth. She's screeching and slamming herself against the door.

"What do you suggest?" I already know he means to kill her, I'm just not sure I'm ready to hear it yet. Ultimately, I don't have a choice.

"You open the door and I'll stab her in the head." The shock on my face has Darren softening. "It'll be quick. She won't feel a thing, I promise." He rubs my arm, but there's no time for warm and fuzzy feelings. "Ready?"

I nod, because no, I'm not ready. Jacinda's the nicest lady, and I'm about to be an accomplice in stabbing her in the head with a fire poker.

Darren stands with his back against the wall, readying the fire poker for the best stabbing angle, and then nods, signaling that he's ready. My hand tightens around the doorknob, as my heart pounds in my ears. I mentally count to three before yanking the door open, allowing a screeching Jacinda inside.

Darren wastes no time and plunges the iron rod into her temple, but she doesn't go down peacefully like he promised. She continues to shriek and flail, now targeting Darren, her fingers splayed into claws. He hits her, pinning her down with his foot, stabbing her repeatedly in the stomach. He tries different angles, not able to get another shot at her head. Unbelievably, she's screaming louder than before, the sound deafening.

A switch inside me flips, and I rush to Darren's aid, stabbing down. The flat end of my iron shovel connects with her neck, leaving a large, bloody gash. I raise my arms up and slam home again. This time, cutting through muscles and tendons. A pained gurgling drifts up to me moments before I slam down for the third time, hearing the crunch of bones, eliciting a battle cry from my lungs. My strikes become wild, killing not only Jacinda, but this entire zombie situation.

"Mya! Mya! Wake up!" Hands grip my arms and shake me. "Come on, babe. You're having another nightmare."

I'm ripped from my dream in a panic. "Darren!"

"I'm here." He reaches out and soothes me, murmuring, "It was years ago. Mrs. Yotti is long gone." He pulls me closer, tucking me against his side. "Try to go back to sleep."

Sleep...I haven't slept well since the night before the Flash. We've made ourselves at home in grandma's house. My mom hadn't touched anything after my grandma's death, leaving the cellar and all its full pantry alone for us to live on. Since Grandma lived in a secluded area on the outskirts of town, we've made this our home base, rarely having run-ins with infected or humans.

On mornings that don't plague me with nightmares, there's a moment between my dreamworld and conscious-ness that is peaceful, normal. A world where there was no Flash, and my mom's alive, sleeping in the next room. Then realization hits, slugging me in the gut repeatedly, delivering its own message.

Welcome to the new world.

ABOUT JESSICA GOMEZ

Jessica Gomez is a bestselling author of Suspense, Romance & Paranormal, Apocalyptic books. She is best known for her Paranormal Flash series. She independently published her first book, After the Before, in 2014, and reached #1 in Bilingual, Suspense, & Romance genres. She recently released book 3 in the Flash series, Evolved. For more about this author, visit one of the sites listed. She enjoys hearing from and chatting with her readers, who have the same passion for reading.

5

―――――

FIRST OCCURENCE

BY JOSHUA C. CHADD

Wednesday afternoon, three days before the official outbreak

Sheriff Gibson walked up to the corpse, his boots sinking into the soft soil. He pulled off his cowboy hat and wiped the sweat from his brow with the back of his hand. Living in Texas his whole life, he'd grown accustomed to the suffocating summer heat, but today was hot even by his standards.

The teenage boy at his feet had been brutally murdered, with his throat torn out and a nasty gash on his head. But the murderer hadn't stopped there. They'd taken chunks of flesh, leaving the corpse barely recognizable, but he knew it was Tedd Harms, a high school student from Hill City.

Someone else had died on his watch, in his town. This wasn't the first person he'd let die when he should've been able to help them, and that wasn't even counting the other deaths this week. His breathing grew frantic as an anxiousness rose within him. Feeling something nudge his leg, he glanced down. Fidel was looking up at him with eyes too intelligent for a dog. He took a deep breath, stroking the brown and black hair of his German Shepherd Malinois mix. After a minute, he regained control.

"Thanks, buddy," Gibson said, patting Fidel on the head.

He looked back at the body. It was the same MO as the others, to a T. It was hard to believe that in the last few days there'd been more murders in Hill City than in the last ten years combined—four in as many days. These weren't random deaths like it'd seemed at first, and it wasn't some rabid animal. This was a person, someone who liked to kill their victims and then eat the bodies—a serial-killing cannibal like some crap he'd seen on TV.

Crouching down, he examined the body more closely. The head wound had been fatal, cracking the boy's skull and killing him before the perp had begun to devour him. He was lucky. The other victims had been alive for that part. More than likely, the fatal blow was sustained when he'd been flung from his ATV after he'd swerved to avoid hitting the perp.

Standing, Gibson took a few steps back, looking at where the boy lay compared to the rolled ATV. His guess was right. Swerve marks in the dirt showed he'd tried to avoid something. He'd been going too fast and wasn't wearing a helmet, and when his head had collided with a large rock on the two-track, it'd killed him instantly. Then the perp had descended on the boy and started eating him.

What confused him the most was why none of the victims had tried to run. The perp had to have been armed with something, like a gun or knife at least. Yet, all the evidence pointed to one simple fact—the perp had never used a weapon, always killing with their bare hands, or more accurately, their teeth. The whole thing didn't feel right, but he couldn't put his finger on it.

Fidel's ears perked up and he looked down the two-track

leading to the road. Someone was coming. A few seconds later, Deputy Randall walked around the tree line where the trail made a hard left.

"He's a little ways back in here," Randall said, huffing as he stopped next to Gibson.

"I don't think it's the distance," Gibson said, glancing down at Randall's belly. "I think it's all those donuts you've been eating."

"It's at least two miles back in here," Randall said, still trying to catch his breath.

"Try just over half a mile," Gibson said.

"Damn, guess I am gettin' a little fat."

"More than a little."

Randall huffed and walked up closer to the body. "Same MO."

"Glad to see that police academy paid off."

"You know what I think?" Randall asked, looking back at him.

"I don't wanna hear it."

"Boss, it's got to be them zombies all the kids are talkin' about these days. I mean, just look at the wounds."

"It's not some fairy-and-magic-horse crap," Gibson said. "It's just some freak who likes eating his victims, nothing else."

"But what if it is zombies?"

"The next time you say the word zombie, I'm gonna pistol-whip you in the jaw."

"Fine, but don't say I didn't warn ya, Boss. When it comes out and we find it is them zombies, I'll have to say I told ya so."

"If that ever happens, I'll buy your next box of donuts myself."

Randall smiled, missing the sarcasm in Gibson's voice.

He usually did, which made it all the more enjoyable. For all the crap he gave Randall, he was a good man and a decent cop. He wasn't going to win any medals any time soon, but he was good at his job.

"Think there's any relation to the other victims?" Randall asked, bending over to look more closely at the boy.

"I doubt it," Gibson said.

"Then what's the connection here?"

"You tell me."

"I'm not sure..."

"Then we're on the same page. They almost seem like opportunity killings rather than thought-out murders, like the perp just stumbled into them. If that's true, we need to find whoever it is because it won't be long before they're in town."

Randall nodded and walked over to the ATV. "You think the perp did this?"

"The marks back there make it look like Tedd was trying to avoid hitting something."

"Interesting," Randall said, scratching his belly. "Oh, Mrs. Henderson said to tell you the Feds called. They're sending in a team to assist with the investigation."

"Assist, my ass," Gibson said. "They're here to take it over."

"I can finish up here and wait for the coroner if you wanna meet 'em."

"Thanks, Randall. I'll do that."

Gibson turned and Fidel finally stood up from where he'd been sitting, following by his side as they started down the two-track. It was funny how most people forgot he even had a dog with him, but he didn't. The constant companionship was what helped keep him calm. Other people just couldn't believe a dog that weighed eighty pounds could be so well behaved and almost invisible. He didn't bark and he didn't growl unless he was protecting Gibson. Then, he got downright mean and his military K-9 training kicked in. Fidel wasn't just his service dog; he was his best friend.

Gibson made it back to the gravel road leading to town where his Hill County Sheriff's Department truck was parked. He opened the door and Fidel jumped in, going over to sit in the passenger seat of the old, single-cab Chevy. After a few miles, Gibson pulled up outside the sheriff's office on the north side of the small town. There were five hundred and sixty-two people living in Hill City. It was a town in the middle of nowhere, and the main reason people lived there was the large pharmaceutical laboratory located fifteen miles north of town. It was owned by LifeWork and was the corporate giant's main facility where they produced all of the generic drugs from Texas all the way up to Montana. They even had some distribution to the east and west coasts, although those had their own facilities.

Going inside the office, he was immediately greeted by Mrs. Henderson sitting behind the front desk. The lady was in her late fifties, and he could only imagine how much of a fireball she'd been when she was younger—a lot like his wife. Fidel nudged up against his leg and Gibson absently scratched between his ears, not even realizing that his heart rate had picked up until he took a deep breath.

"Our illustrious sheriff has returned," Mrs. Henderson said, glancing up at him. "You find the psychopath yet?"

"No, Mrs. Henderson," Gibson said, hiding his smile. "But you're welcome to go out and catch him yourself."

"I'd rather not. That's your job, after all," Mrs. Henderson said, and he nodded. "Someone from the FBI called; they said they're sending a team down to help contain the situation."

"Contain the situation?"

"That's what she said."

"How is this a federal case?"

"Don't ask me. I just answer the phone and file the paperwork."

"When will they get here?" Gibson asked.

"They're sending a team down from Dallas," Mrs. Henderson said. "They called at eight, so maybe in the next hour or so?"

"Let me know when they arrive. I'll be in my office."

Gibson walked through a small room containing the two deputies' desks to get to the back where his office was. He went inside and shut the door behind him as Fidel slipped in by his side. He walked up to the corkboard on his wall and stuck a red thumbtack in the approximate location they'd found the kid's body that morning. The map showed Hill City in the center and the Nechos State Park to the north with the Nechos River cutting through the middle of it. A gravel road led north from town to a campground on the far side of the park. It continued for another four miles, exiting the park and ending at a black circle on the map— LifeWork. Two red tacks were inside the campground while a third was two miles south and now the fourth, four miles south of that. That only left five miles between the last body and town.

There was a red circle around the campground from a recent unsolved case. Last Friday, a woman, Jacinda Yotti, had gone missing. Her tent and all of her belongings were still at the campground, but she'd disappeared. Could she be the killer, or was that case unrelated? Within two days of Jacinda going missing, people started turning up dead, that wasn't a coincidence. There was a connection there; he just had to find it. The missing woman was a librarian who'd come all the way from Kansas City, Missouri on vacation. Gibson had learned this when he'd contacted the woman's husband back in Missouri.

Two days later, Mr. and Mrs. Pennualis had turned up at the campground—dead. The young couple had been on vacation from Houston. The following day, while coming back from the scene, Deputy Henderson had found Ethan Darthu's body in a ditch with his mountain bike laying a few feet away. The man had been the school's PE teacher, an upstanding citizen, and a guy everyone liked, literally. No one had anything bad to say about him, which was impressive in a small town like this. Now, two days later, a high school student, Tedd Harms, was murdered four miles south of where they'd found Ethan's body. All of the victim's bodies had been mangled and eaten on to where they were barely recognizable and oddly enough, they'd all sustained some kind of head wound. Before, the three bodies had made a triangle in and around the campground, but now a new pattern could be seen. The murders had started just south of LifeWork and they were heading towards town.

They'd learned about Tedd's death that morning when his buddy, Francis, had come right up to the sheriff's office on his ATV. He'd been scared, claiming his friend had been eaten. It took five minutes for Gibson to get a coherent story out of the kid. Francis had been farther up the trail when he realized Tedd wasn't following. He'd turned back and found the body, proceeded to vomit, and then he'd come speeding into town.

Gibson glanced at the pictures and evidence pinned around the map. It wasn't like a perp not to leave any evidence that could tip him off—some sign or clue that gave him an idea about what they wanted or why they were killing. He had a way of looking at these cases and putting the pieces together even when others couldn't. He'd even been the youngest on the force in Houston to be promoted to detective. Back when he'd lived there, cases like this weren't as rare. Yet something about this didn't make sense. He couldn't find the clues he normally could. True, the perp may have left some blood at the first scene, but they hadn't heard back from the laboratory in Lufkin yet and probably wouldn't until it was too late. Either this perp was extremely good or ten years in this small town had dulled Gibson's skills.

The phone on his desk rang and he picked it up. "Yes, Mrs. Henderson?"

"Your Feds are here..." she said and paused, "but they aren't like any I've ever seen."

Gibson hung up the phone, checked the Glock holstered on his duty belt, and looked down at Fidel.

"You ready?" Gibson asked. The dog looked at him in that particular way he had and Gibson smiled, patting Fidel on the side. "Yeah, me neither."

Exiting his office and walking through the front doors, he stopped just outside.

What the hell is this?

Six men were standing around a big black armored vehicle, decked out in black camouflage with full tactical gear. Most of them carried ACR combat rifles, while one carried a SAW machine gun and another had a scoped bolt-action rifle. These men weren't FBI or any other federal agency he was aware of. They looked more like a military squad, but they didn't have an emblem on their vehicle or ranks on their uniforms.

"Are you the man in charge?" asked a big man with a red beard, walking up to Gibson.

"I'm Sheriff Gibson," he said, sticking his hand out. The man didn't shake it. "And you are?"

His nametag read Clover, but that couldn't be—

"Clover," the bearded man said. "This is my team. We'll be taking charge of this situation."

"Like hell you are," Gibson said. "You don't have the jurisdiction."

"Night," Clover said, motioning to a hulking African American man.

Night came forward and handed Gibson a single sheet of paper. It was a document signed by Texas Governor Henry Price giving power to a private contracting company called Vindex Corp. Since when did mercenaries get involved with federal investigations?

"I don't care what your paper says," Gibson said, crumpling it up and throwing it at Clover's chest. "This is my town and you're not gonna take my investigation from me."

"I don't care about your investigation," Clover said. "We're just taking the bodies."

"The bodies?" Gibson asked.

"Yes."

"If that's how it has to be, so be it," Gibson said. "But stay outta my way."

Clover turned without saying another word and motioned to his men. They all climbed into the large armored vehicle like a well-oiled machine. They were certainly professionals. The driver backed out while Clover glared at Gibson from the passenger seat. He didn't like this. Those men knew too much—way too much, he realized as they headed straight to the funeral home where the victims' bodies were. He thought it'd been strange when no one from Houston had come down to get the Pennualis's bodies. In fact, they hadn't even called him back. This wasn't a normal case. Absently running his fingers through the hair on Fidel's back, he decided it was time to visit Mrs. Harms.

Might as well get it over with now.

Pulling up outside, he turned the truck off and climbed out. Mrs. Harms met him at the door.

"Is it true?" she asked as he walked onto the porch.

"I'm sorry," Gibson said, taking his hat off. "It is."

She stifled a cried. "I know what Francis said, but I didn't..."

"I'm sorry for your loss," Gibson said. He was tired of saying that. He'd had to do it way too much in the last few days. He needed to find that perp and solve this case, and maybe it'd be better if the perp didn't even get a trial. "I know it's hard for you right now, but can I come inside and ask you a few questions?"

She nodded, moving into the living room, and he followed. He sat down on the couch while Mrs. Harms sat in a chair across from him and Fidel curled up at his feet. She didn't even glance down at Fidel. Everyone in town was used to the dog following Gibson around.

"I'll try and make this quick," Gibson said. "The sooner I get answers, the sooner I find the killer."

"I'm ready," Mrs. Harms said.

"Do you know why Tedd and Francis were in the park on ATVs?"

"I know it's illegal, but Tedd has been so hard to discipline after his father left last year," Mrs. Harms said through her tears. "I tried to stop him, but he wouldn't listen."

"So they were just going for a little ride?" Gibson asked.

"As far as I know. They do that from time to time."

"I want you to think hard about this next question," Gibson said. "Do you know if anyone wanted to harm Tedd?"

"Of course not," Mrs. Harms responded immediately.

"I want you to take a second and think about it. Anyone mad at him lately? Even something small could help with the investigation."

She paused for a few seconds. "My son may have played hooky a lot, but he wasn't a bad kid."

"So no one might want to hurt him?"

"I said no."

"I just want to be sure. Do you have any relatives in Houston?"

"Some extended family, but most live north of Dallas."

The more she talked the more strength she gathered. Tedd's little brother would be home from school in a few hours and she'd have to stay strong for him. Gibson knew personally how hard it was to cope with the loss of loved ones. It could do things to peoples' minds if they were left alone. Fidel rose to a sitting position and rested his head on Gibson's leg, and his hand found its way to Fidel's head.

"Have you ever heard of a Robert and Darcy Pennualis?"

"No. Was that the couple found in the campground?"

"Yes, ma'am. How close were Tedd and Francis?"

"They've been friends since they were kids. He wouldn't do something like this."

"I don't think so either, but I have to ask."

"Do you have many more questions, Sheriff? I'd like to go lay down before Bobby gets home."

"One more. Did Tedd have Mr. Darthu for PE?"

"Yes, he did."

"How was their relationship?"

"PE was his favorite class and he always had good things to say about Mr. Darthu."

"Thank you, ma'am. I'll call if I need anything else."

He stood up and let himself out. Mrs. Harms was taking

the loss of her son as could be expected, and he didn't think she was a suspect. That hadn't even been a question since the beginning, but he liked to check off the obvious first.

After driving back, he walked into the office, noticing both of his deputies sitting at their desks.

"Who were those assholes at the funeral home?" Randall asked.

"Mercenaries sent by the Feds," Gibson said. "They have authority to confiscate the bodies for some reason."

"The letter from Governor Price said the bodies could be contaminated with something," Randall said.

"I didn't read it," Gibson said and then looked at Henderson. "Find anything else at the campground?"

"Nothing, but I've been thinking," Henderson said. "What if it's like a zombie virus or somethin'?"

"Come on," Gibson said, retreating to his office.

"I said the same thing," Randall said.

"If you two morons don't quit it with the zombie crap, I'll can ya both," Gibson said, shutting his door.

He could hear them laughing outside. Sitting down, he kicked his feet up on his desk and grabbed a Shiner Bock from his mini-fridge. He popped the cap off on the edge of his desk, adding another mark to the already scarred surface. Taking a sip, he gazed at the map on the wall. Randall had added new pictures of today's scene to the board. Somewhere within those pictures and dots on the map there was a pattern; he just had to see it.

At the end of the day, he went home empty-handed after chasing a few dead ends. His biggest hunch was that the missing woman, Jacinda, was to blame for all this. But how did he go about finding her and bringing her in?

Thursday morning, two days before the official outbreak

Gibson sat at his desk, staring intently at the map as he'd been doing for the last hour. There was nothing new this morning. He'd learned that the coroner hadn't even been able to touch the kid's body. Those mercenaries working for Vindex Corp. had disposed of all three bodies in the cremator as soon as they'd gotten there. More of their people had shown up last night, setting up a couple of large pavilion-style tents in the empty lot next to the funeral home. Two of their armored vehicles sat next to the tents, along with two black SUVs. He still didn't know how Vindex Corp. fit into this. He'd tried getting answers, but Clover hadn't told him anything and none of the others had even responded to him. They were a bunch of pricks. They might have key information to his investigation and yet they wouldn't say a damn word.

So here he was, spinning in circles, knowing he was missing something. He knew the clues were there. They had to be; they always were. Maybe he needed to go to LifeWork and question them. It was the only lead he hadn't followed yet. He glanced at his watch. It was seven o'clock in the morning, and their offices should be open. Wasting no time, he climbed into his truck with Fidel.

Twenty minutes later, he was sitting outside a gate, and yet he was still a mile from the facility. A small intercom with a large green button and video camera sat on a support post to the left of the dirt road.

"LifeWork front desk," a female voice said. "How may I help you?"

"This is Sheriff Gibson," he said. "I need to talk to someone in charge."

"One second, please."

It was more like ten minutes before the voice came back. "Sir, I'll have someone waiting for you."

The gates swung open and he drove forward onto the paved road. Soon, he saw a large compound with a high fence around it. A guardhouse sat by another gate, operated by a man dressed in a black uniform—similar to the ones the Vindex Corp. men wore. That was an interesting fact, which he noted, as the guard waved him through the already-open gate. Entering the compound, he noticed there were four large buildings on the premises. The signs for each read Production and Management, Research and Development, Front Offices, and Housing. Following the sign for offices, he was awed by how truly massive the place was. There must have been more people working there than the entire population of Hill City.

He parked in front of the large doors to the first building where a man in a white lab coat was standing out front, presumably waiting for him. Climbing out of his truck, he and Fidel walked up to the man. The man was tall—even more so than Gibson's own six feet—and in his sixties with white hair and soft features.

"Sheriff Gibson, I presume?" the man asked.

"Yeah," Gibson said.

"I'm Dr. Hashen," the man said, reaching out his hand, which Gibson shook. "What can I help you with?"

"Can we go inside and talk?" Gibson asked.

"I'm afraid there are no pets allowed in the buildings— FDA policy and all," Dr. Hashen said. "You can chain him up outside."

"I'll chain you up outside," Gibson mumbled under his breath.

"What was that?"

"I said, in that case we can talk out here."

"So what would you like to know?"

"Are you aware of the murders just a few miles south of here?"

Dr. Hashen looked shocked. "No, I hadn't heard. What happened to them?"

"They were murdered, like I said."

"How were they murdered?"

"Looks like they were eaten alive."

The doctor's face turned a shade paler than his already alabaster skin.

"What can you tell me—" Gibson began, but Dr. Hashen cut him off.

"I'm sorry Sheriff," Dr. Hashen said, turning. "I have urgent business to attend to. We'll have to reschedule."

"Like hell we will," Gibson said, grabbing the doctor's arm as he started to walk away. "I want answers. I have four bodies out there."

Dr. Hashen jerked the arm out of Gibson's grasp. "Then you'd better start looking elsewhere because you're not going to find any answers here. Good day."

With that the doctor turned, swiped his keycard, and walked back into the building. Gibson growled in frustration. That doctor knew something, and whatever it was had him spooked.

He walked back to his truck and climbed in behind Fidel. The stress of the investigation was wearing on him. When he'd moved to this small town, he'd been hoping for an easy, stress-free job until he retired. And it had been just that for the last decade, but now this.

His cell phone vibrated in his pocket and he pulled it out. It was Randall.

"What do ya want?" he asked, answering his phone.

"Boss, we've got another body," Randall said on the other end.

Gibson cursed. "Where?"

"The Dobendik place."

"I'll be there in ten," Gibson said, hanging up the phone.

The Dobendik ranch was just south of the park, only a half mile from Hill City, which meant the murderer was closing in on the town. Gibson had just started his truck to head over to the ranch when he noticed one of the armored vehicles the Vindex mercenaries drove pulling through the gate and stopping at the large doors to the offices. Dr. Hashen came storming out, yelling and waving his arms at the man who climbed out of the passenger seat. This man wasn't dressed like the rest of the mercenaries. Instead, he wore a gray suit. He took the doctor by the arm and led him inside. The rest of the armed men fanned out, going in separate directions. It was like they were hunting something within the compound.

What the hell is going on around here?

Regardless, he had another murder to investigate, and he'd have to figure all this conspiracy shit out later. Right then he had a town to protect from a vicious killer he couldn't seem to catch. He sped back down the gravel road through the park, spooking a deer, and its white, flag-like tail waved back and forth as it disappeared into the trees to the side of the road.

Pulling up outside the ranch house, he came to a stop, gravel grinding under his tires. He jumped out and Randall met him at the front door.

"Prepare yourself, Boss," Randall said. "This one's brutal."

"Is it, or are you just bein' a wimp?" Gibson asked, taking out some of his frustration on his deputy.

"It's bad," Randall said, turning and leading him towards the master bedroom.

Fidel walked by his side, nudging up against his leg to be in constant contact with him. It was frustrating because he couldn't walk normally with the eighty-pound dog pressed against his legs. But his anger began to fade, and he found himself petting his companion. It'd been a long couple of days, and he considered going back out and grabbing the pills from his glove box, but he didn't. It was too hard to think while on them, plus it'd been years since he'd needed them and he wasn't about to start again. This investigation was beginning to remind him of his last one in Houston over a decade ago.

He hesitated as he realized Fidel had sat down next to the couch in the living room. Gibson's heart rate had skyrocketed and his breathing was coming in quick gasps. He slumped down against the back of the couch next to Fidel, leaning his head on the dog. All the stress was causing his anxiety to heighten. He closed his eyes but immediately opened them. Just for a second, he'd no longer been in this room but in a different living room, with the corpse of a woman lying on the floor. She'd been carved up, missing her skin like a deer hanging in the butcher shop—gutted alive.

"You okay, Boss?" Randall asked, coming back into the living room.

"Gimme a sec," Gibson said through clenched teeth.

"Sure. I'll just be in here," Randall said and walked back into the bedroom.

Deep breath, Gibson told himself. *Breathe, just breathe.*

Fidel laid his head on his lap, and Gibson rested his head against the back of the couch, staring up at the white plaster ceiling. All he thought about was each breath he took as he slowly stroked Fidel's hair, the motion calming him. It amazed him how the dog knew his emotions better than he did. Even after more than five years, it was still impressive. There was a reason his companion's full name was Fidelis.

Taking one last deep breath, he stood up. "Thanks, buddy," Gibson said, looking down at the dog. Fidel wagged his tail in response and Gibson smiled, giving him a scratch behind the ears as he walked into the master bedroom.

Randall wasn't a wimp. The woman, presumably Kay Dobendik—although it was impossible to tell now—was lying on the bed. She'd been opened up. Her intestines were hanging off the edge of the mattress and the cream-colored sheets were stained a dark crimson. Blood had splattered on the wall above the headboard and a few drops even speckled the ceiling. That she'd been alive when this happened was evident by the shattered glass near the night-stand, the lamp laying on the floor, and the disheveled bedding.

Walking up, he took a closer look. Large chunks of flesh were missing from her body, just like the other victims. Any reservation he had that this might not have been connected fled his mind. This was the killer's fifth victim. As he looked closer, he noticed skin under the victim's fingernails. She'd definitely fought back. Finally, they could gather some DNA and at least have a chance of identifying the killer. He looked at the rest of the body. It was hard to tell, considering how mauled she was, but it looked like this had happened within the last couple of hours. He glanced at his clock— eight-thirty in the morning. There were no missing vehicles outside and the killer couldn't have gotten far on foot.

"You already call the coroner?" Gibson asked Randall, who was walking around the room taking pictures.

"He's on his way," Randall replied.

This was the one thing his deputy excelled at. He could inventory a crime scene like none other. He had an eye for catching things that were out of place and documenting them all.

The front door of the house opened and Gibson left to go meet the coroner, but it wasn't Jerry; instead, it was the Vindex Corp. man he'd talked to the day before.

"What're you doin' here, Clown?" Gibson asked.

"It's Clover," the red-bearded man said.

"Close enough," Gibson said.

"I'm here to confiscate the body," Clover said.

He stopped in front of Gibson as two of his men wearing hazmat suits walked around them and into the bedroom.

"Like hell you are," Gibson said, stepping up and looking down at the man.

While Gibson was four inches taller than Clover, the other man had another fifty pounds of muscle on him. Clover pulled out a new piece of paperwork and shoved it in his face. Gibson snatched it away and read it as Clover's men came back out, carrying the body wrapped in plastic. It was a form stating that Kay Dobendik was now property of the US Government and their acting associates, Vindex Corp. It also stated that the house had been foreclosed by the bank and was also now theirs. The murder had only taken place a couple of hours ago. How could they have already gotten this paperwork?

"This is bullshit," Gibson said, crumpling it.

"You and your deputy need to leave the premises," Clover said, leaning forward. "Now."

Fidel growled from beside Gibson and the other man looked down.

"I wouldn't piss him off," Gibson said. "He's liable to rip your throat out."

"I don't want to have to kill your mutt, but I will if he so much as flinches in my direction."

Gibson's hand went to the Glock on his hip. This man was two seconds away from getting his ass kicked.

"Boss," Randall said from behind him. "Let's go. I got what we need."

Gibson didn't take his eyes off Clover until he stepped aside, motioning towards the front door. "Listen to your deputy."

Randall came up next to him and whispered in his ear. "I have all the pictures and samples from under her fingernails."

His deputy walked past him, and Gibson took a deep breath and walked out behind him. Fidel stayed, teeth bared at Clover.

"Fidel, *Hier*," Gibson said. His dog hesitated only a second before following him out the front door.

Deputy Henderson's squad car pulled up and he rolled down his window. "I just got news. Holly Dobendik was admitted to the clinic an hour ago."

The daughter, of course!

"I'm headin' there now," Gibson said, jogging over to his truck. "Randall, get those pictures back to the station and that DNA sent off. Tell them to rush it. Henderson, keep an eye on these black-uniformed pricks. I want to know exactly what they're doing."

"Got it," Randall said.

"Yes, sir," Henderson said.

Gibson sped off to the only medical facility within fifty miles—a small clinic on the south side of town. He made it there in record time, coming to a screeching halt outside the front entrance.

"Where's Holly Dobendik?" Gibson asked, bursting through the front doors.

"Exam room three," Mary, the receptionist, said. He had already taken off down the hall when she called out behind him. "Fidel has to wait in the truck!"

He ignored her and continued on his way, Fidel right by his side. He knocked on the door but didn't wait for a response, opening it and startling the young teen sitting on the examination table. Dr. Hart, the town's new doctor, sat in a chair, writing on a clipboard. He glanced up when Gibson barged into the room, his stern features turning into a scowl.

"I'm afraid—" Dr. Hart began to say.

"Shut it, Doc," Gibson said. "I need to talk to Holly. You can wait outside."

"I beg your—"

"I said, wait outside!" Gibson shouted and Fidel helped accentuate the point with a low growl.

Dr. Hart called him a colorful name and left the room in a hurry. Gibson would pay for that one later, but right then he had one goal—to catch a killer.

"I need to ask you some questions, Holly," Gibson said, sitting down in the chair the doctor had just vacated. Fidel sat next to him, facing the door.

"Okay," Holly said. He could tell she was nervous and scared as hell.

"What happened?"

"It was dad. He killed my mom."

"What?" Gibson asked. That didn't make any sense. Liam Dobendik was the killer? The rancher who was involved in FFA? "Tell me how it happened."

"I was in bed when I heard mom screaming. I didn't know what to do at first, so I just laid there. Then she stopped and I went into the room. Dad... he was on the bed... he was eating her."

Tears were streaming down her face. He could only imagine what it would be like to see his dad eating his mom—almost like coming home to see his wife and children skinned alive. Fidel nudged him on the leg and he asked another question before he lost control. He hated to push the girl, but he needed answers.

"Then what happened?" Gibson asked.

"I screamed and dad came at me. I just stood there. I held my arm up to stop him but he bit me. I pulled away and ran all the way here."

"He didn't follow you?"

"I didn't look back."

He finally really looked at her. She had her left arm in a bandage, and her skin was pale and shiny with sweat. She looked terrible, but that wasn't surprising with all she'd just been through.

"Do you know why your dad might...?" Gibson couldn't finish the question.

"No," Holly said through her tears.

"Did your dad say anything this morning before he bit you?"

"No, he just growled, almost like an animal."

"Where was your dad yesterday?"

"He spent most of the day on the north section."

"Doing what?"

"There's been a couple hogs tearing up the fields and he was up there trying to kill them."

No alibi and only a mile or so from where they'd found the kid's body yesterday. Crap, maybe it was Liam. He had a deer feeder and hunting blind on the north section of his land that bordered the park. Had he returned there after killing his wife? It was the only lead he had.

"Is there anything else that might be important?" Gibson asked.

"No," Holly said, and then hesitated. "Well, dad came back last night saying he'd been bitten."

"By what?"

"He didn't say, but mom bandaged him up. He didn't even eat, he was so sick. Mom thought it might've been rabies or something."

"Anything else?"

"No," Holly said, then looked up at Gibson with pleading eyes. "When you find him, can you try and talk to him?"

"I will. Thanks, Holly," Gibson said, standing. "I'm sorry for your loss."

He exited the room and passed by a fuming Dr. Hart without saying a word. Jogging to his truck, he climbed inside and took off back towards the Dobendik's ranch. As he drove through town, he noticed a pillar of smoke rising into the sky to the north.

"What the hell is that?" Gibson mumbled.

He sped through town, going double the speed limit. As he drew near the ranch, he could tell the smoke was coming from the Dobendik's house. Pulling into the driveway, he was shocked to find that it was completely consumed by flames. Their small town's fire truck was just sitting there, not even trying to put out the fire.

"What the hell?" Gibson asked, walking up to the fire chief.

"Hey, Sheriff," Ron said.

"Why aren't you putting that out?"

"Because of them," Ron said and pointed to a squad of

Vindex mercenaries, watching the fire. "They said let it burn. Even gave me some fancy paperwork saying the house was condemned."

"This is total bull," Gibson said. "All that paperwork is probably fake."

How could they possibly have gotten the paperwork required to burn down a house with all its possessions, especially when the owner was still alive? That didn't even make sense, but it was a line of questioning for another day. He had to find Liam before he killed again. Then he could stick his boot up Clover's ass.

Gibson left the fire chief watching the burning house and continued north on foot, towards where Liam would have his feeder and blind set up. He walked at a quick jog, hand at his hip and ready to draw. While he didn't want to kill the man, he wasn't going to let Liam get the jump on him either.

After a few minutes, he saw the camouflaged blind sitting in the tree line and a feeder in the middle of the field a hundred yards away. Three white tails faded into the trees on the north. Staying just inside the trees, he snuck around to the back side of the blind. If Liam had a rifle, he sure as hell didn't want to be shot, even if that wasn't his MO. Twenty yards away from the blind, with a view of the back door, Gibson stopped, drawing his handgun. Fidel moved a couple of steps away from him, making it less likely that he'd be hit by a stray round aimed at his owner.

"Liam Dobendik!" Gibson shouted. "If you're in there, come out with your hands in the air!"

He waited for a few seconds, but nothing happened. No movement or sound came from inside the blind.

"I just wanna talk!" Gibson shouted again, slowly approaching.

There was still no response. He was only a few feet from the door and there was no noise coming from inside. Quickly, he closed the distance and flung the door open. It was empty. He cursed. So much for his only lead.

The wind swirled at the edge of the trees and Fidel's ears perked up. Gibson looked down at the dog. "What is it?" he asked.

Fidel was looking along the trees north of the blind, and Gibson lowered his handgun as he walked in the direction Fidel was looking. The dog's ears stayed up the entire time, and after fifty yards he could smell what Fidel had—the stench of decomposing flesh in the hot sun. Just inside the tree line up ahead was a body, and as he slowly approached, the smell became stronger. This person had been dead awhile. No way was it Liam.

The body was that of a middle-aged female. Crouching down, he got a better look and tried his best not to throw up. The woman had a bullet hole in her head, along with three more in the chest. The strange part though was the shots to the chest almost seemed post-mortem. There wasn't nearly as much blood around the wounds as one would expect, had it washed off somehow? It hadn't rained in weeks, and there was still a decent amount of blood on the rest of her body. It looked as though she'd been dead for a couple of days; the more he looked, the more uneasy he felt. There was extensive bruising under the skin, almost as if the victim's veins had burst prior to death. Her eyes were still open and bloodshot. Her chin and upper chest were covered in congealed blood that had oozed out of her mouth. In all of his years as a cop, he'd never seen anything like it. Pulling out a latex glove, he slipped it on one hand and held the body up to look at her back. There were no other visible wounds apart from the exit holes from the bullets. So if the shots were after she was dead, what had killed her?

Setting the body back down, Gibson pulled out his phone and scrolled through the pictures from this case. It was amazing what could be done with technology these days. He stopped at the picture of the missing person and held the phone next to the face of the corpse. Beneath the blood and abnormal discoloration of the skin, it was plain as day. This was his missing person; this was Jacinda Yotti.

This death didn't have the same MO as the rest of the killings. This woman hadn't been eaten, and she'd been shot. Another of Gibson's leads had proven false. Jacinda wasn't the killer because she'd probably been dead before the first murder had occurred. That left him with one suspect—Liam Dobendik—and he had no clue where to find him.

☂⚰⚰⚰⚰⚰

Thursday afternoon, two days before the official outbreak

Gibson sat at his desk with Fidel curled up at his feet. None of this made any sense. The pieces just didn't fit together. His deputies were in town, looking for any clues as to Liam's whereabouts, but nothing had turned up yet. Clover and his goonies had shown up right after he'd radioed into the office saying he'd found their missing person. They'd taken that body as well, carrying her back to their vehicle, hazmat suits and all. A few things were beginning to make sense, but, sadly, none of it was telling him how to catch Liam.

Vindex Corp. was involved with all this somehow, and that meant LifeWork was as well. But how? What did they know that he didn't? An idea had begun to form in his head, but it was a wild one. Holly had said her dad acted almost like an animal, and all the victims had been chewed on—mauled actually, almost like a bear or something. What had Holly said her mother thought it was? Rabies? He got on his computer to look that up and the Wikipedia page told him all he needed to know. It was a deadly virus that was spread through the saliva of the infected creature. What if the reason his perp was eating it's victims was a virus? It would make sense. He thought back to the signs on the different buildings on the LifeWork compound. One had been labeled Research and Development. Was that for drugs or something else? What if they'd created something that acted like rabies, driving the infected person insane and causing them to kill and eat others?

He started to put the pieces together. Liam had been bitten and then turned on his wife and daughter. The other victims had been eaten alive. The Vindex Corp. men were burning the bodies while wearing hazmat suits, and they'd burned down the Dobendik house. That first sheet of paper from the governor had said something about the bodies being contaminated. And hadn't Mrs. Henderson told him yesterday that the Feds were sending people in to contain the situation? They weren't there to investigate the murders. They were there to stop a deadly contagion from spreading to the rest of the state!

The pieces fell into place and it all made sense in some twisted way. It was farfetched but explained a lot of what was going on. There were more questions he didn't know the answers to, like how had it started? How exactly was LifeWork involved? Were others infected? Or was it all a cover-up for a killer who ate his victims? That last one didn't seem logical. Too much evidence pointed to it being a contagion gone rampant for him to ignore. That left the most important question still unanswered. Where was Liam Dobendik? If he was indeed infected by something that drove him to kill, he may not be thinking properly, which meant he would be erratic and hard to track down. What would someone in that state of mind do?

A thought crossed his mind. What if Jacinda had been infected, killed her way south, and then encountered Liam and bit him. Liam killed her and then came home, unaware that he was infected with a deadly contagion. It drove him mad and he killed his wife and tried to kill his daughter. That meant the Jacinda had been the first one infected, but how had she looked so dead already? Had the contagion caused that too? Or had she only been there for a day? The coyotes and hogs hadn't gotten to the body yet, so either they could sense the corpse was contaminated or she hadn't been there long enough to attract them. *Had* Liam, in fact, killed her? He swore the bullet wounds looked post-mortem, but maybe he was wrong, because it seemed like Jacinda had been the first one infected and then spread it to Liam. Now he just had to find Liam and stop this from spreading further.

Picking his hat up off his desk, he exited his office. He couldn't help but feel like he'd forgotten something—there was a nagging dread in the pit of his stomach. He couldn't put his finger on it, but there was more to this.

"Off to find more bodies?" Mrs. Henderson asked.

The woman could be so heartless sometimes, or maybe she used her humor to cover a deeply buried pain, like he did.

"Nope," Gibson said, walking by her and out the door. "Goin' to find a killer."

He was just about to climb into his truck when he heard something to the south that almost sounded like screaming.

Glancing down Main Street to the clinic at the end of the street, he could see a commotion and wondered what it could be. Climbing into his truck, he started it up, and Fidel watched through the windshield. Halfway to the clinic, it hit him. How had he been such an idiot? Liam hadn't just tried to kill his daughter, he'd bitten her. She could be infected. He stepped on the gas and the truck lurched forward.

The scene that greeted him outside the front of the clinic was straight out of a horror movie, and he remembered why he didn't watch those. Real life was much more terrifying.

Holly Dobendik, still wearing her medical gown and with blood leaking from her mouth, was crouched over Deputy Randall. The big man was lying on his back with his stomach ripped open. Gibson pulled the truck to a stop fifty yards away and Holly looked up, the intestines of his deputy gripped in her small hands. This was a lot worse than he'd thought. Climbing out of his truck, he walked forward a few steps, and Holly dropped Randall's innards and stumbled towards him.

"Holly, stop," Gibson said, resting his hand on his Glock.

If this was the work of a contagion, he couldn't just kill the girl. She might not even be in control of herself. She continued to stumble towards him as a low groan escaped her lips. Her eyes were bloodshot and lifeless, just like Jacinda's had been, and her skin shone with bruising. The awkward gait she moved with seemed completely unnatural, like she'd forgotten how to walk or couldn't feel parts of her body. She was thirty yards away when he noticed something else. The handle of a scalpel was sticking out of her chest right where her heart was. She should be dead.

"Holly, you're sick," Gibson said. "Just calm down and I'll get you help."

He glanced past her to Randall's body. The man was

dead, killed by a teenage girl. More than likely, he'd been drawn there by the same screams Gibson had heard. Randall had been doing his job, trying to help her, yet he lay dead on the pavement. Anger rose within him—not at Holly for what she'd done but at the people who'd set this loose on his town.

"Shoot her!" Dr. Hart yelled as he ran out of the clinic's entrance. "She's already killed three people!"

Gibson cursed. Three? Fidel growled next to him, picking up on his tension and the threatening way Holly continued towards them, closing the distance to twenty yards. He drew his handgun.

"Holly, I can get you help," Gibson said.

Her gown was covered in enough blood around the scalpel in her chest that she shouldn't be walking. Maybe that was why she was stumbling, yet why wasn't there more blood leaking from the wound? If her heart was beating, she would still be bleeding. Holly groaned louder as she closed the distance to ten yards. Fidel growled back and then lunged forward, heading straight for her.

"*Fuss!*" Gibson yelled, raising his handgun.

Fidel listened and came to a stop, growling menacingly at the girl. He was only a couple yards from Holly, who now had her gaze locked on the dog. Gibson didn't know if the contagion could be transferred to animals from a human host and he wasn't about to find out. Firing twice at her chest, he watched as the bullets smashed into her. She kept coming, arms stretched for Fidel.

"*Hier!*" Gibson yelled, but Fidel stayed between his owner and the threat.

He opened fire on Holly, hitting her three more times in the chest to no effect. He didn't stop firing. She had leaned down to grab Fidel when one of his rounds took her in the top of the skull and she dropped. He ran up and grabbed Fidel's collar, hauling him back a few feet, all the while keeping his eyes and gun on the girl. She didn't move. Dr. Hart approached him, wide eyes locked on Holly.

"What the hell was that?" Gibson asked, looking up at him.

"I have no idea," Dr. Hart said. "She flat-lined and one of the nurses tried to resuscitate her, but Holly woke up and bit into the nurse's neck! Holly then killed another nurse on her way out. Your deputy heard the screaming and ran up to help, and she attacked him. I don't understand how this happened."

"It's some kind of contagion," Gibson said. "Her father was bitten. He contracted it and then bit her."

"I've never heard of a virus that potent before. She couldn't have been bitten more than a few hours ago," Dr. Hart said, motioning to the body on the ground.

"This morning, but—" Gibson cut off as he heard the sound of gunfire from the northern part of town.

He cursed. This wasn't over yet. He ran back to his truck and jumped in, turning it around and heading toward the gunfire. Turning on Second Street, he saw one of the black armored vehicles parked outside one of the houses. He pulled up next to it and jumped out, grabbing his shotgun. Two of the men were walking up to a body that had the same bruising as the others. It wasn't Liam Dobendik, it was Bruce Bacmen.

"What the hell is goin' on?" Gibson yelled, walking up to the men, who turned, shouldering their rifles. "Easy now!"

"This is none of your concern," said one of the men. "Move along."

"None of my concern!" Gibson stormed up to the young

man. "Kid, this is my damn town. Everything that happens here is my concern! Where's that asshole in charge?"

"Right here," a voice said from behind him.

He turned to see Clover climbing out of the armored vehicle. Gibson stomped up to him, his anger at everything that had happened boiling over.

"You son of a—" Gibson began but was cut off as Clover punched him hard in the face.

The last thing he saw as blackness closed in around him was Fidel lunging for the man, followed by a gunshot.

Friday night, day before the "official" outbreak

Darkness engulfed Hill City to the point where it was almost palpable. Gibson lay on his stomach behind a house on the south end of town, waiting for one of the patrols to pass. He couldn't believe what'd happened in just over twenty-four hours. A three-man patrol passed his position and continued on their way, and he rose to a crouch, running to the heavy-duty fence Vindex Corp. had put up last night, surrounding the town. Pulling the wire cutters from his belt behind his back, he snipped a hole big enough to get through, then held the cut edges open for Fidel to get through as well, thanking all of his lucky stars that the young mercenary had missed his dog. It was a blessing that Fidel had only been lunging to stand over him and that those pricks had spared him after the first shot. They'd opted to leave Gibson lying on the street under guard until he regained consciousness and then he'd been escorted to the school where they were gathering all the townspeople.

After going through the hole in the fence, he entered the

trees and disappeared into the night. They wouldn't find him now, even if they did get one of those choppers in the air to look for him. Hopefully, they wouldn't worry about finding him; it wasn't as if he was infected like some of the others, although that didn't seem to matter since they wanted to keep everyone who knew anything about what'd happened under lock and key.

Not that he really knew what had happened. Clover's boss—the man in the gray suit named Mr. Smith—had told them just enough to keep them scared and compliant. It wasn't much, just some horse crap about an accident with an experimental drug and that they were all safe as long as they complied with the blood tests and stayed in the school. Mr. Smith had made it clear that anyone caught trying to escape would be dealt with accordingly. That was why Gibson made sure to take down the two guards who'd tried to "deal" with him. After that, it'd been easy to avoid the patrols throughout town.

He felt kind of bad for leaving behind all of the people he'd interacted with over the past decade. In one day, both of his deputies had been murdered by a father and daughter high on some drug—if Mr. Smith's story was true, which he didn't believe for one second. The man was lying through his teeth. Even his name was a lie. Mr. Smith? Yeah, right. Gibson knew he should feel bad for leaving them at the hands of those mercenaries, but he didn't. He and Fidel were a team and that was all he cared about. If he could save the whole town he would, but he knew he couldn't. His plan probably wouldn't have worked if he'd taken even one other person with him. They were on their own now, just like he was.

After bushwhacking through the brush and trees for two miles, he thought it'd be safe enough to take the road south.

He hoped he remembered how to get to his destination, but it'd been a few years since he'd last visited.

The call that day was easy to remember—a mother claiming that her ex-husband had kidnapped their daughter. When he arrived at the ex-husband's house and saw the mother, Jane Hashen, banging on the door, screaming, he decided there may be more to the story. There was. The teenage daughter, Alexis, had run away from the mother's home to be with her father. After defusing the situation and begrudgingly sending the daughter back home with the mother and step-father, he'd sat down with the ex-husband. The man had lost his son years before, something Gibson could relate to, and then lost custody of his daughter. He'd then left the Corps to spend more time with his daughter. Gibson'd had a good talk with the man that day.

Hours later, he turned a corner in the dirt driveway and came upon the house. It was almost as he remembered it, except now the windows were boarded up and the souped-up Ford was missing from the driveway. After going around the house twice, he confirmed that all the windows were boarded up tight and the doors were locked. Emmett Wolfe had skipped town, probably getting ahead of whatever was about to happen. He sat down on the front steps and Fidel rested his head on Gibson's knees. The dog knew him so well, more so than anyone had in years—not since the death of his family. He scratched his dog behind the ears, knowing he loved it.

His best chance to get answers was gone and wasn't coming back. Yet, not all was lost; he still had his trusty companion. The name really did suit his dog—faithful. He'd have his back no matter what might be happening. How did that saying go, again? Dogs were a man's best friend? Yeah, that was it.

Gibson stood up, patting his dog on the side. "You ready, boy?" Fidel looked up at him, giving him that same look he always did. "Yeah, me neither."

He gazed to the south. His best bet was to hit US-257 and get as far away from there as possible. Yet his eyes kept being drawn back to the northwest. He didn't owe those people anything. They stood just as good a chance on their own as with him, maybe even better. It was Fidel and him against the world. He stood there for a while, a war waging within him. Finally, he cursed and turned back the way he'd come. He couldn't just leave them there; he'd sworn an oath to serve and protect. Disappearing into the night, he headed back to Hill City with Fidelis at his side. He couldn't shake the feeling that this was just the beginning.

ABOUT JOSHUA C. CHADD

Joshua is a Jesus Freak and follower of the Way. As an adventurous nerd, he loves the outdoors and when he is not found high in the mountains of Alaska, he can be observed living on the rolling plains of eastern Montana with his wife, guns and two katanas. He has a passion for all things imaginary and finds inspiration in the wilderness, away from all the distractions of life. Some of his other passions include hunting, shooting, board and video games, hard rock, movies, reading and the Walking Dead.

6

DOMINION

BY R. L. BLALOCK

A Story of Death & Decay

Day 26
7:38 pm

Elsy's eyes fluttered open. Her vision was blurry. She blinked rapidly trying to clear it.

Where am I?

The room was dark but slowly came into focus. It was empty. No furniture. No decorations. Light trickled in the window, illuminating her surroundings. Elsy cringed. The beige carpet beneath her was dirty. Stains had turned it into a mottled mess. Some were darker than others. She didn't want to think about what they might be.

Her arms ached as she tried to move but couldn't. Snapped from the foggy haze that had clouded her mind, Elsy thrashed against her bonds. Her arms were bound and tethered to the wall above her head and her feet had been tied together.

Where was Vincent? Her heart leaped as she struggled again. He wasn't here with her. Where could he be?

Elsy sucked in a deep breath. Panicking wouldn't do her any good.

She looked down at her clothes. Her black and white polka dot dress was dirty. It had been dirty before, but it looked dirtier. There was blood on it. Was it her blood? Her black Prada pumps were missing from her feet and she fumed at the loss of her favorite shoes.

With a huff, she shrugged off the lost shoes. The world was full of free shoes. Right now, she had to focus on getting out and finding Vincent. She had to think. How had she gotten here? What time was it?

The blinds were drawn on the window, but the light coming through was tinted the deep red of dusk. It had been almost a full day.

What had she been doing? What was the last thing she could remember?

Her mind was still muddled by the haziness of sleep. She had been walking. She had stopped somewhere. Where? A gas station? That sounded right. But what had happened after she stopped. She had locked Vincent in the bathroom so he wouldn't wander while she slept. Could he still be there?

She leaned her head back against the wall and closed her eyes. A woman had happened upon the same gas station. She had started to leave...but she hadn't left. She had stayed.

Footsteps echoed from outside. Elsy quickly shifted back and forth, looking for her weapons. She had dozens that she carried. Knives. Guns. A baseball bat. A hammer. A screwdriver and a few others she had found handy, but they were all gone. Her backpack of supplies was gone as well.

The footsteps stopped outside her door. The voices that accompanied them were solemn. Elsy turned her body toward the door as best as she could, plastering a broad sparkling smile across her face.

The door opened, light from the setting sun burning her eyes after being in the dark for so long. Reluctantly, Elsy turned away when she could no longer bear the light. After a moment to adjust, she turned back.

A man stood in the doorway. His dark brown hair was slicked back making him look like a sleazy car salesman. His round face was lit with a broad smile that created small creases around his eyes and mouth. He wore a pristine white robe with a dark scarlet sash around his neck though he looked far too young to be a priest or a minister.

"Good," the man's voice boomed through the room again, making Elsy's head throb. "You're awake. Welcome to God's Kingdom. The folks around here call me Father Neal."

The man's jovial manner already made Elsy despise him. It was the same as her smile. Fake.

"I'm afraid I'm not feeling too well though."

The man smiled down at her the way a father smiled at a child who had said something silly. She wanted to wipe that smile right off his face. "No, I imagine not. Roofies are a nasty drug, my dear."

The memory came flooding back. The woman had shared applesauce with her at the gas station. As they chatted, she had offered Elsy one of the small individually portioned containers. It had still been sealed, but that doesn't mean it hadn't been tampered with. Elsy chided herself for taking anything from a stranger.

"Where's my friend?" Her voice cracked though she already knew the answer. Her mouth was dry and her throat suddenly felt like it was lined with sandpaper. She didn't want to ask about the woman. She wanted to ask about Vincent. But if they hadn't found him, it was better if they didn't know about him.

"Oh, she's fine." Father Neal waved away her concerns. "You seem like a smart girl. I'm sure you figured out already that she is the one who brought you here." Elsy's eyes narrowed. The man took a few steps forward, crouching down beside her. "But don't worry your pretty little head about it, my dear. The woes of this world are no longer a concern of yours." The man patted her leg reassuringly. Elsy didn't flinch from his touch. She wouldn't allow him to see any sign of fear. "You have a grand purpose now." His eyes lit up with a manic fervor. "You have been chosen to save us all."

"Why don't you let me go? I can't save anyone. Not even myself apparently." Elsy let out a soft tinkling laugh, one that she had practiced to perfection, at her own self-deprecating joke. She had spent years smiling and laughing, even when the act felt like it would rip her in two. It was the price she paid for the life she had lived. This was no different.

"That is not how it works, my dear. God has chosen you and you alone. Your sacrifice will protect the rest of us from the dead rising out of the bowels of Hell. By feeding the dead, we are doing God's will. It is for the greater good. You will be a hero." The fiery glint in his eyes made the man look unhinged.

Elsy spat in his face, the saliva hitting his cheek. "God has nothing to do with what you are doing."

The man stood, calmly wiped the spit from his cheek. "My dear, I am the Lord's messenger. I am charged with caring for his children and saving as many as I can. You may not understand, but that's all right. It makes no difference whether you understand or not."

"Is that what you're doing? Saving people?" Elsy cackled. The maniacal laugh a stark contrast from the pleasant lilt before.

"Not everyone can be saved, but I will save all of those who are truly worthy." Sadness filled his eyes. "Sometimes the needs of the many must outweigh the needs of one. This time, unfortunately, that one is you."

A giggle escaped Elsy's lips. "And how can you save them, Neal?"

The man sneered when she referred to him only by his first name. "When man has sinned, God demands repentance. Sometimes that means a sacrifice."

A snarl curled Elsy's dark red lips. "You're killing off the other survivors you find. That's how you think you'll find repentance with God. You are not a man of God. You are a monster."

"You may think so, my dear, but I am not worried about your judgment." Father Neal took the last few steps toward the door, pulling it closed behind him and leaving Elsy in darkness.

Elsy didn't care for people. Not anymore. Not even really before. People were just as monstrous as the infected, but she had never brought harm on someone who didn't attack her first. She loathed those who had used the chaos of the outbreak for their own personal gain.

The same type of people who had brought a horde down upon her beautiful home and left her trapped. Left her to die. Left the only other person she truly cared about to die. Left Vincent to die.

She had survived those horrific days and she was going to survive this one. And when she walked out, the first thing she would do is feed the holy traitor to the infected. Piece by piece.

Day 28
5:43 am

Elsy's eyes hurt. She wanted to sleep, but she refused to let herself. She wouldn't be taken off guard again.

She had pulled on her bonds until her wrists bled and then continued pulling. The blood that slowly dripped down her arms had dried hours ago. Her wrists burned and her arms ached from the unnatural position. Her stomach rumbled in angry protest to its emptiness. Yet, none of it bothered her. If there was one thing she had learned before the outbreak, it was discipline.

The sky outside the window had only just begun to lighten when footsteps echoed outside the door again. These were different than Father's. They were light and quick. The door opened just a crack at first before a girl stepped in, a large soup pot clutched between her hands. She was young. Perhaps fifteen or sixteen. She could have actually been younger. The fight for survival had aged everyone beyond their years, even children.

"Father Neal sent me to get you cleaned up." The girl's words were barely above a whisper. Her hair fell into her face as she kept her eyes on the ground.

"Why does it matter?" Elsy said with a sigh, leaning her head back against the wall again. "You're monsters. You're just going to feed me to the infected anyway. They don't care if their food is clean or dirty."

"We aren't monsters!" the girl almost shouted. Elsy eyed the girl up and down, she seemed meek but something was bubbling just beneath the surface. Anger? Despair?

"I forgive you…for your cruel words." The girl's voice was quiet once again. "You just don't understand."

The girl kneeled beside Elsy, setting down the large pot she had been carrying. The water inside sloshed back and forth, a rag rolling around the small waves. The girl reached in and rung out the rag. Gently, she wiped the blood off of Elsy's arms. Each stroke was soft and she carefully tended to the swollen irritated skin on Elsy's wrists.

"I understand why you think we're monsters," the girl said, her voice soft and hesitant.

"The world is dying and your feeding the last of the survivors to the dead. I have no idea why I should think that." Her words were sharp despite her calm demeanor. The girl flinched but didn't deny the accusations. She nibbled on her lip as she worked, continuing to gently clean Elsy's skin. As the silence grew heavier, Elsy could see the emotions warring on the girl's face. Pain. Anger. Fear. Guilt.

"We wouldn't do this just for anyone," she finally whispered.

"Then who would you do this for?" Elsy wasn't sure she wanted to hear the answer. Everyone had a sob story now. Everyone had lost someone. Everyone had been hurt. Everyone had struggled. Everyone had some way to justify any terrible thing they wanted to do, but her curiosity had always been voracious.

Before the outbreak, she had satisfied that curiosity by taking up many hobbies. She hadn't practiced them all regularly, but she had taken them up at one time or another just to know how to do it. Horse back riding. Tennis. Ju-jitsu. Fencing. Archery. Even rugby for a while, but that hadn't stuck long. She hadn't liked the way the bruises marred her flawless skin.

"My mother." Unshed tears shone bright in the girl's

eyes and she swallowed a few times before continuing. "Father Neal says that God sent the plague to us because we had lost our way. That we must return to the old ways or we will be cursed like them. But if we are devout, if we make sacrifices, maybe God will see fit to bless us and spare us the same fate as our loved ones."

The girl reached into the pocket of her skirt and pulled out a folded piece of paper. She unfolded it tenderly, careful not to tear the heavily creased page. In her hand was a picture. Her mother had an arm around the girl and the girl wore the forced smile teenagers presented when photos were demanded. A typical family picture.

Tears rolled down the girl's cheeks as she gazed at the photo. She looked like a younger version of her mother. The same strong cheekbones and soft brown eyes. The same jet-black hair. They even had the same body structure.

"Honey." It was all Elsy could say. She wasn't quite old enough to be this girl's mother but almost. The girl looked so lost. So broken. She couldn't imagine what this child must be going through now, though. The world had changed suddenly and violently and now she was alone. "Would your mother want you to do this for her?" she finally asked.

The girl didn't answer. She didn't even twitch. Elsy was fairly certain that the answer was no. No good parent would want their child to inflict pain on others in their name. She could only guess based off the picture but she felt confident in her answer.

"My son would not want me to do this for him." Elsy's voice was soft. "He would never want this."

The girl's head snapped up. "Your son?"

"Vincent." She could still see the happy little boy that climbed into her bed to snuggle in the morning. The little boy that liked to read stories with his mother. The little boy that made her drawings of the two of them. The little boy whose blood had covered her hands when the infected had ripped him to shreds. The little boy she still led around with her, in hopes that one day she could find him a cure.

"What happened to him?" The girl's words were cautious.

"The same thing that happens to everyone now." The two sat in silence for a long while as the words settled around them.

"He's lying to you," Elsy said firmly, staring hard at the girl. "The infected. They aren't lost. But they don't need to be saved by God. They need a cure. Medicine."

The girl let out a long breath but held her silence. Her eyes roved Elsy up and down as if searching for any physical signs of a trick.

"It's the virus that turns them into monsters but a cure might be able to turn them back. They don't need God, they need doctors and medicine."

"We don't have doctors and medicine anymore." The girl stood, gathering her rag and pot. "Those luxuries were taken away with the outbreak. Just like everything else. All we have left is prayer and sacrifice."

"We have each other," Elsy pushed. She knew she couldn't push the girl too hard, but she knew she had gotten under her skin.

The girl stopped at the door, her hand resting on the knob. "I'll pray for you. That your end comes swiftly and you do not suffer."

"Don't." Elsy's voice hardened. "Say a prayer that Neal meets his end before I get a hold of him." The girl's lips pressed into a thin line and she pulled the door closed behind her.

Elsy rested her head back against the wall, imagining the look on his face when she walked away from whatever he had planned for her. The shock and horror.

The fear.

She didn't have to be afraid of him or the dead, but he should be afraid of her. She would dethrone him before he could beg the Lord for mercy.

Day 28

10:00 am

The door burst open unceremoniously. Late morning light spilled in, burning Elsy's eyes.

"Your time of judgment has come, my dear." Father Neal filled the doorway, a mere shadow against the light.

"As has yours, I suppose." Elsy smirked.

"You sure are full of yourself," he sneered back at her. "Pride is a deadly sin, my dear."

"You would know." Elsy set her steely gaze on the man.

"Take her to the reckoning," Father Neal snarled. Two other large men entered the room, heaving her up by her aching arms. Elsy didn't struggle against them as they marched her out of the room. Instead, she matched their long strides, holding her head high. With every step, she defied him. She would not beg. She would not cry.

She didn't need to.

Outside, she stole glances at her surroundings. They were in a motel. One of the crummy ones that lay right off the highway. The outside was dirtier than the inside of her room. The entire place was run down and probably had been long before the outbreak.

Elsy caught one of the guards staring at her and flashed

a smile at him. The man quickly turned away. She loved making men nervous. She always had.

The guards marched her down the road. A crowd was gathered outside of the large warehouse next to the motel. Father Neal stood at a makeshift pulpit on a hastily erected stage.

He beamed at Elsy as the guards pushed her up the few steps. All the eyes of the crowd turned towards her. Elsy surveyed the crowds, taking in the hopeful fervent faces that stared up at her.

Could these people be saved? Or were they too far gone into Father's madness?

"The Lord has blessed us today!" Father Neal's voice boomed joyously over the crowd. "He has brought to us an exceptional sacrifice. One who faces her fate with dignity and grace. Behold, our blessed sacrifice." The crowd rippled as the congregation clasped their hands together in thanks and murmured cheers.

"We have been tried and tested this past month," Father Neal said solemnly. "But our Father has always tested the faithful. Only those who persevere through the worst of times will be rewarded. And we have persevered!" he shouted triumphantly.

"Praise him!" a woman shouted from the crowd.

"Our faith has not been shaken. Our faith has only grown stronger!" he bellowed. "We, the righteous, have seen the flaws in man and we seek to correct them. We have returned to the ways of God. We have humbled ourselves before Him. Put our faith in Him. He has not abandoned us and today we have been rewarded." Father Neal gestured to Elsy enthusiastically. "A sacrifice that recognizes her sinful ways. That recognizes her need for redemption through sacrifice. Who offers herself to God so that we, the faithful, may be blessed." He paused looking out at the crowd as they clung to his every word. "Today is the day that God smiles upon us. Today is the day of our redemption. Praise Him!"

The crowd erupted into cheers. People clasped each other excitedly as they shouted joyously.

Among the crowd, Elsy spotted the girl. She didn't cheer. She didn't shout. Instead, she stared at Elsy, her hands clasped in front of her chest, fear making her look years younger.

The crowd turned and filed into small doors on either side of the warehouse. Elsy was led around the back. The inside was hot, the stagnant air trapped between the metal walls. A staircase led up to a catwalk that encircled the warehouse floor.

The entire building was eerily quiet. The once raucous crowd from outside had fallen silent. Not one person made a sound.

Elsy looked into the pit below her. At least a hundred infected wandered aimlessly on the warehouse floor. The entire building reeked of their stench. Elsy tried to take slow, shallow breaths, trying to minimize the stench that entered her nose.

Father Neal stepped up next to Elsy. He looked to the guards and simply nodded. The guards yanked Elsy forward to the edge of the catwalk. Without warning, they heaved her over the edge of the railing and let go.

Elsy landed right on top of one of the infected, the creature softening her landing. It snarled up at her through mangled lips. One eye was missing along with the entire right side of its face. The flesh had healed in a disgusting knot of scar tissue and muscle, giving the creature's head a lopsided shape.

She scrambled off the creature and to her feet. All

around her, the other infected stirred, rousing from the autopilot they fell into when food wasn't present.

They cast about, scenting the air, but they didn't see her. An infected bumped into her, eyeing her before moving on. The horde grew agitated. The growls of a few stirred the others. The cacophony grew and the infected frantically scratched around the enclosure for the meat they knew was present.

A broad, cat-like grin spread across Elsy's face. She had walked through hordes before, unscathed. She knew that his horde would ignore her.

The first time had been an accident. She had stared into her son's eyes as he had awoken, knowing her time was up. Instead, he had turned from her, disinterested. When she had built up the nerve, she had stepped into a horde in broad daylight, moving amongst them. As one of them. Since then she had walked through each horde untouched.

She scanned the horde, looking closely at the infected. Her son wasn't here. He hadn't been taken with her. But she still needed something and one of the other infected had to have it.

There! A woman shambled about with a steak knife protruding from her neck. Elsy pushed her way through the crowd. She collided with one of the infected, a man. His lips peeled back in a snarl, the dry blood around his lips flaking. Elsy snarled back at him with her own imitation of the growl. The infected turned away, dismissing her.

Elsy darted the last few feet to the woman. They met face to face, but the woman didn't see her. Elsy looked into the woman's eyes. There was nothing there. No recognition. No emotion. Just two empty windows to an empty mind.

Elsy took a long deep breath. The woman may not recognize her, but she recognized the woman. She was the woman in the picture the girl had shown her. The girl's mother.

Without another thought, Elsy seized the knife and pulled with all her might. Scar tissue had grown around the knife where it was implanted in the woman's skin. The woman shrieked, snapping at Elsy. A chorus of moans rose, answering the woman as the infected around her riled.

None of them attacked her.

Elsy gritted her teeth and pulled on the knife again. A wet tearing sound reached Elsy's ears and the knife suddenly popped free, making Elsy stagger backward. Blood oozed from the freshly opened wound in the woman's neck. The woman snarled at Elsy again but didn't take a step forward. Instead, she cast about, looking for something else. Something to eat despite the meal standing in front of her.

The crowd up on the catwalks was still utterly silent. Their lives depended on it. If the infected really got worked up, they might break free. Despite the quiet, their faces were curious, even a bit afraid. Some were even...hopeful.

Elsy stepped forward, placing her hand on the woman's shoulder. The infected growled at her, the way it would growl at another infected who crossed it.

"Don't worry," Elsy whispered. "I'm going to free them from his grasp. Your daughter will be safe and cared for." She didn't know what compelled her to do this. She didn't think they could understand her. She didn't even think they were people anymore. How could they be? But if there was still some minuscule shred of humanity left inside the virus-riddled body, she felt the woman deserved some measure of peace.

Elsy turned back to the crowd, her eyes drifting across the catwalk. "Your God did not abandon these people. He did not abandon you," she screamed over the moans of the infected. She picked her words carefully. She didn't believe in God. Not since the outbreak. She had never been religious, but she had been open to the idea of a higher power. What kind of God would let his people perish in such a horrendous way? What kind of God would allow thousands to be ripped to shreds? But these people believed. They needed to believe and she needed them to believe her. "He never left and he certainly did not send this plague. This plague was made by man. What other creature could create something so awful? And you" —she pointed her knife accusingly at Father Neal— "You walked hand in hand with the Devil to do his bidding." Venom dripped from her words.

Murmurs rippled across the catwalk. All around her, the infected began to moan. Their cries grew desperate as their heads turned up and they finally sighted prey. And yet, Elsy remained untouched.

"It is not I who walks with the devil!" Father Neal cried in indignation. "You! You are a witch sent here to turn us from the true path of God!"

"You murdered the innocent!" Elsy blood boiled. Her fists were clenched so tightly that her nails bit into her palms. "You feed them alive to the infected instead of helping the survivors and rebuilding a society that reflects God's true kingdom! You feed your own sick fetish at the expense of innocent lives. You bathed yourself in power and used fear as a weapon against those who needed you! You are a traitor to God and a traitor to your people and you will be judged!"

Elsy ran at the chicken wire fence, throwing herself at it.

"She is one of the unpure!" Father Neal screeched. "She is wolf in sheep's clothing come to ruin us all. Kill her! Kill her!" Before the words even left his mouth, Elsy had scaled the chicken wire fencing. She reached for the rail of the catwalk and pulled herself over. Neither of the guards moved toward her.

"You are what is wrong with this world. You and everyone else like you," Elsy hissed. Her heart thrummed in her ears. Her anger coursed through her veins like fire.

Father launched himself at her haphazardly, hoping to use his greater size as a weapon. It wasn't hard for Elsy to dodge his attack. As she stepped to the side, she swung her fist around, planting it squarely in his gut. With a sharp cry, Father sank to his knees, gasping for breath.

"You spread lies. You spread fear. I won't let you do that anymore." Elsy turned to the others on the catwalk. "Let this be the dawning of a new age for us! Just because the world has been taken over by monsters does not mean we need to become monsters ourselves." Some of the folks on the catwalks cheered. Some clasped their hands in hope.

A growl from behind alerted Elsy just a second too late. Father Neal wrapped his thick arms around her throat, knocking the knife from her hand and instantly cutting off her air.

Stupid! She cursed herself. *How could you be so stupid as to turn your back on him?*

Before she even finished the thought, he cried out again and released her. Elsy sprung back to see the guards forcing Father Neal to his knees. Blood poured out of a new cut on his temple. She collected the knife from the catwalk, glad it hadn't fallen down into the pit below.

"Time for a new age." One of the guards nodded.

"You fools!" Father cried. "You will burn in hell for this! You all will!"

"No," Elsy said firmly. "We will build a better world. A

good world, but you will never see it." Elsy nodded to the guards and they heaved him up.

Father's eyes grew wide and he realized what was about to happen. "No. No. No. No. No." Each word grew more panicked than the last.

Elsy stepped up to him, her fingers caressing the side of his face. "What?" Her eyes grew wide in mock surprise. "Are you afraid of the death you sentenced so many to?" Her lips twisted into a wry smile. "Burn in hell." The words came out in a vicious snarl. Her hand come up fast, driving the knife up through his chin. She pushed until the knife sunk in to the hilt. Father Neal's eyes went wide as he tried to scream around the knife. Instead, all that came out was a muffled cry as blood poured over his lips. A smile curved the corner of Elsy's lips up. With that, she shoved him hard.

The man hit the railing and teetered for just a fraction of a second before falling over the edge. He landed hard on the concrete floor below, the thud resonating over the moans of the infected. As one, all the infected turned toward him. Their howls filled the empty warehouse, rattling its metal walls. A piercing scream cut through the air as the infected converged on the helpless man.

Elsy stepped back from the railing, smoothing her hair and straightening her dress.

"This ends here. These sacrifices die with Father!" Her voice boomed even over the shrieks of the feeding infected. "The Lord does not need our lives. He already has them. We must rebuild a world that is kind. A world that God wants for us. We will have to fight to survive and make no mistake, we will fight hard, but we will bring peace to this ravaged land."

"And what of the unclean?" a man asked, drawing some

unwanted attention from the infected. "They...they are our families."

"They"—Elsy gestured to the pit below—"will be cared for. They are sick. Maybe one day someone will find a cure. Until that day, we will keep them contained where they can do no harm." People nodded through the crowd.

"If you don't agree with me, if you wish to follow Father's ideals"—Elsy's eyes narrowed as she stared down the crowd—"then leave. You are no longer welcome here." No one moved. She was sure there would be at least a few dissenters and she would make sure they left or they would be dealt with.

"If no one has any objections, I would like to rest. My night was not entirely pleasant." Many people cast their gaze down at the floor. "Good." She nodded and shooed the people to exit the warehouse. She needed to get back to the gas station. She had to find Vincent before someone else did.

At the edge of the catwalk, the girl lingered as the others filed out. Elsy smiled and strode over to her.

"I'm sorry—"

"Don't be." Elsy cut the girl off, laying a gentle hand on the girl's shoulder. "Father had everyone under his spell. People were...vulnerable. They need someone to give them hope and he took advantage of that."

"We should have known..." The girl shook her head.

"Things have changed," Elsy said, nibbling on her lip. "The world went up in flames. Overnight everything we knew disappeared."

The girl was quiet as they descended the steps of the catwalk and exited the building.

"How did you do that? Walk amongst the unclean...the infected?" she corrected herself quickly.

Elsy smoothed her dress again. Her fingers ran down her ribs, unable to smooth out the knot there. "A way that many would be stupid to try and wouldn't survive."

The girl stared back at Elsy, her brow furrowed as she thought about Elsy's words.

Elsy smoothed the dress again. The act like a nervous tick as she tried to smooth away the knotted flesh that would never leave her.

ABOUT R.L. BLALOCK

R. L. Blalock's love of reading started young, but her love of zombies started later in life. In 2008, when R. L. Blalock first watched the remake of Dawn of the Dead she instantly fell in love with the genre. Born and raised in Sacramento, California, R. L. Blalock now lives in St. Louis, Missouri with her loving husband, precocious three-year-old daughter, two dogs, and a bird. Stay connected with R. L. Blalock at **rlblalock.com**!

I would like to give a special thank you to my wonderful and supportive mother who endures the nightmares of reading my work.

The rest of the Death & Decay series can be found at **Amazon.**

7

FORGET THE MALL: FORGET THE ZOMBIES 1.5

BY R.J. SPEARS

[**Author's Note:** *This story takes place inside the first book of the Forget the Zombies series, Forget the Alamo.*]

The little old lady zombie clamped its teeth onto Neal's throat like a lamprey eel, hard and fast with little chance of letting go. It all happened so fast that both Jenkins and I had no time to react or do anything. One moment, Neal was leaning over this old lady in a blue dress with bright yellow polka dots because she looked like she was in distress. The next thing you know, she was on him, yanking him to the floor.

Neal's screams filled the food court, echoing to the heights of the forty foot ceiling and reverberating into the mall. Blood sprayed from the wound, shooting onto the floor like a geyser.

Jenkins backpedaled away, his arms pinwheeling in the air, wanting to be as far away from the old lady zombie as he could be. If he could have teleported, he would have been in Alaska.

Neal's eyes stared directly at me and said, "*Help me!*"

Neal, who managed the pretzel shop. Neal, who loved bulldogs, Australian Shepherds, and nearly all four-legged creatures. Neal, with the broad smile and the kind eyes and chatty ways. Neal, who had lived in Florida and had decided that San Antonio would be a good place to relocate. Neal, who didn't know how badly that would turn out for him.

Neal, who I had only known for less than thirty minutes, but had already felt like I had known him a lifetime. Maybe that's because his lifetime ended right there in front of me.

At that point, my experience with zombies was limited to seeing a man devoured by one outside my hotel and running into another one on the street. That was just the beginning of the fun.

What I did know was that Neal was way past helping. If there was one thing I had learned from the media in the past couple of days, one bite meant that you were infected. Infection meant death and subsequent reanimation.

In other words, Neal was already dead, but he didn't know it. Neal, whose last name I didn't know how to spell because it wasn't on his name tag, but I swear he said it was Smead. Now I would never know his last name for sure.

Still, he fought for the precious few moments he had left, punching at the old lady's head and face. After three quick blows, he dislodged her and rolled away, trying to get some distance from her.

She wasn't done with him, though, and stumbled to her feet, blood dripping from her chin, looking like a dark red bib. She snarled and took a step toward him.

I jumped forward and kicked the old woman in the side. She wasn't all that big, probably weighing less than a hundred pounds. My blow sent her sailing across the floor into a mop bucket, spilling dark gray water on the floor and sending the mop skittering in my direction.

She recovered astonishingly quick and scrambled to her feet. She snarled like some kind of rabid animal and took a step toward me. I knew it was on.

Despite the fact that I had my gun at my side, something prevented me from pulling it and shooting the old lady. Shooting old ladies was against all the rules I had been taught. Old ladies were meant to serve tea and watch soap operas.

So, I snatched the mop off the floor and pushed the mop part into the old lady's torso, knocking her back. That only made her mad. She growled and tried to bat the mop away, but I yanked it back and then slammed it into her again. This time she went down.

"Shoot her!" Jenkins yelled from behind me.

She tottered back to her feet and started toward me again. Still, my prohibition against shooting old ladies restrained me from pulling my gun.

Instead, I put the mop on the floor, lifted the handle, and then brought my foot down onto the middle of it, snapping it in two. I kicked the mop part away and brandished the sharp point at the old lady.

"Listen here, grandma, you better stay back, or else I'll stick you," I said, poking the jagged point at her.

She couldn't have cared less and stumbled my way.

"Stab her!" Jenkins yelled. "Stab her in the face!"

Things were getting nasty.

"She's not an old lady anymore, Grant," he yelled at me. "She's one of those things."

Those weren't magical words, but they broke through all my social inhibitions against killing little old ladies. Jenkins was right. She wasn't an old lady. She wasn't even alive.

She came toward me and I pulled back the mop handle,

getting ready. Her arms were out and her hands clutched the air, wanting a piece of me.

Well, that wasn't going to happen.

With every ounce of force I could muster, I stabbed the mop handle forward, and it flew like an arrow. The trajectory took it right into the old lady's eye socket. Something in my stomach clenched up when I felt the jagged end impact with the back of the woman's skull. I'm a man with a strong stomach, but even I have my limits.

Her arms fell to her side, and she slid off the broken mop handle and went down like a puppet after someone had cut its strings. The sound of her body hitting the floor only increased the sickening feeling in my gut.

Silence fell upon the scene, like someone dropping a curtain. I felt my heart hammering away in my chest.

"Should we check out Neal?" Jenkins asked.

"We?" I asked, looking back at him. "You mean me, right?"

Jenkins had his hands clutched to his chest reminding me of a little girl. "Well, you are the closest."

Killing the old lady wasn't enough, I guess. I had to check on what once was a vital, young man who now was probably dead. With the amount of blood pooling around his body, there was very little doubt of that.

I made my way over to Neal's bloody corpse and looked down. His lifeless eyes peered up and past me, looking into the great beyond. One of his hands still clung to his throat as if he could have kept all his blood in with that futile gesture.

"Is he dead?" Jenkins asked from behind me.

I just nodded my head.

"Do you think he will turn into one of those things?"

My chest tightened for a moment, then I said, "If what the reports say is true, then yes."

"Shouldn't we do something about him?"

"Again with the *we*," I said. "You want *me* to do something?"

"I guess, yes."

"You realize that he died all because you wanted one of those pretzels, right? We came down here from our safe haven because you just had to have one of those damned things."

He didn't say anything.

My vision became blurry, and I saw spots dancing behind my eyes. For some reason, I felt like I wasn't getting enough oxygen. I dug my fingernails into my palms and the pain brought me back from the edge.

"Sorry," was all that Jenkins said.

I refused to look at him. "Get back upstairs. I have to clean up this mess."

I pulled my gun out this time. I had had enough of mop handles. Neal deserved to a better ending, but it was the best I could do for him.

I wasn't good with words when it came to death. I had only known Neal for a very brief time, so a eulogy was out of the question. Besides, there was no one around to hear it.

I did what I had to do and got it over with. Goodbye, Neal. Neal, who had worked at the pretzel shop and served us soft, warm, and salty deliciousness. Neal, who would be among the first of many people I would have to watch die over the next few months.

This is how day one at the mall ended. I hoped the next day would be a better one, but it surely wasn't.

Malls are supposed to be cheery places of vapid consumerism -- until they're overrun with zombies. Who knew a mall could go from a place where material dreams came true to a real nightmare?

Two days ago, I was flying across the country with my protectee, Sam Jenkins, a key witness in a case against a nefarious East coast mobster. As a U.S. Marshall, it was my job to set him up in a new identity in the witness protection program. Sunny San Diego was his intended destination, but instead, we were forced to land in San Antonio.

At first, I thought it was mechanical problems, but once we got inside the airport, rumors swirled about a viral outbreak. Mixed into the morass of rumors and gossip was the news that all flights were canceled. That caused the hairs on the back of my neck to stand on end.

The powers that be said there was nothing to worry about, but I knew that was bullshit. There was no way that every flight across the country was grounded for a little burp in safety and security. That last and only time I remember that happening was 9/11. I learned just how serious it was when Jenkins and I saw a zombie chow down on a man in our hotel. It all went downhill from there. Chaos ensued, and it was every man for himself. Since Jenkins was my responsibility, I didn't have that option. I had to keep him safe and sound.

Call it my overzealous dedication to duty. That or plain stubbornness. Zombie apocalypse be damned. I hadn't lost a protectee yet, and I didn't intend to do it now.

That's how we ran into a cop named McKinney and that's how we ended up at the mall. He said it was safe there, and it was -- until it wasn't. Then things got really ugly. But that didn't happen right away.

"I'm hungry," Jenkins said.

"You look like you're always hungry," I said. Jenkins wasn't corpulent, but it looked like he rarely took only one trip to the buffet table.

"Can we go to the food court?"

We had taken refuge inside a hair salon on the second floor of the mall. I didn't want to be at street level with those things out there walking around. Plus, it gave us a decent view outside through a window in the back hallway. Not that it offered a lot of optimism.

The salon wasn't overly swanky, but it had some decent couches we were using as makeshift beds. It also had a ready supply of water which is necessary for human life. Or so I have been told.

"Do I have to remind you of what happened the last time we went to the food court?"

Jenkins went silent, but that didn't mean everyone was going to remain quiet.

"Mr. Grant, I'm hungry, too." This came from a cute as a button seven-year-old named Martin who had just stepped up beside me. He was part of a family who had taken refuge with us. Well, a partial family. Dad was missing in action with no word on his whereabouts. He had gone missing when the world went to hell in a handbasket.

Mom was there with Martin. Her name was Joni and, on the surface, she came across like any TV-family mom of three -- haggard, but with an underlying sense of scrappiness. She wasn't all that tall but had a runner's body, lean with sinewy muscles. If I had to sum her up with one word, I would say spunky.

The other two members of the family were Travis and

Jessica. Travis was cast as the sullen teenager of fifteen who came across more disturbed that his iPhone had lost service than the fact that the world may be circling the drain. Life without text messages was a life not worth living, I guess. The last member was Jessica, and her role was that of the sassy and precocious nine-year-old.

Joni just seemed ill-fitted for Texas. It wasn't something specific. Just a vibe I got from her.

I turned to Martin and said, "Hey, I told you to call me Grant. Not Mr. Grant."

He seemed to like my lack of formality because he let loose with a big smile that both warmed my heart and caused me concern. Let me state for the records that I wasn't ready to become a father-figure since his dad was MIA.

"Okay Mr. Grant, can we go get something to eat? I sure would love a twist cone from that ice cream store."

I scratched my head for a moment and said, "I guess we could. You'll need to ask your mom first."

His face scrunched up for a moment as he contemplated the request to ask his mother. "Do I have to?" He asked.

"Yes, you do," I said.

He didn't like my response, but he decided it was the only way to get what he wanted. He turned and started trudging toward the back of the salon to his mom, his shoulders slumped, like man on death row.

"How come you decided to go when the kid asked you, but you shut me down?" Jenkins asked.

"Well, he's a growing boy who needs his nutrition and you're a grown man who looks like he has some reserves to live off of." He narrowed his eyes at my playful barb. "Besides, his mom will shut him down, anyway. That leaves me off the hook from being the bad guy."

"Chicken shit," Jenkins replied.

I heard someone clear their throat behind me. A man reclined in one of the salon chairs, a tan Stetson tilted over his face. This gentleman rounded out our cast of zombie apocalypse refugees and was a mall guard named Carl. He was a crusty guy of around sixty, but with his grizzled gray beard, that estimate could go five years either way.

"Yes, Carl?" I asked but didn't really want to hear his response. Carl was the resident know-it-all and one of the few locals still at the mall. I found it very curious as to why he was still here while all the other resident San Antonians who worked at the mall had fled for home.

"Let me tell you, hombre, it's a scary world out there," Carl replied leaning forward in the salon chair. He pushed the brim of his Stetson back on his head revealing his weather-worn face.

"Tell us something we don't know," I said.

"Some of the dead ones got into Claire's --"

"Claire's? Is that someone you know?"

"It's a store. They sell earrings and jingle-jangle thingies for the teenie boppers. You don't get out much, do you?" I didn't answer, so he continued with his story. "Anyways, these dead ones are trapped inside. I think they ate a couple folks."

"How do you know that?" I asked, alarm bells going off in my head. So far, I had only seen two people get eaten, and that was two too many in my book.

"Well, while you all were sleeping, I was out doing my rounds. I know, I know, I'm not on the clock anymore, but old habits are hard to break. Anyways, when I get to Claire's I see what I thought was melted chocolate smeared all over one of the windows."

I sighed inside, knowing Carl was building for one of his long-winded stories.

"As you probably guessed, that wasn't chocolate. It was blood. While I'm inspecting that, one of those dead bastards slams into the window, holding someone's foot. As in a foot no longer attached to a body. And this zombie's chewing on it like it's a turkey leg. I tell you, I just about lost my lunch."

I looked over to Jenkins. His eyes glazed over as the gruesome scene played through his mind. His pallor had shifted from his normal pasty white to a shade of green. Maybe that would squelch his appetite?

"And you decided to wait until now to let us know?"

"Well, they can't get out of there. I shut the security doors." Carl shrugged sheepishly.

"Next time, Carl, let me know sooner about incidents like this. We are only two stores away from Claire's."

Carl sat forward in the chair and gave me what he probably hoped was a hard stare. Instead, it made him look cock-eyed. "Who put you in charge, anyway?"

"I'm not. I'm just trying to save my ass like the rest of us. Well yes, and his ass." I jerked a thumb toward Jenkins. "Zombies down the hall seems like a need-to-know fact that you should have shared."

Footsteps approached from the back of the store. Martin wore a smiled that spread from ear to ear as he bounced toward me and I knew I was in trouble.

He stopped and beamed up at me and. "Mom said I can go down to the food court with you. Jessica's hungry too so we're all going! She said it would be like a picnic."

I couldn't see anything in this scary, new world being a picnic. I probably should have headed out on my own to get food to bring back, but there I was being a people pleaser again.

"You can't very well go without me," Carl replied, holding up the expansive ring of keys he so generously showed us about once an hour. He had the keys to the king-dom, and he was its lord and master.

I let out a sigh and said, "The more, the merrier, I guess."

Jenkins spoke up and his voice cracked a little. "Do I have to go?"

"Well, it was your idea in the first place," I said. "Besides, that would leave you here all alone. You don't want that, do you?"

I saw the wheels turning behind his eyes and he must have come to the conclusion that risking a trip out of the salon was better than being alone. "Okay, I'll go." He didn't look too confident in his choice.

"Jessica, Martin, stay next to me," Joni commanded as she joined our merry little band. "There will be no running off. Do you understand?"

"Mom, shouldn't we stay in here until the police or someone gets here?" Jessica asked as she looked past me and into the mall beyond.

I leaned down and put on a confident smile. "Listen, you know that there is strength in numbers. Right?" She nodded reluctantly. "Good! We can watch each other's backs." I offered my hand in a high five gesture.

She looked up at her mom and then back at me and said, "High fives are so lame."

Joni shut that down fast. "That was rude, Jessica. You apologize to Mr. Grant."

"Please call me Grant," I said.

Looking chided, Jessica said, "I'm sorry, Mr. Grant."

Maybe someday they'd listen and call me Grant.

"That's okay, sweetie," I said. "We'll be okay." I turned back to Carl. "Can you get the door?"

"Travis!" Joni shouted back into the store. "I said now. And put the phone down. There is no service. It's just a waste of time." She turned back to me with a sheepish grin. "Kids. You know?"

But I didn't know. There were no kids in my life and no prospects of them. Maybe never.

Carl went into motion and thirty seconds later the metal accordion door clattered open and we were on our way.

As Carl pointed out, I didn't get out much. My life consisted of work, work, and more work. Maybe that's why my relationships never worked out?

Malls weren't a part of my habit, but let me tell you something; empty malls are creepy. You'd think with all the bright colors that were scientifically proven to get us to buy, buy, buy, the atmosphere would somehow ward off all the doom and gloom of our circumstance, but that wasn't the case.

The salon we now called home was on the second floor, so we were forced to head downward and that got us closer to the roaming dead ones. While we had listened and watched whatever breaking news reports we could until the cell and television networks collapsed under the strain, we still knew very little about these dead things.

I knew enough from my detective days to determine that half of what the news carried was bullshit. The other half was overblown to get ratings, but the little I could discern said we were in trouble. Serious trouble.

This wasn't a localized thing. Reports told us that it wasn't just a national crisis, but a global one. It was rolling like a tsunami across the planet and there seemed to be no stopping it.

To make matters worse, no one knew what caused it.

One day, the dead were dead and the next, they were up and roaming around looking for people to munch down on. The truth was that it didn't matter how it started, it was here and the dead were here, ready to turn us into dinner.

We hit the first floor and it didn't seem any cheerier down there. The whole group felt it and tacitly paused.

Carl said, jangling his large key ring. "Come on, gang. The food court is wide open. Time for some decent food."

As we started forward, Martin slid in next to me and tugged at my shirt. "Mr. Grant, remember, you said I could have a twisty cone," There was a slight whine to his voice.

I leaned over closer to him. "Listen, big guy, we need to just get food." I tried to say this with as much firmness as I could without sounding overbearing. I prayed he didn't say the next words. Then he did.

"But you promised," he said.

Why pleasing a seven-year-old boy mattered to me was crazy, considering what we were up against, but it did.

His eyes brimmed with tears and I knew as soon as the first one streamed down his cheek, I would cave anyway. So, I took the easy way out. "Sure, big guy. We'll see about getting that twisty cone. But don't get your hopes up. We may still have electricity in the mall, but I don't know if they left any ice cream in the machine."

In retrospect, I should have been a hard ass, but off we went.

After walking past empty and closed stores in a long corridor, we turned the corner and came to the food court. It really wasn't much of a food court. There were only four vendors. One served tacos and other Mexican food. The next one was a warm pretzel joint that then now deceased Neal managed. There was a pizza by the slice restaurant, too. The last one was what mattered most to young

Martin. It was a combination ice cream and smoothie place.

All-in-all, it was an underwhelming array of options, but as the desperate sailors say, any port in a storm.

What made this food court somewhat special was that it was on the interior of the mall. Just outside the windows was an expansive courtyard area that included a waterway that connected to San Antonio's Riverwalk. The Riverwalk was what brought the tourists in.

The Riverwalk was an interconnected set of man-made waterways that streamed through the downtown featuring all sort of restaurants, shops, and hotels along each side of it. The city's tourism bureau called it a "World-Famous Destination." While it had been impressive in the few hours I got to spend by it before a zombie showed up to devour a man, I hadn't heard of it before I was forced to land there.

It just so happened that one tributary of the Riverwalk waterway ran into the courtyard of our mall. The waterway made up most of the courtyard with walkways surrounding it, complete with small tables with colorful metal umbrellas. I'm sure without zombies roaming the streets, it had been the place to be. Now, it was just sort of sad, devoid of smiling and happy people.

"I'd love some pizza," Jenkins said, sidling up next to me.

"I don't think firing up the ovens to make a slice is on the docket for the day," I said. "This is more like a snatch and grab. I don't want to be down here any longer than I have to be."

"What about my ice cream?" Martin asked, moving in beside me.

I looked down to him. "What would your mom say about having dessert before you ate your real food?"

Before he could answer, Joni interjected, "She'd say that's a no go. Ice cream is fun food. We eat fun food last."

"Carl," I pivoted toward the older man who was standing fondling his key ring again. "Do your keys open the back rooms of these places?"

"They sure do," he said.

"Jenkins, why don't you and Carl go scrounging for food?"

Jenkins didn't need any more encouragement and he and Carl disappeared behind the door of the Mexican place.

I looked in Joni's direction. "Why don't you, Jessica, and Travis check out the front areas of the pizza and taco places for anything edible?"

"What about you?" Travis asked looking like he didn't want to take orders from me or anyone.

"I'm on lookout," I said. "Me, and Martin." I peered down to Martin. "Right, kiddo?"

Martin beamed at me and echoed, "We're on lookout."

Jessica was compliant, but Joni had to nag Travis twice to follow her over to the pizza by the slice restaurant. That left me alone with Martin and gave me a chance to be the "favorite uncle."

"Hey buddy," I whispered. "Why don't we check out the ice cream place? They might have something there we need."

"Really?" He asked.

"For sure."

We were at the counter of the combo ice-cream/smoothie shop ten seconds later. I hopped onto the counter, reached back, and hoisted him up with me and then dropped him behind where I quickly followed.

There were several contraptions back there for making smoothies and squeezing out ice cream along with a freezer that had an assortment of flavors ranging from vanilla to rocky road to rainbow. All the flavors to delight the palettes of young and old alike.

"It'd be a waste of time if we didn't check to see if this soft serve machine still works, right?" I asked him.

His eyes widened, and he said, "Really?"

I answered his question by grabbing an ice cream cone from one of those nifty dispensers that seemed to hold an endless supply of them. I place it under to the nozzle and pulled the handle for a mix of chocolate and vanilla, then said a silent prayer.

The machine hummed for a moment and made a little noise that sounded like a robot coughing. A second later, ice cream oozed out of the nozzle. I swiveled the cone to make sure I evenly distributed the ice cream into the cone.

It was only a small cone, but it seemed to mean the world to a small child who was looking at the very real possibility he might never see his father again. And I was a hero.

"Let's head back out on lookout," I said and reached under his armpits to lift him back onto the counter. I jumped up beside him and let him down a moment later.

No sooner had his feet hit the ground than I heard the words, "Grant, how could you?"

My hero days quickly ended, but at least she called me Grant.

I slowly turned to see Joni ten feet away, her arms crossed, and her eyes narrowed to slits, sending figurative daggers my way.

"He said he wanted ice cream," I replied, knowing I didn't have a leg to stand on.

"You heard what I said too, mister," Joni snapped.

"Come on, what's so wrong with the kid having a little ice cream?"

"Listen, you don't get to come in here, trying to be dad for a day. He doesn't need that. I don't need that."

"Mom," Martin said from behind me.

"Not now, Martin," Joni cut him off.

Jessica appeared at Joni's shoulder. "Can I have ice cream, too?"

"See what you've started?" Joni said. The heat coming off her stare came close to melting me.

"Mom," Martin said again.

"Martin!" Joni shouted.

"But mom!" Martin said.

"What?!" Joni said just as her temper came close to boiling over to tears.

"Is that grandpa and grandma?" Martin asked.

I turned and saw that he was pointing past Joni to the courtyard. I followed his finger and saw a couple people hustling across one of the walkways that ran along the southmost edge of the courtyard. I could tell they were on the older side. Her hair was silver and what I could see of his was nearly gray. They were not running toward an objective, but more away from something by the way they kept looking over their shoulders. I would put both of them in their late sixties. She seemed sprier than him, but refused to let the man fall behind as they hurried across the walkway.

We quickly learned what they were running from when a group of zombies came into view. Unlike the old couple, they were not spry but maintained a steady shambling pace.

"You think that all old people are grandma and grandpa," Jessica said. She obviously hadn't seen what was following these "not" grandparents.

"Grant, what should we do?" Joni asked and all of her anger was gone, replaced by fear.

I wondered why everyone kept asking me those type questions. Did I have the words "Boss" or "Leader" tattooed on my forehead and no one told me?

I turned back toward the door that Carl and Jenkins had gone into and yelled, "Carl! Jenkins, get out here!"

The two old people must have seen us and ran toward the doors right in front of us. I heard a door open and close behind me. A moment later, Carl asked, "What is it? We were finding some good eats back there."

I pointed toward the doors that led out into the courtyard. "We have two old folks on the run and they're being followed by a few of the dead ones."

Carl quickly appeared at my side. "What do you want me to do about it?"

"Well, you have the keys to the kingdom," I said. "You can let them in."

The old couple made it to the bank of windows and peered in. Their faces were twisted in terror. They began to frantically beat at the windows, beseeching us to let them in.

"If I let them in, then those things can get in." Carl shook his head vehemently. "No way, it's too risky."

Tears welled up in Martin's eyes. "But the monsters will get grandpa and grandma."

When I looked down at him, I could see that he had abandoned eating his ice cream. It melted down onto his hands and dripped onto the floor.

"They aren't grandpa and grandma," Jessica said with no small amount of annoyance. "Our grandparents are in Ohio."

"They're someone's grandpa and grandma," Martin shouted as the tears started to flow.

"Come on, Carl," I said. "They don't have a lot of options."

"Well, neither do we. There's only so much to eat and live off inside here. This is my home and I plan to keep it safe and sound."

There it was. That was why he didn't leave. He was claiming the mall for himself. We had just made it in before the brunt of the zombie storm hit and that's why he let us stay.

"Carl, I think you need to rearrange your priorities," I said. "Those are living people out there and if we don't help, they...they..." I trailed off not wanting to be totally explicit about what was going to happen to the old couple if the zombies got to them."Carl, give me your keys," I said as I turned his way.

He took a step away from me and his hands went to his belt, covering up the keys. "No. I ain't doing it. No way. No how. You can't make me."

"Carl, we really need those keys," I begged. "Those people are going to die."

He didn't respond but just kept backing away.

"Give me the keys!" I yelled.

"Just 'cause you're some fancy U.S. Marshall doesn't mean you have the right to order me around. I'm the security guard here and my rules are the only ones that count."

The zombies were closing quickly on the old couple as they smacked their hands at the glass trying to get us to open up. They were yelling, but the windows just turned their voices into muffled, indistinct sounds.

"Carl, please give him the keys," Joni pleaded.

Carl didn't say anything but just kept backpedaling away from us.

"We need those keys," I said, putting my hand out toward him.

He turned and ran down the corridor, leaving us all stunned. The sound of the old couple beating on the glass seemed to intensify.

I took a peek back over my shoulder and saw that the old couple had twenty to thirty seconds before they were in trouble. I looked back and saw Carl disappear around the corner and out of view.

It didn't take a mental giant to know that if I went chasing after Carl, there'd be no time to return with the keys to open the door in time. And that was if Carl didn't force me to fight him to get them.

I looked to Joni. "Get the kids down the hall and ready to run."

"Grant, what are you going to do?" She asked and I could see fear in her eyes.

I pulled my gun from its holster and said, "I have the universal key right here." I started for the doors, watching the approaching zombies.

Of course, this wasn't a bright idea. If I shot out the windows, then the zombies would come in along with the old people. But if I did nothing, these old people were toast. Toast with bloody jelly on them.

In my mind, it was the only choice and we'd deal with the next step after we saved the old couple. I motioned to the two of them to get away from the door. I'm not sure they didn't initially think I was going to shoot them, but they finally got it. The man grabbed the woman and pulled her out of the way, using his body as a shield from any of the glass that was about to go flying.

I aimed low, then high, pulling the trigger three times.

As expected, the glass shattered and flew onto the walkway, glittering in the sunlight like diamonds.

"Get inside," I yelled and the old couple didn't need any more encouragement. Motivated by sheer terror, they ran inside.

"Thank you, thank you, thank you," the woman said breathlessly. She had the no-nonsense short hairstyle of a woman who wasn't afraid to speak her mind. He was a little soft around the middle and wore one of those herringbone skid lid hats that always made me think of Englishmen. Pip, pip, and cheerio, old chap and all that crap.

To the right of the now windowless door were several tables ready for the people who weren't ever coming back to the food court. They were heavy duty plastic ones with metal legs and hard plastic bench seats.

"Travis, get up here and help me get these tables in front of the doors," I shouted back at the gaped mouth teenager. "I need your help and I need it now!" I shouted.

He started in motion, but Joni shot out a hand to grab his arm. He shook her off and sprinted my way.

The zombies were less than twenty feet away when he and I got behind the first table and started pushing it along the floor like one of the tackling sleds that football players use. We had to be careful not to shove it too hard or else we'd break out more windows. He got it without me having to say anything and pulled back as we approached the broken door.

We both did some mental calculations, and he said, "Let's put it on its side."

I didn't think we had time to Jenga it in place, so I just helped him lift onto its side and we rammed it into the now gaping hole in the bank of windows.

"Let's get another one and jam it into this one," I said.

He didn't need any more directions. Just as we slammed it into the upended table, the zombies hit the windows and the table we had placed in the hole. I wouldn't call it a jarring impact, but it was clear to see that this was a temporary solution at best. With us holding the second table in place, we could probably keep the zombies out, but that wasn't really a viable long-term option. Holding a table in place for hours on end wasn't the job I had signed up for. But I had no one else to blame because I let the old couple in.

More zombies poured onto the walkway, drawn in by my shots. They started stacking up outside the window like planes at O'Hare airport, ready for a landing. The ones that could see Travis and me holding the table in place tried to do what they could to get at us.

The other zombies ended up pressing themselves against the glass and I got this distinct feeling that this was how fish felt. We were on the inside with the predators on the outside looking in.

"Hey, can I help?" A voice asked behind me. When I glanced back, I saw the man who had just come inside. He was still huffing and puffing from the exertion.

"Not sure if you're up to this, old timer," I said.

"I'm not that old," he replied and I could see him suck in his gut a little while inflating his chest.

"It's okay. We've got it."

"But for how long?"

I wanted to congratulate him for being Captain Obvious but decided I'd be better off keeping my mouth shut.

"What's your name?" I asked.

"Oscar," he replied. "And that's Minnie." He pointed back at his wife. "Listen, we're really grateful for what you did."

"Think nothing of it," I said. "I'm sure you would have done the same for us."

Something thudded against the our temporary barrier and I felt the table we were holding onto move back an inch or two.

"Grant!" Travis said with some alarm.

When I looked back out the windows, I saw a gargantuan zombie butting his body into the upended table. He looked like a giant mated with Big Foot. He was shirtless and had an expansive belly with a disgusting amount of body hair covering it. Some things can never be unseen.

I bent my back and pushed back for all I was worth. We regained an inch of the two we had lost, but I knew if two giant zombies started pounding away, we'd be in real trouble. Our only upside was that these things didn't think. If they had decided to cooperate and push all at once, Travis and I would have been ten feet back into the food court and on our asses. It would be like taking the proverbial cork from the bottle because the zombies would have flooded inside.

"Grant, what are we doing?" Joni asked from behind me. I could hear fear on the edge of her voice.

"Can anyone find Carl?" I asked.

"He's long gone," Jenkins said. I took in a deep breath, looking down at the floor as the zombies pushed against our makeshift barrier, then let it out. "Listen up, folks. Travis and I will hold this in place for as long as we can, but I can't think of a long-term solution for keeping it here. If Carl were still here, he might have some idea of what we could use to keep these tables in place. At least temporarily. But we're on our own. So, everyone needs to get back up on the second floor. Once Travis and I let go of this table, it will only be a matter of minutes before they get inside."

I made a quick assessment of the zombies outside and guessed there were at least forty. The ones at the windows pawed and slapped at the glass. Every once in a while, one would slam its head into the glass with a sharp thud. I wondered what pounds per square inch of pressure it took to break that glass?

"What then? Joni asked.

Gigantor the zombie slammed his bulk against the table and this time it gave almost three inches.

"We'll have to take it from there. Now, you have to go."

When I looked back, I could see the reluctance on Joni's face.

"Don't worry, both Travis and I are fleet of foot. We can outrun these undead bastards."

It wasn't much of a sales speech, but she bought it, mostly because she had no other choice. She shouted commands at the kids to get moving. Martin's ice cream was nothing but a melted mass dripping off his hand and glopping down to the floor. Oscar and Minnie joined Joni and the kids and they were off and running. Not being fleet of foot, Jenkins followed up the rear.

"Travis, I'll hold it for now," I said. "See if you can push another table up here."

He looked scared witless, but he let go, found another table, and started pushing it my way. It screeched along, the metal legs dragging across the tiled floor. Just as he had it at my back legs, I looked around and said, "We're going to lift that one on top of the other one. It won't keep them out, but it will slow them down."

"You mean, they're really getting inside?" He asked.

"Yes. There's no stopping them."

I could see his lower lip start to quiver.

"Travis," I said with a bit of sharpness to my tone. "What

we do right now could make the difference between whether your family lives or dies."

It took a couple seconds for that to sink in, but he slowly nodded his head.

"Grab the other side," I said, and I moved to the opposite side of the table. "Now, lift."

It wasn't exceptionally heavy, but still, it took some effort. We dropped it on top of the other table indelicately. The sound of it clattering down excited the zombies outside.

"What now?" He asked.

"We run."

That was something I didn't have to work to sell. Less than a minute later, we were up on the second floor, standing next to the other members of our little group. Joni positioned them to have a view down onto the food court. Together we stood, waiting and watching.

It was sort of like waiting for a volcano to erupt. You felt the tremors and a few burbles of lava had broken through the earth's crust, but you knew deep down that real trouble was coming. The big blow was inevitable, and it was going to be messy.

We watched as the zombies pushed the upended table inward, slamming into it again and again. Each impact moved it a few inches. Hands pawed around the sides of it.

That wasn't the worst of it though. The forty or so zombies were adding to their total as more and more zombies came from wherever they had been.

"What do we do now, Grant?" Joni asked.

"First, I'd like to throttle Carl, but that won't get us anywhere," I replied.

"Who's Carl?" Oscar asked.

"He was a security guard here at the mall," Joni replied.

"He was downstairs with us, but he ran off after he refused to use his keys to let you in."

"Sounds like a selfish asshole to me," Minnie said.

"I'll second the motion," I chimed in.

"Are there other ways out?" Oscar said.

"We could make a run out onto the street, but, and please don't take offense, but you and Minnie don't seem to be up to sprinting."

"I'm not sure the kids are, either," Joni added.

"Where does that leave us?" Oscar asked.

"Well, fu--" I started but stopped myself and looked down at Martin and Jessica. "Screwed." I knew that didn't go over well. "But I have this idea."

I looked at the rest of our group and they actually leaned in closer to me like I was a stockbroker with some great insider tip.

"Look over there." I pointed out of the windows and past the zombies gathering there just past the waterway. "Do you see any of them in the water?"

"What are you trying to say?" Oscar asked. "That they can't swim?"

"No, I'm just saying they are avoiding the water."

"Maybe it's because there are no humans in the water," Travis said.

"That could be," I said.

"Where's this leading?" Oscar asked.

"Those waterways lead out of here."

"And?" Oscar asked again.

"We need to get into that waterway and use it to get away."

"If you hadn't noticed, those things are out there."

I felt like I had to be overly confident because my slow developing plan was bordering on preposterousness. "I've got that." Again, I pointed out the window. "You see those awnings leading out the second floor?"

"What about them?"

"Grant." Travis tried to get my attention.

"Hold on a second, Travis. We bust out the windows and we slide down the awnings, drop into the water, and we use the waterway to escape."

Oscar looked at me like I was from another planet. "You make it sound so easy. If you hadn't noticed, I'm not exactly James Bond. Hell, a fall from there'd probably break my hip or throw my back out."

"Mr. Grant," Travis insisted. This time with more pitch and volume.

"Hold your horses. I'm talking with Oscar. It's not that far and there's water to break your fall. Besides, once those things are inside, all bets are off."

Travis leaned between Oscar and me. "They're inside."

I quickly turned my attention back to our makeshift barricade and saw two zombies in the food court and two more wriggling their way in. Gigantor had his head and shoulder through and once his wide girth gut made it through, a river of zombies would flow inside.

"Times up," I said. "Unless you have a better idea in the next fifteen seconds or less."

"Won't they just come over to where we are jumping, water or not?" Joni asked.

"That's where our diversion comes in," I said.

"What's our diversion?" Joni asked.

"Me."

✕✶✕✶✶✶✶

Nobody liked my plan, least of all me, but we were out of

time and out of options. Joni and Travis took the others down the corridor that led them to the windows over top the waterway. First, they would get the windows open however they could. The next step was the biggest one. Sliding down the awnings. For that part of the plan, Joni and Travis would take one of the younger kids on the plunge into the waterway. Oscar and Minnie would have to risk the fall or find their own way out of the mall on their own. Jenkins still wanted teleportation capabilities, but settled on my plan.

I, on the other hand, was bait for the zombies.

"Woooooooooo-hoooooo, you ugly sons of bitches," I yelled at the top of my lungs as I stood at an intersecting corridor a hundred feet from the food court. All sixty of the zombies shambling around in the food court took immediate notice. It would have been so much easier if they had decided to get a slice of pizza or a couple tacos, but I was on their menu and nothing else would do.

My yell was all it took, and they were off and running. Well, really shambling.

There was little doubt I could outrun them, but sooner or later I was going to run out of real estate or be forced to exit out a door on the other side of the mall into unknown territory. Who knew how many deaders were outside any door I might open? Not I, and that's why I was planning to draw them deep into the mall, away from Joni and the others. Then I would find a way upstairs where I would sprint across the second floor, out the window, and into the waterway, joining the others.

It was a bad plan with many holes in it, but it only got worse when a wild card got played by an unexpected hand.

I couldn't go too far or too fast or else the zombies might forget I was there. Then they might turn around and head back toward the others. So, I ran fifty feet, then turned around and taunted them. (If zombies could really be taunted.)

"Hey you," I yelled at one of the lead zombies wearing a bright Hawaiian shirt. "You call that a shirt? Did your momma buy it for you?"

I didn't say that I was good at taunting, now did I?

In reality, I didn't have to be good at it. My voice was the siren song drawing them deeper into the mall. Stumble, shamble, or wobble, they followed my voice.

That part of the plan was working as intended until it stopped working.

Just as I was getting closer to the end of the corridor and the stairway door I had planned to take upstairs, a shot rang out. The report echoed loudly inside the empty mall with the only competition for noise being the moans and grunts of the zombies.

My first ridiculous thought was that zombies had learned how to shoot guns. If that were true, we were done for.

The second shot discouraged me of that idea as a bullet whizzed by my head. When I wheeled around to find the source, I saw Carl slipping his arm around a corner, gun in hand, pointed in my direction. It wasn't much of a gun being a snub-nosed .38. Accuracy was terrible with something like that, but still, he could get lucky.

"You son of a bitch," he screamed. "You ruined everything. Those things are in my home now."

He fired off two quick shots and one whizzed by me, the second chipped some faux marble off the wall behind me.

"Carl, I don't have time for this," I yelled.

"I had a perfect place here," he said. "I let you people in

and look what you did. The zombies are inside and it's all gone to shit."

"Carl, how long could you have really stayed here?" I asked.

"Forever," he wailed.

"Forever until the electricity ran out," I replied, looking back over my shoulder. The distance between me and the zombies was diminishing rapidly. There was no time for a debate about what had happened.

He was silent for a few moments. "I would have figured something out. Me and that little filly you brought in with you. We could have been king and queen here."

"Joni?" I asked. "She's already married. Besides, what would you have done with the kids."

"No room for kids here." He fired off another shot. This bullet pinged off the floor in front of me, then chipped back into the mall.

It was more than obvious that he was off his nut, but that made me question my intuition. He had seemed all right when we came to the mall. Then again, maybe I was a little distracted by the impending zombie apocalypse.

"Carl, that's not going to happen."

"All because of you," he stuck his head around the corner to take another shot at me and I had had enough of that. I yanked up my pistol and fired off a shot forcing him to pull away.

"Two can play at that game, Carl," I shouted. "And I think you're a shitty shot."

He stayed behind the corner and shouted back, "I don't have to be good. The zombies will do my work for me."

I glanced over my shoulder. The pack of zombies was just seconds away from overrunning my position.

I guessed that Carl thought I wasn't willing to approach

his hiding spot because he could shoot me down. In reality, if it came down to being mauled to death by zombies or being shot, I'd take being shot any day.

I pulled up my gun arm and aimed at the corner he was hiding behind and started toward it at a light jog. Maybe he suspected I was too scared to do that, but he was about to find out that I had taken the lesser of two evils. I wondered if he could hear my footfalls over the moans and groans behind me.

Well, my wondering ended when he popped around the corner. He had hoped to get the drop on me, but instead, I had him. It only took me three quick trigger pulls. A spray of blood filled the air, then he spun around and out of view.

I hadn't wanted to kill him, but then again, that's what he was trying to do with me. Turnabout is fair play, right? Still, I felt shitty about shooting him.

As it turned out, I hadn't killed him. As I edged around the corner, I saw him lying on the ground, his face locked in a grimace, and his hand clutched onto his shoulder. Blood seeped between his fingers. His little .38 sat on the ground about ten feet away from him.

"You shot me," he gasped between ragged breaths.

"To be fair, you shot at me first."

"You screwed up everything. My plans. My home. Everything." I could swear it sounded like he might cry.

"Come on," I said. "I'll help you up. The zombies are coming."

His eyes snapped open wide. "I don't want your damn help and I don't need it."

"Suit yourself. I'm not waiting around and I'm not asking twice."

I ducked out of the little side corridor he had been shooting from and saw that we had thirty seconds before the point of no return. They'd have us trapped with no place to go. I only had so many bullets. My choice would come down to whether I saved one for myself.

"Come on, Carl," I said.

"You do what you have to do," he said.

"Have it your way." I shrugged and sprinted for the stairwell to the second floor. This stairwell had a door and that was good because I didn't think the zombies were smart enough to open it. But a minute ago, I thought they might be able to shoot guns, so all bets were off.

I looked back at the corridor where Carl was and didn't see any movement. A part of me was telling myself to go back and help him, but the deep down part of my brain that was all about survival shouted down any other voices. That's when I heard the shot echo out of the corridor.

Carl had taken away any of my options to save him.

A moment later, I shut the door behind me and bounded up the stairs to the second floor. When I made it there, I peeked over the balcony. I saw the zombies in a huge scrum, pushing and shoving to get into the corridor to get a piece of Carl. A peek was more than enough, and I was off and running across the second floor to get to Joni, Travis, and the others.

The wonderful thing about this mall was the openness. The windows gave a panoramic view of the courtyard and this allowed me to see Joni sliding out onto one of the awnings that hung over the waterway below. She had her back to me and was reaching up for a reluctant Martin who looked like he wanted no part of my plan to jump off the awning into the water.

Travis followed his mom's lead and climbed onto an adjoining awning. He reached back for Jessica who was less reluctant than Martin. Maybe Jessica goaded Martin into making his way out, but it was only a couple seconds after she moved out onto the awning with Travis that Martin slowly climbed out. It was then that I became really concerned about how much weight those awnings would hold, but in the end, we were way past worrying about things like that.

I continued running the length of the mall to get to them. I caught glimpses of their progress through the different windows and obstructions on my way. I was about halfway there when I saw a show stopper.

Drifting into the waterway beneath Joni, Travis, and the kids was one of the riverboats meant for carrying tourists on relaxing tours of San Antonio's picturesque Riverwalk. What took my breath away about this little tour was that the boat was filled with zombies. They were stumbling about in the boat, bumping into each other, fortunately not noticing the tasty humans above them.

Somehow this brought forth into my mind the Disney theme park ride the Pirates of the Caribbean -- only it was more like a dine-in booze cruise where people were on the menu. Don't ask me why I thought this. My thinking is sometimes warped.

I put myself into high gear and was on an approach path to Oscar and Minnie, who stood at the windows, looking out over the awnings. Minnie's eyes were wide and Oscar wore a scowl on his face when faced with the prospect of taking the plunge. Nope. This little plan to jump off into the waters below wasn't looking all that peachy.

They turned at the sound of my approach, their brows furrowed and lips pressed into a thin line.

Oscar whispered to me, "Grant, I don't know about this."

"I hear you, Oscar, but we don't have a lot of choices," I

whispered back. "Those zombies down on one are going to venture up here sooner or later."

"Grant," Joni said in a hushed tone as she looked down below. "What do we do?"

I leaned past Oscar. "Be quiet and wait for them to drift by. Then we jump."

"We?" She asked.

"Well, you."

"Thanks," she responded, then added, "a lot."

It was too late for me to take her place with Martin. The combined weight of two adults and a child looked to be too much for the already straining awning.

Seconds ticked by and the boat packed with zombies slowly drifted fully into view. It took what seemed like an eternity for it to slowly float along to the other side of the waterway where it bumped into the walkway and stopped.

They hadn't noticed us yet. "It's go time. Martin, hang tight onto your mom. Joni, slide off but grab the awning, then hang drop off into the water. I'm guessing you're falling no more than ten feet and water will soften the impact."

I had to sell this crazy idea somehow.

She looked up to me with doubt in her eyes, but she was smart enough to know that this was the best way to go. I watched as she built up the courage.

Then she looked to Travis, who was on the next awning with Jessica.

"You ready?" Joni asked him.

"But my phone will get wet," he said with a real look of concern on his face.

Joni leaned over to him, snatched the phone from his hand, then tossed it down into the waterway below.

"Mom!" Travis said in shock.

"Shhhhhhh," I said, but it was too late. His voice carried

back to the boat of the damned and the zombies took notice. "Time to go!"

Joni saw the zombies, too. She took a deep breath, let it out, and I saw the expression on her face shift from worry to determination. She was a fighter.

She slowly slid down the awning with Martin holding onto her like a little spider monkey. The two of them slid over the edge and the only thing I could see were her hands straining to hold onto the metal bar hidden under the fabric of the awning. I could also see the awning stressed to the max by the motion.

A moment later, her hands let go and then we all heard the splash below.

There wasn't time to make sure the landing was safe. Some of the zombies were abandoning ship and falling over the side of the riverboat into the waterway, while others climbed onto the walkway. The ones on the walkway would have a long path around the courtyard to get to us. The ones in the water looked quite graceless as they floundered around looking more like they were drowning than anything else.

This brought forth the question on whether a zombie could really drown? I quickly put that aside for the task at hand.

Travis followed his mom's lead and went over the side of the awning.

"Minnie, let me help you out," I offered.

She didn't need any coaxing and neither did Oscar. Just as they slid to the edge of their respective awnings they reached out to each other and squeezed each other's hands. In any other circumstance, it would have been endearing. Actually, it was, but there was no time for a Hallmark moment. They went over the side with a splash.

The zombies weren't making good progress in the water, but it wouldn't be long before they made it to us. So, I climbed onto the awning and slid off it without trying to hang drop.

A moment later, I splashed down and went under the water.

As it turned out, the waterway was only four feet deep, so when I stood, the water was only up to my chest.

I sputtered water out of my mouth and wiped my eyes in time to see all of our group looking at me, their expression looking like a question mark -- what next?

"Go out the way the zombies drifted in," I said. "The zombies don't move well in water, so we'll use that to our advantage. We'll find a new safe harbor somewhere outside the mall."

And that was my plan. It wasn't much of one, but whoever had a contingency for a zombie apocalypse in their back pocket? Certainly, not me.

ABOUT R.J. SPEARS

R.J. Spears splits his writing time between mystery/crime and horror. His stories have appeared on A Twist of Noir, Shotgun Honey, Flashes in the Dark, and the Horror Zine along with other sites. His zombie series Forget the Zombies and Books of the Dead can be found on Amazon. You can learn more about his writing at: rj-spears.com

8

FIRST JOB (THE ZEE BROTHERS)

BY GRIVANTE

I. Zombie Exterminators?

"So... you want us to pretend to be exterminators?" Jonah scrunched up his face, locking eyes with Dr. Natasha Nitsau, who sat with her legs crossed behind her desk.

She leaned forward smiling, placing her hands over her nylon covered knees and staring right into him. She wore her white lab coat, black business skirt and a white blouse which was open at the top. "Not pretend, no. They'll all die in the end but I want you to collect them for me first. There's lots you two can do for me. If you're willing." Her gaze turned to Judas, and she mashed her red-coated lips together, slowly spreading them into a smile.

Judas shot his brother a quick look and let out an audible gulp.

"And what do you want with these zombies we'll be collecting?" Jonah asked.

"They're needed for my research."

"And what kind of research is that?"

The doctor's gaze narrowed, looking him over as he

stood there in his black Nitsau Corporation security uniform. "Anti-aging." She removed her hands from her legs and uncrossed them, looking Jonah directly in the eyes. "So that you understand, what I'll be paying you for is to do as you're told. Asking questions is not in the job description."

"I, uh," Jonah stammered. "I'm just trying to understand what you want of us." He wiped a hand across his brow as she continued to stare him down. "I just want to make sure we get it right."

The CEO's gaze held steady, then relaxed as she moved her chair under her desk and picked up a stack of papers. "Very well. These are the forms you'll need to file with the U.C.A. to be properly licensed and then you can begin your studies of my archives. You will be an independent company but you will use Nitsau Corporation assets and continue to be paid as security guards by us. To be clear," she paused, looking them both hard in the eyes one at a time, smiling as Judas averted his eyes from her gaze, "you work for me. Understand?"

"Yes," they both answered.

"Good. You'll find everything you need in warehouse nine. There's a loft in the back where you'll find my research archives. Start there. The main warehouse is stocked with equipment and weapons for your use. You'll have everything you could need. I'll be assigning one of my engineers to train you and help you with any needed modifications." She thrust the papers forward.

Judas stepped forward, clamping onto the forms. "Thank you, Natasha."

Dr. Nitsau's lips tightened into a thin line and her hand clamped onto the papers, refusing to let them into Judas's grasp. "No." Her dark eyes pierced into his. "It's Dr. Nitsau, always. Ma'am is also acceptable." Her eye's continued to bore into him. "Understand?"

Judas's face reddened, sweat dripping from his brow. "Y-yes, ma'am." He stumbled back as she released the papers into his grip.

"Ma'am, may I ask what happened last week?" Jonah asked her.

Her eye's darkened. "Always with the questions, hmm, Mr. Zee?" She didn't wait for an answer but asked another question. "Why?"

He put his hands behind his back and stood taller. Judas noted his posture and assumed the same position. "To better understand the things we might encounter."

She smiled at his posture and her eyes softened. "You may."

"Thank you," Jonah nodded in acknowledgment. "What happened there and how did it get out of control?"

"Hmm," her lips squeezed together, and she brought her hands in front of her, forming a steeple. "An experiment that went too far."

"Too far?" Jonah nodded, brow furrowing. "How far was it supposed to go? Everyone in there but you was dead."

"We were testing a new serum on a few test subjects. The technician in charge didn't make sure the subject was secure before starting. One of them got free and my former bodyguards failed to keep the situation contained."

Jonah's forehead wrinkled even further. "And this was an anti-aging serum?"

Dr. Nitsau opened a side drawer on her desk, pulling from it a small silver case and a long black tube. She opened the case revealing a half-dozen slender cigarettes, took one out, stuck it in the holder, held it to her lips and lit it. After a long pull, she blew the smoke out directly at Jonah.

"I run a pharmaceutical 'research' company. We have many trials going on, treatments, antibiotics, vaccines, etc. Some of which overlap with others. So, yes, anti-aging."

Jonah breathed in the smoke as it wafted over him. He cleared his throat. "Thank you for clarifying. You mentioned vaccines. Since collecting the undead for you will be rather dangerous, is there a zombie vaccine we should receive?"

Dr. Nitsau let out a long laugh. "That is an excellent question to ask me, Mr. Zee. The first question that hasn't made me reconsider offering you this position. The answer is complicated. We have some experimental vaccines that have shown potential in lab animals, however, there are many causes of zombification as you will see when you study my record on the subject. My research has shown there isn't likely a singular vaccine. It's similar to the flu virus, there are thousands of strains and quite possibly it's the same with zombies. While the flu is always a virus, some causes of zombification are not and they are impossible to prevent but I'm hopeful with you and your brother's work," she glanced at Judas who beamed at the mention, "we'll have plenty of new subjects from which to further our exploration into the possibilities."

Jonah nodded again. "Ok. So bringing you zombies from different outbreaks will help you develop a better vaccine?"

Another long slow puff. "Yes, among other things." She set the cigarette and holder on her desk. "Now boys, enough with the Q and A. You've got homework to do."

II. Edja-Macation

The brothers held their tongues until they left the lab

building and were out of earshot of other Nitsau Corporation employees.

Judas put a big wad of chewing tobacco in his mouth and looked at his older brother, who chewed on his lower lip, brow furrowed in deep concentration. "What's the matter, bro?" he spat a black gooey stream onto the concrete.

Jonah glanced at him while pulling a cigar out of his pocket and lighting it. He took a few puffs and blew them out before answering. "I don't know. Something doesn't feel right about this job." He took a long puff. "No, not the job, her. Dr. Nitsau." He looked at his brother as they walked past the first of the many generic looking warehouse buildings on the property.

"What?" Judas looked up at him, his head cocked to the right and his forehead scrunched. "She's eccentric and a little stern but I kinda like that. Plus, she's hot, rich and owns her own company. What's wrong with that?"

Jonah waved his cigar around in front of him. "No. It's not those things. It's her attitude. She's so... cold. All those people died in her lab last week and she doesn't seem to care."

"Scientists can be strange," Judas said, shrugging his shoulders.

Jonah huffed. "And how many scientists do you know Judas?"

Judas spat, his face souring. "None, but the professor on Gilligan's Island was kind of a strange guy."

"Gilligan! Really, Judas?" Jonah took his hat off and smacked his brother on the head. "That's as close to Gilligan as this situation is. You can't base your views on the world off of what you've seen on television shows."

Judas shrank away, raising his arms. "Sorry, bro. I just don't think she's that bad."

Jonah shook his head. "You're just smitten."

Judas smiled. "I'm okay with that."

They came to a stop outside building number nine.

"We're here." Jonah put his cigar out on the concrete and opened the door to a blast of music. Nirvana's 'All Apologies' played from deep in the rear of the building. The warehouse was vast, with a huge high ceiling running all the way to a loft section they could only partially see at the back.

Four large, black, unmarked BMW transport vans stood in a line down the center of the building. Racks and locked cabinets filled with various weapons, ammo, and other implements lined the walls. They sauntered past the vans to where the music originated. A man with a mass of wavy red hair pulled back in a ponytail to his waist, sat at a workbench. His head banging to the music as he cranked a wrench, fastening a long silver tube into place on a half-finished, multi-barrel gun.

Tools and parts littered his workbench, including blades of different sizes and bullets of various gauges. Mounted on the wall above the workbench stood three customized guitars, the likes of which the brothers hadn't seen before. Giant metal sprockets and weird tubes speaking of steampunk designs adorned them.

The brothers watched him work in silence. His focused intensity as he tightened bolts and moved to put another barrel into place, all while rocking out, was something to behold. He wore blue jeans and a sleeveless denim jacket, both stained with spots of grease.

Not wanting to startle him and interrupt his work, Jonah waited until a pause between songs and then coughed. "Excuse me, Sir?"

The man continued working. The next song blasted from the speakers mounted on either side of the workbench. Jonah looked at Judas, raising his eyebrows. Judas shrugged. Jonah stepped to the right and noticed in addition to the loud music, he also wore earbuds. Jonah waved his hands in the air to get the man's attention until he tilted his head to the left and peered back.

He wore round-rimmed glasses with orange-tinted lenses over the regular ones that hung at the tip of his nose. He flipped them up, then used his thumb and pointer finger to smooth out the long red whiskers of his greying horse-shoe mustache.

The man reached into a pocket, pulled out an iPod and hit pause, then pressed a button on a computer behind the giant gun he was working on, bringing Kurt Cobain's grunging vocals to a halt. He took in both brothers and then held out a hand.

"You must be the Zee brothers. I'm Hank. The boss sent me an email saying she'd found someone to take on this particular project of hers. Welcome aboard."

"Thanks," Jonah took his hand. "I'm Jonah, this is my brother, Judas."

"Nice to meet you. I'm glad to have some company around here. It's been a while since the last ones."

"Why'd you have the headphones in and the stereo blasting?" Judas asked.

Hank shrugged. "Loud music keeps people from coming in and asking me to come work on something for them. Plus, when I'm creating something like this beautiful beast of a gun I love the sounds of Beethoven." He wiggled the earbuds in his fingers.

Jonah smiled at Hank's taste in music. "What do you mean, 'the last ones'?"

Hank looked him square in the eyes. "This isn't a cupcake kinda job, boy. It's dangerous. Fuck up and it means your life." He looked at them both and smiled. "That's what I'm here for though. I'm in charge of keeping you safe. Arming and armoring you so that when you go out on a job, you come back. More importantly, that you come back with what the doctor ordered." He laughed, picked up a washcloth off the bench and ran it along one of the barrels, wiping away an oily smudge.

"What is that you're building?" Judas asked.

"This?" Hank beamed. "Just something I'm making to pass the time. I call her Dee-Dee. It's a hundred caliber machine gun, something I'm building just in case that big z-day finally happens. It'll turn a horde of zombies, or just about anything, into Swiss cheese with the pull of the trigger. Of course, I've got to find something to mount it on. I'm not sure the good doctor will let me put it on one of her company vehicles."

"Damn," Judas said. "That's impressive. Why Dee-Dee?"

"It's short for Death Dealer."

"I bet," Judas chuckled and reached out to touch the gun.

Hank's hand flew up and smacked it away. "Not now boy. You've got some edja-macation to get to before you get to play with the toys. Stairs are over there." He pointed to the right where a wooden staircase led up to the office loft above his workshop.

The brothers entered the room and found stacks of papers, pictures, books and a few computers.

"Where do we even start?" Judas asked.

Jonah picked up a stack from the nearest pile with a shrug. "Here's good."

Days later, Jonah flipped through a binder looking at images of different zombies and their causes.

Judas stared at the wall, blinking.

"Wow. It says here," Jonah turned the page toward his brother, "that there are voodoo curses and black magic spells that can turn people into zombies. There's even a handwritten note from Dr. Nitsau that no vaccines are likely to prevent it." He turned the page. "Here's one that says some native American tribes could even control those they turned. She put a big asterisk next to that part. That's crazy don't you think?"

"Hmm," Judas glanced over, "what about her?"

Jonah's eyes narrowed, noticing his brother wasn't even facing his work area. "Are you paying any attention? Have you even opened your binder this morning?"

Judas bent his head and shook it. "No. I got bored and started daydreaming about when we might get to go bash some heads... I mean capture them. Then you mentioned Dr. Nitsau and I started wondering when we might get to see her again. It's been three weeks."

"Judas, are you crazy? Do you really think the CEO of a major pharmaceutical company is romantically interested in someone she hired as an exterminator?"

Judas's face warmed and he shifted in his seat. "It could happen," he mumbled without looking at his brother.

"What?"

"Interoffice romances happen all the time."

Jonah spun his head around, looking around the room. "Really? Cause all I see in this office is you and me!"

Judas's shoulders sank. "It's not impossible."

"Sure," Jonah said with a sharp nod. "Now, how about you get to studying the different zombies that will be trying to kill us so we can get to the fun part?"

III. The Mama and the Papa

Hank moved a lever back and forth on the pole causing the hoop at the end to cinch tight and then release.

"If there's just a few, you can use these to capture them and keep them out of reach. I've got a prototype around here somewhere for a version that'll deliver a 100-megawatt jolt and fry em like a piece of over-cooked bacon in three seconds flat. Smells like holy hell but gets the job done."

"Sweet!" Judas said, moving the lever back and forth on his own pole. "When do I get to play with that one?"

"You don't." Hank set his pole down. "I haven't figured out how to insulate it properly yet. It can fry the wielder just as quick as the wearer. Besides, she wants them 'living' dead, remember?"

"Yeah," Judas sighed. "Living dead, check."

"That said," Hank walked over to one of the many cabinets lining the wall. "If an outbreak gets out of control, there will be times you'll have to exterminate a bunch before you can round up samples to bring back. You boys know how to handle a firearm?"

"Oh, yeah! Time for the good stuff," Judas grinned.

"Yes," Jonah added, "we've been shooting since we were little."

"Good." Hank opened the cabinet, revealing a row of black polished assault rifles, handguns and more. "Let's take some of these to the range for practice."

The next morning, the brothers were back in warehouse nine going over implements with Hank when the phone on the wall rang. Hank walked over answered it, listened a moment, then turned to Jonah and Judas with a huge smile. "It's for you."

Jonah took the phone, uncertain what to do as Hank grinned at him. "Hello?"

"Yeah, hello," a man's voice answered. "Is this the zombie removal and extermination services?"

Jonah's eyes shot wide open and he looked at Judas motioning him over. "Uh, yes sir. My name's Jonah, how can we help you?"

Judas leaned in and put his ear next to the phone.

"My neighbor's zombies got out again and now they're at my back door trying to get in and eat me and my kids. I've had it and I want them gone. They terrify my girls. If my wife comes home and finds them loose again she will lose it."

Jonah looked at Hank wanting to ask him what to do but the man just grinned at him, stroking the sides of his mustache, excitement radiating off of him.

"What do you mean your neighbor's zombies got out again?"

"Douglas keeps them in a tin shed out back. They were family members that got turned during an outbreak overseas or something. Somehow he managed to smuggle them out of the country and into the US. He doesn't want them put down, which I understand but when my little girls are outside playing and his dead mom bursts through the fence and tries to eat them, I've had enough!"

"I understand, sir. What's your address?" Jonah grabbed a pen and paper from Hank's workbench and scribbled as the man spoke. "Okay, sir. Please stay inside and close your blinds. We'll be there as soon as we can." He hung up the phone.

"Have we got a job, Jonah?" Judas's eyes were wide and glistening with excitement.

"Yeah, we do, though I've no idea what we do now."

Hank's face split in a wide whiskery smile. "Yahoo! It's time to load you two up with weapons and gear and get you outta here!"

"Ok," Jonah nodded, adrenaline flooding his system. "I'll go get Sasha and we can load up."

Hank's face scrunched up, causing his mustache and beard to blend into one mass of hair. "Who's Sasha?"

"That's our truck," Judas said.

"It's a 55 Chevy Step-side. Used to be our dad's. We've been restoring it," Jonah added.

"That sounds like a sweet ride. I'd love to see it some-time but you two will take a company vehicle." He nodded toward the row of black BMW cargo vans. "You'll need space to put the zoms. She'll want at least three, no more than five. You can terminate any excess. If there's freshly turned and old dead, make sure to get some of each."

"What do we do with any we put down?" Jonah asked.

Hank shrugged. "Burn 'em."

❡❡❡❡❡❡

The van stopped at the address written on the scrap of paper in Jonah's hand. "What do you think, we ready?"

Judas studied the ordinary looking house. "Guess we kinda have to be, huh?"

"Yep," Jonah nodded, opening his door. "Let's do this."

They met at the van's back door, Judas slipping a large wad of chew into his mouth.

"What are you doing?"

Judas shoved the tobacco in with his tongue and spat. "What?"

"Now isn't the time for chew."

"Why not?"

"It's not professional, Judas. We're going into someone's home. Plus, what if things get out of hand and you ended up swallowing it and getting sick? That's not how we make a good impression."

Judas grimaced then reached into his lip, swiping out the wad of black gunk. "Fine." He flung it to the ground with a splat.

They opened the back of the van and examined the assortment of equipment Hank had prepared for them. Catch poles, knives, guns, a few axes, and other blades. There were even spears and a pair of assault rifles next two extra sets of body armor, gas masks, and two helmets.

"What do you think we'll need?" Judas asked.

Jonah reached in and grabbed a catch pole, then handed it to Judas. "Two of these to start. We should each have a knife and a handgun. There should only be a couple of them, so we can come back and grab more equipment if needed."

"Ok, sounds good." Judas hopped in and looked at the knives and guns. "Nice Glocks. You want one of those?"

"Sure," Jonah nodded. "Wish I'd thought to grab Brutus out of Sasha." He took the gun his brother offered, popped the magazine and checked the chamber before slipping it into an empty holster on his belt.

As they headed for the front of the house, a cream-colored sedan pulled into the driveway next door. The man driving it, a tall thin man around six-foot tall with a pencil-thin mustache running across his upper lip, got out and looked at them, eyes widening, then rushed into his home.

The brothers paid him little attention as they stepped onto the concrete slab at the front door, both shuffling their feet and fidgeting with their equipment. Jonah knocked on the door and they waited.

"We should have a business card or something like we used to have at Pests B' Gone," Judas said.

"That's a good idea. We'll have to ask—"

The door opened and a young Hispanic-looking man answered, two grade-school aged girls huddled behind him.

"Hi, we're—" Jonah started.

"Come in," the man waved them inside. "We closed the blinds but they haven't stopped pawing at the back door. Their moaning and groaning is scaring my girls." The two children whimpered, sniffing the snot running from their noses in unison.

"Please do something," the man asked.

Jonah stood taller. "We'll take care of things for you, sir. Don't worry." He smiled at the girls, hoping to calm them.

A thump from the dining area alerted him to where the problem was. They made their way through the living room and up a small step into the dining room where the sliding glass doors were. Jonah grabbed the plastic rod and slid the blinds open, revealing two very dead people. A man and a woman appearing to have been in their sixties when they died, both pawing at the glass. When they caught sight of Jonah, they let out a loud growl and banged against the door.

The two girls shrieked behind him, causing Jonah to jump and spin around. Fresh tears stained their terrified faces. "Dammit," he muttered under his breath, then turned to the homeowner. "Sir, maybe it'd be best if you took your girls and locked yourself in a back room until we're done."

The man nodded, grabbing each of the girl's hands and turning them away from the scene. "Yes. Good idea. C'mon, Rosey. C'mon, Esme. Let's go play with your dolls, while these nice men..." he looked back to the dead creatures at the door, "clean things up."

Jonah and Judas studied the zombies through the glass. Their grayish-green skin cracked and peeled in places, with brown spots of long dried blood here and there. The male's left arm dangled as if it might fall off at any moment.

"Siblings?" Judas asked.

"No," Jonah shook his head. "I think they were a couple. See their wedding rings."

"Oh." Judas nodded. "So what do we do, Jonah?"

"I'm not sure yet," his brother said, taking in a deep breath.

Judas leaned in and stared through the glass. "It's strange seeing them up close. These have been dead a long time, not like in the lab where it felt like we were killing living people."

"Yeah, it sure is." Jonah looked at the catch pole in his hand. "We're supposed to bring them back alive for Dr. Nitsau, so..., I'll open the door enough for the first one to come through. Then you grab it with your pole, take him and pull him in, then lead him out front. I'll close the door, then we can come back for the second one or I'll use my pole on her and we can get them both out front and into the van. Better if we can secure them one at a time but we'll do what we need to do."

"Ok, sounds good." Judas adjusted the hoop on his pole open and closed twice to make sure it was working.

Jonah grabbed the handle of the door and flipped the lock to open. "Ready?"

Judas huffed out a big breath, bouncing on the balls of his feet. "Yeah, I'm green. Let's do it!"

The door opened and the male zombie shoved his hand through the opening, their groans filling the room, followed by the stench of long-dead flesh.

"For someone who's been dead a long time, he sure is strong," Jonah said, struggling to keep the door from opening too far. "Here he comes," The door opened letting the dead man in.

The zombie growled, looking at Jonah but stumbling toward Judas. Judas swung the catch pole toward his head but overshot, missing him with the hoop and hitting him upside the skull with the pole instead. It tore free a piece of his scalp, the flap of rotted flesh and gray hair falling to the floor.

"Sorry," Judas scrunched up his face, then shook his head muttering, "what am I apologizing for?"

At the door, the dead woman lurched forward, grasping at the air. Jonah slammed it shut to stop her from getting in but caught her arm in it instead, severing the limb from the body just above the elbow. It fell to the white tile floor, writhing and oozing black blood everywhere.

The woman tried to pull away, only to find herself stuck by the bits of flesh and parts of her dress being pinched tight in the door. A dark thick goo dripped from the wound coating the glass.

"Perfect," Jonah said, clicking the locking lever in place. He turned to see how his brother fared with the man, then let out a cry. "Oh shit, Judas!"

Judas tried repeatedly to get the hoop around the zombie's neck, opening it as wide as he could get it but still struggling to slip it over the head of the moving target.

"This was much easier when Hank had us practice on dummies," he said to himself, backing up further as the corpse approached. "Stand still!" He grit his teeth and ran his tongue through his empty lip, wishing he had a chew in.

Distracted as he was, he didn't see the small ledge that stepped down into the living room from the dining area behind him. "Ahhh!" he cried out as his foot found nothing to stand on and he fell over backward, thrusting the catch pole into the air and through the ceiling where it stuck. It dangled there, mocking him as he fell.

He smacked onto the ground, getting the wind knocked out of him. Gasping, he stared up at the approaching zombie as it stumbled forward. Judas threw his arms up, covering his face as the dead man lunged off the step.

Judas waited for the impact, wheezing in a hollow desperate breath, the rush of blood pounding in his veins overwhelming his senses. A dozen rapid heartbeats passed and he opened his eyes. *Why am I not being eaten alive?*

He moved his arms and looked up to see the zombie leaning off the edge of the stair but suspended there, grasping uselessly at the air a foot away from him.

"Wh-what?" Judas gasped, then the zombie rose as Jonah yanked on his catch pole, the hoop securely around the creature's neck.

"I got him, Judas," Jonah panted. "You okay?"

"Yeah," Judas sat up, gasping. "Just winded. Thought I was... zombie chow."

"Not this ti—"

"Mama!" A loud voice rang from out back.

Jonah froze, listening.

"Mama, what are you doing out there? I told you not to bother the neighbors. Get over here right now."

The dead woman at the door groaned and pulled away from it, tearing the sleeve of her dress and the bits of rotted flesh free.

"Oh shit," Jonah growled and turned to Judas who rested on his elbows, still struggling for a full breath. "Judas, I need you to take this one, quick!"

Judas nodded and struggled to his feet.

Jonah shoved the zombie out of the way with the pole and handed it to Judas. "You got him?"

His brother, pale-faced and still wheezing, took the pole in both hands. "Got him. Go, bro! We don't want anyone dying on our first job. That might start a trend!"

Grabbing the dangling catch pole from the ceiling, Jonah yanked it free, bringing with it a chunk of the ceiling and a plume of dust. The debris smacked onto the floor and Jonah scrunched up his face. "Whoops." He rushed to the back door.

Outside, he found the tall thin man they'd seen in the neighboring driveway earlier, pushing the dead woman toward his house. "Let's get you home, mama. Then I'll find dad and your arm." The man wept as he spoke.

"Sir!" Jonah stood tall and walked after him. "I'm a zombie exterminator and we're here to deal with this. We're professionals. I'll take care of that creature."

The man looked over his shoulder, saw Jonah approaching in his black fatigues, body armor, and the catch pole. His eyes shot wide, pupils narrowing into tiny dots amongst the bulging whiteness. He shoved the zombie forward, tripping it and knocking her to the ground, then spun to face Jonah.

"You are not exterminating my mama!"

"Wh-what," Jonah stopped short as the angered man charged toward him.

"Did you hurt my pops? Where is he?" The man pushed the catch pole aside and walked right up to Jonah. A few inches shorter, he craned his neck staring up at him.

"Sir, we're—" Jonah started but the man wouldn't let him speak.

"What? Here to break up our family, like my crackhead ex tried to do with my children? We've been through hell and stayed together through it all. You're worse than those people from immigration. They're not deporting my parents and you are certainly not departing them."

Behind them, the man's mother got back to her feet and with her one remaining arm outstretched made her way toward them.

"These creatures aren't safe," Jonah tried. "They were terrorizing your neighbors and we're here to help."

Mention of the man's neighbors caused him to turn and look at the house, Jonah's gaze followed. Through the sliding glass door, they could see Judas pushing the man's father around with the pole, struggling to get him under control.

"Hey! What's he doing to pops!"

The man turned, knocking the catch pole from Jonah's startled grasp with a kick and charging toward the house. Jonah dove for the pole, snatching it up and getting back to his feet only to find the woman's small shape lunging for her son.

Jonah shouted an unheard, "No!" and closed his eyes as the inevitable happened.

Douglas Kay-Fraser reached for the handle of the sliding glass door and then screamed as his mother dove in, biting into the flesh at the back of his neck, tearing free a strip of fat and gristle. "Mama, no!" The man fell to the ground, curling into the fetal position and bringing his mother with him. He wept and howled, feebly smacking at his mother with one hand and sucking on the thumb of his other as she feasted on his flesh.

Jonah stepped in behind the woman, slipping the loop over her neck, cinching it and yanking her back.

From inside, behind the glass slider, Judas stared, eyes wide. Jonah shoved the woman forward and moved to the door.

"Let's get these two loaded up and..." he glanced back at the sobbing man, "come back for him."

Part IV - Undead Delivery

Her red-painted lips spread until they formed an open-mouthed smile. "Excellent!" Dr. Nitsau beamed at each of the brothers in turn. "You boys have done well." She turned to examine the two older specimens. "They were turned in England?"

"No, ma'am, Scotland," Jonah answered.

"And they bit their son while you were there?"

"Yes."

"Was he the one who called you?"

"No. He... it was his neighbor. A dad concerned for his girls' safety."

"Hmm, were any of them bit?" She cocked her head and eyed Jonah.

"No. We kept it well contained, there was only the one... collateral damage, ma'am."

She nodded and looked at the couple's son, the fresh wounds on his back still oozed blood. "It's rare to get samples that originated abroad. So hard to get them into the country legally. I wonder how he did it." She walked around the three chained zombies, her heels clicking on the concrete. "These two look at least a decade dead and to know that they are still infectious after all that time is fascinating. They'll make for an excellent study to further my research."

Dr. Nitsau pivoted on her right heel and faced the brothers. "Put them in the cold storage on sub-level B. You'll find places to chain them up in the freezer. The cold will slow them and I'll have someone collect samples later." She turned to Judas and gave him a slow smile that made his cheeks warm. Then, she turned to Jonah. "Next time, don't be overly concerned with collateral damage. If it happens, that just means more samples to work with."

Jonah's eyes widened and he opened his mouth to speak but the way her eyes flicked up and bore through him silenced the protest he wanted to muster. He took a deep breath, nodding. "Yes, ma'am." He moved to undo the younger man from the bolt securing him to the wall.

Behind him, he heard Dr. Nitsau's heels click their way to where Judas stood. The CEO whispered something to his brother and the hairs on the back of Jonah's neck stood up. He turned to see what she was doing and saw her leaned in, face right next to Judas's ear. His brother had wide eyes and bright red cheeks. Jonah took his time undoing the zombie, trying to keep quiet, so he could hear but he couldn't make out anything she said.

When he heard her heels clicking away across the concrete, he waved his brother over. "What was that about?"

Judas didn't look at him, instead, he studied the floor and muttered something Jonah couldn't make out.

"What?"

Judas met his brother's gaze for a moment, then looked back at the floor. "She told me we did a good job."

"Ok... so why are you lit up like a Christmas tree?"

Judas let out a huff and looked up, shuffling his feet. "She touched my face, said she was proud of me and appreciated how well I followed orders."

Jonah's brow furrowed, he turned, watching as the woman disappeared down a hallway.

What is she up to?

ABOUT GRIVANTE

Grivante, pronounced "Gri-von-tay" for anyone wondering, is the author of The Zee Brother's series. What you have just read is part two in a special origin story that tells us how the brothers got into zombie exterminating in the first place. It also deepens the mystery surrounding Dr. Natasha Nitsau.

Special thanks to Jack Appell for his editing skills in fine-tuning this story into all it could be!

The Zee Brothers series can be found on **Amazon** and on their website www.thezeebrothers.com

9

VALLEY OF THE SHADOW

BY L.C. CHAMPLIN

As Amanda plopped down between her two daughters on the couch, the lights and TV went out. Darkness enveloped the house.

"Aw man," whined Denver, the younger of the two siblings at nine years old. "The power's out?"

"Maybe it's a breaker," responded Taylor. The twelve-year-old took the older-sister role seriously.

"Hang on." Amanda pulled her smartphone from her pocket. After activating the flashlight, she went to the living room's bay window. She pulled the slats of the blind apart. Night darker than any she'd seen in years filled the neighborhood and obscured the neat, upper-class houses that lined the street. In the north, where San Francisco usually glowed, more blackness festered.

"It's not just us," Denver remarked, suddenly at her mom's elbow.

"Let's see what's going on." Amanda turned off the flashlight, then loaded the local ABC News app. Crap, no data. And no cell service. She wet her suddenly dry lips. She ran her hand over her dyed-blonde hair, which a braid kept out of her face. No power and now no way to communicate. Maybe a sunspot or something had knocked out the systems.

"Taylor, where did we put that emergency radio?" she asked, keeping her voice calm as she reactivated her flashlight.

"I'll get it!" Denver called as she bounded into the darkness. Sounds of rummaging came, then the crackle of static. "I'll find a news station." The static shifted, like the sound of a restless winter sea against the coast. "Huh, I'm not finding much." Eyes on the radio, she returned to the living room. Her neon pink and green hair hung in her face.

"*—Authorities say to stay where you are. If you need emergency support for life- threatening conditions, contact 9-1-1. Be advised, due to the situation, response time will be extended—*"

"What situation?" Taylor looked up at Amanda with anxiety.

Amanda shook her head. "Let's keep listening." What kind of situation? An earthquake? She hadn't felt anything. A tsunami? No, that would give warning. A gas-line explosion? Or a—

"*—Authorities confirm that the Federal Reserve was attacked. There are reports of other locations as well. If you are unable to find shelter, proceed to the safe zones—*"

"Attacked?" Denver squeaked.

"Shh." Amanda placed a gentle hand on her daughter's shoulder.

"*—Terrorists may be responsible, but there's no hard evidence—*"

"What do we do?" moaned Taylor. "Are they going to attack us *here*?"

"I don't think so, honey. We're in Silicon Valley, but we're not very close to the big tech buildings." Google and Facebook owned offices to the south.

"This is like 9/11," Taylor murmured.

The trio looked out the front window as the news reported poor traffic conditions, people assaulting one another, explosions—

Taylor sniffed. "I don't want to listen anymore."

"I'll get my headphones," Amanda decided. "I'll listen for any emergency updates." The sisters would have nightmares for weeks about this. They hadn't experienced the terrorist attacks of 9/11, but she had. The feeling of an abyss opening below her heart returned.

As she rejoined the sisters, she paused at the window. Across the street, their neighbor Jeremy Nelson stood beside his car with the driver-side door open. He held his cell phone to his ear. Evidently having zero service too, he angrily shoved the device into his pocket.

Amanda bolted to the door. Slinging it open, she yelled, "Jeremy, what are you doing? They said to stay put."

He stopped to look over his shoulder at her. The dome light showed the anxiety in his face. "Jennifer's out there. She was working late at the lab, and now—"

"Stay inside," Amanda ordered the girls before hurrying out to meet her neighbor.

"I can't leave her out there."

"The radio said the roads are clogged. What about Zander? Who's keeping him?" The four-year-old couldn't stay alone.

"The Singhs are going to keep an eye on him. I—"

"You can't, Jeremy," Amanda insisted, catching the car door to prevent him from closing it.

His normally cheerful, open expression turned cold. Though not outspoken in the least, he did value his family.

They often took family trips, and played or relaxed in the yard. "Amanda, what would you do if someone you loved was out there?"

"I would want to go, but what could I do for them? Data and cell service are down, so you can't call her to see how or where she is."

Jeremy sagged against his vehicle. "I can't stand being useless."

"If she can get here, she'll get here. She might be in one of the safe zones. You know, staying safe." Possibly the worst comfort she'd ever given anyone. She winced internally.

By this time, other neighbors had begun stepping out of their homes. Like moths to a porch light, they congregated around Amanda and Jeremy. Questions and speculations flew.

"Why don't we all go back to our houses?" Amanda suggested over the chatter.

A white SUV rolled down the street toward them. It stopped, then a distinguished, middle-aged woman stepped out: Carolyn Blum. Amanda let out a sigh of relief. If anyone could handle this mess, Carolyn could. She headed up the neighborhood homeowners' association. Amanda served as second to her.

"Everyone," Carolyn began in a clear voice that carried over the fear and consternation. "I know there's a lot going on in the city right now. But nothing has happened *here*. The safest option is to stay in your homes. Please, go back inside, lock the doors, and keep your radios on. I'm certain the authorities will get this sorted out soon.

"Yeah, right, keep calm and carry on?" sneered a short, Hispanic man from the rear of the crowd. Eduardo. He regularly offered dissenting views at community meetings.

"Yes," Carolyn responded. "Keep a level head, everyone." With that, she climbed back into her SUV.

"Come on." Amanda took Jeremy by the elbow and led him back into his house. "Jen will be back when she can. There's no sense putting yourself at risk too." If something happened to Jennifer, losing Jeremy would orphan poor Zander. Amanda blinked. Way to jump to the most pessimistic outcome! "Let us know if you need any . . . any help." But what could she do?

🏃🏃🏃

After a night of fitful slumber, seeing the sunrise came as a relief. The alarm clock beside the bed remained blank. No power. Still no data or cell service, either.

Amanda fixed breakfast with the items in the fridge that would spoil the quickest. She didn't have much appetite, but the girls wolfed down leftovers from supper.

Steeling herself, Amanda turned on the radio, keeping the earbuds in and the report away from the girls.

"*—Authorities are doing their best to restore power, but civil unrest has made repairs difficult. We can't stress enough the importance of staying where you are if the area is safe. Now we have a report from Josephine, one of our correspondents in the field.*"

"*Thank you, Steve. I have a witness to the civil unrest. What did you see, sir?*"

A nervous voice responded, "*People are being crazy! I saw four guys jump on another guy. I don't know if it was gang bangers hopped up on some drug, or what. They just started chewing on him like they were animals! I—*"

"*Thank you, sir. It's clear that the attacks are taking a toll on the most fragile among us.*"

Amanda switched off the radio. "When the power and phones come back on, we'll know the city's gotten things straightened out."

"No electricity," Denver sighed. "This is going to be really boring."

"You have homework to do. Both of you," Amanda added before Taylor could say something condescending to her sister.

Amanda stepped outside. She should speak with Carolyn and see if any of the neighbors needed help. Jeremy's car remained in the driveway. Common sense had prevailed, apparently.

As Amanda started down the sidewalk, an Escalade rolled down the street. The SUV pulled into the Nelsons' driveway. "Jennifer?" Amanda stopped.

The door to the Nelsons' house burst open. Jeremy dashed out, with little Zander trotting behind him in the clumsy run of a preschooler.

"Jennifer?" Jeremy used the car to stop his momentum, then yanked the door open.

"Mommy?" Zander asked, stopping a few feet behind his dad.

"Are you all right?" Jeremy supported his wife as she eased out of the vehicle.

Amanda jogged across the street. "Do you need help?"

Jennifer took a gulping breath. Pale, sweaty, she looked like she'd caught the flu. She coughed, covering her mouth. It sounded wet. "I—" She coughed again.

"Take your time, honey. I'm just glad you're home." Jeremy laughed in nervous relief as he stroked his wife's long, blond hair.

"Mommy, we missed you!" Zander exclaimed as he ducked under his father's arm to crawl up with his mother.

"Hi, baby," she wheezed. "Now get down. Mommy's not feeling well."

"What is it?" Jeremy asked, as pale as his wife.

"I—" She coughed into her elbow. Her blood-shot eyes attempted to focus on his face. "Was leaving work. Caught in traffic. Saw somebody on the sidewalk. He looked sick. Thought I recognized him from the gym—" She stopped for more coughing. "I tried to help." Another fit of wheezing seized her. "He coughed on me, then he . . . he threw up on me. I took my jacket off. Think I still got . . . some on me." She slumped back into the seat, gulping air. "Not sure, but . . . maybe it's something we were working on. It didn't escape our lab. It couldn't have. We don't have it." Her eyes went wide. Panic drained the last of her color.

"What is it? Honey"—Jeremy leaned closer—"you're not feeling good. You feel hot. I think you might be—what is it, delusional?"

"Delirious," Amanda supplied. "Come on, Jeremy, let's get her inside."

Between them, they half led, half carried Jennifer into the house.

"Is Mommy going to be all right?" Zander quavered.

"She'll be fine, Zander," Amanda assured him over her shoulder, forcing a smile.

When they reached the bedroom, they lowered Jennifer onto the queen-sized bed. Sweat beaded on her forehead and soaked her shirt. Jeremy gathered pillows to prop her up and ease her breathing. "I can call 9-1-1," he panted. "You might have a really bad case of the flu. They—"

"I'll do it," Amanda volunteered as she went to their landline. She picked up the receiver, but no dial tone greeted her. Still no cell service, either. Great, now what could she do?

She returned to the husband and wife. "The phones aren't working." Mouth dry, she gripped the door jamb, nails biting into the wood. "We'll just have to keep her comfortable."

Jennifer doubled over in a coughing fit. Blood spotted her arm as she lowered her elbow. She stared at it but either didn't comprehend or didn't truly see it. Then she jerked as if coming out of a dream. "Jeremy, promise me, if I get really sick—if I don't act normal—you'll keep me safe. And keep Zander safe. Just—" She gagged. Her face muscles twitched. "Tell him I love him. Keep him safe." A tear rolled down her cheek as she collapsed against the pillows.

"Mommy?" Zander whispered from beside Amanda.

"Come on, kiddo," Amanda encouraged the boy as she directed him away from the room. "Are you hungry? Did you have breakfast yet?"

"Is Mommy going to be okay?" He looked back at the bedroom.

"Sure." *Hopefully.* Amanda forced a smile.

She found breakfast half-eaten in the kitchen. "Mac and cheese, ooh! Looks good. Finish up." She guided him to his plate.

"It's cold." He frowned at the yellow mess.

"All right. I'll see—"

"Jennifer, what's the matter? What are you doing? No—" Jeremy's voice rang from down the hall.

"Stay here." Amanda patted the boy's shoulder as she dodged around the kitchen island.

She hurried down the hallway. Ahead, Jeremy backed halfway out of the room. He stared into it with utter confusion and shock. Wheezing came from within. He stepped inside again.

Amanda slowed as she reached the doorway. Jennifer

was crouching on the bed. Her skin had turned as pale as a chicken before it's cooked. Her mouth hung slightly open. Black drool dribbled from the corner. It looked like oil. She let out a wheezing hiss: *Ssssaaaahhh.* The room's murk hid the details, but the woman's eyes bulged, and blisters stood out on her face.

"I'll get help, honey." Jeremy retreated, one hand out toward his wife. "Stay here."

She crawled forward, her gaze locked on the man. Another hiss like static escaped her. Then she lunged off the edge of the bed. Her claw-like fingers missed Jeremy by inches.

"Move!" Amanda yelped as she jerked Jeremy into the hall. She slammed the door closed. She couldn't lock it from here—

Thuds, scratching, and hissing came from the other side. The doorknob rattled but didn't turn. Had Jennifer's delirium made her forget how to use a knob?

What did the guy on the news say? A gang jumping on people? People attacking one another like animals? And then what Jennifer said about the lab . . . But she worked at a company that developed *anticancer* drugs. The fever must have impaired her thinking.

"Jennifer," Jeremy panted. "Stay here. I'll get help. I won't let anything happen to you. I promise," he choked, grimacing as if undergoing an amputation without anesthetic. Leaning his head against the door, he sniffed back tears. One escaped.

Amanda put her hand on his back. "I'm going to get Carolyn, all right? I'll take Zander. Stay here; make sure Jennifer is . . ." What? Contained? "Is safe." Leaving him might not prove the best idea, but what choice did she have?

"Come on, Zander," she said as she scooped him up.

Grunting, she maneuvered him onto her hip as she made for the exit.

Surely Carolyn would know what was going on. A few neighbors had RVs with satellite TV, and a few others had generators. Carolyn would check the news reports on TV.

Speak of the devil: Carolyn's white SUV appeared at the intersection and turned down Keelson Circle, Amanda's street.

As Amanda crossed to her house, Carolyn pulled into its driveway.

"What's the matter?" the older woman asked, exiting her vehicle.

"Jennifer Nelson isn't feeling well. Um, Zander"—Amanda looked down at the inquisitive boy—"go in and say *hi* to the girls."

"Okay." Scuffing his feet, he traipsed to the door.

The sisters watched from the window, their faces pale. Images of Jennifer's bloodless visage flashed in Amanda's mind. She shook her head. "Carolyn, what does the news say? Is there some sort of weird sickness? Because she—Jennifer—tried to attack Jeremy. She's drooling black mucus and looks like death warmed over." Hearing the description made it sound all the more preposterous—and horrifying.

"I've seen some of the reports." Carolyn cast a concerned glance after Zander. He went inside, out of earshot. "It looks like the news networks are attempting to suppress the information, but a few scenes did get through. They appeared, at least at a distance, to show people similar to your description of Jennifer. They were attacking other people."

"We have to get her help—"

"That's part of why I came to find you, Amanda. The Army has come with a truck of water and canned goods. It's not much, but they said more will be on the way."

"Maybe they could help her!" Amanda brightened.

"I . . ." Carolyn looked compulsively at the Nelsons' house. "There are also reports of military and law enforcement killing people like her. They warn not to engage the . . . affected."

"You mean—" Amanda stared at the older woman. "You mean we might have to—"

Carolyn put a hand on Amanda's arm. "If Jeremy can keep her safe and managed, she might be better off than if we tell the Army about her. We should wait, in my opinion, until we have more information. I want to keep everyone together as much as we can. We're safer as a community. And, Amanda, if you're willing, I need your help. I can't keep us together by myself." She suddenly looked ten years older.

"I . . ." Amanda had to protect her girls and her community. She could handle this. At work, she evaluated employees' performance, suggested candidates for employment, and organized HR projects. How different could this be? She met Carolyn's steady gaze. "I'll help."

Amanda and Carolyn arranged for a few of the neighborhood residents to assist with getting Jennifer into the Nelsons' garage. They chose that location due to the risk of contagion Jennifer's black vomit and saliva posed.

The neighbors blocked off the hallways, forming a chute into the garage. Then they positioned the nervous and heartbroken Jeremy at the end of it as bait. Amanda winced at the word. Not bait, but *encouragement*.

Poor Jennifer, who knew what horrors she suffered in the delirious dream world in which she existed? Was she aware of her actions? Did she watch herself attack her own husband, all the while struggling to stop? Or had her conscious mind slipped into darkness?

Amanda opened the door to the bedroom before darting back behind the plywood chute wall.

Shoulders back, head forward, Jennifer shuffled out. Her body twitched as if random electric currents arced over her muscles. She hissed to herself.

"Jennifer? I'm here, honey," Jeremy's voice echoed down the hall.

Her head shot up. "Sssssaaaaaaahhh." She shambled forward, dragging her left shoulder along the wall to support herself. Black oil dribbled from the corner of her mouth. In the light, her eyes appeared rust orange. Blisters marred her face, a few draining clear fluid.

She rounded the corner and disappeared. A moment later, hissing followed, then the slam of the garage service door.

"All clear," called one of the neighbors.

With a sigh of relief, Amanda slumped against the wall. "Thank God."

She located Jeremy. "Are you all right keeping an eye on her?" she asked, taking him by both shoulders so he had to meet her gaze.

He rubbed his eyes with his shirt. "Y-yes. I'll keep her safe, like I promised her."

"We can watch Zander—"

"No, I want us together." Misery contorted Jeremy's face. "He's had enough stress; I want him to be with me."

Doubt's cold breath chilled Amanda. "I'll go get him."

The rest of the day passed uneventfully. Darkness fell —*hard*. Here and there, lights glowed in windows.

Amanda sent the girls to bed but stayed up for a few hours to keep watch. She leaned against the sill of the living-room window, toying with the tail of her braid.

Outside, near the Nelsons' house, a figure moved. Amanda froze, breath dying. Looters? Terrorists?

Two people wandered onto Keelson Circle. They looked about in apparent bewilderment. Their unsteady gait resembled the stumble of drunks. Then one threw back its head like a wolf howling. The moonlight caught his pale skin. No, maybe the illumination just drained the color—

Then the man took a few running steps. With each step, his torso fell farther forward. Then his hands hit the ground as if he set up for a push-up. His rear legs came up; he lunged forward. It resembled a twisted version of a lion's lope. His companion joined him as they bounded down the street. The darkness swallowed them.

Amanda gulped. Why didn't the stupid news play anything useful? Like, what the hell this infection was, and what it did to the people who contracted it. She lowered the blind, then checked every lock in the house.

* * *

Sunday morning, thirty-six hours since the attacks. Still no power, no cell service, no data. Radio broadcasts warned not to drink water from the tap without purifying it first.

Amanda and the girls had eaten through the refrigerator's contents. Now Amanda cooked a steak on the grill. It sizzled, juices glazing its surface. She lifted it onto a plate. Then she splashed steak sauce on the meat. Some of the dark liquid splattered the white glass. Scenes of Jennifer and her black drool shoved their way into Amanda's mind. Grunting, she shook her head.

"Breakfast's ready, kids," she called as she stepped inside the house.

"Great!" Denver exclaimed. She and Taylor took seats at the breakfast bar.

A knock came at the door.

When Amanda reached it, she pressed her eye to the peephole. Carolyn waited outside.

Amanda opened the door. "I'm glad to see you. I was going to contact you after the girls had breakfast. I saw something last night—"

"Many of our neighbors did." Carolyn looked grave. "There were strangers here, apparently."

Thank God someone else saw them. "They seemed like they might be under the influence, or sick." Sick like Jennifer. Like the people on the news who attacked others.

"We will begin posting guards to warn us of trespassers. Even if the affected—that's what the news is calling them—aren't as dangerous as the authorities say, looters may find us soon. It's been almost two days since the power failed. Law enforcement is having difficulty restoring order in the city."

"What about the Army?"

Carolyn opened her mouth, but a vehicle's horn cut her off. Down the street, from the intersection of Davit and Keelson, came a black pickup truck. A man rode in the back, wearing the same kind of gear as a SWAT team member and holding a megaphone. "Everyone, come out of your houses and proceed down Marlin Drive to the tennis court at the intersection of Marlin and Redwood Shores Parkway. Go now. It's critical to your safety."

"Is he with the police?" Amanda wondered as the truck

rumbled around the corner. The man repeated his message. "Maybe he's with the Army. They said they'd be back." Let the government come and make everything all right. Let *someone* come and make everything all right.

"I'm not sure."

Already, neighbors had begun emerging from their houses. They looked questioningly at one another. Some declared they weren't going, while others responded that if it was critical to their safety, they didn't have a choice.

"*We* at least have to go," Amanda decided.

"I can go alone. You stay with your girls—"

"They'll be fine here. I said I'd help keep the neighbor-hood safe." Amanda leaned back to call into the house, but both of her children waited a few feet behind her.

"What was that?" Taylor asked.

Denver ducked under her mom's arm to look out at the road and neighbors. "Are we going? I don't think the Nelsons are."

Amanda hadn't told her daughters about Jennifer, other than that she didn't feel well. "Jeremy's probably looking after Jen. Girls, I'm going to see what these people want. If I don't come back in a half an hour, gather up the emergency kit that we made. Go over to the Singhs and stay with them." Then what? What could the Singhs do? What could anyone do in this situation?

They could move forward. One step at a time.

⁂

Amanda parked her Genesis behind Carolyn's SUV. Ahead lay the tennis courts. Several pickup trucks ranged about, blocking the parkway to prevent anyone from traveling down it and off the peninsula that formed Redwood Shores.

Something felt off. No Army trucks or Soldiers in camouflage appeared. Numerous Redwood Shores residents did, though.

A gray Ford F-250 rolled into the center of the parking lot, engine rumbling. Then it fell silent. A mountain of a man stepped out. Bald save for a fuzz of hair on his bullet-shaped skull, he had the look of a soldier who had seen more than his fair share of atrocities. And he'd come out the tougher for it, eating concertina wire for breakfast. He probably used Napalm for aftershave. He glared about at the people as he climbed into the bed of his truck, where he picked up a megaphone.

"People of Redwood Shores, the world has changed. If you want to survive, you will do as you are instructed." He spoke like a drill sergeant, yet showed zero emotion. That cool, impassive expression made Amanda edge closer to Carolyn. "We will protect you from looters and the affected—those oil-drooling monsters. In exchange, we ask for a third of your supplies in the form of food and water. Bring them here by eleven o'clock this morning."

"You're stealing our supplies?" a man yelled. The speaker pushed to the head of the crowd. Eduardo.

Amanda groaned. "Shut up," she breathed.

The hulk glowered down at the gnat. "We will protect you."

"This is ridiculous," Eduardo retorted. "We're not going to submit to this. You can't just march in here and steal everything! We'll starve." With the last sentence, he threw his arms out as he looked about at his comrades—the same ones who usually agreed with him during community meetings.

People began murmuring.

"Get out of here!" someone cried.

"We'll call the police!" screeched another.

"If you do not comply with our conditions," the protection-racket bastard went on as if explaining a contract's terms, "we will take your supplies anyway."

Carolyn stepped forward. "I am the head of the homeowners' association here. We won't stand for people taking our property."

The bald man held up his fist. The doors of the surrounding trucks opened. His cronies stepped out, all wearing similar body armor. They carried black assault rifles.

"Our demands aren't excessive when you consider the alternative," he declared.

The residents exchanged glances, but most said nothing. The shock of the demand on top of the continuing disaster rendered most of them incapable of making rational decisions.

"I want to speak with your leader," Carolyn decided, standing tall.

"The hell we do!" Eduardo bawled, face red. "Get out of here! We haven't had any looters before *you* showed up, and we haven't had any trouble with the affected. The Army will come and put you in your place—"

"It looks like you need some education," the brute growled. "I don't think you understand your situation." He motioned to a few of his flunkies. "Give me seven. Take the young ones and the pretty ones. We can sell them."

"What?" Carolyn stared at him, appalled. "You can't do this."

"Are you going to bargain with us?" He folded his arms.

She sighed. "All right, we'll give you the supplies you asked for. We'll give you even more if you let us have our people back." She did an admirable job hiding her emotions.

"I'll need the Chief's approval on that. But I'll cut you a deal. If you give us half of your supplies, we'll think about giving the collateral back."

"Think about it?" Eduardo raged. "You can't—"

A pistol seemed to teleport into the lieutenant's hand. It pointed at Eduardo. "Unless you want to be one of them, shut up. You have no one to blame but yourselves."

He snapped his fingers. His men advanced.

People yelled and pushed. They ran for their cars, but the men with guns moved faster: a few positioned themselves in front of the vehicles. Warning shots cracked.

Like hyenas tearing into a herd of confused zebra, several of the raiders surged into the crowd. They grabbed four women and three men. Before anyone could make a move, the kidnappers had dragged their prisoners to a white moving van. More of the bastards swung in to guard them, guns raised.

The thugs at the neighbors' vehicles retreated to their own trucks. With the way clear, the Redwood Shores people bolted for the escape route. Those associated with the victims cried and pleaded, but they didn't dare approach the gunman. They had little time to react beyond that, because the van pulled away.

"Eleven o'clock," the lead monster called. "Don't be late." He vaulted over the edge of his truck onto the ground, then hopped into the driver's seat.

Amanda stood frozen as the invaders roared away. "What..."

Carolyn made a choking sound. She passed her hand over her eyes.

Amanda returned to her senses with a start. "Carolyn—"

"We do what they say. For now." The older woman pulled herself erect, mustering the last shreds of her dignity. "We have to protect our people."

⁂

Amanda gripped the Genesis's steering wheel, knuckles white. She pulled into her home's driveway.

As she went in the house, she called, "Taylor? Denver?" No answer.

Heart thundering in her ears, she swung around the counter to check the notepad where they left messages to each other. Taylor had scribbled, *Went to watch the news at Chas's house.*

That bought some time. She looked about the kitchen. A flat of water bottles sat on the counter. Several pots held bleach-purified water. The refrigerator had already yielded up its contents. As for canned goods, who had any of those around—unless collecting for a food drive, of course. The Army had given them some packaged food, but not much.

"How much is enough? How will they know if it's half?" Frustration constricted her heart. Years ago, she might have broken down and cried. But life had taught its lessons well. It had taught her she couldn't rely on others, especially if that *other* was her husband. And she didn't *need* to rely on anyone, either.

She took a deep breath, then began collecting what she could spare.

⁂

Eleven o'clock came more quickly than Amanda could have imagined. She stood with Carolyn in front of the pile of food and water. They waited near the tennis court as instructed. A score of neighbors—mainly those with kidnapped loved ones—waited at a distance.

The white moving van and a few pickup trucks trundled up Redwood Shores Parkway to meet them in the parking lot.

"We'll get through this," Carolyn reassured Amanda, but it sounded as if she tried to reassure herself more.

Amanda could only nod.

The grey Ford F-250 came last and took its central place in the lot. The raiders' spokesman emerged. His toadies also stepped from their vehicles, keeping their guns ready.

The hulking brute strode forward. "Let's see it." He circled the pile, then kicked through into the center. "Not bad."

Amanda held her breath. *Please let them just take this and go!*

"Not good either, though." He turned to them.

Amanda's heart sank to somewhere around her ankles. Dread overshadowed her like a thunderstorm.

"Red Chief, our leader, has given me permission to give you back three of your people."

Carolyn stiffened. "But that means four—"

"I can subtract. The four are our collateral." He glared about at the citizens. "We want to form a long-term relationship with you. Things aren't going to clean up quickly, and you'll need our protection. We'll be back in a few days for another payment. By the way, I don't care how you get the supplies. Just make sure they're here when Red Chief wants them."

Amanda stared. She should protest or argue or—or do *something*. But what could a neighborhood of affluent Silicon Valley residents do against these monsters?

"All right," the leader called to his men at the moving truck. "Give me three."

The Redwood Shores neighbors watched, stunned, as the men brought out three captives. The families to whom the victims belonged gasped, or let out sighs of relief. The families of those who remained in the bastards' chains broke down sobbing. A few looked ready to argue, but the machine guns of the men and the relief of their neighbors shocked them into silence.

By the time the people had recovered, the raiders were on the way out. The gray Ford F-250 acted as rear guard.

"Now what?" Amanda murmured.

"Now we have a community meeting," Carolyn managed.

While the neighborhood would have held the meeting in the local elementary school like usual, the people who held the keys had failed to return to Redwood Shores. So the residents gathered in Carolyn's yard. Even those who normally had no interest in the community suddenly found it relevant to their interests. Onlookers filled the street and surrounding yards.

The Denver and Taylor remained at home, safe for the moment. Amanda stood with Jacinda, a librarian who'd lived in Redwood Shores for ages. Of medium height and build, she wore glasses und kept her long, dark hair pulled back. Her kind but firm expression fit her profession.

"Amanda," Jacinda whispered, leaning in, "don't worry; we'll make it through." She patted Amanda on the back. "I bet I can take on at least a few of them." The forced smile should have added humor, but it fell short.

"You're studying Muay Thai, so I wouldn't doubt it," Amanda responded, not nearly as reassuring as Jacinda deserved.

"Thank you for coming." Carolyn projected her voice like a theater actor. "You all know what has happened. I cannot in good conscience allow these people to run roughshod over us. This is my suggestion: we make roadblocks at the entrances to the neighborhood. The Belmont Channel protects us on the north, and the wall along Redwood Shores Parkway protects us on the southeast." The wall enclosed the neighborhood, just as a wall enclosed every backyard. Typical for a California suburb. "In the southwest, Davit's intersection with Marlin is the most vulnerable ingress."

Amanda cleared her throat. "We are also going to make caltrops—spikes that deflate tires. We'll have volunteers keep guard. We'll know when the looters are coming." But what could they do against the guns?

Beside her, Jacinda nodded. "We're not helpless."

"Well, well," Eduardo sneered, elbowing to the front of the group. "Look who's finally agreeing with me. Maybe we should have stood up to them at the start—"

"How?" Amanda snapped. "You saw how easy it was for them to grab us when we were standing there like sheep."

"What about the people they kidnapped?" one of the victims' family members demanded, her eyes puffy.

Amanda paused, but Carolyn picked up: "We will do what we can to get them back. But right now, we have to think about the larger group."

"There's no dealing with those sons of bitches!" Eduardo cried for the crowd to hear. "Let's get ready to fight them if it comes to it."

His sympathizers cheered, but the other neighbors looked nervous.

"With what?" Jacinda demanded.

"What's that?" someone at the far edge of the gathering asked, fear in his voice.

All eyes turned in the direction the young man pointed. A group of ten individuals appeared at the intersection of Davit and the side street the residents occupied. The intruders moved with a predatory, inhuman hunch in their shoulders and bend in their knees. The newcomers glared at the people.

Then the front rank charged toward the residents. With each step, the invaders' torsos fell forward until they landed on outstretched arms. Their legs shot forward to push them ahead in a lope. The *affected*! The monsters the news said to stay away from. The infected people like Jennifer Nelson, who had attacked her own husband.

Shouts of *Run!* rang. People scrambled to get into their vehicles. Amanda, Carolyn, and Jacinda began yelling for neighbors to help one another and avoid contact with the affected.

With their first charge largely foiled, the infected attackers slowed. Their heads swiveled from side to side in search of targets.

Panic froze some people in place. One young man stood on the sidewalk some distance away, paralyzed with fear. Hugging himself, he stared at the predators.

Then they turned to stare at him.

"Move!" Amanda yelled. "Run!" She took her own advice, but sprinted toward the victim—and by extension the enemies.

But Jacinda moved faster. She barreled up to the man. Grabbing him by the arm, she tried to drag him toward the nearest vehicle, but terror had made his brain go offline. He gaped and shook his head at the incoming horde.

The affected fanned out, blocking the escape route and cutting off Amanda's way to rescue. She halted.

The infected invaders fell on their victims. Or tried to. Jacinda's side kick slammed into the first attacker's chest. As the man stumbled back, a hissing, orange-eyed woman lunged. Jacinda pivoted to catch her with a knee, then drop an elbow into the back of the neck.

A third enemy charged in, only to have Jacinda's elbow crash into his jaw. Black, oily drool flew from the affected's mouth. It splattered Jacinda and the young man. Jacinda bared her teeth as she wiped it from her face with her baggy purple sweater. The young man, though, clutched his arm where the drool touched, and began screaming.

The two grounded attackers struggled up as the others closed in around Jacinda and her charge. One of the affected dropped to all fours, dry heaving like a dog. Then the infected man let loose a stream of black projectile vomit. The second it hit the young man, all the maddened assailants threw themselves on their victims.

The young man went down screaming, but Jacinda went down fighting: punching, kicking, kneeing, elbowing. The affected in the lead sank their jaws into the easy target's neck. He cried and thrashed, but this only encouraged them to a feeding frenzy.

They dragged Jacinda down by sheer mass. Her roar of defiance ended in a gurgle.

Amanda's body wouldn't move. Her mind wouldn't think. "Cannibals?" her mouth blurted.

"Amanda, get out of there!" Carolyn called.

Legs moving on their own, Amanda fled to her car.

Shaking, Amanda pulled into the driveway of Chas's mother's house. Images of Jacinda and the man falling under the cannibalistic attackers looped through Amanda's mind. She remained in the vehicle, breathing hard.

A moment later, Denver and Taylor emerged. They climbed into the car.

"What's the matter?" Taylor asked.

"I . . . I have to tell you girls something." Then it all poured out: the looters, the demands, the kidnappings, the monsters.

The girls listened, solemn.

"I'm sorry I didn't tell you earlier." Amanda took a breath. "I was in denial. But this seems to be the world we live in, at least for a little while." She forced a smile that fell short of reassuring.

Denver shook her neon-striped hair out of her eyes. "It's all right, Mom. We'll get through it." She wore an expression of determination.

"You can count on us," Taylor agreed, for once on the same side as her sister. "We'll do everything we can to help us and the neighbors."

"Thank you, girls." Amanda's voice broke with the last word.

Due to the affected, most of the neighborhood stayed indoors.

The idea of owning a firearm had never occurred to most people here, including Amanda. Now she would love to have a gun in her hands, even if she didn't know how to use it.

Instead, she collected makeshift weapons: Denver had a BB gun, which she claimed would make a healthy person think twice. Taylor found a dandelion weeder; it resembled a spear with a forked point. And Amanda settled on a baseball bat.

The rest of that day and part of the next morning passed uneventfully. For the most part, the infected people left this section of Redwood Shores in peace. Did the raiding kidnappers actually keep the affected at bay? Did having safety mean handing over lives and goods to criminals?

The tension and lack of electricity turned the hours into years. In the cabin-fever insanity that ensued, it almost seemed better for something to happen just to get it over with. How did the kidnapped neighbors fare? Had the raiders killed them—or worse? Amanda pushed the thought out of her mind. She had her own family to worry about.

✶✶✶✶✶✶

Monday. No work, of course. Would she ever return to the office?

That afternoon, after returning from checking on a few of the neighbors, Amanda sat down to listen to the news on the radio. "I must be a masochist," she muttered as she reached for the earbuds.

A man's voice came from outside.

She crept to the window, where she peeked between the blind slats. A tall, fit blond man in glasses and casual clothing stood on the sidewalk. He waited for another man, who knocked on the neighbor's door. No one had seen that neighbor since Friday morning.

The man returned to the sidewalk. He had tan skin, black hair, and a goatee. He was slightly taller than his companion and wore jeans, sunglasses, and a leather jacket. The two exchanged words, then the dark-haired man pointed to Amanda's house.

Amanda's eyes narrowed. She reached for the bat.

While the blond waited, his friend strode down her walkway. His knock echoed. "Hello? I'm here to help, but I need your help first. I'm not going to hurt you, I promise. Hello? Is anybody there?"

A door in the rear of the house slammed. Denver and Taylor stalked down the hall, arguing.

"Shh!" Amanda hissed.

The kids went silent as they hurried over. "What is it?" Taylor whispered.

"Get your weapons. We have to be ready."

Denver squinted between the lower slats. "Who are they? They look familiar somehow."

"Maybe they were on TV," Taylor responded.

"Yeah, but a lot of people have been on TV."

"We've wasted enough time," the knocking man told his cohort, who joined him on the porch. "Somebody may have already broken into the truck and stolen the water."

"Perhaps we should return to the vehicle and await assistance?"

"Maybe. It's too bad. These people need help."

"As do we."

The black-haired one turned back to the door. "If you can hear me, we can help you."

Something about the pair, as if . . . as if they handle situations like this every day. *Capable* described the impression they gave. Still, strangers were strangers.

"Maybe they really are here to help." Hope shone in Denver's eyes.

"Maybe," Amanda murmured. But what could these men do? They had no army, no weapons. How could they stand against the raiders and cannibals?

The visitors moved off down the sidewalk. Then their attention snapped rightward, toward the Nelsons' home. The next moment, they hopped over the neighbors' hedge and took cover.

Across the street, a woman emerged from the bushes. Jennifer!

Denver started, but Amanda put a hand on her back. "Shh."

Jennifer looked even more out of it now. Black sludge still dribbled from her mouth. She meandered through the picket-fence gate, onto the sidewalk.

Behind her, a window in the Nelsons' house opened. Zander leaned out. Amanda bit back a gasp.

Taylor grabbed Amanda's arm. "Mom—"

"I know."

Zander climbed out the window.

"No," Amanda breathed. "Get back inside!"

Jennifer swung about to stare at her son. Mouth open, he gawked at her.

The men hiding behind the shrubs split up, with the blond jogging stealth-style parallel to the street.

The remaining guy, apparently the one with the leadership role, stood. "Get back in the house, kid! That's not your mom. Now!" He stepped over the hedge and onto the sidewalk. Clapping, he called, "Cannibal! Come get me!"

Jennifer took a wary step toward him and away from Zander.

"See?" Denver hissed. "He's trying to help. Can't we help *him*?"

"I don't—"

Denver scooted toward the door. Amanda reached but missed.

"Denver—"

She whipped it open. "Hey, you! Come here!"

"Are you stupid?" Taylor blurted as she grabbed the dandelion weeder / spear.

Swallowing a choice bit of profanity, Amanda hurried to the door. "Spread out. Get ready to—to defend yourselves." *What am I doing!*

If Amanda stood back, the kitchen window to the left of the door provided a view of the scene outside. The black-haired man eased toward the escape Denver provided. Not until Jennifer dropped to all fours in that appalling lope did he head for safety. Wincing, he kept his left arm wrapped about his torso as he jogged toward Amanda's porch.

In the Nelsons' yard, Zander climbed back into the house, his attention on something to the left.

"Oy! Here!" the blond called, pushing out of the Nelsons' bushes. He tossed a—a yard gnome? It shattered ahead of Jennifer.

"Come on!" Taylor encouraged.

The man charged in, then slammed the door behind him. Ignoring his rescuers, he pressed his eye to the peephole.

A *thud* reverberated through the door. The knob rattled.

He clicked the lock and shot the bolt.

"Turn around with your hands up," Amanda ordered.

Hand still on the bolt, he turned. Confusion furrowed

his brow. At this distance, Amanda could see bruises and scratches on his face. Taking in the defenders and their weapons, he raised his hands, his back against the door. "Easy now."

"Don't move," Denver snarled as she raised her BB gun rifle.

"I'm not moving, see?" He lifted his sunglasses to reveal dark brown eyes.

"What do you want?" Amanda adjusted her grip on the bat.

"Ma'am, I'm here to help." Calm filled his deep voice.

"*Sure* you are," Taylor sneered. "We're not stupid."

The door handle rattled again and another *thud* came. The stranger looked out the peephole. "No, but you are trapped."

"She'll wander off eventually," Amanda returned. *I hope.*

"Let me reach into my bag"—the shoulder satchel under his jacket—"and get my radio. My friend Albin can lure it—her—away. If you lend me your spear, I'll subdue her. I won't kill her."

"No." Amanda shook her head. "As soon as Jennifer leaves, *you're* leaving." She raised the bat an inch more.

"Jennifer?" the man repeated. "You know her?"

Explaining it to this invader didn't seem right.

"I see." He looked disappointed. "People like it—*her*—will kill anyone they encounter. She was going to attack her own son."

"No." Or would she?

"Listen—sorry, I didn't get your name. I'm Nathan."

"Amanda." Shit! Reflex answer.

"Amanda, if I don't stop her, she will hurt people. If she bites you, you'll become like her. You'll attack your loved ones."

No. *No.* "She's just sick. It's a drug or illness—"

"It's infecting people."

"Then the government can quarantine them until . . . until they—"

"Mom," Taylor urged in frustration, like she always did before an argument. "Chas said he saw video of them killing people. The Army's shooting them!"

"Zombies," Denver confirmed.

"Worse. Trust me." Nathan winced.

"Mom, we should listen to him." Taylor lowered her spear.

"Taylor—"

"Amanda." Nathan raised his hands again. "We came here to bring supplies, but our truck suffered two flats—"

"Mom." Denver turned to Amanda, pleading gaze at full force. "We're almost out of bottled water."

"Denver . . ." Maybe he told the truth. His story *did* make sense. Amanda let the bat fall to her side. "Go ahead, Nathan. You can't be with those raiders if you helped Zander."

He withdrew a walkie-talkie. "Albin, distract the cannibal."

"*If you are certain.*"

"H-here." Taylor offered her spear to him.

He received it. "Thank you; this is excellent."

After squinting through the peephole again, Nathan opened the door. He swung around the frame. Jennifer, now at the sidewalk, had her back to him as the blond—Albin—distracted her.

Nathan closed in.

Taylor gasped. "Now I remember! He *was* on TV. He and his friend—"

"Fought terrorists!" Denver finished, eyes wide. "They *are* the Good Guys!"

Outside, Nathan chambered the weeder, ready to swing.

"Jen!" Jeremy's voice rang from across the street. He charged around the corner of his house. "Get away from my wife!"

Nathan halted, spear still poised.

"Honey?" Jeremy eased toward her, hands out. "Come into the garage."

She stopped and watched him.

"Come on back, Jennifer. We'll get you help." Sorrow filled his entire being.

Jennifer took a faltering step in his direction.

"That's right." Jeremy forced a miserable smile.

Then she dropped to all fours.

Nathan cocked the weeder like a bat. "Hey!"

Jeremy retreated to the knee-high picket fence. Jennifer lunged. The fence tripped him, sending him onto his back. Jennifer's swipe missed his throat by a hair. Her momentum carried her into him.

Nathan jumped the fence. As he landed, he swung the weeder. It crashed into Jennifer's back. This grounded her, but in an instant she rolled onto all fours, ready to leap.

The blond man joined Nathan, a rake in hand. The two garden tools caught Jennifer on the back of the head. The picket fence hid the severity of the attack, but it still drew a wince from Amanda.

The newcomers backed up a pace but kept their weapons ready.

Amanda growled as she gripped the bat. A coil of rope she'd been intending to string up for vines to crawl up lay amid the shoes beside the door. She snatched up the line. "This is getting out of hand. Stay here, girls."

Jeremy rushed toward his wife.

Nathan stepped between them, holding the distraught husband at spear-point.

Amanda dashed toward the scene. "Jeremy," she barked. On the ground, Jennifer lay unconscious. Blood poured from beneath a flap of skin the strikes had sheered from her skull. *Damn it, maybe I made a mistake with these people!* "Don't touch her. The blood—"

"She's my fucking wife!" Jeremy roared. "They *killed* her!"

"She is functional," Albin related in a matter-of-fact tone. He gestured to Amanda's rope. She tossed it to him, then he began tying a loop.

"Functional?" Jeremy hauled back his fist—

Amanda grabbed his arm. "She attacked you!"

"W-we love each other."

Nathan eyed him. "She doesn't understand love anymore."

"You don't know that! Have you seen anybody like this hurt people they loved? Well?"

"I never waited to experiment, but I can recognize danger."

Meanwhile, Albin slid the rope loop down the rake handle and around Jennifer's neck. Like . . . like a dog. And like a dog, she would attack. Amanda moved to tie her hands with the rope-end that hung from the noose. "Jeremy, this is the first time she's gotten out of the garage?"

"Yes."

Albin ran the rope around one of the porch's brick pillars. He tied it around a nearby sapling.

"Jeremy." Nathan pointed the weeder at the man. "You can keep her in your garage or barn or wherever you please, but it's your fault if she hurts anyone."

Amanda looked from the unconscious wife to the devastated husband. "She might have attacked Zander, and she did attack you. These guys saved you both. If they hadn't shown up, well . . ."

"You would be mourning two family members," Albin announced, apparently nonplussed by the situation.

A white SUV tore around the corner. It screeched to a halt beside Amanda and the others. Carolyn jumped out. "What's going on? Who are these people?"

Amanda stepped up. "They saved Zander and Jeremy. They came to help us." If only they'd come in time to save Jacinda.

Trusting these two seemed like a long shot. Still, she could hope. And where there is life, there is hope.

ABOUT L.C. CHAMPLIN

Writer, traveler, adventurer. Lover of all things Geek and Dark. I admire villains, antagonists, and rogues more than a little. They really do have more fun, and they can teach us important life lessons.

I write fiction because the characters in my head have too much attitude to stay in my skull, I want to see the world through different eyes, and I want to live life through different souls.

I write zombie apocalypse/horror/thriller books because it's in the dark that we see a person's true character. Plus, who doesn't like shooting zombies?

Check out my site lcchamplin.com for book updates, and blog posts about villains, weird science, and more.

AIRBORNE

BY ARTHUR MONGELLI

Kristen stepped toward the counter with her boarding pass in hand. She had been listening to her mother arguing with her father through the phone for nearly five minutes.

"Mom. Mom. Mom, I have to go!" she called into her Iphone. "I'm about to get on a plane, Mom. I have to hang up."

"What's that, Kris?" her mother replied.

"I have to go, I'm about to board."

"Oh, well, I wish you didn't always rush me off the phone. It'd be nice to get to talk for more than a few minutes at a time, you know."

Kristen's eyes rolled back in her head at the comment. It seemed like every time she spoke with her mother she got to speak less and less. Usually she was forced to patiently listen to an hour of what TV shows her parents had been watching and what meals her mother had prepared. Between telling the same stories repeatedly and her short temper, she was beginning to think that her mother was suffering from the onset of Alzheimer's. Still, despite it all, her mother always managed to throw some guilt her way.

"I know, Mom. I'm sorry. I'll be back in Boston this evening, we can talk then."

"Okay, Kris. Safe travels."

Kristen looked up from the phone and met eyes with the counter clerk at boarding. The woman's eyes shined with pleasantry, tinged by a subtle hint of annoyance.

"I'm sorry!"

"It's okay, I have a mother too." the woman replied with a wink. "Boarding pass, please."

Kristen tensed at the request. She held her breath as she handed the computer printout across the desk to the woman. Going AWOL was a cardinal sin in the military. It had been drummed into her head since basic training that desertion, abandoning your brothers and sisters, was one of the worst transgressions a soldier could make. She also knew that with everything going on, her absence mere hours before, would likely be insignificant if it was even noticed. In her haze of guilt, she pictured the airline attendant pressing a secret button under the desk and a handful of MPs swarming out to arrest her.

"Welcome, Ms. Harris. Please have a seat, we will start boarding by sections momentarily."

Kristen let out the pent breath in a gasp and hoped the woman didn't notice. She stepped away from the counter and moved across to the wall of windows overlooking the tarmac. For what she thought would likely be the last time, she looked out across the city of San Diego. Numerous plumes of smoke crept skyward from the sun-baked city beyond the fences of the airport. She wondered, for perhaps the hundredth time since the day before, if she was making a huge mistake by leaving like this.

She had been operating in near complete panic for the past eighteen hours, since the orders came down. The civil unrest that had begun the day previous was steadily intensifying. The National Guard was completely unprepared and had no time to recall its troops. The men and women that were available to them, on active duty, were spread too thin across the major cities. Their efforts had been largely ineffective. That's when the orders came down, when they called on the rest of the branches of the military to help quell the madness. Kristen knew that the orders were illegal. The military was prohibited from acting on American soil by the Posse Comitatus Act.

The fact that the orders had been given at all told her beyond a shadow of a doubt that things were not okay. She figured that once the troops were en route to the riots, they would get ordered to treat US citizens as enemy combatants. She knew that she could not follow that order if given and feared the penalty for that would be much worse than going AWOL. The only other reason she could think for troops getting sent in, was that some kind of coup was happening. Either way, it was not what she had enlisted for. She knew that she needed to get home to her family.

She looked at her boarding pass once more, reminding herself that she was seated in Economy, row 25. She concentrated on regulating her breathing as the feelings of panic started to creep in. She knew that people went AWOL all the time. As long as they weren't in active combat, the most that usually happened was that they got sent an inflated bill for gear that "Wasn't returned". With the scene before her, San Diego in flames, she was worried that this was different. She worried that the penalties, in what might be a domestic war zone, might be much harsher. She also felt guilt for letting down her brothers and sisters in arms, but she would not, she could not raise arms against American civilians. She wondered if she could claim conscientious objector if her case were ever tried.

Any disabled persons, Military personnel, and people who have purchased an additional room seat may now board, squawked the intercom.

Kristen started forward but caught herself mid-stride, reminding herself that she was a civilian now. The last thing she wanted was to draw attention to the fact that she was deserting. She needn't have worried, as soon as the call for boarding began, the entire gathered crowd of nearly two-hundred people rushed the gate. For the first time, she noticed that the crowd around her wore faces of thinly masked fear. The attendant behind the counter shouted into the loudspeaker, but it was too late, the floodgates had been opened. The throng of panicked people surged down the boarding tunnel, past the captain and first officer, and onto the plane. Kristen followed behind the mob.

The madness of the rush of people continued onto the plane. The fuselage was a tumult of activity as people shoved past, or through, one another. Looking to avoid the chaos, Kristen slid through the crew area between business class and economy. A moment later she slid into her seat; row 25 seat F, an aisle seat at the very front of economy class. She was grateful to have found her seat. After a few minutes of watching the frenzied passengers board, a woman moved to the seat next to her. The woman's husband or travel partner sat in the seat directly behind her and the two conversed quietly over the back of the seat. The frenzied scene calmed gradually as more and more people found their seats, stowed their overhead baggage, and finally sat.

"Oh my god, as if I need to see that when boarding a plane!" the woman next to her said, aghast at something.

Kristen sat up a little, peering over her and out the window, to see a pair of coffins being loaded into the cargo bay of the plane.

"That doesn't seem like a good omen to me," replied the man traveling with her.

"I'll just be happy once we are airborne," Kristen interjected. "Can't wait to put this mess behind me."

"If you look at the stuff people in Boston are saying, it's not much better over there," the woman replied.

"Really?" Kristen asked, growing suddenly nervous. "I was just on the phone with my mother, she didn't say anything about that."

"My cousins posted some pictures on Facebook, here I'll show you."

Kristen really wasn't interested in seeing the woman's cousins' pictures, but feigned interest and looked at them out of politeness. They didn't show much, just crowds of people, it could have been anything from a street performer to a car accident. A moan from beyond the curtain ahead stole her attention away after a few seconds. It was a moan of sickness or pain. Kristen unbuckled her belt and started to rise when a flight attendant came rushing over.

"Ma'am, please remain in your seat, we are about to start taxiing for take-off. If you have to use the loo, you'll have to wait until we hit cruising altitude and the pilot turns off the seatbelt signs."

He gestured toward the seatbelt indicator on the overhead panel, that was lit up.

"Someone sounds sick or hurt up there," Kristen replied as she sat back in her seat.

"Oh, are you a doctor?"

"No," she replied, suddenly embarrassed at seeming like a busybody.

"Okay then," he replied, clapping his hands together and moving away, through the curtains separating economy from business class.

When the curtains parted, Kristen caught sight of a gentleman, three rows into business class, whose face was lathered in sweat. His head lolled a bit toward the aisle and his skin was ashen. The curtains flapped closed after a moment, leaving her cringing at the thought of such a sick person in an enclosed air environment. Her germaphobic mind could almost see the particles of sickness drifting into the air circulators and coming out of the air vent above her. She shuddered at the thought.

Finally, the massive 767 lifted lazily into the sky. Kristen watched the city below through the windows as the plane circled, gaining altitude. When the clouds blotted out the signs of chaos on the streets below, the tension finally started to leave her body. Her packing, planning and preparation over the last eighteen hours, all in a haze of panic and doubt, meant that she had been awake since the morning previous. The pilot's voice came through the intercom, sounding staticky and garbled. Kristen didn't hear any of the words as the tension departed, she drifted into unconsciousness.

"Ma'am. Ma'am," came a voice, shaking her out of her nap. "Please lower your tray, your meal is here. Hindu vegetarian?"

"Yeah," she replied, rubbing a stream of drool from the corner of her mouth.

Kristen wasn't vegetarian, but she was extremely partial to Indian food, especially when the alternative was a microwaved meatloaf sandwich. She had learned a few tricks from her father, who often flew for business over the years and this particular tip had paid off. The tray of chana masala the flight attendant set in front of her smelled marvelous. Her stomach responded to the aroma by grumbling loudly. She realized that she hadn't eaten since breakfast the day before. Without even waiting for the woman next to her to get her tray, she stripped the plastic off her spoon, took the lid off the tray, and dug in ravenously. The woman next to her stared longingly at her food.

"Wish I knew that was a choice we had," she said indignantly, looking at her own bland tray as the flight attendant handed it to her.

Kristen finished her meal and washed it down with a hot, flavorless cup of coffee. She wiped her mouth with the crunchy little napkin and turned her attention to the in-flight movie. It was what looked like a remake of The Fugitive. She enjoyed the Harrison Ford version quite a bit, having watched it with her dad on a lazy Sunday afternoon many years before. The movie held her interest for only a few moments, it seemed they made up for a lack of quality acting with and over-abundance of special effects. She flipped through the SkyMall catalog absently as her mind drifted back to her predicament.

A series of odd sounds issued from business class ahead, a gurgle followed by a thump and some shuffling. It immediately drew her attention from the magazine and her own thoughts. A moment later, the same flight attendant from earlier rushed forward from the rear of economy. He spoke in an overly light, faux-feminine voice calling "excuse me" and "coming through" as he moved up the aisle. He ripped the curtain open and moved in to help before closing it completely, offering Kristen a clear view of what was happening. The sick passenger she had seen earlier was seizing on the floor, laying partially in the aisle. A handful of passengers stood far off to the side, displaced from their seats by the efforts of the flight crew. The crew was gathered around, mostly watching, except for two who were trying to prevent the passenger from striking his head on anything as he thrashed about in the throes of a seizure.

Kristen watched in fascination. She had never seen an active seizure before and couldn't tear her eyes away. One thing she noticed as the man writhed about, was that his shirt rode up and out of his waistband. When it did, she could see a blood-soaked bandage on his left side. A body moved in front of her view, blocking it out entirely. She looked up and paled at the sight of the flight attendant giving her a haughty look as he ripped the curtains closed with a huff.

Kristen was left feeling shamed, and in equal part, nervous. She feared for the man, but also felt a deeper, unsettled feeling start to form somewhere in her gut. Before she could sort out her feelings, the overwhelming urge to evacuate her bowels came over her. She unbuckled, slid out of her seat, and moved quickly forward through the curtain to the restrooms. If the urge wasn't so strong she would have retreated to the rear of the economy section to use the bathrooms, and avoided the flight attendant altogether. Instead, she hustled to the first unoccupied booth, averting her gaze from the scene entirely. Even looking away, she could tell immediately that the sounds of the man seizing had ended.

As she slid the lock home she could hear a steady, rhythmic sound that she immediately recognized. It was the sound of CPR being performed. Her heart sank into her stomach as she sat on the toilet. With all the chaos of the past day, something like a man fighting for his life on the floor of the plane humbled her and put her own problems into perspective. *It's not a big deal, Kris. You just need to pick a new path in life. You need to re-enroll in college and finish your degree,* she reassured herself about her decision to leave the service. *There are more important things than your duty, especially when they are breaking the law.*

The rhythmic thumping of chest compressions ceased a couple minutes later, followed by the low murmur of voices. The voices were muffled by the door and Kristen couldn't tell what was being said, but the low tone gave her the impression that things didn't end well for the man. She flushed the toilet and washed her hands in the little sink, taking a moment to compose herself before walking out. She was wracked with sadness for the man, who she assumed had died. She also recognized that most of the emotion she was feeling was pent up anxiety, and worry for herself and her own plight. Regardless of the source of the emotion, she didn't want to show it. *Don't act like you're weak and they wont treat you like you are,* she reminded herself, a mantra from basic. Not crying was something that she learned early on in the service. She took a couple deep breaths to steady herself and bite back the emotion, before sliding the lock back and pulling the folding door open.

The sound of pained screams came to her as soon as the door opened and she stepped out into the aisle. The scream startled her, and she froze mid-stride. She had intended on escaping back to economy the same way she had come into business, with her head down. Her head snapped up from her shoes and spun around, where her eyes locked onto a gruesome image. The sick man wasn't dead at all, he was up and moving. It took her a moment for her eyes to focus and for her mind to absorb what was happening. The man had bits of bloody gore hanging from his mouth and the flight attendant that had shamed her was laying on his back, clutching at his throat, just a few feet in front of her. Blood poured down from beneath his hands and he had a shocked and terrified look on his face.

Everyone was screaming. Those who were already standing ran, either forward toward first class or through the curtains, back into economy. Those who were seated struggled with their lap belts as the man stalked in, halfway across the row, just ahead of where she stood. He knocked aside the defensive hands of a boy who couldn't have been older than six years old. Kristen stared in a stupor, watching in disbelief as the man leaned down and began to eat the child. The boy's shrill screams died out after a few seconds and blood began to pool on the floor at his feet.

Just to her left, coming through the curtain, a flight attendant shrieked in horror at the scene. Kristen's head snapped to the woman in surprise. When she turned back, her eyes locked with the attacker's. They were the eyes of a predator, soulless and devoid of any trace of humanity. His face was covered in blood and he let loose an unearthly sound as he turned to face her fully. The flight attendant shoved her forward mightily, still screaming. The spell of the moment broke with the shove and Kristen started running up the aisle toward the front of the compartment, urged on by the steady, insistent shoves of the flight attendant.

"Stop!" called a man's voice from off to the left as they ran.

Kristen glanced to the side as she was shoved down the aisle. She could see a heavyset man holding a pistol and a badge moving across the last row of seats, toward the aisle. She also saw the visage of the bloody, screaming man tearing across the row as he moved in pursuit of them. His screams sounded inhuman and sent a small sprinkle of urine down her leg. The man's eyes boring through her as he single-mindedly ran after them, sent a jolt of terror down her spine. *He's going to catch you and when he does, he's going to eat you,* a small voice whispered in the back of her mind. With her next breath, she joined the flight attendant, screaming out of shock and fear. There was no longer a need for the flight attendant to shove her, they both ran headlong up the aisle, away from the man.

"Federal Air Marshal! Stop or I will shoot!" the man shouted.

Kristen blew through the curtains that separated business class from first class, tearing them off the overhead sliders completely. She nearly fell when a hiccup of turbulence hit and the plane lurched up momentarily. The people in first class slid away from them, across the rows of seats. When their pursuer came into sight, a new volley of screams and panicked noise cascaded through the cabin. Kristen hesitated, seeing the locked door of the cockpit ahead. She looked furtively around for escape. The rough hands of the flight attendant propelled her forward once again.

"Cockpit!" the woman screamed, nearly in her ear.

The two women hit the cockpit door at speed. The reinforced door held and Kristen's hands stung from the impact. The flight attendant fumbled with the number pad on the door, struggling in her panic to punch in the code. A steady stream of curses left the flight attendant's mouth as she furiously punched her fingers on the number pad. The man giving chase was only ten feet away, running headlong with his arms spread as if to grab them in a hug.

He left his feet, diving in toward their midsections. The impact of his body, colliding with them, came at the same time as a series of three beeps from the door. Kristen was blasted down to the ground, just inside the flight deck. She rolled to her back and kicked with her legs to push herself deeper into the cockpit and away from the man. The bloody man was biting and tearing at the flight attendant, who flailed her arms and kicked out in defense against the brutal onslaught. Kristen's back hit something hard and metal, causing her to rise and try to move around it. As she stood, she could see the Federal Air Marshal taking aim with his pistol. Looking down the barrel herself, she instinctively threw herself back to the ground.

The shot rang out, sounding hollow and amplified in the pressurized cabin. Kristen was sprayed with gore as the bullet tore through the man's chest. She let out a shriek of surprise and disgust before wiping it from her face with the sleeve of her shirt.

"Fuck!" shouted a voice from behind her. "Fuck!"

Kristen hazarded a glance back and could see in an instant that things had gone from bad to worse. Sparks and a small fire erupted from the control panel.

"Get that fire put out!" the captain called as he flipped some toggles and tried to get control of the stick.

The first officer stood, removing his headset, and shoved past Kristen as the chime and buzz of alarms began to sound.

"Ground this is GE6104 flying over 40.7387 degrees north, 73.9901 degrees west, requesting a vector for emergency landing," the captain said into his headset a moment later. "Repeat: Ground this is GE6104 flying over 40.7385 degrees north, 73.9961 degrees west, requesting a vector for emergency landing."

She followed the first officer's movement for a brief moment when another form came and took him to the ground. The impact of the two men striking her knocked her to the side, where she landed heavily in the flight engineer's seat. Her jaw dropped in shock and disbelief at seeing the man who had chased her across the length of the plane attacking the first officer. She had seen him get shot center mass and could still feel the blood dripping on her neck from it. A hand gripped her ankle as the two men struggled at her feet and she responded with a flurry of kicks, shoving both forms a foot further away form her.

"Can't hail anything on comms, Dave, and shit is getting worse. Get your ass back in your seat and buckle in," the captain called. "We're going down."

A weird warbled shriek came from the throat of the first officer as the other man's teeth sank home in his throat. The scream raised in pitch and volume for a moment, sounding eerily similar to an air raid siren, before his voice box was crushed into silence. From overhead an oxygen mask dropped, striking her on the shoulder and startling a frightened gasp from her.

"What the Jesus fuck!" the captain shouted, snapping his head around in time to see the conclusion of the struggle.

The smoke filling the cockpit, mingling with the numerous buzzing and chiming of alerts, was disorienting. A moment later the controls went dark, silencing the racket. Kristen was nearly thrown from her seat when the plane pitched to one side and started a rapid descent. Everything was shaking and rattling in the cockpit. The two men on the floor started sliding back toward the door of the cockpit.

Kristen was screaming in terror as the whine of the descending plane increased in pitch and volume. She barely noticed the hand that gripped her ankle as she struggled to buckle the unfamiliar belt, that came up to her shoulders where it connected. Only after she was secured did she recognize the unsettling sensation. She lashed out again and again with her other foot, smashing the heel of her sneaker into the man's face. He seemed unfazed by the barrage and continued to struggle toward her. She pulled the oxygen mask on as the smoke stung her eyes and her lungs. Everything started rattling; the seats rattled on their rivets, the numerous compartment doors around the flight deck rattled, even the control panel spitting sparks and fire rattled.

Her stomach crawled up into her chest and Kristen knew this was it. The clouds parted and the ground, appearing straight through the cockpit windows, crept ever closer as she was pressed back against the seat. A single tear escaped from the corner of her eye. She knew this was the end of her life.

The airplane bucked and heaved mightily, and everything went black.

Kristen started drifting back to consciousness with the unsettling feeling of being dragged across the ground by her foot. The memory of the man clutching her ankle lit fear in her and she rolled over in the grip, clutching and grabbing at anything that her hands came upon, hoping something would help her. Dirt, crumbled rock, and dried clumps of dead grass were the only things her hands came across, however.

"You're awake, good. You can walk on your own now," the captain said, as he unceremoniously dropped her leg.

Kristen rolled again and sat upright. The captain was bloody, his uniform was torn and burned, and he held his left arm limply at his side. He paused long enough to make sure she could move of her own accord before turning back to trudge slowly up the shoulder of the highway. She sat there for a few minutes, trying to get her bearings. *I'm alive?* her inner voice asked, perplexed.

She had lost all hope when the plane started going down. But now, here she was on Terra Firma, seemingly relatively unscathed. She wanted to leap in the air, pump her fists and shout a cheer of joy at being alive. A stiff, chill wind whipped in from the north and sapped her strength and the last of the warmth from her body, pulling her attention to the rural stretch of highway they were on. She stifled her laughter of relief and tried to get a handle on her surroundings.

In the distance behind her she could see the flames and black smoke from the wreckage lifting into the gray sky. There were a handful of vehicles scattered about the highway, apparently broken down. She could see movement coming from within some of them. She stood slowly, taking a full measure of her own condition as she did. Aside from her entire body aching as if she had done the world's worst belly-flop, she felt okay. She shuffled slowly toward the closest car, a Volkswagen broken down in the slow lane.

When she got within twenty feet, she could clearly see that there was a person inside.

"There's something wrong with them," the captain called back from about a hundred feet ahead. "I wouldn't get any closer. They're all messed up, like the one on the flight deck."

Kristen stopped where she stood and watched the person inside the vehicle. It raged and thrashed about, seeming intent on getting at her, but it made no attempt to open the door. She was horrified and mesmerized by it. It smeared its face across the glass and gnashed its teeth, as if it were trying to bite her through the glass.

"What the fuck?" she whispered to herself.

Her eyes panned across the highway at the scattering of vehicles, to see similar forms in some of the others, all fixated on her or the captain. A shudder of fear and revulsion wracked her body and spurred her to movement. She took off at a jog, despite the aches and pains, to catch up to the man.

"What the fuck is happening? What is all this?" she panted out, once she got close.

"Same as on the plane, I'd guess," he replied. "Same as what's going on everywhere, maybe. I'm John, by the way."

"Kristen," she replied. "Wait, everywhere?"

She didn't expect an answer, as it became obvious to her that this was why her battalion was ordered stateside for policing. It hadn't been because of a coup, nor were the riots caused by normal malcontents. They had been mustered to stop whatever was causing the madness overtaking these people. She plodded on in silence while digesting this knowledge, and the impact of the decisions she had made. A creeping unease settled over her, caused not by the revelation or knowledge of what was going on, but the unanswered question as to what was wrong with these people. Every time they drifted near one of the cars she let her eyes linger, hoping to make sense of it all. Each time her dread grew.

"They aren't alive, are they?" she finally asked, on seeing a grievously wounded woman thrashing about on her entrails in the rear of a station wagon.

"If they are, they certainly don't feel any pain," John replied.

"So what do we do? How do we get help?"

The silence lingered for a moment, then, as if in answer, they rounded a bend in the highway and spotted a police cruiser in the distance. Its flashing lights signaled like a beacon.

"We can start there, I think," John replied, smiling slightly through his pained grimace.

The people inside the vehicles faded into the backdrop of late fall in the northern climes. Both Kristen and John hugged themselves and rubbed their bodies, trying to stay warm as they hustled up the roadway toward the cruiser. It was parked halfway up an exit ramp, about a mile ahead, just behind a handful of other parked cars. John was in pretty rough shape, his arm hung limply and his uniform was in scorched tatters. His face hung and his breathing came in short gasps. He could barely move faster than a walking pace. Kristen could see the pain in his eyes and wanted to give him a chance to rest for a moment.

"Hold up a second, John. Gotta catch my breath."

He stopped where he stood and leaned on the guardrail, using it to support him.

"Where are we anyway, John?"

"Not entirely sure, Northeast Pennsylvania, New York State, maybe. To be honest, I was deep into a crossword puzzle when that asshole shot up the controls. The plane does all the flying for the most part," John gasped out the words as he spoke, struggling with some syllables more than others.

"What do you know about all the rioting and stuff?" she asked, more to extend the opportunity for a break than actual desire for information.

"Not much more than talk. I was on a red-eye into San Diego from Tokyo last night. Overheard a couple of the flight crew talking about it. The stuff they were saying sounded pretty far-fetched, though. I thought they were a little bonkers, or reading the Enquirer or something."

After a few minutes, Kristen got them moving once again. She could tell that the man needed much more than a breather on the side of the highway, he was in desperate need of medical attention. As they walked, they could hear the sound of gunshots in the distance, heightening their tension. John made it a few hundred more yards before he started falling. She did her best to support him and help him along, but he was a foot taller and close to a hundred pounds heavier.

By the time they made it to the foot of the exit ramp the cruiser was on, Kristen was fully winded. Her own breathing came in great blowing gusts, nearly equaling in volume the sounds of the howling winds coming from the north. John was moaning, low and pained, as he shuffled along with most of his weight resting on her. The police officer came into view a hundred feet ahead as they approached the rear of the cruiser. He was attending to someone wounded on the roadway, with his back to them, giving CPR from the look of it.

"Help!" Kristen gasped as they staggered up the ramp, her weak voice getting lost in the wind.

She continued to plead for help every five or ten paces, whenever her hoarse, strained breathing would allow. Alarm bells started going off in her head when they reached the rear bumper of the cruiser. She pulled up short, seeing a pool of blood on the ground around the officer, fifteen feet ahead. John toppled forward at her sudden stop, tripping over his own dragging feet. He managed to support himself for two more weak steps before he tumbled alongside the cruiser. His shoulder connected with the side-view mirror on the way down, shearing it off the vehicle. The sound of his body thudding onto the roadway was drowned out by the shattering of the mirror. The tinkling of glass on the roadway hung in the air for a moment as the police officer turned toward them.

Kristen froze in terror at the grim visage before her. Half of his face was missing. A deflated eyeball sagged down from an empty socket, hanging limply onto bone, muscle, and sinew. As he stood to face them, she could see that he had been disemboweled and his upper thighs were stripped of flesh and muscle. His condition horrified her and she rubbed the side of her neck to try and prevent passing out at the wretched sight. This one was not like the man on the plane, it was slow, stumbling almost lethargically as it approached the prone form of John.

"John get up!" she shouted. "John!"

John didn't respond, he simply lay face down on the tarmac as the horrible thing staggered toward him. She tried to force herself forward to help John up, but no matter how much she wanted to, she simply couldn't force her feet to move closer to the thing. *If you don't get moving and help him, you are going to be alone out here, Kris,* her inner voice urged.

Her terror finally broke and she forced her legs forward. She gritted her teeth and charged at the officer, who was now just a few feet from the prone form of John. With a roar of fear and revulsion she threw herself at the cop. She planted both her palms on the center of his chest and shoved with all her might. His mouth snapped hungrily at her arms and his hands pinched and scratched at her face. She was able to overcome his weight with her momentum and when she stopped her roaring charge, he tumbled backward down onto the pavement. He immediately struggled to pursue, but she was back out of reach, slapping John along his head and back as she moved toward the rear of the cruiser, away from the officer.

"John! Get up!" she screamed.

There was still no response so she quickly rolled him onto his back, hiked his feet up into her armpits, and started dragging him behind her like a travois.

She managed to get twenty feet back down the ramp before his legs jerked heavily under her arms and his weight doubled. She looked back in terror to see the police officer laying atop John. Her sanity snapped at seeing the officer dig his teeth into John's stomach and the ensuing bloodletting. She roared in rage and pain, and tears shot from her eyes. She considered for a moment laying into the cop with her hands and feet, but kept enough of her wits to check his waist. His Glock sat there, still in its holster on his hip.

"Don't you fucking move!" she screamed at the officer as she stalked in.

If he noticed her, he didn't lift his head from John's stomach. She circled around to the officer's right side and leapt in. In one swift move she unbuttoned the holster and slid the weapon free. She raised the weapon as she stepped back away from the two. Her heel struck the blacktop wrong and she fell on her backside in her haste. She scrambled back a few feet as the officer turned his head toward her and started to stand. A low plaintive moan escaped his lips and she squeezed the trigger. She fired a single shot into his face. The officer crumpled immediately, falling down on the roadway, laying half across John.

"John!" she screamed, afraid to move closer to the policeman. "Are you. . .okay?"

As she rose back to her feet, it became instantly apparent that John was not okay. She turned away from the gory mess before it could come fully into focus and released the undigested chana masala onto the roadway next to her. She was on her hands and knees, purging her stomach, when a voice startled her back to reality.

"You okay, Miss?" the voice called.

She spun and scrambled away from the voice, bringing the weapon up and to the ready. A heavyset man in sweatpants and a Dallas Cowboys jersey stood on the ramp just beyond where the police officer had initially been. He held his hands out, hesitantly, at the sight of the brandished weapon.

"What the fuck is going on?" she replied, shouting.

She was still scared and traumatized by the events of the past few minutes, but seeing another normal human being got her back to her feet. She moved closer to the man, who appeared to be in his late forties, with salt and pepper hair and a goatee. Having seen people devouring each other multiple times in the past few hours, she exercised caution and stopped once she was within earshot, still more than a dozen feet from the man.

"Dunno, to be honest. I was running to town to fill up the gas tank and get some food and water. The emergency broadcast said to stay indoors, but its hard to keep food around with a couple teenagers in the house," he started. "Never made it into town, though. Those things are everywhere. By the time the Tops market came into view, I knew there was no way I was going to set foot outside the car. I probably look like a fucking steak to them things. I just turned around and headed home. Ran out of gas just up there."

He pointed up to the cars sitting idle on the ramp.

"That cop came staggering down the ramp lookin' all fucked up like that. He seen me and tried to get at me for half the morning, 'til that poor sucker caught his eye," he gestured to the partially devoured corpse laying a few feet to the side. "I been stuck in the truck for the past five hours or so, too afraid to come out. You got a car?"

She took a moment to try and absorb all that was said, and all that was implied, by his statement. She was struck by the pictures the woman on the flight had shown her, of Boston. She wondered how far she was from home.

"Wait, where are we?"

"Huh?" he replied, confused by the question.

"What state, county. What town are we in?" she barked back at him.

"New York, Fishs Eddy," he replied, taking a step back away from her and eyeing her suspiciously. "Where are you from, lady?"

"I was flying from San Diego home to Boston. Plane went down."

"Ho-lee shit, that was a plane that went down?"

Kristen nodded.

"Hot damn, I heard the sound and saw the smoke and fires. I just thought a gas station went up or something. You were on it?"

"Listen, what's your name?"

"Darrell, Darrel Harbaugh. Pleased to meet ya."

Darrell rushed across the gap with his meaty paw extended in polite greeting. Kristen took a hesitant step back, but held her ground and shook the man's hand when he approached.

"I'm Kristen. You live around here, right? With your family?" she asked, trying to voice the question as innocently as possible.

As happy as she was to see another normal person, she wanted to make sure that she would be safe around this guy. If he had a wife and kids at home she would be much more comfortable with the idea of heading in that direction. More than anything, she wanted to head directly toward Massachusetts, but she had no vehicle and no real idea how bad things were. The thought of safety behind a locked door and four walls was too compelling for her to turn down.

"Yeah, Tina and me been married twenty-seven years come next April. Our eldest, Darrell junior, moved out already, over to Chenango. He got a job working on Harleys at Southern Tier. Toby, our middle child turned sixteen last month, and Tanya is fourteen going on twenty-five," he finished with a hearty laugh at his own mirth.

"Can we walk to your place from here?"

"'Bout a mile over that way, as the crow flies," he gestured with his stubby pointed finger. "Take us a bit longer on the roads, maybe thirty minutes to walk it."

"Okay, Darrell, let's get moving."

It took nearer to an hour to make the trek. Darrell was extremely out of shape and needed to 'take a minute' every hundred yards or so. When they finally arrived at the house, which was set back from the road a hundred feet or more, there was someone waiting on the front porch with a rifle in hand. Kristen spotted him from the road and froze alongside the garage that sat out front, refusing to move any closer. Darrell took a few steps down the walkway before he noticed her hesitation.

"Come on, Kristen. This is it." he gasped, red-faced with the effort of the walk.

He stared at her, confused, for nearly a full minute before realizing the sight of his son, nearly a grown man, with a rifle in hand might disturb a woman traveling by herself.

"Toby, get your ass inside the house and send your mother out here," he called back.

"Don't mind the boy," he said to Kristen. "Fancies himself a big-time hunter ever since he nabbed a twelve-pointer last year. Luck is what I say."

The boy scrambled inside and a moment later a heavyset middle-aged woman came out onto the porch. She wobbled a little when she walked, which tickled Kristen a bit. By the time she moved down the length of the walkway to her husband's side, her cheeks were rosy and she was out of breath. Kristen smiled broadly at the woman, despite her reservations.

"Well, don't just stand there, girl. Get inside and out of the cold. You'll catch your death out here."

Kristen allowed herself to be led inside the turn-of-the-century foursquare style house. The warmth inside was uncomfortable after barely a moment. She had been out in the cold for so long, the heat inside felt like it was burning her skin. Darrell put a crocheted blanket around her shoulders and led her down the hall to the kitchen at the back of the house. He sat her in a chair at the table, closest to where the wood-burning stove sat. She still held the pistol in her hand, refusing to allow herself to feel safe.

"Kristen, this is Tina, my wife. Tina, this is Kristen. I found her by the roadside, couldn't leave her out there," he winked at Kristen, in acknowledgment of his exaggeration. "It's a goddamned nightmare out there."

"What's happen-" Tina began.

A harrowing roar echoed down through the forests across the street, accompanied by frenzied hammering on the front door. Everyone froze and stared helplessly toward the front of the house. Kristen steadied herself with a breath and let the blanket drop to the floor as she stood. She stalked to the corner of the kitchen and peered down the length of the hallway. Through the myriad designs of etched and colored glass inlaid in the front door, she could see the forms of at least two people. One of them locked eyes on her and started shouting.

"Let us in, please!"

Kristen could see the hysteria in his eyes and knew immediately that the man was desperate. She lowered the pistol to her side and glided down the hall to the door, throwing the latch and stepping clear. The weight of three bodies pressed the door open and spilled them onto the floor in front of her. She stepped back and raised her pistol slightly, at the ready. The man she had locked eyes with scrambled around, slamming the door shut. He locked the dead-bolt and pressed his back against the door while the other two, a boy and a girl, both teenagers, looked nervously from the door to Kristen's hand gripping the pistol.

Kristen opened her mouth to utter a reassurance when a shadow came across the window. The flash of movement barely had time to register before the window smashed inwards and the upper half of a body came through. Everyone started screaming. The thrashing thing came fully through the window and into the foyer and the three newcomers scrambled away from it, moving into the front room of the house. Kristen retreated a step further back into the shadows of the hallway as the man stood and roared in fury. The sound sent a shiver of fear down her spine. Flesh rent by the glass hung in ribbons down the front of his face and congealed blood coated the front of his coveralls. His skin was grayish-black and mottled, not that she noticed. She was fixated on his eyes he had the same predatory eyes as the man on the plane.

When the man lurched off in pursuit of the three, Kristen's hesitation broke. She moved to the door and shouted into the front room.

"Hey, asshole!"

She raised her pistol, but the chaos of movement inside the room granted her no clear shot. Through the tumult of activity, those eyes came into focus, locked on her own. Then the man was running toward her. She fumbled with the dead-bolt and got the door open just as he arrived. She took a single step to the open door as he dove in. He slipped on the scattered glass and he bounced off the left side of her hip, sending her careening, crashing through the screen door and onto the wide front porch. The pistol flew from her grip as the back of her head struck the column at the side of the stairs. She could hear the cacophony of cascading glass and a heavy thump as she worked to remain conscious. She slid backwards down the stairs as the man skidded on the broken glass and came out the door after her.

Kristen crawled to her feet, quickly scanning for the pistol but was forced into a run at the sound of rapid footfalls coming down the stairs behind her. She was screaming and she didn't care. All her aches and pains from the past hours vanished as the adrenaline coursed through her. Her legs pumped furiously to keep ahead of the rabid man. She looped around the garage by the road, tossing the garbage cans to the ground behind her, when she remembered the people trapped inside cars on the highway. Those people weren't as angry as this guy was, but hope sprung in the idea that she might be able to trap him in the garage. On her next circuit around the garage, she tried the side door. The knob turned and she threw her weight into it, crashing through and into the side of a big SUV inside.

As she turned, the ruined face of the man came into full focus, bearing down on her. She slid her body toward the rear of the Jeep a split-second before the man collided head first into the side of the vehicle. The dull metallic thud sounded loudly in the small space. She paused, watching for a moment, hoping that the force of the impact had rendered him unconscious or better, dead. Her brief hopes were dashed when the man immediately turned and scrambled on all four to come after her. She dodged to the side, narrowly avoiding the clumsy tackle and stepped toward the open door. Three more strides carried her out of the garage, where she slammed the door shut behind her. Without a moments pause, she ran to the front of the garage. She knew that the flimsy wooden side door couldn't contain the enraged man, she figured that her only hope of keeping him inside was to distract him away from it. She slammed her hands noisily on the roll-top door while shouting:

"Over here! I'm over here!"

She leapt back and screamed in terror as the man threw himself bodily into the roll-top door. The sound of the door shaking on its metal rollers reverberated loudly, echoing off the forest and throughout the area. Kristen backed away from the garage slowly. She watched the garage door shaking for a long while before finally breaking away. She moved south on the roadway and made her way back to the house in a wide, circuitous route.

"-are you sure, Darr?" Tina asked her husband as Kristen approached the two on the porch.

"Of course I'm sure, you think I wouldn't recognize him, Tina? Hey, you okay, Kristen?"

Kristen nodded as she mounted the steps.

"You guys got a spare vehicle I can take?" she asked. "I appreciate you taking me in, but I need to get home to my family."

"Out of gas on the exit, where I ran into you." Darrell replied, shaking his head to the negative. "Tina's car is down at Ricky's, waiting on a back-ordered starter."

"What about that Jeep in there? You have the keys to it?"

"That's my brother's, been keeping it here since the

divorce. He keeps the keys on him, though. You should've asked him when you met."

Kristen looked at him blankly, having no idea what he was talking about.

"He's the one that was chasing you just a minute back." Darrell replied with a big, mischievous grin on his face. "Now, I think we'd best be getting inside. It looks like all the commotion brought some unwanted attention to us."

Tina smacked Darrell on the back of his bicep as the two moved inside. Kristen turned, looking out off the front porch. As her eyes focused she could see a great many forms converging on their location. She paused long enough to scoop up her pistol from where it lay on the browning grass before following Tina and Darrell inside.

ABOUT ARTHUR MONGELLI

Arthur Mongelli spent his formative years in the 1980s. Growing up in the shadow of the Cold War and the heyday of apocalyptic cinema left an indelible mark. The lingering fascination with zombies and the apocalypse in general is the theme of most of his body of work. He is the author of Harvest of Ruin (Severed Press 2017), The Dead of Winter (Severed Press 2017), and A Spring of Sorrow (Severed Press 2018). Additionally, he has had short stories published in Undead Worlds: A Reanimated Writers Anthology (2017) Mad Like Me (2017) and the upcoming Undead Words 2 anthology (2018), His current work in progress, tentatively titled 'Sand' is a non-zombie, dystopian/post-apocalyptic tale.

11

BREAKFAST IN HELL

BY DIA COLE

CHAPTER ONE

"It's a good day to die," Trish said, pointing her semiautomatic assault rifle up at the cloudless sky.

Her words made the fine hairs on the back of my neck prickle. "Don't say that. Don't even think it." Keeping my fingers tightly wrapped around my tactical knife, I wiped away the sweat on my forehead. It was only late January, but the stifling heat wave was a familiar prelude to a scorching Saguaro Valley summer—a summer we probably wouldn't live long enough to see.

Trish swiped her frizzy auburn hair out of her face and flashed me a feral grin. "We all got to go someday. Why not today?" She moved farther out into the debris-covered street, her face shadowed by the Festival of Lights banner doing the splits between two palm trees overhead.

"Hush, you two," ordered Eric, pressing himself flat against the abandoned Suburban we were using as cover. He glared at his younger sister who shared his slight stature and light brown eyes. "Get back here if you know what's good for you." At twenty-three he was only a few years older than Trish and me, but he loved to boss us around.

"You know, you're my least favorite brother." Trish blew a raspberry at Eric and bounced up and down on the balls of her sneakers like the overexcited puppy my sister had once rescued. Of course, that had been long before the canine flu vaccine brought about the zombie apocalypse. Now the human species needed rescuing far more than any animals.

Trish rubbed her belly. "I'm starving. Why did we have to skip breakfast for this stupid field training test?"

My stomach rumbled at the reminder of our missed meal. I'd given my sister most of my MRE last night, which made missing the single protein bar we were rationed for breakfast hurt more than usual.

Next to me, Eric shifted his shotgun. "Shut your mouth. They'll hear you." He jerked his beard-covered chin at the crowd gathering in front of the Euro Gift Shop down the street.

I tensed, glancing at the mob.

Even with their heads and limbs bent at odd angles, the shambling bodies could almost be mistaken for normal people. *Almost.* But a closer look at their milky eyes, uncoordinated gait, and rotting skin gave them away. *Biters.*

Trish scoffed. "They're all the way over there."

She can't be serious. We all knew how dangerous Biters could be when they gathered together, and that pack was the largest I'd seen since the day the world went to hell over a month ago. The memory of the zombie horde smashing through my house had me shivering despite the warm temperature.

Trish held her fingers to her lips and mocked her brother by making loud shushing noises.

Neither the desert heat nor Trish's cavalier attitude was

doing anything to thaw the ice water running through my veins. *Why did I volunteer for this? Oh wait. I didn't.* Sergeant Dominic Rosario, the leader of our group, ordered us to accompany him on this training mission. Before he'd left to scout ahead, he'd announced we'd be tested on our survival skills and our knowledge of his rules.

Ugh. He has so many goddamn rules. Living under Dominic's command kept us alive, but sometimes I wondered if we'd embraced the devil in an attempt to survive hell.

I rubbed a sweaty palm on my jeans. *I have to pass his test.* Those that failed were exiled or assigned the most menial jobs back at the school where we were staying. Although being shackled with latrine duty wasn't the end of the world, being thrown out of the safe house without the protection of Dominic and his soldiers would be. Even worse, my sister and close friend would insist on leaving with me. *I can't keep them safe by myself. Not with those things out there.*

As if sensing my fear, two of the Biters down the street lifted their heads and sniffed the air.

I froze, not daring to move a muscle.

After a tense moment, the creatures turned back to their shambling.

I let out a relieved breath. Thank God we were all wearing heavy perfume to disguise our scents. We didn't know how or why, but Biters seemed to rely on their sense of smell to hunt.

"Those Biters have the right idea. We should get breakfast there." Trish pointed at the gift shop. "They have the most amazing fruit pies. They're better than sex." She smacked her lips. "Anyone want to get a pie with me?"

Eric gritted his teeth. "No one is getting a pie with you. Now be quiet."

Trish flipped him off.

Eric and I shared a troubled look. Although sassy as hell, the pixie-sized girl was normally razor-focused in the field. Her strange mood only made my anxiousness grow.

"I'm getting breakfast." Trish spun on her heel and marched down the street.

Has she lost her damn mind?

"Stop her," Eric barked into my ear. "She listens to you more than me."

Making a sound of frustration, I ran after my friend and snagged the strap of her weapon with my free hand. "Do you have a death wish?"

She winked at me and mouthed, "Play along." The overpowering scent of marijuana wafted off her clothes.

I gasped in disbelief. *We're out in one of the deadliest parts of the neighborhood, and she's high? Great. Just great.* Not only weren't we going to pass the field training test, she was going to get us killed. I cast a quick glance at the Biters. Thankfully, they hadn't detected our presence. *Yet.*

"Let me go," she exclaimed, trying to shake me off.

Years of spinning around a pole, along with Dominic's daily defensive training workouts, gave me the strength to reel the smaller woman in. I dragged her behind an overturned gray sedan trying to ignore the blood-streaked windows. "Dominic ordered us to stay by the Suburban." *Rule number one, follow Dominic's orders.*

Trish gave a dramatic eye roll. "He's been gone too long. He's probably been eaten."

My stomach dropped. *Not Dominic. He can't die.* Despite my conflicting feelings on the handsome sergeant, I couldn't bear to consider anything bad happening to him.

I shook off her words. "Seriously? The man could take out a horde with his bare hands. You don't want to piss him off."

Trish scoffed. "Just because you have the hots for one of the scariest mofos still alive on this planet doesn't mean I'm going to roast my lady balls off waiting for him." She whipped around and elbowed me in the gut.

I doubled over with a grunt, losing my grip on her. "Why the hell did you do that?"

She glared at me with her hands on her hips. "I'm getting that fruit pie."

"Not only is that suicidal, you know we're never supposed to travel anywhere alone." *Rule number eight, always travel with backup.*

She arched a brow. "So, come with me."

Movement over her shoulder quickened my pulse. Two zombies peeled off from the pack and lurched our way. "Biters, eight o'clock!"

The closest flesh-eater wore teal medical scrubs, and a nurse's ID badge linking her to the retirement home up the street. The shredded skin of her throat revealed a half-eaten trachea, the same color as her sunken white eyes.

Close behind her shambled a hulking, male Biter, wearing a blue polo and bloodstained chinos. Maggots danced in and out of the gaping hole where his nose had once been.

I gulped. These Biters weren't like the toothless, armless ones we'd practiced fighting back at the safe house. *These monsters will fight us to the death.*

Trish spun around, her eyes narrowing. "I'll teach these cock blockers to get between me and my breakfast." She shouldered her rifle and pointed it at the nurse.

"What are you doing?" I grabbed the weapon and ripped

it from her hands. "Guns are only used as a last resort." *Rule number five.* "The noise will attract the others."

"You're right. Damn, I forgot my spear. Can you handle them?"

Crap! I gave Trish her rifle back and pushed her behind me.

The nurse was only a few yards away. Seeing us, she clicked her bloodstained teeth together in frenzied anticipation.

Terror slammed into me. My muscles froze and my heart hammered so hard I feared it'd burst through my chest like some kind of alien monster.

"Snap out of it, Lee!" Trish whispered hoarsely. "You have to do something or we'll die."

CHAPTER TWO

Realizing the nurse was almost on us, I took a deep breath and immediately choked on the pungent, rotting-meat stench of her. Quickly switching to mouth breathing, I focused on Dominic's training. The words he'd drilled into my mind came back to me. *Attack. Don't react.* Stiffening my shoulders, I raised my knife and ran at the flesh-eater head-on.

She opened her jaws and reached for me.

Avoiding her long, jagged fingernails, I stabbed my blade straight through her milky eye. It exploded like an overripe grape. *Ugh.* I ripped my blade free, and she collapsed to the street, lifeless.

Before I could congratulate myself on the kill, the male Biter shambled over her body and tackled me to the asphalt.

Shit! The air whooshed out of my lungs and my knife flew out of my hand.

"Kick him off!" Trish cried.

Adrenaline roared through me as I fought to keep the Biter's snapping jaws away from my throat.

"You've got this," Trish called out, suddenly becoming my personal cheerleader.

No, I don't. It's too strong. My arms shook with the strain of trying to hold off the freakishly huge creature.

It gnashed its teeth and several writhing maggots fell onto my face.

Oh, God! I couldn't stop the impulse to shake them away. I lost my grip on the Biter.

He lunged for my throat.

Letting out a foul curse, Trish swung the butt of her rifle into the temple of the Biter, knocking him off me.

I scrambled away as she brought the rifle down on his forehead, crunching in its skull like an eggshell.

"Th-thanks," I stammered wondering why she'd waited so long to help.

She let out a heavy sigh. "You may not thank me in a few minutes. Just remember whatever happens, it'll be okay."

I looked at her in confusion. "What will be okay?"

Ignoring my question, she looked up at Eric who'd run over to join us.

He frowned as he clapped his hand on my shoulder. "Maybe you'll have better luck next time."

"If Dominic gives her another chance," Trish added, shaking her head.

I blinked in slow understanding. "Wait, you mean you guys staged this?"

The Miller siblings shared a guilty look.

"I don't understand. Aren't you guys being tested today too?"

"We passed our field training two weeks ago," Trish replied in an apologetic voice.

"Oh," I said, feeling a bitter stab of betrayal.

"Please don't be mad. Dominic didn't give us a choi—" Trish broke off as a large shadow fell over us.

All six-foot-six muscular inches of Dominic stepped around the sedan. His dark close-cropped hair, tactical vest lined with throwing knives, and shiny black combat boots marked him as the Special Forces soldier he was.

"You three, over here," he rumbled in a deep voice.

Not wanting to test the sergeant's limited patience, we hustled to follow him down the street.

A small gasp of surprise escaped my lips when I spied the carnage in front of the gift shop. The entire pack of Biters lay motionless on the ground—a single knife wound in the center of their skulls. *Dominic's calling card.*

As I stepped over the piles of bodies, I realized the sergeant must've been inside the shop watching us the whole time. No wonder the infected were gathering in front. *Way to be observant, Lee.*

Dominic's flint-black eyes bore into mine as he propped the door open to the gift shop. His silence was damning.

A sinking feeling grew in my stomach. *Crap. I really messed this one up.*

"Get inside. I've cleared the shop," Dominic said, his massive shoulders filling the doorframe.

My heart raced as I squeezed by him and entered the small shop. The welcoming scent of floral potpourri failed to take the edge off my anxiety. Ignoring the rows of nesting dolls and colorful wooden bowls on display, I studied

Dominic. It made no sense that he could scare the hell out of me and intrigue me at the same time.

The ever-present dark scowl on his sinfully full lips should've been enough to dampen my attraction. But despite his dangerous aura, or maybe because of it, he had me seriously rethinking my lifelong vow of abstinence.

Not that he'd be interested. In over a month of living with him, he'd never spoken to me without either barking an order or glaring at me. Which was fine, I needed a man like I needed a bullet to the gut. Especially an alpha male soldier like him. *Like my father.* I shuddered hoping that monster was roasting in hell.

"Attention," Dominic called out.

Trish, Eric, and I fell in line, our backs against the cash register counter.

Dominic paced in front of us. "Did you wake with amnesia this morning, Miss Walker?"

I flinched at the ice in his tone. "No, sir."

"Then explain why you seem to have forgotten every goddamn thing I've taught you."

Sweat trickled down the back of my neck. I curled my hands into fists to keep them from shaking. "Um—"

Not giving me a chance to respond, he continued, "Your defensive skills are piss-poor, and you showed a complete lack of awareness out there. Do you want to be zombie chow, Miss Walker?"

"No, sir." My stomach knotted. "Did I fail the test?"

A muscle ticked in his jaw. "Of course you failed the test. If Miss Miller hadn't saved your ass, it'd be in pieces on the street."

Trish stiffened. "Lee did take out the first Biter, and she showed a clear understanding of the rules."

I gave her a look of appreciation. I could almost forgive her for setting me up. *Almost.*

Dominic let out a cold laugh. "Like rule number nine?"

Never leave a weapon behind. Oh, crap. I looked down at my empty knife sheath.

"Looking for this?" Dominic held up my blade and waved it under my nose.

When I grabbed for it, he pulled it out of reach. "You won't need a knife like this where you're going."

And where will that be? I curled my hands into fists. "Am I going to be exiled?"

"We'll discuss it on the way back to the safe house." He looked over at Eric and Trish. "You two go on ahead. Dismissed."

"Yes, sir," they said in unison.

Trish flashed me an apologetic look. "Lee, I—"

"Out." Dominic pointed at the door.

"Come on." Eric dragged his sister forward.

"Wait." Trish stopped at a row of gift baskets stacked near the door. With a hesitant look at Dominic, she snatched one.

"I saw that, Miller," Dominic called out as Trish darted outside.

A moment later the door opened and Eric flung the gift basket back inside. "Sorry about that," he said before closing the door.

No fruit pies for Trish today. I let out a choked laugh.

"Pull yourself together. There's no crying in the apocalypse," Dominic chided.

As if. I fisted my hands. "I don't cry."

Dominic's expression hardened. "I'm your commanding officer, you will address me as sir." He gave my knife an appreciative look and then slid it into his tactical vest.

What's he doing? "Can I please have my knife back, sir?" The blade was much more than a weapon to me. It symbolized me conquering the nightmares of my childhood and I intended to carry it until my dying breath.

"It's mine now. If you ever demonstrate sufficient skill to wield it, I'll return it to you." His mocking tone indicated how unlikely that was to happen.

Red crept across my vision. For the past several weeks I'd been forced to eat tiny amounts of tasteless food, spend all day in training exercises, and exist on meager bits of sleep. *And for what?* The protection of this man who'd just taken the only thing of value I had left.

Suddenly, the idea of being exiled didn't bother me. *Fine, let him throw me out. I won't be as safe, but I'll have my freedom.*

Decision made, I let out a deep exhale. *Since I have nothing more to lose...* I leveled Dominic with a hard stare of my own. "Give me back my knife, Sergeant Pain in the Ass."

He jerked his head around so fast he might've gotten whiplash. "What did you call me?"

"Are you hard of hearing?" I couldn't believe the suicidal words coming out of my mouth, but I wasn't about to back down. "Give. Me. My. Knife."

His eyes glittered with challenge. He pulled my blade out and raised it over his head. "Make me."

I jumped for it, but he raised it higher.

Damn it. More games. I'd never get my knife from him that way. And the very idea of me trying to take the massive soldier on in hand-to-hand combat was ridiculous. Unless I used an entirely different set of survival skills.

Channeling my brazen stripper persona, I unzipped my jacket and let it fall to the ground. The air felt so amazing on my heated skin, I went ahead and slowly peeled off my sweat-dampened T-shirt too. That left me in only a sports bra and jeans.

He inhaled sharply. "What are you doing?" It might've been my imagination, but the pulse at his neck seemed to kick up a notch or two.

Good. The sergeant isn't immune to my charms. I moistened my lips. "Just getting comfortable. It's so hot in here."

"Put your clothes back on," he growled, his gaze tracking the sweat trickling between my heaving breasts.

"Make me," I said, throwing his words back at him.

CHAPTER THREE

He looked as if I'd smacked him on the head with a two-by-four. His hand, still gripping my knife, fell to his side.

A thrill shot through me. *It's working.* Making no attempt to take the blade, I sauntered over to him wearing the come-hither expression that'd made me the headliner to one of the most popular strip clubs in town. "You've got to be burning up in that." I reached out and touched the front of his tactical vest.

He swallowed hard and stepped back toward the door. "Stop whatever this is right now."

"What do you mean?" I looked up at him through my lashes while raising the bottom of my sports bra.

He opened his mouth and closed it.

Excellent. I released the bottom of the bra with a snap. "Why don't you show me some new moves? You said it your-self, my fighting skills need work." I stepped closer, forcing him to brush against me or step back.

He stepped back. Something dangerous blazed in his midnight eyes. "You—"

"Shh," I whispered, placing my finger against his warm lips. This close, the masculine spice of his cologne played havoc with my senses.

My breath caught as an unfamiliar ache pulsed inside me. My insides melted and a hot rush of desire pooled low in my belly. *No. I can't let him affect me.* Battling my body's traitorous response to him, I aligned our hips and lifted my mouth toward his.

His breathing shallowed. He whispered something that sounded like my name.

Now. Using the element of surprise, I yanked my knife from his hand at the same time I hooked my foot around his and swept it out from under him.

He fell back into the gift baskets with a crash. Packaged food, crinkle-cut colored paper, and cellophane exploded around us.

I kicked aside a box of candied almonds and waved my knife over him in triumph. "Looks like your defensive skills could also use work."

He said nothing for a moment. "You may be right." His lips quirked up.

My mouth fell open in shock. *Is he actually smiling at me?*

Dominic pushed pieces of broken basket off his chest and sat up. "Your methods are unorthodox, but you got the job done. You can keep the knife."

"Thank you," I muttered. *It figures he's turning my act of defiance into one of his tests.*

"Help me up," he ordered holding one hand out.

I looked at him through a narrowed gaze. *Another test?* I could just imagine him yanking me to the ground to teach me a lesson. My breath caught as my inner tramp warmed to the idea. *Maybe he'll roll on top of me and...*

"No tricks," Dominic said as if reading my mind.

I sheathed my knife and reached over for his outstretched hand.

His fingers wrapped around my wrist.

The sensation of his flesh against mine made goose bumps dance across my skin. I couldn't help noticing how the muscles in his neck flexed like rip cords as he moved. Unable to tear my gaze away, I watched the sleeve of his sand-colored T-shirt ride up. It revealed a blood-crusted oval on the side of his huge bicep.

What? The air froze in my lungs. The mark was unmistakable. *He's been bitten.* Horror had me twisting my hand free and shoving him back.

"What the—" Dominic broke off when he saw my gaze on his arm. He quickly tugged his shirtsleeve down.

"Is that a bite?" My voice shook.

An impassive mask fell over his face. "It's nothing for you to worry about." He pushed himself to his feet.

Like hell. "Were you bitten by a zombie?"

Confirmation was in the stiffening of his shoulders. "We should get back to the safe house."

I shook my head. Emotions blew threw me—shock, denial, and unexpected anguish. The idea of losing this insufferable, stubborn, domineering man gutted me. "S-safe house," I echoed weakly.

He nodded. "I've got another training mission at nine hundred hours."

Dominic's cardinal rule ran through my mind. *All infected must die.* Under no circumstances were any infected survivors to set foot inside the safe house. *He can't go back.* I couldn't allow my feelings for him to endanger the safety of everyone else.

Dominic bent down and picked something off the

ground. "This must be one of those damn fruit pies Trish was going on about. It looks safe to eat."

With shaking hands, I reached for my knife. *Wait. I can't just knife him in the head like the monsters in the street. He deserves a better ending than that.* I grabbed my gun.

Dominic studied the brightly colored package in his hand. "I'll send a team back to gather the food here—" He broke off when he saw my gun pointed at his face. "What are you doing?"

"I can't let you go back to the school with a bite. I'm sorry." My eyes burned as I released the safety. Every muscle in my body tensed. The gunshot would draw Biters. I'd have to run like a demon the moment I pressed the trigger.

"Christ, wait!" He licked his thumb and rubbed it vigorously over the bloody mark on his bicep. "Look." Tension rolled off him as he held out his arm.

I blinked in disbelief. There was nothing under the blood but pinkened flesh. *No bite.* "Thank God." Letting out a shuddering breath, I lowered my gun. The loss of adrenaline left my knees weak and rubbery. "That looked just like a bite." So much so I couldn't imagine anything else that would've left a mark like that.

Dominic's gaze narrowed. "You were ready to kill me."

"I-I'm sorry," I stammered. *Crap. Well, if I wasn't getting thrown out of the safe house for failing the field training test before, I certainly am now.* Wanting the floor to open up and eat me, I studied the tops of my sneakers.

Dominic's shiny black combat boots stomped into view. "Lee, look at me."

Bracing myself for his rage, I slowly looked up into his eyes.

"I'm not mad."

"Y-you're not." I searched his face trying to translate his unfathomable expression.

"Christ, no. That was a very brave thing you did. You've passed the field training test."

My mouth dropped open in shock. "What? You're shitting me." I'd nearly killed him, a commanding officer, in cold blood and he was passing me?

He pressed his lips together as if fighting a smile. "I assure you, I'm not."

A wave of dizzying relief swept over me. Despite my bravado, the idea of trying to keep my family alive outside the safe house terrified me.

Dominic cleared his throat. "Today, you've demonstrated resourcefulness under pressure and a solid understanding of the rules of survival. Here." He pressed the fruit pie into my hand. "Go ahead, have some breakfast, you deserve it."

Eyeing him warily, I opened the palm-sized package. The intoxicating aroma of baked apples filled the air. It'd been weeks since I'd smelled something so divine. With a moan, I bit into the decadent pastry. Each bliss-filled bite was more delicious than the last. Only when I was licking my sticky fingers clean did I realize he was watching me with rapt fascination.

A flash of self-consciousness had me wiping my mouth with the back of my hand. "Did you want one?" I gestured down at the scattered pile of pastries on the ground. "They're amazing. Trish said it's even better than se—" I broke off before I could totally embarrass myself.

Dominic's gaze fell to my lips. "I doubt that." His voice was low and rough. He took a step forward, closing the distance between us.

My mouth went dry and the pie wrapper fluttered from my hand. Suddenly, all I could think about was pressing my mouth against his. Unable to stop myself, I tilted my head up at the same time he lowered his. My eyelids fluttered shut as the warmth of his breath ghosted my sensitized skin.

Bang.

I jerked my eyes open and found a scrawny Biter slamming into the window behind the cash register. The creature's rotting face left a revolting trail of zombie goo on the glass.

Cursing, Dominic stepped away. "Get your clothes on and knife out. You're going to put this one down. This time, remember your training."

Welcome back, drill sergeant. With a deep sigh, I yanked on my shirt and jacket. By the way Dominic averted his gaze as I dressed, it was clear whatever connection we'd temporarily made was gone.

Bang.

The Biter hit the glass again.

I eyed the creature without a trace of fear. How could I be afraid of that sad, skeletal husk when I'd just gone toe-to-toe with one of the most dangerous men in the world, and won. Smiling, I drew my knife.

Dominic eyed my weapon. "You'll have to keep proving you're deserving of that blade."

"Oh, I will...sir." I returned his challenging stare with one of my own. *And you'll have to keep proving the safety you offer is worth putting up with your high-handed attitude.*

His dark eyes flashed with something I could've almost sworn was approval. "Then let's move out." He shoved open the shop door and led me back into hell.

ABOUT DIA COLE

Dia wanted to be a writer from the time she could hold a pencil. A lover of science fiction, urban fantasy, horror, and paranormal romance, she writes action-packed stories featuring kick-butt heroines and the alpha male heroes who fall for them. She is currently working on a post-apocalyptic paranormal romance series.

12

ALONE AGAINST ZOMBIES

BY ALATHIA PARIS MORGAN

It was time for my monthly trek down the mountain and into civilization. While I loved my life as a teacher in this rural community, it was so nice to visit the city.

Most of the time, I got up before it was light, loaded the cart and hitched it to the horse to get a good start down the mountain. The small place I'd grown up in was made up of only a couple hundred people who had never seen a TV or eaten at a fast food restaurant. People told me I was crazy to go back home to teach, but someone needed to give the children a taste of the outside world in case they wanted to try it out sometime. I knew firsthand how much the "outside" world, as the townsfolk called it, was a shock if you weren't prepared for it.

So I made my monthly trip down to bring the "outside" world homemade goods, like quilts and canned vegetables, to sell in exchange for things the town couldn't make or buy for themselves. What I didn't tell the folks was that I enjoyed the outside world, but I wasn't going to find a man in town to marry, and the trips down the mountain gave me a chance to be myself for just a few days. I was related to most of the guys that hadn't left Bethel, and the others were more old-fashioned than I really liked. In the last hundred years, the only people that had stumbled upon our fair town were moonshiners trying to hide or hunters that were lost.

The truck that the town had bought for bigger trips into the world was sitting in a shed to keep others from messing with it in-between trips. It didn't take long to unload the cart's contents into the truck and put Elmer into the corral with food to last for the three days that I would be gone. Also, my Uncle John had a house about a mile over, closer to the road. He would check on Elmer in case I didn't come back on time.

While the truck still looked new, it was over thirty years ago that my dad bought it, before he had returned to the mountain with my mom. It was normal for the guys to go out and find a wife, and then tell her where their family was from after the day long hike up to the town.

I flipped on the radio, but all I heard was static. "Huh, that's weird," I muttered.

The antenna was still attached, but that didn't mean anything, really. I shrugged and pushed the Loretta Lynn tape in the slot, glad that the tapes still worked, even if the radio didn't at the moment.

After what seemed like hours of driving, I began to get this strange feeling as I reached the outskirts of town. Something was off because it was just after daylight, and normally there would be cars on the road, hurrying to work before the weekend got started, but there were no signs of movement anywhere.

The closer I got to town, I realized that the few cars I was seeing were pulled to the side of the road, abandoned. Buildings were boarded up where the windows had been broken, and the intersection's light was blinking instead of turning red or green.

I pulled up and stopped, which seemed silly since there wasn't anyone on the road, much less a car driving on it. Lee's house was only a few blocks from the intersection, but with the abandoned feel of the town, I was pretty certain I wouldn't find him at home.

Approaching his driveway cautiously, I scanned the windows for some sign that he was alive. The empty windows still held the glass, but there was no movement to show that anyone was lurking inside. The worry I'd been holding back grew as I grabbed the rifle from the rack behind the seat of my truck.

Unsure of what I'd find inside, I lifted the gnome and took the key from the bottom where it was hidden, and put it in the keyhole.

"Lee, are you in here?" I called out quietly, not wanting to yell for fear that something would pop out.

Silence greeted me as I moved farther inside, making certain that the door latched behind me. There was a layer of dust on all the furniture, and the house gave off that smell when it's been closed up for a while.

"Where did you go?" I mumbled as I made a sweep through the house to reassure myself that it was empty. The lack of people was starting to remind me of that time when I'd watched the *Twilight Zone,* and all the people had mysteriously vanished.

Trying to decide what my next course of action would be, I noticed a note taped to the fridge with my name scrawled in Lee's handwriting.

Sarah Beth,

If you're reading this, then I'm most likely dead or at my brother Chase's house in Gatlinburg. The zombie apocalypse started about two weeks ago, and I wanted to be with my brother and his kids, but there's no guarantee that I made it there. Cell phones quit working days ago because they were overloaded, so try to call his house phone number before you try to go there to find me. Stay away from the big cities because the zombies look like people, but they will kill you if you're not careful. If I don't answer the phone, go home and don't come back down for at least six months. Maybe by then this sickness that leads to death will have run its course and things will be safe again. Take care of yourself.

Lee.

I yanked the note off the fridge and walked over to the counter where Lee's house phone was located. I dialed the number he'd left and waited for an answer, but it just continued to ring.

Now I had a choice to make: go back up the mountain or go find Lee. When he mentioned zombies, my first thought was that someone had raised the dead and was controlling them, but that didn't seem to fit the rest of his description for what was going on.

I would only worry if I went back up the mountain and didn't at least try to find out what happened to him. While we could potentially wait out the world and come down when it was over, we would have no idea what we were walking into at the edge of our mountain after that time.

Mind made up, I went to open the garage to load the extra gas cans I knew Lee stored there in case of emergencies. While the crates of stuff really wouldn't be needed for resale, there might be someone who needed these items more than I did where I was going.

I finished up and closed the garage door before heading inside, hoping that someone would answer the phone so that I didn't have to go out there and look for Lee.

Again, no answer, confirming my fears that the world had gone crazy and I was about to head out into it for a man that I just hadn't said yes to yet. I patted the gun laying on the seat next to me, just in case I needed it to survive the zombie things.

The same emptiness that had filled the small town was everywhere the closer I got to Gatlinburg, but there were more people just wandering around in the fields, or simply sitting in their cars, heads turning to follow the noise of my truck as I passed them. Nothing about this was feeling normal, and the hairs on my neck were starting to stand up, warning me that something evil was around the corner.

Gatlinburg's outskirts gave way to the heart of the bigger city. I understood what Lee had been trying to warn me about; a bigger city meant more people. While I didn't drive very often, I always tried to follow the traffic rules, and yet when I stopped at the light, which was still working, the group of people that were bunched across the street began to move toward me. I sped up, trying to hurry past them so that they didn't surround my truck. The sound of the muffler made the zombie things move faster, and they continued to follow the trail behind me as I turned down a few side streets, hoping to lose them before I reached Chase's house.

There weren't as many wandering people in the neighborhood, but groups of two or three aimlessly walked around, lifting their heads as I passed by, going too fast for them to move in my direction.

Chase didn't live too far away from the center of town, but his home was boarded up so I couldn't tell if they were inside or not. I glanced up and down the street as I parked in the driveway to see how far away the wandering people were to me and the distance to the front door. He kept a key in the same place as Lee did, so I knew getting inside wouldn't be hard if they hadn't blockaded the door.

They hadn't even locked the door when they left because it opened to my touch. The place had been trashed and was much worse than I had imagined it could be. Someone had put the dining room table against the French doors because the glass was cracked, and they had shoved the couch up against it to help hold it in place. Even the bedrooms had a story to tell, but it was the master bedroom that held a gruesome twist. Blood was spattered on the wall. It had dried, running down to a puddle where the imprint of a head was, the only clean spot on the dirty pillow.

It looked like someone had died, but there wasn't a body lying there anymore, and the house didn't smell like someone was laying around decaying. "They must have buried it outside before they left." The sound of my voice startled me in the quiet of a home with no electricity running throughout it.

I made my way over to the window, careful to step over the blood. Seeing a mound with a cross in it in the back yard confirmed my fears.

"Oh, my God. Chase, or Lee, are dead," I whispered quietly, sinking to the ground with my back against the wall.

The sun was starting to set when I finally roused from my trance. I needed to secure a place to stay safe until morning. In the garage was the safest place to stay that didn't have windows and wouldn't draw the wandering people to me while I managed to try and sleep during the night. Thankfully, it wasn't too cold since it was almost summer, but the concrete floor kept me from getting hot through the long night. My last thought before I drifted off to sleep was, "Tomorrow, I'm going to find them, even if I have to brave the larger city to do it. I have to know if Lee is still alive because I need to say three words to him."

The next morning, I got up and looked through the house, hoping there was something to eat, but it was empty of food, and the water had been shut off. "I guess I'll have to wait until I find them and hope they have some food," I mumbled to myself. There was only one place they would have gone for shelter and safety once their own supplies ran out, which was the church Chase helped at in Knoxville. The church fed the homeless and gave showers to those that wanted them, so the likelihood that whoever was alive would have taken the girls there was pretty high. Staying at the house wasn't going to solve anything, so I made a quick dash to my truck without any of the wandering things trying to get me.

It was over an hour's drive to Knoxville, but the hunger pangs from the past twenty-four hours without food were starting to set in and take away my common sense. I continued to pass fast food places, and the cravings for a burger were growing stronger, especially since I only got to eat them once a month.

When a gas station appeared on the right, I pulled off the road in hopes that there might be food somewhere inside that would keep me from starving. I kept forgetting that the truck was noisy in the quietness from no planes in the sky or cars driving by. The world had grown quiet. There were a few of the wandering people that I'd hoped would stay away, and they looked a little lost when I turned the truck off, making the noise they were drawn to disappear.

Abandoned cars were still sitting at the pumps with doors left open, so I went to grab the rifle and realized that I wanted to have my hands free, but wasn't sure how to make that happen if I carried it inside with me. I opted to leave it on the seat and went to try the door that I was happily surprised to find unlocked. I wasn't sure if this was a good or bad sign. The store was a little off the beaten path, and it looked like I had hit the jackpot because there was still food on the shelves.

I took the bags that were hanging on racks for sale and started filling them with as much food as I could put in them. I had four bags filled and was about to hit the candy bars when a series of thumps came from the back room. "What the hell was that?" I looked around frantically for something to defend myself with, because I was fairly certain that whatever was behind the employees only door was going to try and kill me.

On my right were packages of cupcakes, and on my left was a rack of umbrellas and canes. Not exactly the best choice of weapons, but they were better than nothing. I gripped a cane with both hands and approached the back slowly, taking time to look through the doors of the walk-in, hoping that I could see something that would let me know what was making all the noise.

The doorknob turned and I pushed the door open, holding the cane in front of me. "I should've brought the gun inside with me. I'm so stupid," I muttered as my eyes tried to adjust to the back room, which was much darker than the front. I crept inside, jumping when the door slammed behind me.

I couldn't see anything, but the thumping was louder

and closer to me as I tried to see. The exit signs were still working and cast a red glow, allowing me to make out something in the back corner that was moving. It looked like a person, but I'd already come this far, and it might be someone who needed my help.

A shadowy figure moved between the shelves and jumped out at me as I rounded the corner. The figure landed on top of me, but it wasn't what I expected. It was a cardboard cutout that had fallen over when the cat knocked into it. The kitty jumped down and rubbed itself along my body and nuzzled my face.

"Aw, you poor thing, all cooped up in here by yourself. You must've started making noise to get my attention." I patted its head as I rolled onto my knees.

Another noise had me reaching out for the cane that had fallen, but I was too late. An arm reached though the shelves and pulled on my hair as I frantically tried to reach behind me and get released from its grip. All I could feel was saggy skin that tore, leaving me holding the bone connecting to an arm. I just needed to break the arm, and the boxes sitting on the shelf between us would do that if I could push them down onto the person on the other side.

Everything crashed down around me and the thing on the other side, causing the arm to separate, but left a still moving hand stuck in my hair. Crawling toward the doorway and freedom, I left it hanging from my hair. The knob slipped in my fingers because they were covered in skin, so I pulled the edge of my shirt up and turned the knob, watching the cat scurry out the door before me. I made sure that the door closed after us so the thing wouldn't be able to get out.

Now that I wasn't fighting for my life, I reached up and yanked the hand from my hair, becoming frustrated as the fingers pulled at my scalp. When it finally came free, I threw it across the room, hoping to put some space between us. I spotted a sink next to the food area, so I grabbed a gallon bottle of water and poured dish soap over my hands, leaning the gallon on the side to rinse with. I scrubbed and rescrubbed my hands until my skin turned red. I wasn't going to hang around to pack up anything else, but as I scooped up the four bags that were packed and headed to the door, the cat let out a horrible sound.

"All right, you can come with me." I balanced the bags and hoped that the cat was friendly, and didn't scratch the hell out of me when I picked it up.

"Here, kitty, kitty. Come on and play nice with me. Let's go." It let me pick it up and cuddle it in the crook of my arm.

Amazed, I backed through the swinging front door and made a mad dash for the truck. I didn't want to let the food or the cat out of my sight, so I opened the passenger door and placed everything on the seat. If the cat jumped out before I got in the truck, then it would have to find a way to survive on its own.

Oddly enough, it was sitting in the center of the seat like it owned the world. She—and it was a she because I caught a glimpse of its parts—just sat there looking at me. "Yeah, yeah, I'll get going." It must be the end of the world because I was talking out loud to a cat.

The truck backfired as I started it, and I didn't try to be quiet since I was moving quickly. Knoxville was only ten minutes up the main highway, but I wasn't going to go on any major streets, so it would take closer to twenty if none of the roads to the church were blocked.

Each street I crossed held more of the wandering people in groups that were becoming more dangerous. I had to reverse and turn around several times to take another longer route. The groups of people were close enough that I could see blood dripping from their noses, and the sagging skin hanging off their bodies. I wanted to pull over and puke, but there simply wasn't time if I was going to make it to the church. I gripped the wheel harder and tried not to look at the horror of the people around me. My truck was drawing these things toward me, and I had no idea how long it would be before they completely surrounded me.

I spotted a parking garage and drove up into it, turning the engine off and sitting quietly. I was hoping that the crowds of dead would keep walking in a straight line, leaving the road free for me to go back over to the area where the church was located. This idea was beginning to seem dumber by the minute. If the streets were this full, then why was I holding out hope that a church full of people would be holding some live ones?"

The wait seemed like forever, but was only an hour before my view of the street showed it to be empty. I hated that the truck was so noisy, but there wasn't anything I could do about it at the moment. The church appeared to be empty as I got closer, and I was afraid that everything I'd gone through would be for nothing.

In the bell tower of the church, I saw movement and parked the truck on the edge of the lot. I didn't want to bring the wandering people to the church, and I could make a run for it. Now, if they would just let me into the building, but I figured I should leave the food until I'd found out what the situation was.

A bus had been pulled in front of the doors that led to

the Red Cross safe area. When I approached, the back door flew open, and a guy with a gun stepped out.

"This way, miss. Hurry." He waved toward me.

I scooped up the cat and closed the door quietly, taking off at a run. The guy stood in the emergency doorway and pulled it shut behind me, and walked the length of the bus to the front door that opened into the church.

The cat jumped out of my arms once we were inside, but then were filled by Chase's daughters, Hope and Charity. Relief that they were alive flooded me, but then I looked up to see Lee standing just a step behind them, waiting for them to move. I met his gaze and saw the sadness lingering there. Chase was dead.

Yet, tears of joy streamed down my face, and I knew that no matter what choice I made for my future, it was going to be by Lee's side for as long as he would have me. I wanted us to have a life together, even if it was a shorter version of it.

For more of Lee and Sarah Beth's story, check out Churches Against Zombies

ABOUT ALATHIA PARIS MORGAN

Alathia Paris Morgan is a part-time writer. With the death of her brother in 2013, she decided life was too short to waste the ideas she was given. Since she'd always had stories floating around in her head, she took a shot at writing them down during a NANOWRIMO Camp. She realized quickly that her characters had more than one mystery to solve, which resulted in her Nova Ladies series.

With the support and love of her husband, Alathia continues to bring new worlds to life. Their three daughters and three dogs are more than enough to keep her busy when she is not delivering orders or lost in her imagination.

In her free time, she loves to read and add to her personal library, which has over six thousand books. She also enjoys quilting and watching TV shows while hanging out with her daughters.

13

GODS AND MONSTERS

BY RICH RESTUCCI

University of Oxford. Oxford, England. 2018 AD

"And, as seen in this map, the city of Thanatos was once a travel hub for caravans from the east. Exotic furs, scents, meats, and of course, salt was traded in its vast marketplace." The professor used a laser pointer to indicate a small area on a huge pull-down map of Greece attached to the wall of his lecture hall.

The professor continued, "Now, history tells us that the city was sacked by an unidentified enemy, pitiless and without mercy. The state of the ruins and some of the bones found indicate the citizens of Thanatos died violent deaths, indeed." He held up his right index finger, "But! Other ancient accounts claim that a horrible disease struck the city and the entire populace died overnight." The lecturer shook his head. "No one dared enter the city for almost two hundred years after that fateful event. In the wake of the disaster, the name of the city was associated with the god of death, or even death itself."

"Like we needed more gods back then," a woman in the

very back of the hall whispered to her companion. There were a dozen rows of seats between the two of them and the rest of the students.

The man with her harrumphed, patting the printed leopard on his sweatshirt and adjusting his sunglasses. He pointed to the map, "I remember the whole episode differently. And as I recall, a few more gods might have helped."

The woman reached into her jacket with something between her fingers. The head of an owl tentatively reached out, grabbing the offered morsel and swallowing. The animal receded back into the folds of the jacket immediately. "I'm surprised you remember anything. You were drunk the whole damn time."

"I'm the fucking god of wine, sister. I *invented* that shit. What, was I not supposed to drink? What kind of message would that have sent?"

"You spent two thousand years shitfaced. Congratulations, it's a record."

"I guess the memory is a bit fuzzy." He pointed to the professor, "This guy is wrong anyway. Well, half wrong." He shook his head, "Fucking mortals."

"No, brother, he's more right than he knows."

Acharnae, Greece. 612 BC

"We must flee, Antrius! They are upon us! The city is lost."

The small boy looked to his mother in fear, "Where is father?"

"Athena preserve him, he battles to give us time." The woman grasped her terrified son by both shoulders, sinking to one knee to match his eight-year old height, "We must not waste this time! Take up your sword. I have packed us provisions for a few days." She stood and pulled her long dead father's shield from its place of reverence on the wall.

An evil had sprung up in her city. She had been witness to this creeping evil earlier in the day. Several people, bloody and screaming, had leapt upon some citizens when she was at market not two hours hence. When the men and women began to rend and bite their victims, she had dropped her basket and run. She had hoped the soldiers would slay the evil, but the horrible noises, the smoke, and the sound of the Great Horn told her she and her son were in danger. The Horn had called both the guard and the militia to fight off whatever had come.

She pulled the iron handle to open the cracked and warped wooden door that would lead them into the city. She and her husband raised their child on the outskirts and this could be their salvation. She cast a quick glance left, the way looking clear. A glimpse to the right, down the hill, and she beheld the city she had called home for nigh thirty years.

Acharnae burned. Her beloved temple of Demeter was afire, as were a dozen houses and the market. Between the flames shadowy figures leapt on fleeing citizens, bringing them down. She could see the militia, of which her husband was a captain, fighting the things in the streets with sword and spear. The enemy needed no such weapons, but instead brandished tooth and nail.

"Now, Antrius!"

Mother and son bolted from their home down the cobbled street toward the city wall. The door to everything they had held dear left open behind them. Not fifty steps from their dwelling, a dark-haired woman stumbled from the foliage on their right. She held her right arm with her left hand and even in the semi-darkness, it was easy to see she was injured.

The woman noticed mother and son. "Desma?" she asked through obvious pain.

Desma knew this woman. She had met her when she had fetched a scroll for Desma in the library near the temple of Apollo some twenty years past. They had become fast friends, as had their families.

"Jacinda?" Desma questioned. "My friend, what has befallen you?"

"They came in the night. Demons in the form of men. Savage ghosts wearing the flesh of the living!" Jacinda retched, obviously ill. Even through the gloom of the evening, Desma could tell her friend's color was that of rancid cream.

Desma pushed Antrius behind her and raised her shield slightly, "Ghosts?"

"My mother, dead these two days, came to us from her grave under the olive trees." Jacinda gritted her teeth as she spoke, blood flowed from between her fingers in crimson torrents. Fat drops struck the cobbles beneath her. "My husband heard her in the garden and went to help. She bit into him, scratching and tearing! She devoured him as he screamed!"

"Devoured him? Gods, what devilry is this?"

"I do not know! I pushed her away from him and struck her with my shovel, a blow that would have felled a Roman barbarian, but she wouldn't stop and came at me. She bit me here before I was able to flee into the house and bolt the door."

Jacinda showed her friend her arm. A large chunk of the forearm was missing, the wound horrible. She crushed her eyelids together in agony.

"I ran from the house, but before I left, I saw my husband was screeching and pounding on the rear door aside my mother. It was not him, Desma, it was something else."

"What else?"

"A demon had taken him," Jacinda cried, fear and confusion briefly replacing the rictus of agony on her face.

"Fly with us to the wall, Jacinda. We will seek shelter with the guard or flee the city."

The three of them made for the city gates. Desma knew that even with the attacks happening inside the walls, the guard would never leave the gates. She tugged at Antrius, her son was small, but too large to carry should she need to use her shield.

They were within sight of the gate torches when Jacinda dropped to one knee, her hand palm down on the ground. She didn't glance up when she said in a choked voice, "Leave me, Desma, I am spent."

Antrius knelt beside her. He reached under her arm and tried to stand and carry the heavier woman, but he lacked the strength. He struggled until his mother knelt and did the same with Jacinda's left arm. Even through her bloody tunic, Desma could feel a fever raged. Her friend's skin gave off heat like a furnace. They were able to get the woman on unsteady feet and they moved forward. The pride Desma held for her caring son was interrupted by a figure who burst from the cypress bushes to their left. The figure, a woman by her dress, stood partially hunched over and heaving, staring in the direction of the city. Antrius let loose with a quick gasp and the stranger whipped her head around to glare at the trio of Archarnians. The woman raised her face to the heavens and shrieked, long and loud. The sound sent tendrils of terror down Desma's spine. It was a screech no mortal could make.

The thing righted its gaze and Desma could see sadness

in its face. For an instant she thought everything would be fine, then the thing's lips curled into a snarl as sadness transformed to rage. The woman-thing sprinted toward the small group and Desma was forced to let go of Jacinda. She brought her shield to bear just as the creature reached her, the impact sending them both sprawling. Astride her, the thing scratched and snapped at the shield between them, trying to pull it away to rend the flesh behind it. Desma began to scream as she realized the teeth and claws would reach her in moments.

Salvation came in the form of Antrius' short sword. He thrust the blade into the side of the creature, who paused for the briefest of moments to glare at the boy. The stab should have felled anyone, but this thing only showed more rage. Antrius yanked the weapon from the attacker, raising it high as the thing leapt at him. Desma felt the creature's weight shift and reached for the thing's ankle to slow it, but she was woefully short.

Antrius yelled as he brought the dripping blade downward upon the thing's crown with both hands. He had trained with his father in the sword, remembering a killing blow when he saw one, and this was no exception. The blade cleaved the woman's head in two, the evil in it released in death. The thing fell to the cobbles, lifeless.

"Mother," the boy shouted, a smile on his face, "did you see? I killed it with my sword!"

Desma stood coming to her son. The shield was heavy, and her arm sore from the thing that had been atop her. "I saw, my son. You saved us. Your father's heart will swell when he hears of this, as does mine." She hugged him, holding him close, her love resolute.

A growling hiss came from behind them. They both

spun to see their wounded friend hunched over and shaking.

"Jacinda?"

Jacinda jerked her head up and stared at them. Desma lost her water as she looked into the eyes of the thing before her. There was nothing left of Jacinda in the obsidian orbs that stared back. Gone was her family friend of twenty years. Gone were mercy and compassion. These emotions had been replaced with a black malice and incomprehensible hunger.

The thing that had been Jacinda shrieked and scrabbled toward them on all fours. There would be no time to get the shield in place and Desma lived a lifetime in the next few moments. She felt something fly past her right ear, her auburn hair moving slightly with the wind of the object's passing. A shaft protruded from Jacinda's left eye and she tumbled to the ground. Three men approached, two holding spears and one with a bow. Instinctively, Desma attempted to push her son behind her, but the boy stood firm, sword clasped in both hands.

The torch in the fist of one of the spear holders illuminated the men enough that Antrius yelled, "Father!" and rushed to the bowman. The man knelt to accept the boy's small frame in a fatherly embrace.

"Antrius. You are well?"

"Yes father. I slew a demon!" The boy turned and pointed at the thing on the ground.

"The blood of Ares must flow through your veins, my son!"

Desma rushed to her husband and embraced her family. She let loose a sigh of relief, "Pelias. I feared you had fallen."

"Many have," he stated simply. "You have your father's shield." He nodded in approval, "You'll need it."

One of the spearmen, Abantes, pointed down the street toward the market square, "Pelias!"

Everyone peered through the darkness. The flames in the city proper exposed a mob of slavering things dashing up the cobbled road.

Pelias scooped up his son and the five of them sprinted to the gates. A mere hundred yards and the things chasing them had more than halved the gap. Upon reaching the gate, the two spearmen took up defensive positions on either side of the inner eastern tower door. Pelias rushed through the door with his son, his wife immediately behind.

"Come!" he bellowed to his spearmen. Both made it inside and they were able to slam the heavy oaken door and shoot the three bolts home before the vanguard of the horde hit it. The things stretched torn and bloody limbs through the barred viewport in the gate, reaching with broken fingers toward the flesh they hungered for.

The tower was made to repel invaders, constructed of massive granite blocks mortared together. Both towers had stood for three hundred years. Pelias added two stout oaken bars to the braces on the back of the door for extra protection. The other spearman, Theras, lit two more torches with his torch and passed one to Pelias and the other to Abantes.

"The tower is secure," Theras stammered. "They cannot get in."

"Nor we out." Pelias stared at the things reaching for them not a yard from where they stood. He recognized the butcher's son, a good young man who now wanted nothing more than to rend and tear. "Let us move to the top of the tower to better see the city and our fate."

Dawn peeked over the eastern horizon, the white stone catching and reflecting the rays. Sunlight showed a group of five perched atop the eastern tower gate of Archarnae. They stared down at thousands of the people of their city. The citizens stared back, reaching and clawing at the walls of the tower. Inhuman shrieks made Antrius cover his ears. The square below seethed with writhing bodies, all seeking the flesh of the living.

Pelias regarded the things. All sported horrible wounds, some were missing limbs. One such creature dragged itself down the street toward them. It had no bottom half and entrails dragged behind it painting a crimson swath in the dust.

"They are all dead," the soldier lamented.

"This cannot be..." Desma breathed, "they are dead but alive..."

Pelias reached out to his son, Antrius moving to his father. He pulled the boy into a kneel, indicating Desma should follow. "We must pray. We must ask the gods what we have done to bring their wrath upon us, but more, we must know why we were spared and what we must do."

They clasped their hands together and bowed their heads as one. The spearmen lay their weapons on the stone and knelt as well.

Olympus.

The throne was cold today. Cold and hard. Some days he didn't feel it, but today... today screamed of violence and deceit. Lightning coursed across his fingers as he heard his sister call him.

"Zeus! Zeus, have you not seen?"

Demeter burst into the council room. Spying her brother on his throne she rushed over and knelt before him.

"Rise, sister. "What ails you?"

"My city," she cried. "My greatest temple! Gone!"

"Gone? Gone how?"

"Come, brother. Away to the Pool!" She reached her hand to him, a small breach of etiquette which he always overlooked. Zeus loved his siblings. Most of them. He took her hand and she pulled him to the Gazing Pool.

They stared at a great marble basin, five yards across at least. The water within began to ripple slightly, then a picture of a burning city took the place of the shimmer.

Zeus shook his head, "Fools. We swaddle them in our love and they squander it with battles and blood. Have you spoken with Ares? This looks to be his doing."

"No, brother, look again!" The picture changed, and Zeus watched a nightmare unfold. Thousands of drooling citizens prowled the city in the morning light. The men and women were bloody and filthy, many sporting wounds that no living mortal could endure. Zeus watched as a man made a run from a doorway. The things spotted him and gave chase, bringing him down in moments. They tore into him with tooth and claw, ripping his entrails from his still screaming body and biting his flesh over and over. The scene was done in just a few seconds, and the things stood, dripping. The Lord of the Sky gaped when the man who had just been killed stood and joined the very group who had just murdered him. They sprinted down the street, shrieking. The man had been dead for certain and then had risen. This infuriated Zeus as only the gods should possess immortality.

Zeus pointed in fury, "What is this?" Before Demeter could answer, Zeus bellowed. The sound shook the very foundations of Olympus itself, the Pantheon being called to the council chamber.

The Twelve sat in their chairs, all having seen the

horrors the Pool had to show. Seven others stood behind the council, awaiting what was to happen.

"Tell me," Zeus demanded. "Tell me which of you is responsible for this treachery." He stared intently at each of the eleven gods seated around the table. None had spoken, and this further incensed him. Thunder boomed and lightning crackled as he brought his fist down on the thick, white marble. The table split in two and several of the gods knew fear.

"Tell me!" Zeus bellowed again.

A helmeted god balanced his spear against the broken stone and put his hands on the table, cords rippling. He attempted to becalm his enraged leader. "Set your mind at ease, father. None here would dare destroy your precious mortals without your permission." The God of War gave a half-smile, "Can you not think of who might have constructed a living death for mankind? What an insult this must be."

Ares' passive aggressive attempt at tranquility worked, but his suggestion as to the cause of this betrayal fueled Zeus' considerable rage.

"HADES! TO ME!"

Ares smiled when Hades failed to show. "Looks like he might be busy, father."

Acharnae

"I am frightened, father"

Pelias nodded in agreement, "As am I, Antrius. Only a fool would have no fear when looking upon this horde." The soldier bent a knee to speak to his son directly, "It is how we handle ourselves when fear takes hold that dictates our fate."

One of the spearmen picked up a heavy rock usually spent on attackers outside the gates and threw it down on the beasts below. The stone struck one of the things in the shoulder, crushing bones and drawing blood. The creature howled and screamed, but not in pain. It was hunger these things felt.

The defenders had tried oil as well, heated by a sconce beneath the cauldron. The boiling liquid poured down on the former Acharnians, but they paid no heed as flesh melted away. Pelias fired a flaming arrow into their midst, setting the oil ablaze. Dozens of the things collapsed after being roasted by the fire, but for every one that dropped three took its place. They burned as well until the flames burnt out.

The horde was thick. Two hundred deep on this side of the wall at least, but very few on the other side. Pelias considered this as he glanced at his son. An eight-year old would not be able to make the eight-mile run to the sea. Pelias doubted he could finish the run himself with the dead on his heels.

He was watching the center of the mob when he noticed a golden gleam. The gleam intensified until it exploded into a light too bright to look upon. A thunderous explosion rent the air sending dead Acharnians flying out from the epicenter. In the now clear center of the square, stooped upon broken stone, knelt a figure in gilded armor with a golden Spartan helmet. One fist upon the ground, a golden spear gripped in the other. The massive weapon reached eight yards at least. The helm's red plume shifted as the figure turned its gaze toward the dead knocked down by his arrival. He stood, his height topping four yards.

"Fear me mortals," the figure roared. "Ares is come!"

The fallen dead also stood. They echoed the godly roar with malicious shrieks, sprinting toward the towering figure. Muscles rippling, the God of War swung the spear in a wide arc, slicing through the vanguard of the deep ranks of dead. Again, bodies flew, this time sundered. Ares thrust and spun, using his spear to keep his assailants at bay. They fell like wheat before the sickle, but they were too many and felt no fear. The ones split asunder crawled beneath their brothers, intent on the flesh in front of them. They didn't differentiate between gods and men.

An eagle alighted on a rampart near Pelias and his family. The majestic bird watched the battle unfold below, glancing once at the humans in the tower before focusing on the fight for some minutes. When Antrius looked for the eagle again, it was gone.

Ares thrust his spear behind him and drew a gleaming sword. He brought the spear back over his head, struggling figures impaled upon it, and smashed it into the surging tide of death. Two dozen dead were pulped and the swing of his sword split a dozen more. He strode forward, his gilded sandal lashing out to crush four of the dead Acharnians who had gotten close.

The humans atop the tower, rapt with the destruction the god dealt, failed to notice several of the things closing in on Ares' blind spot. Save one. "Ares, behind you!" screamed a terrified Antrius through cupped hands.

Ares swung his spear to the rear as he swung his sword to the front. He spun in a circle, once, twice, then a third time, slicing through the dead that encroached upon him. The move slowed the front ranks considerably, but only the foes who lost their heads ceased to attack. He suddenly felt one such undestroyed on his back, scrabbling for purchase, but just as suddenly it fell away, an arrow in its skull. The son of Zeus noticed several more of the monsters down, their skulls also pierced by feathered shafts. A quick glance to the towers showed a bowman raining darts down with godly accuracy.

Ares took quick stock of his situation. He had never beheld opponents such as these. No matter how much effort he expended on their destruction, he lost ground. As the things closed, something unfamiliar crept into Ares' very soul: fear.

"Oh shit..." he said as the things leapt the final yards toward him.

Olympus

His chin in his hand, Zeus looked old. Ten thousand battles commanded on ten thousand fronts and never had he seen death and destruction like this. Even the battles with Cronos paled in comparison.

"Six of my human cities lost," he whispered to no one. "The dead feed in the mountains of Ionia and legions of them reap the plains of Thrace. Ares battles them in Acharnae, Athena in Delphi. Poseidon mows them down in Knossos and still they come." The King of Gods angrily brushed eagle feathers from his cape. "Enough! Hades will pay for this treachery! His time has come." Zeus stood. His robes burned away to reveal hidden armor of blue and white with gilded edges. Lightning flashed as he flexed his fingers.

Hera, wife and sister to Zeus, rushed to his side. "Husband, where do you go?"

"Tartarus!" he roared and disappeared in a flash.

His wrath knew no bounds as Zeus materialized into Hades' palace. "HADES," he bellowed, "you go too far! Face me, brother, do not cower! Fear does not become you!"

Zeus pointed his palm at Hades' gilded throne, white lightning lancing from his fingertips. The chair exploded, sending stone fragments throughout the vast room. "Where are you?" he demanded.

Only the echoes of his yell and the rain of dust from the destroyed throne answered him. Zeus noticed a hulking mass, bloody and unmoving some four dozen yards away. He strode across the chamber, his brow furrowed in confusion. The King of Olympus knelt next to the lifeless body of Hades' favorite pet. He sighed, placing his hand upon the ebony fur and stroking it for a moment in grief.

"Cerberus. You did not deserve this, my friend. Hades crimes will not go unpunished, I swear on my throne."

Zeus cocked his head to listen to sounds emanating from the halls behind him. A scrabbling noise, which bolstered as it came closer, made the god smile. A shimmering bolt of lightning grew in his fist like a spear, "Finally..."

The Thunderer was completely unprepared for what came next. The vanguard of ten thousand souls burst through the towering bronze doors, all chasing a larger figure. "Brother!" Hades screamed as he ran, "Help me!" The things leapt upon the God of the Underworld as he struggled to escape them. He tossed them away, thrusting with his bident. The fire which shot from his fingertips roasted three dozen of the things, but there were too many. Hades went down under a hundred of the creatures, and there were thousands more to come.

Zeus' hesitation was only momentary. He threw his bolt at the revolting creatures which began to fill the massive room. The bolt struck the front ranks of the teeming dead, incinerating some and tossing others several yards in the air. They landed broken and burnt, but not destroyed. The rear ranks trampled the fallen to get at Hades and his brother.

"Not today, vermin!" bellowed the King of Gods. Another bolt formed in the fist of the massive figure. He strode forward swinging the bolt as he would a sword. Lightning flew from his free hand as he swung the bolt back and forth, crisping his brother's attackers or outright disintegrating them. Zeus grabbed Hades by his robes and threw the God of the Underworld behind him, where he rolled to a stop against the shattered throne. Zeus continued to fire chain lightning and swing his bolt as the creatures advanced. They were utterly fearless, careless even, with their own existence as they ran heedless into lightning. The Thunderer regarded the situation as he destroyed the dead by the hundreds. He then did something he had only done once before; he backed away from a foe. All of Tartarus seemed to stream through the massive doors into the throne room, spreading like a malignant plague across the marble floors and edging ever forward. Hundreds of thousands strong, the host of obsidian-eyed things raced at the gods.

Zeus made a powerful bound, landing next to Hades a few hundred feet from their attackers. He noticed that the robes of the powerful Underworld God were ragged and spattered with vile fluids. He grasped Hades by the shoulder and dragged him to his feet. Hades pointed out the gothic window of his palace into Tartarus, "Look, brother."

As far as his vision would stretch, Zeus saw millions upon millions of the denizens of Tartarus racing across the vast plains and craggy red peaks of the Underworld. They came like a black tide, screaming as they dashed toward the palace with a single-minded goal.

"Impossible..." he breathed. He turned his gaze upon his brother, "Hades, what have you done?" Grasping Hades by the arm, Zeus transported them both to Olympus, the wails of the dead echoing behind them.

Zeus stood tall on the marbled floors of Olympus, but Hades landed in a heap. Ten of the council members sat in their chairs around the great table. Only Ares was unaccounted for.

The King of Gods pointed his finger down upon Hades, "EXPLAIN!"

Hades glared up at his brother, "Look upon me, Zeus! Drink deep this sight, and despair, for I have not the power to accomplish this!" Hades held out his forearms. Deep furrows ran down his left arm, and two small bites adorned the right. Already a puddle of red seeped from beneath his robes. "I bleed, brother!"

The council stood as one, some gasping, others crying out in disbelief.

"This cannot be..." marveled Zeus.

Acharnae

Ares leapt almost two hundred feet from the square to the western tower. He crashed through the flimsy thatched roof of the tower cap landing on the top floor. The door to this tower had not been sealed, dozens of the dead already sprinted up the wooden stairs. Ares made a much shorter leap to the eastern tower, landing amid the living humans. Several of the dead leapt off the tower after him to plummet fifteen yards to the square below.

Four of the humans fell to their knees when Ares landed, their foreheads touching the ground. Antrius remained standing, his mouth agape. The bowman reached up to drag the child to a more respectful position and Ares smiled.

"Rise, mortals."

The humans lifted their eyes and gazed upon Ares in awe. Only the boy stood. "You, boy," the god began, "you had the courage to give warning and the bravery to stand before me first." Antrius could barely discern anything over the din of the dead in the square, but the voice of Ares was like nothing he had heard before. "I would give you the gift of unfailing valor, but it seems you have it aplenty already. These will have to suffice." A golden sword and shield appeared in the boy's hands. "Strike the sword on the shield, boy."

Antrius did as he was instructed. The sword was instantly enveloped in flames. He held it at arm's-length, so as not to be burned.

"The sword will not burn you boy, and any weapon that strikes your shield in malice will shatter. Use them wisely." Ares cast his glance at Pelias. "Bowman, your aim is true. Let it remain so. You will never want for another shaft. Nor your spearman for javelins."

Ares focused on Desma. "Woman, this honorable man has taken you for his own and together you birthed the child before me. I bestow upon you the gift of sight. Danger will never come without prior knowledge."

The mortals fell to their knees in front of their god and he smiled again. "Rise once more, mortals." Ares glanced over his shoulder at the yowling creatures at the foot of the tower. "I must away from this place. The city is lost, and these things disgust me. Where I go you cannot follow. I will bring you anywhere you wish to go, but only this once."

The humans stood as one and regarded each other.

Pelias put his hand on his son's shoulder. "Mighty Ares, we thank you for these gifts. We will use them to clear our city of these foul creatures."

"Be certain, mortal. I offer transport but once."

Pelias gripped his son as he looked to his wife. Both of his spearmen also nodded. "We will stay and fight, if it would please the God of War."

Ares laughed. "What a creation Zeus has wrought! You creatures have the capacity for such cowardice and such courage. Rarely have I seen valor such as this. I bid you good fortune," the god concluded and vanished inside the same gleam of light from which he had arrived.

Desma turned and screamed, pointing. Where Antruis had been stood a warrior, fit and strong with the sword and shield Ares had gifted to her boy. The man looked himself over and laughed. He took a knee, placing the sword on the ground, "Mother, it is your son grown. Ares has bestowed a second gift." Antrius stood and looked to his right, "Father, shall we rid Acharnae of these vermin?"

Olympus

The throne room was vacant when Ares appeared near the Pool. Several of the stone chairs were overturned, one broken. A tattered robe lay on the ground, gold-red fluids staining it and the floor around it.

Ares usually arrived to some flourish from Aphrodite and glances of hatred from Hephaestus. Neither were present. In fact, no one was present, and this struck Ares as odd. There was always one god or another in the room. Where was Zeus? He should have been on the throne or by the pool directing the other gods on how to destroy the evil that was ravaging his precious humans.

No god, save perhaps Zeus, had seen as many battles as Ares, and he knew a battlefield when he saw one. A battle had raged here. A clash between gods was not unheard of, but it was *never* carried out on Olympus. No god would desecrate their home by physical combat, that is what the earth was for.

A scratching sound on the far side of the huge marble table caught his attention. Ares strode past the end of the slab to see a figure slumped in a bloody heap on the cold stone floor. The figure raked its broken nails over the floor once more before it pushed itself from the ground with one hand. It rose on unsteady feet, heaving and making odd and terrible sounds.

"Hermes, what has transpired here?" demanded the God of War.

The figure pivoted its head to glare at Ares.

Ares drew a quick breath, "Brother, no…"

Obsidian orbs burned into Ares' very soul. Red-gold blood seeped from a ragged hole in Hermes' neck further soaking his stained tunic. Ares blinked, but before his lids had finished moving, the thing was upon him. Ares brought his spear to bear, but he was not fast enough, for this was Hermes, the God of Speed. The dead thing clawed at its living brother, slashing bloody channels into the neck of the God of War. Ares pitched the thing away from him, the body of his brother crashing into the side of the Pool. The creature was up in an instant, but Ares was ready. He thrust his spear into the chest of his brother, who grasped the shaft and pulled the spear deeper. Penetrating the skin of a fellow god was impossible, but the spear had pierced the flesh easily. This thing was no longer a god, but it possessed the speed Hermes had in life. Ares smiled and brought his sword down upon Hermes' left shoulder. The blade bit deep into the flesh, lodging halfway down the side of the carcass. The dead thing struggled down the length of the spear to reach Ares, but the living god let loose with a tremendous kick, sending the dead god sprawling yet again.

It was Ares' turn for speed, and he leapt into the air, drawing his spear back then thrusting it forward into Hermes' side, pinning the dead god to the marble tiles. The creature's struggles ceased when Ares brought his gleaming sword down upon the thing's ruined neck. The head of Hermes came away cleanly, a golden winged circlet rolling off into a table leg with a metallic ring. Eyes as black as pitch rolled back into the thing's skull, the lids closing slowly.

Ares took a huge breath and let it out slowly. He didn't know if Zeus would praise or punish him for killing another of the gods. Any other time he would have either been imprisoned in Tartarus, or had his immortality stripped away by his father, but this time... Hermes was clearly no longer a friend to the gods, or even a god himself. Perhaps Zeus would forgive him for this transgression?

As the God of War pondered his fate, his brother's eyes opened, and the mouth began snapping, teeth clicking together loudly.

"Enough!" Ares roared, the tip of his spear piercing the severed skull. He picked up the head by the hair and placed it on the edge of the pool, the red-gold blood of a god dribbling down the white stone.

Ares felt an odd sensation nip at his throat, the god absently brushed at his neck. He failed to notice the stain on the back of his hand. He trod down the halls of Olympus, seeking out his family.

Acharnae

"I feel them, but I don't know where they are." Desma searched in several directions "I can't see them."

"Nor can I," one of the spearmen added. He lowered the palm he had held over his eyes to shield the sun, and glanced below at the piles of truly dead Acharnians. There were thousands heaped upon one another. The cobbled streets ran red with the blood of the citizenry; men, women, and children in a great pile at the base of the tower. One such thing, a dark-haired boy, climbed from under several heavy bodies. It howled at the living humans atop the tower, breaking its nails on the stone in its haste to tear into them.

"Forgive me, child," Pelias whispered. He drew back the string of his bow and a wooden shaft appeared, nocked and ready. He let loose the arrow, the child-thing below released of its misery. Hundreds of shafts protruded from the skulls of the fallen.

"Three days we have destroyed these things with spear and shaft," said Theras, "and still they come." He pointed to one of the things streaking toward the tower. He drew back his arm, the shaft of his spear steady. The thing sprinted, bloody and howling. The spearman threw his projectile, striking the creature between the eyes. It tumbled to the cobbles, landing at the feet of a dozen of the destroyed, all with similar wounds. The throw had been impossible. Thirty yards and perfectly on its mark. Theras held his hand out, the shaft in the skull of the creature quivering slightly. Suddenly the spear shot back to its owner alighting perfectly in his hand.

Pelias regarded his band of slayers. Two were his family, two his friends. He knew what was to come next and he dreaded it. His son, grown from boy to man by the will of a god, was difficult to look upon. Pelias loved him still, but felt they would both miss the child's life the boy should have had. Growing, learning, laughter, and tears: gone. The bowman glanced at the heaps of dead, many of them children, and cursed himself a fool. If not for the gifts of Ares, his son would have been dead these three days past. He shook his head, silently begging Ares to forgive his sentiment.

"We must leave."

The spearmen and Desma turned to Pelias questioningly.

"We must rid the city of the rest of the dead. None must escape. When we are done, we must head to the docks at Penteleimon. We must warn the council of what has happened in Acharnae. They will send the Hoplites to other cities to ensure none of the dead escaped here to spread this plague."

Antrius gazed upon his sword, the blade cool and sharp, "Finally."

"Do not wish for war, my son, or you will find it," Pelias admonished.

Antrius lowered his head, "I only wish to end it, father."

As the group strode down the street, weapons bristling, Desma glanced back at the tower she had called home for almost four days. Both sanctuary and prison, she thanked the gods for it. She also gave thanks that her son had been spared the fate of so many other children.

They weaved between the corpses now rotting in the sun, taking care to make sure nothing moved. They were already beginning to smell, and as Desma brought her wrist to her nose in disgust, she felt a tingling from her right side. She quickly turned her gaze in that direction, her vision able to pierce through buildings and the aqueduct. She spied three red pulses coming from a few hundred yards to the right. They were coming fast.

"Danger from the north!" she whispered.

The four warriors faced north, but only a bloody fountain and an overturned vegetable cart greeted them.

"There," she pointed, "beneath the aqueduct."

"I see nothing," one of the spearmen offered.

Antrius touched his sword to his shield and it erupted into flame. Two of the infected sprinted under one of the arches of the aqueduct followed closely by a third. "I see them, mother. Stand ready!"

Pelias drew his bowstring back to his cheek, a shaft appearing on the nock, both spearmen raised their weapons ready to cast. The first of the creatures shrieked, the horrible sound echoed by the second and third beasts.

At the same time, tingling sensations erupted across Desma's mind, coming from all directions. "Danger comes," she cried.

"We see them," Pelias told her, "there are but three."

Desma tore her gaze from the oncoming trio of monsters searching the city behind her. A tide of death dashed toward her and her group, the red pulses too many to count.

"Husband, many more come from other directions, we must flee!"

Pelias let his arrow fly, the first infected flopping on the street, a shaft in its eye. The spearmen also let loose, both spears piercing the skulls of their opponents. Holding their hands out, the spears returned, glowing a slight gold.

Answering shrieks from the unseen horde rent the air. Dozens of the things came into view, the vanguard seeing their prey and redoubling their efforts to gnash and devour. Spears and arrows flew, but it was too little too late, and in moments the dead were among the living. The spearmen now thrust with their weapons and Pelias brandished his bow as a club keeping the things at bay. Antrius stepped forward, slashing with his flaming blade and bashing with his shield. Two of the things were beheaded with his first strike, the weapon searing the flesh of the dead things and setting clothing alight. He was like a man possessed, stabbing through the skull of a creature which had leapt upon his shield, and bringing the blade backwards to lop off the leg of one which had slipped behind him below the knee. Pelias had never seen such ferocity in a fighter.

The things came from all directions now, the group of humans realizing that they may have left their refuge a bit too early.

One of the things bounded toward Desma, but Antrius beat the thing to her and smashed it away with his shield. The dead woman slashed at his shield, her hand breaking into bloody bits on contact. "HA," the boy bellowed. "Hail Ares!" He swung his sword in a vicious sideways arc, slicing through four of the things and setting them ablaze. Two were destroyed, two severed in various places, each piece of them afire. Antrius stabbed into the skull of the first, the second stopped moving when a spear thrust pierced its skull. Antrius nodded to Abantes as he swiped at another dead man.

Pelias screamed at his warriors and wife, "Retreat back to the tower!"

Desma smashed her father's shield into the face of a looming creature, the blow enough to destroy it. She ran, her husband and son protecting her. The spearmen sprinted behind them, the dead on their heels.

The group dashed through the open doorway of a stone house, Abantes barely getting through before Pelias slammed the door closed and shot the bolt home. A dozen thumps resounded through the antechamber as the infected crashed into the oaken entry from the other side. Antrius heard his mother scream and turned to see a white-garbed horror on the back of one of the spearmen. He threw the thing off him, the beast slamming to the stone floor hard enough to kill a living human, but the impact did nothing to this dead thing. A thrust from Antrius' sword ended its mewling, the howls from outside the only source of sound now.

Arms thrust through the high open window, reaching for soft flesh, but the opening was too small to allow entry. Fists hammered the heavy door and stone walls outside the building.

"We must get to the..." began Pelias before he noticed Abantes, who had been attacked. Blood streamed from between his fingers as he held his right shoulder.

"Let me see," demanded Pelias.

"It's nothing," the spearman countered. "We must away from this place before we are killed."

The group moved from the foyer through the house, finding a smashed door. They entered warily, the horror of what resided in the room a sight none of them would ever forget. A mother held her child in her arms, both with cut throats. Desma burst into tears, and the group fled the room. They climbed stone stairs to the second floor of the lavish house. All the homes in this section of the city were connected and perhaps they could leap from roof to roof to escape the horde, or rain death down upon it with arrow and spear. They soon stood on the roof balcony, a wooden ladder having given them access.

Forty of the dead shrieked and screamed in frustration when they saw the living out of reach. They leapt at the stone walls of the house, tearing off fingernails in their haste to taste flesh. No purchase could be had though, and they fell back to the street.

"This is a familiar predicament," Theras said aloud. He drew his spear back and let it loose. In twenty minutes, the dead were truly dead.

Pelias looked to Desma. "I feel no danger," she told him.

Pelias noted that his friend and soldier was sweating profusely and bore a sallow pallor. He stood beside the spearman, placing a concerned hand on his uninjured shoulder, "Are you well?"

The wounded man drew the top of his forearm across his brow and sat on the stone. "I am weary. These things are legion."

"Let us bind that wound," Pelias told him. "Perhaps we can find some unspoiled herbs for a poultice within the house. We will stay here tonight and resume our hunt on the morrow."

Pelias and Theras searched the extravagant home, taking note of several marble statues and busts. Theras found the pantry, and together the two of them brought as much medicine as they could carry.

When they reached the roof, they saw that Abantes was ill. A foul black ichor with a green tinge dribbled from between his fingers as he clasped his wound. The secretion reeked as well.

Pelias made to help his friend, but Theras stopped him with a hand. "Don't. The wound is but hours old and already it putrefies? Something is amiss."

"Theras speaks the truth," Abantes told them all through gritted teeth. "Touch me not. I can feel it in me, this disease, and I wouldn't pass it to you." The spearman swallowed, and everyone could see it was a struggle to do so. "It seeks to change me, this sickness. I can see now its cause."

Pelias looked confused, so Abantes continued with difficulty. "It is the bite, dear Pelias." Abantes pulled his hand from his wound and beheld it. He turned the palm to face his friends, the ichor on his hand a disgusting sight. "This black ooze will slay me, then bring me back to fight for it." He stood, a monumental effort. He slammed his fist against his chest in salute to his Captain and friend.

"I fight for Acaharnae," he said. "For you." He tossed his spear to Theras, who caught it and placed it at his feet. Abantes searched the eyes of each of his friends until he stopped at Antrius, "I will not become as them." He fell to one knee in front of the boy, "What better honor than to fall to a gift of Ares?" The spearman lowered his head.

Antrius looked to his father, who nodded.

Four Acharnians left the exquisite marble house the following morning. They began their search for the dead anew.

Olympus

A body, burned and black, lay in a heap of scorched robes on the white marble floors outside the door to the Gazing Pool. Perhaps Zeus had finally had enough of Hades' insolence and had roasted him with a thunderbolt? Before today, Ares would have thought that feat impossible, but he had just killed his own brother, the messenger to the gods, moments ago. In truth, he had destroyed a dead thing which had once been his brother.

A horrendous sound assaulted Ares' ears as he trod further down the halls of the home of the gods. The great doors to The Hall of Judgement stood closed for the first time in ten thousand years and Ares could see why. Hera and Demeter, revered mother and aunt to Ares, scratched and clawed at the white marble doors. The same vile fluids that had leaked from the now dead Hermes dripped from the stained tunics of the two goddesses in front of Ares.

Anger took the God of War and he strode forward, his sandals slapping the marbled floor. He had known they were infected. He had known these two goddesses, capable of great love and great treachery, who had nurtured him when his father had been so cruel, were both gone. Yet when they turned to face him, obsidian eyes burning holes through his soul, he took a step back. Hera leapt, and Demeter sprinted at him, their single-minded desires clearly present on their ravaged faces. He thrust with his spear, piercing Hera's chest and swung his mother into his aunt, both smashing into the stone wall outside The Hall of Judgment with a thunderous crash. They began to get up, but Ares finished both with one swing of his sword. The lopped heads rolled, coming to rest against each other near a column.

"Forgive me," lamented Ares. He ended their suffering with two powerful thrusts of his spear. Glancing once more at the carnage in front of him, he gave an involuntary shudder. Three gods dead by his hand, another in a pile of charred clothing by the Gazing Pool.

Ares balled up his fist and gave three powerful hammers to the doors of the Hall of Judgement. "It is I, Ares. I live when others do not! Open! Open, I say!"

The door opened a crack, the bearded face of Hephaestus warily staring out at Ares. The God of War stood with his arms folded, regarding his brother with contempt. "Perhaps you should send out your wife, brother. She has more courage than you."

Hephaestus' face grew red with rage and he tried to slam

the doors closed, but Ares jammed his foot between the gates. He pushed the door all the way open and stepped into the room.

Another charred body lay twisted and broken on the floor. Ares stared at it, not knowing which god had fallen on this side of the great doors.

"Hestia," came a deep voice from his left. Ares shifted his gaze left to see Zeus sitting on the steps to the council seats. The great god sat with his forehead in his palm, regret and sadness on his countenance. Zeus pointed at the body, "It is Hestia."

Ares was overcome with sadness, "I am sorry, father." He searched the room, "Where is Poseidon?"

"He waits at the bottom of the sea. I bade him beneath the waves until we sorted out this business of the living dead. One of the Three needs to remain intact. I did not know if I would survive a battle with infected gods, and Hades has already fallen."

Ares was shocked, "Zeus is... uncertain?"

"Do you mock me, boy? These... things are like nothing we've seen. They can harm us."

"No, father. I do not mock you." Ares sat with his father, putting a hand on his shoulder in comfort. Zeus covered the offered hand with his own. "What happened on Olympus today?"

Zeus' rage began to show anew, "The impossible. The unthinkable." He slammed his fist on the marble stair, the step cracking and sparks shooting from the impact. "Gods have died!"

Ares drew the back of his hand across his brow. "How? How is this possible?'

"I know not. Whatever this thing is, it has the power to turn even a god from the light. I thought it was some hateful plot of Hades, but he was the first of us to fall. I also thought that we were all powerful, but clearly, that is not the case."

"There is always someone stronger," Ares said, again putting his hand on his father's shoulder. "A very wise god told me that once."

Zeus smiled. Hephaestus and Aphrodite appeared next to Ares and Zeus on the stairs. "What is next, Mighty Zeus?" asked Aphrodite.

Before Zeus could answer, Hephaestus stumbled forward, placing his hand on one of the marble steps. He made a sound of anguish, pain stitched across his face. He collapsed on his chest, a black arrow protruding from his back. Another arrow struck the stone near the God of Lightning and he shot to his feet. Aphrodite screamed, rushing to Hephaestus' aid. "Husband!"

Apollo and Artemis stepped from the shadows, both with short bows. Apollo had an arrow nocked, the shaft point dripping with a foul black liquid.

"My twins!" bellowed Zeus. "What is the meaning of this?"

"You said you wanted to know how it was possible to kill a god, *father*," Apollo had sneered his last word. "I am the god of plague. This sickness brings the dead to life. The dead hate the living, father, and they *hunger*."

"Yes, old-one," continued Artemis nocking an arrow of her own, "it was we who killed your precious mortals, those you revered even over us. It was we who culled our family."

"Jealousy?" screamed Zeus. "The end of things is because you covet my *love*?"

"Yes," both twins answered at the same time. Apollo gave a wry smile. "Behold, father, your son rises."

Zeus glanced to the left. Hephaestus pushed himself up and turned his gaze upon Zeus and Ares, his eyes black as pitch. The thing drew a breath to utter a shriek, but Athena drove her hands into the creature's back, ripping out its spine as she withdrew. The dead god collapsed, unable to move. Athena threw the spine at Artemis, who deftly ducked, the vile thing flying past her head. Athena was there to receive Artemis as she stood back up, Athena's hands dripping with the infected fluids of her deceased husband. She raked her nails across Artemis' face, digging red-gold furrows down her sister's cheek.

"Goddess of strategic warfare, bitch!" screamed Athena.

Artemis put her palm to her face, drawing it back to stare at it. Enraged, she kicked out, sending Athena sprawling. Both twins drew their bows and fired at Zeus. Ares threw himself into the path of the incoming arrows, taking both in the chest. The horrible plague-infused arrows pierced Ares' golden armor as if he wore but a sheet of linen.

Zeus put his hand forward, both bows tearing from the hands of his children, sailing across the vast room and into his fist. He crushed both weapons, staring at his twins in a rage he had not felt before. Apollo and Artemis tried to disappear to Earth, but Zeus held them firm with his will.

Zeus shook his head, sadness overtaking his rage. "You have succeeded in killing a god," he told his progenies. "Before this, the only way to remove a god was to send him to Tartarus as I did Hades. Enjoy eternity in hell, my children." The twins screamed briefly before they vanished.

Zeus knelt next to Ares. "Fool. You should have let them take me."

The God of War coughed, a great gout of blood expelled onto the steps. Athena was by their side in an instant. "Use my spear, father," Ares pleaded. "You must pierce the skull else I will return as a slavering monster, witless and without mercy."

"You describe your father, my son. I am sorry for everything."

"At last," Ares said, and died.

Dionysus appeared, weapon at the ready. He rushed to Zeus' side, noticing the dead gods and The Hall of Judgement soaked in blood.

"Zeus, what has happened here?" he begged.

Zeus did not look from Ares's face when he said, "The end has come, I think." He stroked his son's face one last time and stood, lifting Ares's spear.

Tartarus

Artemis glared at her twin shaking her head, "Yet again, I am punished for your foolish ideas."

"It worked!" countered Apollo.

Artemis strode to the center of the vast room, spinning and glancing about, "How did this, in any way, *work*?" she demanded.

Apollo smiled. "Most of the gods are dead. The humans have been dealt a huge blow. We are safe and will remain down here," he stared at the roof of the throne room, "for the time being."

He turned his head slowly to gaze at her, "Of course, then there is the matter of you?"

"Me?"

"Yes. Athena scratched you. She could not have done so unless she had plague-blood on her fingernails." He smiled wider, "You are infected."

She put her hand to her cheek in shock. "*No...*" she whispered.

Apollo shrugged. "I don't need you anymore, sister." The Sun God heard something then. It sounded like thunder from his father.

Thousands of infected poured into the throne room. They came from all directions, shrieking and drooling.

Artemis laughed, "Your plague. It raises the dead. Tartarus is full of the dead, fool."

Apollo leapt over the rubble of Hades' gigantic throne, landing atop the Lord of Tartarus' wife, Persephone's, equally massive seat. He desperately searched for an avenue of escape. Artemis just lowered her head as the throngs of undead tore her to pieces. Legions of the things climbed and scraped at the stone chair, but they could not reach the Sun God. He stared at them, fifty feet below. The entire room, acres of stone floor, teemed with the dead.

"Shit," croaked the Sun God.

Knossos, Crete 610 BC

"Pull the Halyard, Antrius. That's it." Pelias smiled at his son as the sail raised. The sloop moved slowly toward the dock at Knossos.

"I feel them," Desma told the crew of three. "There are but two left."

The boat thudded against the wooden dock, Antrius and Theras fastening lines to a piling. Pelias helped Desma step to the dock as the men gathered their weapons. In the two years since the dead rose, the group of four had been to several cities, helping the citizens clear the towns of the evil that had befallen them.

Knossos, like Acharnae, had been one of the unfortunate cities to completely fall to the undead menace, no living person having set foot there for nearly two years.

"One comes," Desma warned.

A dead man came at them from down the dock. Withered and frail, the thing shuffled toward the humans at a pathetic pace. The group of slayers had learned during their hundreds of battles that without fresh meat, the dead wasted away and began to rot. They slowed down and were easy to kill. Still deadly though, and best slain from a distance.

A spear pierced the creature's skull, Theras holding his palm open for the weapon's return. "We have not heard reports of any dead walking in weeks. Could these be the last?"

Desma took a deep breath, "I do not feel their power as I once did."

A second creature stumbled toward the dock on unsteady legs. Pelias ended its misery with his bow. When the thing collapsed, Desma felt a great tide of relief wash over her.

"That... that was the last of them. Our world is cleansed!"

"Father," a young boy's voice blurted. Pelias and Desma regarded their son. He stood as a child once more in armor that no longer fit. "Mother, I am a boy?"

"My son," Pelias cried, "the gods have seen fit to return childhood to you!"

The boy smiled, looking toward the sea. His mother hugged him on the dock, his father standing proud. The boy had but one question as he stared at the waves, "Can we go fishing?"

University of Oxford. Oxford, England. 2018 AD

The professor ended his lecture and dismissed his class. The students began to pack their belongings and started to file out of the lecture hall. A bloody man burst through the door, searching wildly. The man sprinted toward the group of students, leaping on an unfortunate one and using his teeth to tear a great chunk from the pupil's neck. Several of the group began to scream, others rushed from the scene. Not one tried to assist the hapless victim.

Dionysus, the God of wine, sighed from his seat at the back of the hall. "This shit again?"

His sister Athena stood, throwing her coat to the floor. "At least you're sober this time."

"Are you kidding?" he lamented, "I'm hungover as fuck."

The two of them strode through the seats toward the feasting creature. Athena brandished a golden sword. A gleaming chrome shotgun rested on Dionysus' shoulder. He used his off hand to pull a cellular phone from the back pocket of his jeans. "Better get dad on the horn."

ABOUT RICH RESTUCCI

Rich Restucci is a practicing chemist living in Pembroke Massachusetts. He resides with his lovely wife, three children, a portly cat, and a crazy dog. Rich enjoys drinking beer, stocking up on weapons and supplies, playing with explosives, and reading/writing anything zombie related. Rich has been fortunate to have two series published, The Run series, and the Zombie Theories series as well as many shorts for anthologies. Rich is currently working on publishing several other novels and is always ready to jump into an anthology. Visit Rich's Amazon Author page for updates and a listing of his works.

14

———

ZOMBIE BEGINNINGS: THE ORACLE

BY JAVAN BONDS

CHAPTER 1

What A Day For A Daydream
Prophecy from *The Book of Smokes:*

Much thought is given to life and the role each individual is here to play. Theories abound concerning the origin of life and the frustration of not knowing the answers. Wars rage for decades with nothing to show but bare bones. Civilizations rise to new heights and crumble into the ashes of history all according to the script. Still no one knows.

There is one that does know, The Screenwriter. Some may call this omnipotent presence God, The Director, a Puppet Master. For the chosen few with direct connection to this unique existence, they are given a small fraction of understanding. Their lives are choreographed preternaturally with the lives of others. These others may or may not realize the association between The Screenwriter and The Oracle.

The Oracle is often seen as a prophet, visionary or soothsayer; they are a mouthpiece for The Screenwriter. Though at first glance, the character may appear an entirely unlikely choice for this task, a supernatural knowing of future events, scenes and scenarios will validate the seers visions to be true. Even The Oracle may initially question the uncanny gift or refuse to accept the power. Witnessing the precise timing and unfolding of events as scripted will prove to the character that this role must be accepted as something that is supposed to be.

A tiny, plastic garbage can stood in the corner, overflowing with crumpled York Peppermint Patty wrappers and empty Newport cigarette packs. The sole resident of this small dimly lit apartment, Marlon "Smokes" Williamson sat in his ragged chocolate stained recliner, completely alone. At least, physically alone. He had been in the company of and conversing with an unseen presence for almost a week.

Smokes would have been considered clinically morbidly obese. Though it could be disproven by glancing in his closet, it seemed he was always wearing a red T-shirt. Along with his customary shirt, the self-proclaimed gangsta wore a pair of giant blue jeans. Completing his attire, several wristwatches encircled both forearms; from diamond encrusted to gold. Silver to platinum, every make, model, and brand of wristwatch was sported by the gangsta.

"Today is the day. You only have a few hours. There is no doubt you will see this through, but be wary." The ethereal voice spoke from within his consciousness.

He was uncertain if it was speaking or just pressing thoughts through his mind. Regardless, it would be thought of as a voice, aware of everything almost as if it were directing a play. There was a compulsion to give this omniscient voice a name. It would forever be known as The Screenwriter.

The Screenwriter never seemed to have any sort of gender. Decidedly a voice, it never showed emotion or any kind of inflection. Since appearing in his mind, it hadn't stopped choreographing Smoke's every move.

He realized today was May 5. Guntersville's first annual Cinco de Mayo parade would be underway shortly. Being in a large crowd at the beginning of the zombie apocalypse was not where he wanted to be. Staying away from that would be a good idea.

Some type of strange infection had broken out days before down in Mobile, Alabama and a few other port cities across the country. Expectedly, the world did its best to ignore a rapidly spreading virus. Having been described as ignorant for calling the plague victims what they appeared to be; blue zombies, the descriptor "peevie" had been casually coined. If you were a realist like Smokes, you could see Guntersville being overrun by these plague victims in the first wave.

The city government had only just started securing downtown from the south entrance onto the island. It would be discovered soon that these last-minute measures should have been taken hours, if not days, ago. Now, nothing could stem the tide of crazies. Once the wave of infected got here, it would simply sweep through Guntersville like it had, and would, through any major metropolitan area. Almost every single member of the human population would become another blue naked peevie to add to the growing ranks. Almost every.

Throughout his short life, he had seen all the Romero Classics. Following Robert Kirkman's graphic novels, delving into every type of zompoc fiction imaginable, he was an expert of the genre. Smokes knew exactly how quickly a sickness that altered people's personalities could spread: turning them from civilized humans into bloodthirsty animals. It would happen just like in *28 Days Later*. Society would ultimately deny it was on the verge of catastrophe. That is, until it had already plummeted from the cliff and was in free fall. At that point, it would be too late.

Zero day was the first of the month, May Day. Within four days, Guntersville, the state, and most of the country would quickly become no man's land. In the eternal nanosecond it took for time to blink an eye, the United States and the entire world would be brutalized and desolate.

Smokes was worried about his pawpaw, Sojourner "Soje" Williamson, the only family member in the area. He wished a member of the fading Greatest Generation didn't have to go through these trials and tribulations. Pawpaw didn't deserve to have to deal with troubled times like these. Everyone already had troubles enough back in the day. He might be worried, but he would have to trust when The Screenwriter foretold that no harm would come to the senior.

Besides, Smokes knew his grandfather would be prepared when it came to any sort of disaster. Not that the old man was a prepper or a survivalist, he just knew how to survive. The old-timer had been living off the land long enough, Smokes was confident he could keep on living.

If The Screenwriter was to be believed, the majority of the Williamson family would soon be reunited. Speaking with such certainty on every topic, the voice of The Screenwriter was nearly impossible to doubt. If the next few days happened even close to the way The Screenwriter summated, it would solidify his faith.

Smokes didn't feel he was a part of some deity. Not a third of The Trinity or anything like that, he wasn't in collusion with The Screenwriter. Moving the chess pieces was not his role, Smokes was only able to know the movements before they happened. He would be The Oracle, unable to do anything more than see what was coming.

There was no way to understand why he had been chosen for this task. Nowhere near physically fit, he was a broke ass nigga, unprepared for anything. All he achieved in the few short years after high school was success as a thug. His pawpaw would be justifiably ashamed. He thanked black Jesus his mama wasn't alive to see him.

Well, he had briefly gone to community college before dropping out, later enrolling in piloting school. Wanting to fly planes, his dreams of reaching the skies had floundered. The Oracle understood if he had received his piloting bars, he wouldn't be at this place at this very moment.

"You's always at da place you is always post to be." He calmed himself by once again repeating the phrase in his own words. That wise saying projected to him by The Screenwriter.

Even with all his faults, The Screenwriter had chosen Smokes to know what was going to happen next. Was he the only one with this ability or were there others? Perhaps The Oracle could be plural. All his queries on the subject had gone unanswered. So something was coming and as far as he'd seen, he was the only one ready.

He scoffed at the thought his thuggery was anywhere close to successful. Smokes couldn't remember the last time he had bumped his reputation, improved his street cred, or even scored with a shorty. The Screenwriter gave him the impression none of that mattered. Maybe he was prepared, after all.

Having been accurate so far, the voice had to be trusted. Smokes would continue to follow the commands until it was proven wrong, or he wound up blue.

Life for everyone was about to change. Brave reporters had risked their lives to cover the growing epidemic spreading from a few seaports across the country. Many were attacked by plague victims. Strangely, they were completely ignored after a single bite. Injured bystanders and media personalities alike were immediately treated. No one understood the cause for such violence against innocents and people wearing PRESS badges. The motive for the attacks was unknown, but appeared to be driven by an unquenchable hunger. Initially, the reason wasn't understood, but hours later those that had been attacked realized that something was wrong. Upon returning to their hotel rooms with doctored injuries, the reporters grew sicker with every passing minute. It was no different for info babe, Megyn McKelly.

Eventually Megyn, as all the infected, collapsed. After appearing to be dead, they would rise up, as if for the first time. None of them had a single memory of life before waking. Now the infected peevie would immediately remove all of their clothing and begin excreting a sticky tar colored substance from its anus. Ravenously hungry, the only urge it now had was to feed on living flesh. For Megyn who was alone in her hotel room, it was no different. The metal barrier with the silver handle posed no trouble. Finding a warm, uninfected human body was now the sole priority of the blue, naked former reporter.

Hotel patrons were not expecting screaming and barking coming from the hall. One man stepped out to see what all the ruckus was. He was instantly pounced upon by a naked platinum blonde with breast implants and bluish skin. For some reason, this blonde bombshell also sported yellow eyes. Most men were not accustomed to being assaulted by what could be a playboy cover girl ready for a shoot. Jimmy Sardinia was no exception to this rule.

Jimmy came to Mobile yesterday to pick up a package for Mr. Falcone. Orders were to defend the delivery with deadly force if prompted. This woman had to be after the briefcase. She probably works for Cerimele, only coming at him showing skin to distract him. With his back to the wall, Jimmy reached for the piece in his shoulder holster. *Orders is orders.*

As he pulled it free, the lunatic woman lunged at him again, pushing his elbow down, rotating the muzzle of his .45 to aim opposite of where he intended. The crazy blue lady pushing her beautiful breasts all over him grabbed at everything within reach. The knockout blonde slid a finger in the trigger guard and accidentally, unknowingly, unthinkingly pulled down. The pistol went off, blowing straight through the Mafioso's chin.

Bullet liquefied bone and gray matter as it rocketed through the cranium, exploding from the top of the skull. Jimmy Sardinia had just become an all-you-can-eat buffet. Small spasms jolted through the fingers, extremities, and finally bowels voided before the body went slack.

The female was elated beyond belief. A plate of fresh, juicy, warm, raw meat waited before it, blood still pumping.

The hunger would not be satisfied for long, but eating the entire body would quell the thirst for flesh, temporarily.

⁂

"Go to the door. Unlock it. You will soon have a visitor." The Screenwriter broke Smokes from his reverie, shaking him from a memory that wasn't really his. This was an unusual command. However, The Oracle wanted to see the results.

Standing from watching the director's cut of *Zombieland,* he made his way to unbolt the door. The Oracle began blindly sliding back all the locks, as instructed. Unbolting the final slide, sounds could be heard coming through the closed portal.

A loud crash came against the door before a voice with a Hispanic accent pleaded, "Dios, let la puerta be unlocked!" Smokes stepped back and watched a young stranger fall into his apartment.

The frightened man collapsed to the floor. Smokes quickly reached to pull the door closed, as if this had been rehearsed. He had all the bolts pushed over and down in what most would consider record time. They were now alone and safe from whatever the man had been running from. Wearing his customary red T-shirt, Smokes slowly turned to settle his knowing gaze on the newcomer.

The Oracle decided he would pretend to have no clue what was happening. "Da fuck is you and da fuck you doin' in my crib?"

CHAPTER 2
Blackout

"There's loco people in the hall, homes!"

Smokes waited with a tapping foot and crossed arms for a further explanation from the stranger.

The young man continued. "I didn't mean no harm bro. Honest."

The other tried to appear distrustful, furrowing his brow. Gaining confidence in the face of getting his ass beat, the intruder went on. "I ain't gonna steal from somebody living in the building. I got respect, yo!"

Playing it clueless, Smokes walked toward the door as if to open it. "Ain't shit out dere, foo!"

The interloper put himself between the other and the door, throwing his arms out. "Hold up, cuz!"

Trying to appear chagrined, Smokes was unable to work his way around the wiry Hispanic. "Mufucka!" Stepping back, obviously bested, he shrugged. "What yo name anyway, bra?"

Diego Diego detailed an extremely brief life story to the man that had just saved him. American-born to Cuban parents, he was adamant that he was a legal citizen. Smokes concealed a bitter laugh with a cough. *Legal ain't gonna mean shit no mo. Not afta what comin'.*

Was Smokes the only one with this miraculous trait? If there were others, they were as secretive about it as he. Being knowledgeable while everyone around you remained completely ignorant was a depressingly lonely state. Perhaps he would come across others in the know throughout his travels. Purpose and destination might not have yet been foreseen, but there would definitely be treacherous journeys in his near future.

Cocking his head to the side, the gangsta smiled. "You gots two first names? Or is dat two last?"

Diego blinked hard. "Fuck you, ese. Heard it before!"

The smile on Diego's face let Smokes know he wasn't really angry.

"Man, yo mama musta hated you if she give you a name like dat."

His new friend smiled. "Sometimes I think the same thing, homes."

What a strange feeling. Was this similar to something he had experienced or was it a feeling almost like something that was going to happen? Smokes shook off the creepiness with a laugh. "I'm a call you 'Double D.'"

Diego shrugged. "Most people just call me 'D.'"

Nodding , Smokes acquiesced. "Dat coo, D.

The Oracle gestured to a pair of faded, tattered, threadbare recliners. "Sit yo ass down and gimme da mufuckin' scoop, cuz"

"I was in my pad, getting ready to go see my chica when I started hearing fighting in the hall. Dimitrius was the loudest one yelling. Sounded like he was about to pull out his chrome .45 and I knew somebody was about to wind up dead." D stopped to take a sip from a glass of coke Smokes offered him before starting the story.

"Just as I peeked out the door, some naked dude tackled Dimitrius. The pistol bounced away when the crackhead took a bite out of Dimitrius's bicep. It was barely a bite and I didn't see blood. But Dimitrius started screaming like crazy. Now that I think about it, he was probably more mad than he was hurt. The naked dude got up and started walking away like Dimitrius wasn't even there. Big fucking mistake." He paused for questions or interjections, but Smokes remained silent, listening intently.

"So Dimitrius got up and drop kicked the motherfucker. He hit the Loco with both feet in the lower back. I don't know if that guy was able to walk, but before he could get up, Dimitrius was already standing at his side, kicking the shit out of him. The nut case's guts were definitely ruptured. I mean, Dimitrius's boot was even juicy!" Diego paused again for dramatic effect.

Shaking off the grizzly scene replaying in his mind, he continued. "Dimitrius stopped kicking after probably breaking a few of the guy's ribs. Hocking up a loogey, he spit on the naked man. 'Motherfucker!' he screamed down. Next, he kicked the limp body and walked away."

"It deserved it!" Quickly catching himself, Smokes attempted to recover.

"Mufucka don't even get to be called a man no mo afta doin' dat crazy shit!" Promising himself to never make a mistake like that again, appearing to be clueless would be a top priority. Brushing it off, he added. "So what you do afta dat?"

D continued, "I started down to the stairwell. Luisa and her madre live on the second floor. Before I got down the flight, I heard people screaming like the building was on fire. I just knew it had to be more of those dope fiends chasing people down, probably heading my way next. All I could think was that crackhead that jumped Dimitrius. Figured I needed to go get the piece from my crib. When I got back up to the hall Mrs. Ramsey, the crazy old librarian, was standing in front of her casa. She was hollering to everyone about it being the end of the world and to repent. I stopped outside my apartment to listen, not thinking about the blue lunatics charging up the stairs. That is, until they busted through the entrance." D grew silent and tilted his ear in the direction of the door.

Confident nothing could be heard, he continued. "All the people listening to Mrs. Ramsey started panicking and running. The old lady grabbed her chest and fell over with a shout. Must have had a heart attack or something. The crazies jumped on her and started ripping the Señora apart. It was fucked up! They went to tearing into her, chomping on the raw meat like cannibals or some shit. They were going to town, fucking blood and shit flying everywhere!" The young man had to stop and regain his composure.

"I just started running as fast as I could. Thank Dios you opened the door when you did. Or they woulda done to me like they did to Mrs. Ramsey!"

Both sat in the dimly lit apartment, not making a move. Bill Murray taking Columbus's rifle round was just audible in the background. Smokes glanced up at the wall clock just as the lights flickered once, twice, and finally went off.

Dat da last lectricity we gonna see fo a while.

Hoping against all hope until this very second The Screenwriter was wrong, the omniscience of the voice was again proven to The Oracle.

I'm a finish dac cookie dough ice cream in da freeza while it still good!

Finally, D spoke after a long bout of utter silence. "So... we just gonna sit here?"

Seemingly absentmindedly, Smokes brushed him off. "Waitin', mufucka."

The Latino nearly felt insulted. He would've compared it to someone speaking on one of those damn bluetooth headsets. As far as you know, you're the only other person in the bathroom. When you respond to whatever he said, the jackass rolls his eyes, turns to you, and violently jams a finger to the thing in his ear. Smokes might not have done that exactly, but it felt like he was having a conversation with someone else.

After another eternity of complete quiet, D stood up. "Can I go check on my mamacita?" *Do I really gotta ask permission?*

Defiantly moving to the door, he made an addition. "Oh, and I got a pistola at my crib..."

Pausing to wait for acceptance or confirmation from the other end of the phone that he wasn't on, Smokes finally replied. "Naw, cuz. We gots to sleep here."

"But–"

"Homey... Who saved yo ass?"

In response, D hung his head and grunted. *Am I really doing what he says just because the door was unlocked?*

The Oracle's smile was nearly audible. "Damn straight, dawg. Now, we stay here till da mornin'."

Diego had to question his new friend. "Where we sleeping?"

Snorting out a laugh, Smokes responded. "I'm a go to bed. Yo ass sleepin' on da couch. Dis ain't no fuckin' sleep ova!" He threw his new friend a blanket and turned, disappearing into the darkness.

Lifting his hand to check his digital wristwatch, D shouted after Smokes. "But it ain't even that late!"

Sighing, The Oracle spoke. "Don't cur, foo. You gonna be glad fo da rest when tomorra get here."

Actually, D could think of nothing better to do. No electricity cut their options of entertainment down. "Fine, ese. But you better be up bright and early."

He simply nodded as he walked into the other room. "Fo sho, cuz."

When morning came Diego opened his eyes to see Smokes sitting in the recliner with his fingers steepled, staring at him. Overall, the scene seemed strange to D. *Fucking creepy Smokes was watching me sleep for Dios knows how long!*

Jumping up, the first thing Diego did was go to unbolt the door. "Now I can go?" *The fuck is wrong with me?*

The Oracle nodded. "Yo prerogative, homey. I be here when you get back."

Well, at least he thinks I'm coming back. Alive, hopefully. D stopped as he unbolted the locks. "You better be waiting, ready to unlock the door when I come knocking."

The large black man scoffed. "Course, wheat bread."

"*Wheat bread*, Really?"

Smokes shrugged in the early morning sunlight. "Fittin'." *The moniker just seems to work.* And The Oracle had a strange feeling he would be using a similar designation for another companion in the near future.

In acceptance and agreement with the new nickname, D nodded once before cracking open the door. Deciding to stop by his apartment to grab his gat before going down to check on Luisa, he listened for any movement. Hearing nothing, he stepped out the door and slowly closed it behind him. *Here goes!*

CHAPTER 3
Nobody's Home

Diego Diego started down the carpeted hall, in a silence that was almost loud. It was unexplainably disturbing to move through an apartment building now seemingly inhabited by no one. Well, other than him and Smokes.

Every single door on this level was closed. He certainly wasn't going to knock or jiggle knobs to see if any were open. *Those Loco meth heads could be inside!*

Random splatters of what he was pretty sure was shit accented the beige carpet. Not even sniffing, D immediately picked up on the indescribably horrible smell. The putrid aroma was obviously coming from the black, wet spots peppering the hallway. Dark and watery, it looked like a giant bird had been through there.

Glancing to the spot where Mrs. Ramsey had fallen the day before sent chills up his spine. What looked like chunky motor oil had saturated the carpet, mingling with splotches of red. This nightmarish scene was encircled by a few scattered, gnawed clean bones. *Did those fucking crazies really eat the old lady down to nothing?* The thought was disgusting, but the scene appeared to indicate that must be the truth.

There hadn't been time to notice if those naked people had been shitting out what looked like baby diarrhea, but the drying skid marks surrounding the bones was clear indication they created this filth. D could've swore there was something on the news about people infected with that monkey virus "having no bowel control" or some shit. *These crazies must have been sick with that same thing! How did they make it all the way up to Guntersville without anybody knowing? And if it was them, now what?* Diego had never been much of one for television, but he was now wishing he had paid a little closer attention to some of the news channels.

What if there are loonies in my place? I ain't got nothing to fight them off with! Just as he thought this, he noticed a folded automatic stiletto lying in a puddle of black slime. Supposing it was Dimitrius's forgotten blade, he bent over to pick it up, turning his head as his hand came into contact with the sloppy stain. Well, better to have shitty fingers than wind up like my poor old neighbor!

Gently cracking his apartment door, he eased himself into the dead quiet unit. Thankfully, nothing moved. Was he alone? *Fuck if I'm calling out!* Making his way down the dark hallway to the bedroom, he pulled the knife from his pocket, getting ready for a brawl.

If one of those sick nuts came at me, what the fuck was this little thing gonna do? Yeah, it might eventually bleed out, but not before I was torn apart! Oh well, if it survives, it'll always remember that it fucked with Diego Diego.

No longer would he think of the infected as people. From now on, D decided, he would take the wise words of his new companion to heart. *People that eat other people ain't people no more!*

Nightmarish images filled his mind. He imagined one of the infected jumping out of the bathroom door, tackling him. Though multiple stab wounds would be inflicted on his attacker, it wouldn't stop the crazy! Hearing one's own neck being bitten into would be the most terrible sound imaginable. Popping and crunching of ligaments being pulled away and arteries being ruptured would be horrific. He might be able to stand and fight, even kill the psycho, but pain and blood loss would soon tire him. Diego would sink to the floor, knowing he was beaten. Eventually, the Cuban-American would fade away into nothingness.

Upon reaching the nightstand in one piece, he smiled. What waited in the top drawer would keep him and his new friend alive. There was only one full magazine, but just the sight of such a famous weapon would surely strike fear into anyone... *or anything, no matter how naked and Loco it was. The MAC 10 would scare the shit out of the shitting freaks!*

Going down the flight of stairs, D was thankful Luisa lived only one floor down. Constructed strangely, each floor was only accessible from opposite ends. This meant to get from the ground floor to the next level above; one would have to go all the way to the end of the hall. To reach the next story, passing every single door to get to the other end would be required. Though he had grown accustomed to the weird engineering, it was a hassle to get from the ground to his apartment on the third floor in a hurry. *Fucking government contractors!* Maybe it was a good thing during this situation; those crazies had farther to travel to get to him.

Crazies... Plague victims... What was it they called them on the news? "Peevies?" He would do his best to save Luisa from the peevies.

Nearly running from the stairwell to the closed door leading to the hallway, all he wanted was to see his woman. *She's okay, just waiting for me. They didn't eat her. Her madre's at work. We can just use her cell phone to call the policia to come lock up the locos. Everything will be back to normal by tomorrow. Wait, today's already tomorrow! Does that mean she came home yesterday? Did she look for me? Is she at home now? I bet she's worried.* Trying to convince himself, the Latino just couldn't shake the terrible feeling in his gut.

He wanted to save his chica, but he had to come to a stop at the exit from the stairs. *There's no saving anybody if I get eat!* His mind raced. *What do I do even after I rescue her from the peevies? Back upstairs with Smokes!*

Cracking the door, he heard no charging from the shitting, maniac peevies. He listened before finally peeking out the cracked doorway. *Nothing!*

Groaning and creaking all the way, D eased the door

open to stand in a hallway bathed in complete blackness. Well, a little light did show from under the cracks of some of the doors. *Thank Dios for that, at least!*

Now, I have to make my way to my señorita's casa. It sucks that she lives halfway down the hall. Could be worse. Could be all the way at the other end! Good thing all the doors between here and there are closed. Diego flipped out his blade, trying to be as ready as possible.

Luckily, no hostile's moved on him. A pin drop would have made him shit himself as he reached the intended door. He gently turned the knob, hoping against all hope. *Shit, locked!*

In case of emergency, he thankfully always kept a bobby pin in his pocket. Lifting it from his pocket, he began the tedious process of breaking and entering. *It's bueno,* he supposed, *Louisa don't know what I used to do.*

Quietly shutting the door behind him, he was immediately sprang upon by what he called "Sonja's Diablos." A gaggle of Louisa's madre's Chihuahuas, pugs, terriers, and even one English bulldog threw themselves at D. Barking, panting, and yipping amazingly didn't seem to be drawing the peevies. *Locking the door behind me would be a good idea.*

He tried to give each of the demonias enough attention that they would at least allow him to move. Finally, he got ahead of the pack and started down the short hall in the back of the apartment to Louisa's room. The door to the room was standing wide open, but she wasn't in it. He briefly panicked until he thought about the whole scene. *The door was locked, none of the dogs appeared any more upset than usual, and there was none of that black shit anywhere. Maybe she just went out or is looking for me and will be back soon.*

Do I wait here for her? Should I go back to Smokes? He

might get worried. Don't want his fat ass coming after me. There's no way he could out run one of the fuckers. Well, at least that would give them a target besides me, he chuckled quietly to himself.

Racking his brain for an answer on what to do, his eyes grew wide when he heard something he knew couldn't be the demonias. Diego stopped in place and lifted the gat from his waistband. Heavy knocking came from the apartment's front door. *Louisa?*

CHAPTER 4
Blessed Assurance

Looking through the peephole, he was surprised to see Smokes standing there casually, completely unguarded; his black friend stood ready for nothing. Diego lowered the muzzle of his pistola. Blinking, he continued to stare out the aperture.

Narrowing his eyes and putting his hands on his hips, Smokes screeched in an entirely too loud volume. "Da hell you starin' at, mufucka? Get yo ass to gettin'!"

Without further delay, D swung open the door, wrapped his fist in Smokes's collar, and tried to yank him inside. Smokes didn't budge when pulled but proceeded to casually walk in and D closed the door behind him. "The fuck wrong with you? Be quiet, dumbass. You trying to get us killed? Don't want to let them know where we are!" he whispered harshly.

Refusing to lower his volume, Smokes continued screeching. "Ain't shit to worry bout, wheat bread. Mon, foo."

The Oracle brushed down his shirt and stepped to the

door. Turning the knob, he gave a command. "Sko, mufucka!"

D planted his feet. "If they ain't in the building, what makes you think they won't be outside?"

Snorting, Smokes turned. "Dey ain't gonna be in da sunlight. Trust me. We got dis, cuz!"

"Why the hell you think that?"

In answer, The Oracle only walked out the door. Turning to go downstairs, D waited for him to turn around, admit he was wrong, confess he was afraid of the dark, and beg forgiveness. *Should I really go? What if Luisa comes back? Why am I willing to go with him?*

Automatic dog feeders, lots of water, the dogs will be okay for a while. Guess I'm really doing this. Pulling the chain from around his neck that sported a medallion emblazoned with the name of his lover, he looped it over the doorknob in a position so the door wouldn't latch. Not bothering to lower his own volume, the Latino hollered after his compatriot. "Wait up, homes!"

✶✶✶✶✶✶

Not understanding why, D hesitantly followed Smokes, choosing to walk past every doorway on the first floor and toward the front entrance of the building. It was beyond the Latino why he didn't just use the emergency exit in the final stairwell. But finally, their exit from the complex was looking like it was going to be successful.

Before exiting the complex, D glanced up at the mailboxes, inset into the wall. In the section for the third floor... *There! Ramsey... Jacinda so that is...was.... Her name. Sorry, Jacinda.*

Surprising, to Diego, they didn't meet a single individual or even a peevie on their trek. After a short walk they were now standing at the corner of Taco Bell and US Highway 431. D looked up and down the hi-way and had to question. "The fuck everybody at, ese?"

"Dey's gone or dey's blue." Smokes stated flatly.

This was shocking. The Oracle couldn't remember the last time he walked even a quarter of this distance. Panting and sweating were the results of just walking from his apartment to the front door of his building. Barely retaining consciousness and vomiting always came from walking just a few hundred yards. Now though, Smokes wasn't even winded

Though The Oracle noticed, it slipped by his new friend. *Maybe he just don't know what to look fo.* Surely, there would be those that would realize his miraculous ability to never tire. Smokes decided from now on, with anyone else around, he would do his best to appear ridiculously unfit, like he definitely was until recently. *Dis gots to be Da Screenwrita's doin'.*

Standing at the point where hi-way 431 broke off into the southbound Gunter Avenue and northbound Blount Avenue, The Oracle spun on his heel to move south down the four-lane. Not falling into step behind him, D spoke. "Dude, the police station and all that shit this way." He pointed North up Gunter. "Why the hell you going the wrong way?"

"Not da wrong way." Smokes said with authority. It seemed to the Latino that his new friend must have a guardian angel on his shoulder. *The guy moves with some kind of purpose, a knowing.*

"Shit, fine!" Diego turned to face south. *He's the reason I'm still alive, I should stick with him.* Hesitantly, D began following the leader.

⫻⫻⫻⫻

Passing Arby's, Burger King, the Jet Pep gas station and several other abandoned businesses, the two survivors saw absolutely no one. *431* was the busiest road in Marshall County, yet they had not seen a single moving car the entire time they had been traveling right down the middle of it. D had never experienced anything so creepy. *Are we completely alone? Where the hell is everybody? I ain't even seen no bones!* He shuddered, remembering Mrs. Ramsey in the hallway.

"Madre de Dios!" Looking over to his left and crossing himself, D walked backwards in a hurry.

There were at least a couple bodies lying in the parking lot of Bottom Dollar Pawn Shop. Initially, it would've tensed him just to see corpses. After a moment, he was horrified to realize they were wearing clothes. *These were people, not peevies! Whoever did the shooting better have had a damn good reason.* He shrugged, *it was a pawn shop, maybe they was stealing.*

Keeping his eyes forward, The Oracle ignored the bullet riddled bodies. "Gonna be mo, just wait." There hadn't been visions detailing the full backgrounds of the people laying in the parking lot, the others that would be, their executioner, or even the reasons they would be shot. However, Smokes at least somehow knew those wouldn't be the last bodies seen there.

⫻⫻⫻⫻

Why we doing all this walking? We done passed a hundred cars I could've got into and boosted. No way Smokes ain't wore out. I sure as hell am! D was about to head over to The Magnolia on the right, opposite the pawn shop and maybe find a sweet ride in the parking lot.

Just as he was about to offer his jacking expertise, Smokes shot a finger forward. "Look at dat, homey!"

Squinting, D could make out several cop cars parked across the highway on the causeway before them. *The po po!* He had never been so glad to see law enforcement. Both men hustled past the Best Western on their left and the Exxon on the opposite side of *431*.

I know what I'ma find. D don't need to know I know. The Oracle sometimes felt guilty because he had to hide his unexplainable knowledge. If he actually told Diego or anyone he had seen into the future, would they believe him? Would it hurt to try?

"No one can know. Keep this connection secret!" That was jarring. Though The Screenwriter had given him instructions to be followed immediately several times before, this was the first time he could recall it was apparent the voice was listening.

Commanding from a distance was the feeling he got most of the time. Now he knew The Screenwriter was eavesdropping and spying on his every move since showing up in his mind. He nearly gasped. *Dat means it's seen da movie I was watchin' last night!*

When they came to within a dozen yards of the police barricade, Diego slowed to a complete stop. He nearly broke into tears. "What? Where...?" Not a soul was anywhere in sight. D trotted to the opened door of one of the cop cars and reached in. Pulling the handset from the radio, he clicked it and turned the knobs on the radio. Dead. "Why?"

Smokes didn't understand it, himself. The car door hadn't been standing open more than a few hours yet, but dead it was. *Dead, it gots to be. By da will of Da Screenwrita.*

As Diego exited the car to go to the next, The Oracle leaned into the vehicle. Thumbing up the lock on the opposite door, he again stood up and smiled. Not knowing exactly why, only that this was ordered by the voice, the job was now complete. Only one more task in the vicinity must be finished.

"Every fucking radio in every fucking car! What the fucking hell?" All the radios were dead. Diego Diego was furious. Raging, he couldn't do anything but storm away in a fury.

His new friend caught up with him and easily matched pace. "Take it easy, bra." Gesturing to the gas station up ahead, he offered to try and ease the troubled Latino. "Wanna grab a coke." Shrugging, D supposed it couldn't hurt.

𝕂𝕚𝕜𝕚𝕜𝕜𝕜

Entering the parking lot of the gas station, Smokes walked directly along the curb between the convenience store and the highway. His friend slowed and watched with confusion. When Smokes was nearly even with the entrance to the business, he made a ninety degree turn to head straight toward the door. He passed a closed Frito-Lay truck; he nonchalantly flipped the latch to lock the rear roll down door. Grinning from ear to ear, he felt The Screenwriter was now satisfied. The reason may not have yet been known, but this was what The Screenwriter commanded.

After completing both tasks, he was now free. At least, for what was left of the day. He could grab a shopping bag once inside the store to load down with packs of Bubbli-cious and Reese's Cups! For some reason, his nicotine craving didn't seem to be present. Newports were on his mind every time he stopped at a convenience store. Now though, grabbing some smokes didn't even cross his mind. Maybe after a considerable time of not nursing his habit, the urge would strike him.

Getting a Dr Pepper from the cooler and dumping a box of beef sticks into one of the pockets of his cargo shorts, D looked at his friend. "We probably ain't got time to walk back to The Hill before it gets dark. You wanna make camp here?"

Smacking at least four entire packs of bubblegum, The Oracle gestured to the door. "Naw dawg, Publix." D wasn't sure if he understood that final word around the pounds of watermelon flavored gum.

"The grocery store?" Smokes nodded and started walking out the door. Diego began a question to his exiting friend's back. "But...?"

He would just say, "Trust me, wheat bread." It ain't like he ain't been right so far. The Latino began walking out the door, putting his faith in The Oracle. *Doing what he's said has kept me alive so far. I better stick with him.*

"Aye aye, Capitán! I'm right behind you,"

Convincing his Hispanic friend it was safe to enter the large supermarket was difficult. Hesitation and slow acceptance have been foreseen, but The Oracle didn't realize his friends stubbornness would be such a pain to get around. Eventu-ally though, both survivors stood inside Publix, entirely unmolested. D finally felt comfortable enough to put his gun back in his waistband and move around the cavernous building freely.

Though the two of them had taken what they wanted from the Exxon, it just now dawned on Diego that everything in the store was now free. Realizing there were no peevies in the grocery store, he ran to the aisle containing Fritos, laughing maniacally the entire way. He shouted out a poor attempt at Singing. "Ay yI yI yI yI! I'm a Bandito, I love corn chips, I do. I love corn chips, I take them from you!"

Smokes finally rounded the corner, shirt smeared with what looked like ice cream. He rolled his head to the left and spun on his heel. "Mon, mufucka. We gotta get our shit set up."

Diego followed, not understanding. Once at the spot, it made sense to him. Smokes was laying out blankets as pallets and fifty pound bags of dog food as pillows. *At least we gonna be comfortable even if we sleeping on a linoleum floor.*

The record screeched to an abrupt stop in his mind. "Fucking seriously? You really think I'm sleeping on the floor with those things everywhere? Let's at least go to one of the back rooms. I'm sure there's a manager's office or–"

"No." The Oracle interrupted authoritatively.

"But we could at least–"

"I done told you, wheat bread. No!"

"Motherfucker." D clenched his fists. "Why?"

The heaviest of the duo closed his eyes for an exceptionally long blink. "Listen. Dey don't like big buildins, dey in small rooms." D looked as if he was about to question The Oracle who beat him to the punch. "Trust me, scats."

Arguing was pointless. There was no reason for the Latino not to trust him. In fact, trusting Smokes was why he was still breathing. *If this shit goes bad, I'm 'blaming him. A lot of difference that would make,* he smiled bitterly.

When he broke his silence after an eternity, he spoke through the darkness. "If we get jumped before the sun comes up, I'm gonna kill you, homes." It might have taken several hours or only several minutes, but Diego finally lay down and drifted off. Little did he know, his large black friend was asleep long before his final words.

Smokes wasn't afraid. Though he sometimes wished to be like everyone else, for the ability to fear the unknown, he could rest at peace. Was this Blessed Assurance?

You's always at da place you is always post to be.

CHAPTER 5
Boulevard of Broken Dreams

Surprisingly, D slept solid through most of the night. There had been no naked plague victims breaking into the store and assaulting the survivors. Assuming the thick glass of the sliding doors kept sound from getting through, he hadn't even been awakened by noise from the crazies outside. It made him wonder if there actually had been any blue infected people. *Maybe me and Smokes are just two homeless nuts sleeping in an abandoned building!*

That was his thought just as he cracked his eyes open. Laying on his back, he could make out a figure standing over him in the darkness. Color might not have been discernible, but he could have guessed the shade of the naked form looking down at him and smiling. His gaze couldn't break away from what looked like the end of a misshapen hot dog resting on a couple of shriveled figs. This was of course surrounded by a bush of matted hair.

A dark spray of something resembling slimy Gak was being expelled from the rear of the peevie. This broke his concentration away from the spectacle of miniaturized genitalia long enough for him to look up at the solid orbs grinning down at him. Before he could move his hand to the machine pistol laying at his side, the thing let out a roaring gurgle that could have been a laugh before it dropped its teeth on his neck.

✶✶✶✶✶✶

He shot up, panting and sweating. Reaching for his gat, he peered around for his compadre. *Thank Dios, only a dream! Where Smokes at, anyway?*

Before he was able to call out for his friend, he had to reach up to feel his neck. It wasn't wet. No pain. Nothing felt ripped or torn. The dream just seemed so horribly vivid, D was astonished there were no teeth marks.

Standing, he looked up and shouted. "Yo, homes!"

The prophet stopped at the end cap, drinking an instant breakfast. "Da fuck you want, wheat bread? I ain't got time to wait on yo slow as." He raised his hand and pointed at his many wristwatches. "It da 7th! We gots things to see and peoples to do."

Smiling at the intentional mix up, Diego was about to ask if he had gotten an extra breakfast shake. Just then, The Oracle tossed something underhanded at him. Catching it, he looked at the can. "Slim Fast, really?"

"Gotta watch yo Figga. Sko, homeslice!"

✶✶✶✶✶✶

Exiting the supermarket with nothing more than full bellies and some grab bags of Fritos, the pair of wanderers started across the parking lot. Not heading straight north, D was confident they were moving in that general direction. It was so quiet, a person speaking anywhere in the county could've been heard.

Diego clicked his tongue to make an echo that seemed to reverberate for a considerable time. "Another lonely day, right ese?"

Speaking over his shoulder, The Oracle chuckled flatly. "Maybe fo you, wheat bread."

⸎⸎⸎⸎⸎⸎

Again reaching the point where the four lanes split, they traveled north, right up the middle of south bound Gunter Avenue. The party would not stop unless commanded, or if they were to stumble upon an ice cream truck.

Most of the journey was made in relative silence. This bothered Smokes to no end. Peacefulness only gave The Screenwriter more opportunity to play and replay events in his mind; events that had already occurred and were yet to take place. From now on, he would do his best to always keep himself occupied, quieting the voice.

With his chin quivering, he almost broke out into sobs passing McDonald's. Though the building would be used by humans, at some point, for some reason, Smokes knew he would never eat another Big Mac. At least, not from this location.

Suddenly, Smokes nearly screamed to his friend, seemingly the only other uninfected person in the city. "So you thank zombies is livin' dead or undead?"

We really talking about movie shit? Lifting his shoulders and lowering his head, trying to make himself smaller, D whispered harshly. "The fuck wrong with you, homes? Keep it down!"

Not lowering his volume in the slightest, The Oracle continued screeching. "Man, da sun up. Dey ain't gonna getcha!"

Peering around and not seeing a single hostile, D loosened. Noticing the other cut his eyes at him, he had to think about it. *Night of the Living Dead?* "Suppose they'd be living–"

"Mufucka! Da hell you thankin', wheat bread? Dey ain't vampires."

The argument continued for several blocks.

Even passing through the residential areas of town, the surroundings remained completely still. With heavier tree cover, D expected to see or at least hear some of the peevies. It would have made him put more trust in what Smokes said about them not liking sunlight. There wasn't necessarily the feeling of being watched. More bothersome to Diego than being attacked was the notion that they were totally alone.

Not hearing a single bird tweet or chirp only magnified the creepiness for the Latino. People and animals disappearing was strange, but fowl also vanishing sent chills up his spine. Random splatters of black goop being swarmed upon by various insects were the only indication anything other than the two survivors lived. *Ain't much, but at least it's something!*

Coming within blocks of the county courthouse ahead and to their right, the comrades halted at an intersection. The Oracle closed his eyes and grew still. After a pause, he opened them and looked to his friend. "We prolly needs to get on dat sidewalk." Gesturing to the curb on his right, they stepped up onto the concrete walkway.

Though willing to follow the orders, D wanted to question his black friend's reasoning. Keeping an eye out for anything fishy on the other side of the road, Diego saw no movement and couldn't tell if there had been any recently. *Dry cleaners, nail salon, Excelsior Comics, a thrift store, nothing unusual. All of these places just looked empty.*

Luisa ain't crossed my mind since we left the apartment. Hope she's hunkering down at the hospital with the rest of the nurses. It seemed peculiar that Smokes could somehow make him forget everything else. *It don't matter, I guess. Can't do nothing for her from here anyway.*

They finally reached the courthouse. It was massive compared to every other building in the city. Conversation on more insignificant movie trivia had begun, but abruptly died when closing on the large complex. The silence was nearly overpowering.

Smokes' finger followed an invisible pointer. It landed on a metal ladder attached to the side of the courthouse building, reaching all the way to the roof.

"We gots to see what we can see, homey."

Understanding his friend wanted to get a better view of the surrounding area, D made an offer. "Si, ese." He reached down to his MAC 10."I got a gat. I'll go up and check the coast is clear." *Even though it's the middle of the day and they afraid of sun, if Smokes is to be believed. At least I'll look useful.*

It was almost surprising Smokes didn't correct or refuse him. He gestured for Diego to take the lead.

"Sho as shit, wheat bread. Ladies first." he joked.

D laughed, simulating a curtsy as he passed The Oracle. He

was over halfway up the rungs when a jolting cry from below him made him stop. "Fuck naw, ain't doin' it!"

CHAPTER 6
Post To Be

Stopping his upward movement, D looked below at his friend after the exclamation.

"Everything all right down there, homes?"

The Oracle, who was still standing at the foot of the ladder, lifted his hand to signal *OK*.

"We good, dawg. Keep movin'."

Though his voice almost broke when doing it, Smokes played everything off as cool. Diego might have found it strange that his friend would call out for seemingly no reason, but he found everything about the gangsta strange. When the Latino made it nearly to the top, Smokes placed his hand on the ladder rung to begin his journey up.

It had been like a dream. A dream he couldn't control. The type of dream one knows is a dream, but it's still completely horrifying. The Oracle saw himself reach the roof; D was standing on the north side of the building, holding his hand up to shade his eyes. The only route to where his friend waited would take Smokes directly by a door. That door opened into a small shed that contained the stairwell leading down inside the building. Passing by the door, he lightly turned the knob just enough to unlatch the bolt. The action went entirely unnoticed by D who was still scanning the area. Now, Smokes continued moving forward to stand beside him on his right. The Oracle did everything in his power to halt the dream; the command, the orders being given to him, the scripted events, and the vision of things that were supposed to be. This demand was something he didn't want to partake in.

"Fuck naw, ain't doin' it!" As far as he could recall, this was the first time he had directly refused the control of The Screenwriter. Smokes may have been willing to play his role, but there was no way he would willingly murder or allow Diego to be murdered. He couldn't bring himself to do it.

But there was no choice. Things had to play out exactly as foretold. Demands of The Screenwriter were impossible to refuse. Smokes was able to see now, it wasn't something that had to happen, it was something that would happen, something that might as well have already have happened. *Cept fo da hurtin'*. It wasn't his decision, so he felt a little better about it.

Opening his eyes he was still standing on the ground at the foot of the ladder.

"Everything all right down there, homes?"

"We good, dawg. Keep movin'."

As he made his way up the rungs, he begged, debated and tried to bargain with the voice. With each handhold, he slowly understood the reason for the task. Though acceptance was growing, he still wasn't happy about it.

Take Dis cup from me!

Smokes pulled himself onto the roof. There stood his

friend on the far side, shielding his gaze from the sun with his hand, just like in the vision.

Thank Black Jesus he got his back to me.

Sneakers crunched on the gravel as he walked. Turning his head for the briefest of seconds, D only did so to signify he was aware of the other's approach.

What if I don't? Say I just keep on walkin'. What you gonna do bout it? The Oracle mentally stood defiant.

"Do not think you can decide!"

Not by his own will, Smokes' hand lifted and ran over the doorknob, softly turning it. He had just sealed his friend's fate, whether it was actually his doing or not.

Should I holler? Give my bra warnin's?

"Even if you did, how would you explain what you just did?"

Perhaps he had planned to say something, but the words wouldn't come. Was it possible to defy The Screenwriter? Did anyone truly make decisions on their own fate?

You's always at da place you is always post to be!

But that begs the question, how long has The Screenwriter been in control? How far-reaching is his mastery? If there is a script, is there also an audience?

Standing to the right of his friend, Smokes pointed to the double bridges of Highway 431 across the Tennessee River. "One bridge blowed up." On the north bound side, there was definitely a wide gap in the concrete. Just to the right of the bridge, docked at the Marina, some type of boxy, old wooden sailboat could be seen.

Briefly placing his hand on D's shoulder, the door creaking open behind them was only audible if one listened closely. After giving his shoulder a light tug, Smokes lowered his hand. This caused the Latino to turn his head from facing forward and slightly in the direction of his friend. Catching a hint of blue, D spun.

"Yo, we got atacar... sneak attack, compadre!" He pulled the machine pistol from his waistband, lining up on the approaching peevie.

Maybe it was true, the thing was stumbling around and covering its eyes. *But why's it out in the middle of the day?* D thought that maybe it had just been sleeping inside the stairwell and had awakened to the smell of humans. What woke it up?

The monster kept its face down, only occasionally glancing up to see what was before it. Painful screams came from the creature, but it knew food was almost within reach. Taking his time, D lined up his sights on the downward facing forehead. Squeezing the trigger briefly, a single bullet projected from the muzzle.

Headshot! Diego watched his single improvised sniper round slam into the infected cranium. Just as the demonia glanced up, the tiny piece of lead made contact with the bridge of its nose.

Its face briefly sank in before exploding as bone, mucus, and bloodied hamburger meat erupted from the upper half of the skull. Yellow eyes simply vanished in the torrent of expelling organic material. Dropping to the ground in a twitching heap, the orbless peevie would only void its bowels for a final time.

Before the round collided with the face of the blue nudist, three more bumbled out of the door. Understanding in which general direction the uninfected meat lay, they stumbled around and screeched an earsplitting squeal akin to that of bats or monkeys. Fighting through the pain, one was able to keep its eyes up for a fraction longer than the others. It moved more fluidly than the other two stragglers.

Unfortunately for Diego, it was not one of the first recipients of high velocity metal.

Out of the three, D sent a burst low at enemy number one. Four shots made contact with the area of the right knee. Kneecap seemed to invert before shattering into uncountable pieces. Every vein transporting blood from the upper body to the lower leg had to be ruptured. As the creature collapsed onto its side, it was apparent the only connection that remained to the calf was stringy tendons and some ragged skin. All the animal could do was scream in unimaginable pain and violently squirted something akin to baby diarrhea from its rectum.

Third in this lineup of peevie received the next burst. A couple rounds punctured the top of the left shoulder. Three more bullets destroyed the collarbone and punctured life-sustaining arteries in the neck. D didn't know if it was the jugular or carotid, but blood definitely shot like a geyser from the burst throat. Even if the animal was technically in the fight, it would be technically dead in just a few minutes. Impossible gallons of black sewage rocketed from the blue ass.

It's said two out of three ain't bad. Whoever coined that phrase never dealt with three rampaging cannibals at the same time. Luckier and much more agile, the still attacking peevie charged blindly in the direction of Diego. By the time the other two bodies dropped in their own steaming pools of feces, the comer was closer than anticipated.

Shouting in surprise, D sprayed a wild burst of automatic fire at the charging monster. The right pectoral muscle was ripped into shreds; nipple bounced away and seemed to disappear. Before pain could be understood, tip of the tiny, erect penis was impacted by a metrically calibered piece of lead. Blood freely ran from the shaft as the head launched between the legs and disappeared into the chunky liquid seeping from the anus.

Clearly, the beast wouldn't be alive more than a few torturous moments. The demonic former human was entirely unable to stop its own forward momentum. All it wanted was to curl up on the roof to seek a fraction of comfort, burying its face in the gravel to keep the UV rays away from its yellow eyes. Basically plummeting straight ahead, the thing collided with D.

A horrified spectator, Smokes was only able to regretfully survey. Wishing he could reach out to grab his friend, The Oracle could do nothing but watch what was supposed to be. Could he have changed the outcome in the slightest? *Maybe I just aint tryin' hard nuff.*

Going airborne, Diego Diego was about to impact the concrete below. Smokes looked him in the eyes. "I'm sorry!" he mouthed.

Toppling to his catastrophic end, D held eye contact with his amigo for that fraction of a second that seemed to last forever. In that brief instant, Smokes knew that he knew. Diego understood, Smokes had somehow already seen this. The fading light in comprehending eyes seemed, at least to The Oracle, to shout out. "You could've prevented this!"

I do dat? This had not been foreseen. The Oracle was unsure if he had chosen to mouth that. Of course, he wanted to, but he was beginning to understand choice meant very little in this new world. Or perhaps, maybe there never was a choice in anything.

Since his friend was seconds from death, would it have made a difference if D suddenly gained understanding? Maybe it was a choice! Did it matter? If that was his choice, was there any choosing at any other point? This inner debate could go on for ages. Would the truth ever be discovered?

Looking down now at the unmoving corpse of his friend on the sidewalk, it seemed, at first, Diego remained totally unharmed. A blue, naked, shit covered body lay on top of him, but he appeared to be nothing more than asleep at first glance.

A growing, crimson halo told the predestined truth. Morbidly angelic, twistedly sainted, disturbingly beatific, bloody cherub. The only living person he'd seen in days had now fulfilled his role.

The Sacrifice.

"It is finished. Now, the script must move forward."

Turning to face the South side of the roof, he noticed D's machine pistol lying on the gravel to his side. Conveniently, he reached down picked it up and placed it in his waistband, like it was supposed to be there. As he made his way across the top of the building to climb down the ladder, he was already being prepared for what was to come.

Walking north, straight up southbound Gunter Avenue, The Oracle noticed the occasional unlit but reflective taillights of stopped or parked northbound vehicles. His thoughts were interrupted by nothing.

Just my thoughts? His consciousness was continually assaulted by the ever present voice. Human camaraderie would be needed soon; this deluge of impossible information was unbearable. Infeasible prevision would drive the most adept mind into the bowels of insanity.

Unsure what the reason was, he began moving up the road toward the northbound bridge. *But dis bridge got a hole in it! I guess it post to be.* Putting one foot in front of the other, he had just reached the totally concrete section of Highway.

One foot in front of da otha. The thought made him glance

down, noticing his shoe had somehow come untied. After bending down to fasten the bands, he began to stand. *Da gat in my hand?* Strange. He didn't remember pulling it from his waistband.

As he raised, he forcefully smacked his elbow on the driver side rear view mirror on the closest vehicle. "Mufuckin' piece of bitch!" Dropping back down, he rubbed his impacted funny bone.

Holy shit! He knew what was coming. His actions had been destined. *Had I seen dis befo?*

Whether or not this had been foreseen, it now became immediately familiar. Everything happened exactly as it had so this event could take place. Occurrences laid out far into the distant future in his mind. Though major happenings in the hereafter were now foreseen, The Oracle was to continue to appear entirely clueless. A gracious smile beaming down from The Screenwriter could be felt.

Far to his right, he heard the halting command he expected to hear. "Freeze and put up your hands!"

Fingers opened to drop the MAC 10. Raising his hands before standing, he wiped away his smile. The Oracle mumbled to himself the mantra that had kept him sane for the past week.

"You's always at da place you is always post to be."

THE BEGINNING...

ABOUT JAVAN BONDS

Javan Bonds is the Amazon Best Selling author of the Zompoc series, Still Alive. This series includes Book One: Zombie Lake, Book Two: Zombie Island, Book Three: Zombies On A Plane, Book Four: Zombie Oasis, and now Book Five: Zombie River Run.

The Still Alive series follows a small group of survivors in a small southern town as they try to keep their wits about them and make a new life in a world overrun by naked, blue-skinned, yellow-eyed zombies that are nocturnal and spew shit on everything. Not to mention that they are intent on chomping all the uninfected in an attempt to infect or devour every last piece of flesh on their bones. Fun times!?! Think WW Z, Zombieland, and Shaun Of The Dead, only better.

Bonds has had to overcome numerous obstacles in writing as well as living his daily life. Diagnosed at the age of eleven with Friedreich's Ataxia (FA), (a progressively degenerative neuromuscular disease under the umbrella of the Muscular Dystrophy Association), he has slowly been robbed of his physical abilities through the years. Bonds became wheelchair bound in 1999 but that was only the beginning of his setbacks. His sight began to diminish in 2010 to the point he is now legally blind and his hearing began failing to the point he now can't hear individual voices in a noisy room. In spite of all of this, he continues work tirelessly seven days a week on his writing.

Bonds never let his disability rule him and has lived, loved, and laughed often.

In late 2015 at only 28 years old Bonds was told he may have only a short time left due to the ravages of FA on his heart. After learning this he has been hard at work to complete his other novels and have them finished before his time in this world runs out.

In mid-2016 Bonds published his first novel FREE STATE OF DODGE, the first book in a dystopian series about America in decline and its rebirth.

Javan has these words of wisdom to offer for others stricken by a life-shortening illness:

Live your life. Light your candle on both ends and let it burn. It may burn out faster but your flame will burn brighter than some who live much longer.

Keep an eye on his flame, watch it burn!

Bonds hopes you enjoy the Still Alive series with its humor, pop culture references and excessive zombie killing action. Oh, and there is a pirate ship too.

15

PICKING IT UP IN THE MIDDLE

BY E.E. ISHERWOOD

I

"So. Is this your idea of a first date?" Melissa whispered as if she were in church. "If it is, I'd say this was a dud."

"I'm not sure. It isn't how I imagined it, though. I thought there'd be fewer zombies. Less sweating. A lot less screaming." Phil chanced a look out of the thick blood-splattered window of the mine-resistant ambush protected, or MRAP, military truck he shared with the pretty blonde he often called Mel. They'd already survived for almost two weeks since the zombie plague swept over St. Louis, and they'd just helped most of their party escape onto a plane, but the two of them had chosen to stay behind.

"What have I done?" she asked in a hollow voice.

A pair of tilt-winged Marine Corps V-22 Ospreys had landed inside Busch Stadium, but only one of them managed to clear the chaos on the field and fly to freedom. The other was overwhelmed with zombies as it took off. It hovered twenty feet above third base but then veered into the lower seats where it split open and was fed upon like a bloated carcass on the high savanna.

His young friend Liam had gotten his great-grandma onto the first plane, which was cause for celebration because she apparently carried the cure, but both Ospreys and a lot more survivors would have made it to safety if Melissa hadn't driven through the outfield gate in the first place. The Boy Scouts riding with them had tried to close the gate after they entered, but when that failed the whole city of zombies followed the truck into the stadium. Things fell apart with the speed of a lightning strike, and Melissa took responsibility for it all.

She remained seated halfway down the bench of the rear cargo hold, well out of the line of sight of any zombies looking in through the front windows.

"You want to talk about it?" He scooted next to her and put her sweat-drenched hand in his. She braced a semi-automatic pistol on her far leg, probably to hide the fact she was shaking uncontrollably.

Since the day they'd met, Melissa seemed like the kind of woman who always knew what she was doing. At first glance, she appeared to be a soccer mom with refined tastes in clothing. She wore tight khaki shorts, a white long-sleeved shirt, and name brand hiking boots, like she was on safari. However, she was more than a suburban mom taking kids to the game. She'd driven the six-wheeled MRAP like she'd been doing it her whole life. He'd navigated for her from the passenger seat, so he saw her expertise first hand. Everything about her impressed the hell out of him, but he couldn't ignore what just happened.

"Which part? I've had ten disasters in a row. The TV station? The drive out there in the streets? The gate? The plane crash?" She laughed quietly but she sounded near hysterical.

"It's okay," he said in a comforting voice. "All this isn't our fault."

Melissa had gotten the MRAP onto the baseball field right up next to the open ramp of the giant plane, but when it came time to open her door and get out with the others she panicked worse than a rookie officer at their first bar fight.

"I—I just couldn't move, Phil." She squeezed his hand. "I saw the Marines get slaughtered by the zombies. I saw Liam slide down the windshield and fall over the side because of all the blood out there. I thought our whole party was going to get eaten on the AstroTurf. I couldn't make myself go out there and die, even after all he did for me."

She released a few sobs.

Of all the people he'd met since the world ended almost two weeks ago, she was one of the strongest. They'd talked about their pasts in the extended periods of tedium during that time, but the most he could get out of her was that yes, she did serve in the military and no, she didn't want to talk about it. He'd seen her do some amazing things recently, not the least of which was drive the MRAP like a race car. Pretty hard to do with a vehicle that handles like a freight train.

"You know, I was in the same spot as you not long ago."

He gently tugged at her hand to get her to turn to him.

Phil continued. "It was the first time I met Liam, Victoria, and Grandma Marty. After I, uh, talked to my dead wife through Marty, I got them all across that bridge. Liam asked me to get them home. Practically begged me. I figured I owed 'em one, so I gave them a ride in my patrol car. His house wasn't that far, and I intended to drop them off at the first opportunity I had, but the town was in full on train wreck mode. Those sirens sent the world into a tailspin, and everyone from St. Louis flooded my little town."

It was his turn to get choked up. Melissa knew the back-story well because she was in his town when it happened, but he'd never told her the next part.

"That's when my partner Billy was shot dead in my front seat," he said with finality. "I pulled over a few minutes later and made a big deal about dragging him into the woods to give him a safe resting place. I made sure I was alone. I'd like to say I stood there and saluted like a proper color guard, but I more or less blubbered over his body because I couldn't hold it together."

He let that sit for half a minute. Melissa sniffled and glanced down toward the blood stains on the floor. The tears wanted to come out for him, too, but he had to bite his lip to keep them at bay.

"I almost gave up, Mel," he said with a wobbly voice. "I had the gun in my hand." She turned back and looked him in the eyes, which didn't help his emotions.

"I seriously thought about it for the longest minute of my life, but I came to accept something larger is at work here. If it's God I don't know, but somehow Beth talked to me through Grandma Marty on the bridge, and she didn't tell me there was no hope. I'm never going to give up. Not on myself. Not on you. Not on the world."

He made a valiant effort at fighting the tears, but one escaped down his cheek. It merged easily with the beads of sweat and fell off his face before she saw it.

"What's done is done, Mel." He thought of the woman in front of him, but also, he was ashamed to realize, of how he wasn't there to protect his wife when she slid off that road six months ago. "You did good getting us here. You helped our friends escape. Be proud of your successes, not ashamed of what else you could have done."

She leaned in, and the floodgates opened as they hugged.

2

Later, as Melissa's confidence replenished her empty reservoirs, she sat next to him with no tears or shaking. She holstered her pistol without further incident and they listened to the endless shooting spree outside the metal walls of their 120-degree sauna on wheels. They took turns nursing their last bottle of water.

"I'd love to air this thing out," she said as a suggestion.

"Me too, but we can't risk a stray bullet coming in a cracked window."

"A/C?" she said hopefully.

"If we start using equipment, it may bring the wrong crowd to us." It was almost worth the risk, because he desperately wanted to cool off, too, but the zombies were relentless once they had a target. The virus burned through the living and made them bleed through their eyes, ears, and noses a lot like Ebola, but it could only be transmitted through biting. That was the only piece of good luck about them, however, because every zombie and everything they touched ended up covered in the red stuff. If they were discovered in the truck, the zombies would crawl all over it and probably drip blood right through the open windows. For now, he preferred heat over blood.

Phil craned his neck to see out the front.

He'd been waiting for survivors to fight their way out to them, but the zombies on the field never seemed to clear away. Starting the engine or internal systems might make the infected stick around. On the other hand, the longer they stayed quiet and hidden in the truck, the less likely anyone would try to get to them.

It had been over an hour since the plane took off, and he spent most of that time coaxing Mel back from the edge. Every so often a metallic, "ping," would indicate they'd taken fire from impatient or inaccurate shooters in the stands.

"That's a .22 round. Very small." Phil tried to keep the discussion light and topical, and not dwell on the fact there were still survivors fighting zombies in the stadium or that they had no way to help them.

A moment later a series of hard clangs hit the truck.

"Probably an AR or Mini-14. Sounds intentional." Over the past two weeks, people shot at the MRAP everywhere they drove. It was probably a desperate way to get their attention, but it happened so much it became simple background noise. He hated the new reality, but he stopped feeling guilty after the fiftieth time.

A blast a few minutes later had to be from a shotgun. The little pellets sounded like a handful of gravel had been thrown at them.

When he mentioned this to her, she came out of her shell and laughed a bit.

"So, this is definitely a first date," she said as she leaned against his shoulder. "You're giving me a wonderful play-by-play of our meetup here in the romantic city."

He stroked her wet hair. "I can't deny you're mildly attractive—" He intentionally cut himself off, as if he'd said too much.

"Mildly?" she said with fake concern.

A witty comeback sat on his tongue, but it would take

some time to accept dating was even in his vocabulary anymore. This was more like grabbing the first normal person of the opposite sex and refusing to let go for fear of never seeing such a rare creature again. But he could say with certainty it was more than infatuation. They'd shared a bond driving the MRAP all over the apocalypse and the cramped space and high stress didn't send them screaming to get away from each other. He could have walked off the back deck and gotten on that plane, too, but he stayed with her, and didn't regret the decision. That all had to count for something.

"Beth, do you like her?" he thought.

Was his dead wife now an invisible angel hovering nearby, watching him fight for his life? Maybe she tipped the scales for him many different times, and not just on that bridge. Imagining her as a helpful angel made her death hurt a little less than it normally did.

He struggled not to think about his daughter, even though she died in the same wreck. The thought of her as an angel would be comforting to a degree, but she was already his angel when she was alive, so he pushed it away.

He hated himself for wondering if they were better off already dead, instead of having to survive in the lawless world of zombies. It was one depressing thought after another if he dwelled on his little girl or his wife. Other than saving grandma Marty, he didn't have many victories or happy moments since the sirens.

Being with Melissa could be a new happy moment, he insisted to himself.

They stayed on that bench for several hours as the pitched battle played itself out in the stands. The fighting went up into the highest rows as the survivors kept retreating from the zombies on their tails.

"There's not a damned thing we can do for them," he said. He sincerely hoped the living were able to escape out of the ball park, but he was also glad he didn't have to turn people away from the MRAP. The Marines guarding the Ospreys had to use guns when their planes reached capacity, but the one crumpled in the stands didn't do a good enough job of it.

He shuddered but felt better as soon as she spoke again.

"We could have made a big mess out there if we had rounds for the minigun up top, you know?"

They ran out of ammo getting into the city earlier in the day.

"You like shaking things up, don't you?" She'd turned his life upside down the moment they met back in front of Liam's house.

"Do I scare you?" she asked with surprise in her laughter.

"God, yes." Despite being surrounded by a city's worth of zombies, he admitted he hadn't been as nervous around a woman since his first date with Beth.

"I like scaring tough guys." She gripped his arm while they sat hip to hip.

He tried to think of a witty reply to her, but nothing sounded right. By the time he was ready to talk about something else, she'd fallen asleep on his shoulder. Except for the buckets of sweat, and chaos outside, it was what passed for a pleasant afternoon for him.

The day wore on into evening and eventually the gunfire dwindled to almost nothing, at least inside the stadium. The faint rumble of guns and explosions continued in the city of St. Louis beyond the gates of the iconic ball field.

"Mmm, I don't want to move from this seat," Melissa cooed when she woke up.

He drifted off a few times as well, but he'd been up for the last hour listening to things settle down around them.

"Me either," he agreed. "We can survive a long time in this tin can, but things are going to get real once we need a bathroom break."

"Ewww," she replied.

"Ha! I'm sure you've loved spending the day clearing your pores as much as I did, but when the zombies thin out, we have to move somewhere."

"I feel totally refreshed, but we can go if you'd like." She brushed the wet, matted hair from her forehead like it was a delightful new hairstyle. "Maybe we can go back to the Boy Scout park?"

They'd spent a lot of time in a Boy Scout camp deep in the woods south of the city, but zombies ruined most of it before they left to rescue Liam and Grandma. It took a miracle to find Liam in the chaos of downtown and they needed a second one to get him and Marty onto that plane. It was probably an act of God he was still alive to reflect on it. Maybe it was fate he and Melissa were brought together in the truck at that moment, or perhaps Beth did have her cherub wings, so she could interfere at will. Still, he heard no little voice telling him where to go next. It was like his direction had left when Marty and Liam got on the plane.

"That would take us south. The Osprey was going that way. What are the odds?"

"Not good," she replied. "We can't count on luck. We have to pick somewhere based on sound military doctrine and find a place with fortified defenses. A prison—"

"No way in hell," he shot back.

"Oh. Right. I bet you locked up a bunch of the inmates." She giggled in a playful manner, but they both knew it was true. "Then, how about..." She clicked her tongue several times while she considered where to go. "A shopping mall?"

"Almost as bad as the prison. It'd be a lot like being inside this truck. We'd be safe behind the gates of one of the stores, but once the walking sick found us we'd be stuck there until the food ran out."

"But they always go there on TV," she said thoughtfully.

"That's why we have to avoid them. I bet every shopping mall has been looted and destroyed because people were desperate to get there before everyone else. If it's something they know from television, you can count on people to ruin it."

"Wow, you're a real downer." She pressed her lips against her tongue and made a silly sound.

"Hey now. I'm a cop. I basically babysit adults for a living. You learn to think the worst of most people."

She continued. "Okay, copper, you want to shoot down my next idea?"

"Fire away."

"Okay, give me a minute." She stood up but had to hunch over a little to avoid scraping her head on the roof. She got in front of him and used both hands to steady herself on the ceiling straps. "You're going to love this one."

"I'm waiting." He smiled broadly, catching her spirit.

Melissa held the straps on the ceiling and he couldn't help but admire her. She was filthy from the endless sweat and dirt of the last few days, but it didn't take away from the sweaty glow of her face, the twinkle in her lovely eyes, or the way she bit her lip while she thought. After many seconds of watching her hang there, he caught on.

"You have no idea, do you?"

Her Cheshire Cat grin suited her. "Nope. Not a damned clue. How about you?"

"We should go south," he said while trying to sound confident.

"Why?"

He shrugged despite himself. "The plane went that way."

"That's how we're playing this? We're going with luck, after all?" She chuckled, then offered her hand to pull him up. When he took it, she yanked him off his seat, surprising him yet again at how strong she was. As they met in the middle of the confined hold of the armored truck, he appreciated how feminine she was under all the grime.

His weathervane spun wildly as his conflicted feelings about his dead wife lashed against his uncertain future with Melissa. In that moment, however, he accepted the roll of the dice fate had given him.

"My luck has been pretty good on first dates," he said while looking at her lips before falling into her deep, blue eyes.

"Is that so?" she said as if daring him to kiss her.

Despite the open invitation, he pulled the emergency brake at the last possible moment. Instead of kissing her, he brought her into another hug.

It was a colossal disappointment to him, but she didn't seem to notice his conflict as she held him tight.

"Yuck. You're all sweaty," she said with an ironic laugh because they were both soaked to the bone.

3

"Let's get the hell out of here," he said a moment or two later. No matter how much he wanted to keep his arms around her and work on his dating confidence, the blood-splattered, oven-temperature truck interior wasn't the right place.

"We are going to continue this, Phil," she said as if to reassure him.

"I know. Our date's not over by a long shot, but I like to show a woman a good time, you know? See the town. Burn a few bridges. Stuff like that."

"I can't wait," she said with a final tight squeeze before letting him out of her grasp.

Talk turned serious as they went toward the front of the MRAP. The dark gray shadows of dusk consumed the wreckage of the Osprey and made it difficult to see the zombies in the stands and on the field nearby.

Melissa jumped into the driver's seat. "So, we're in agreement. We'll head out the gate and turn south, correct?"

"Take me home, or lose me forever," he suggested. He was fairly certain the angry citizens of St. Louis had burned his whole town to the foundation, including his humble block. He had more of a home in the front seat of the military rig than he had back there, but it was just a dumb joke.

"Home it is," she countered.

Getting into the city to rescue Liam and Marty that morning was a lot of luck mixed with an equal amount of skill. The roads were choked with abandoned vehicles facing south, especially at the bridges, but Melissa figured out how to ram derelict cars aside and make enough room to slip through. They might be able to escape St. Louis by retracing their route.

She started the motor, then glanced over with an expectant eyebrow. "Full air conditioning?"

"You don't have to ask. Crank it up!"

They both put their faces up against the vents on the

dashboard. It wasn't immediately cool, but the moving air was relief enough.

She leaned back in her seat. "You ready, sheriff?"

It was their little joke. He was no longer an officer and was never a sheriff.

"I'm ready, Melicious," he snickered as the air continued to bathe his face.

She revved the engine to warm it up. "That better mean I'm sweet and dainty," she jibed. While he watched, she unbuttoned her shirt and tied it off just under her breasts. She patted her bare tummy. "I needed to cool off."

"Yeah. Dainty. That's you, Ms. MRAP." He laughed, appreciating the irony of the feminine pin-up sitting in the cockpit of the big military truck.

"I like that name better." She buckled her seatbelt and pulled her ponytail across her shoulder, so it wasn't behind her. "Let's do this."

The nearest zombies moved closer and confirmed what he feared the whole day. The noisy engine alerted them to the potential presence of food.

"What's up with the headlights?" He'd seen her toggle them, but there was barely any light out in the field.

"Yeah. I think they're covered with blood or got broken by those we hit before. Mind hopping out and cleaning them?" Their journey through the city earlier in the day could be summed up best by imagining the sound of hundreds of heavy phone books getting tossed onto the outer hull. He didn't want to remember those, "books," were once human beings.

"I really shouldn't. Doctor said to avoid high stress and intense situations."

"Give me his name. I'm going to let him know what you've been doing with me."

"We haven't done anything," he almost stuttered.

She looked over with mirth in her eyes. "I'm talking about the driving. The shooting. Et cetera. What did you think I meant?"

Melissa didn't wait for a reply. The blonde-haired driver dropped it into gear and spun the steering wheel as she executed a slow turn into the crowd of zombies. It only took about twenty seconds before she hit the first one. They weren't going fast enough to splatter debris onto the front grill and hood, like they'd done earlier in the day. Instead, the truck rolled over the fallen speedbump with a muffled crunch.

He gave her a pretend frown, which she noticed.

"What? I can't help that they're so stupid," she said with all seriousness.

In that moment she seemed more like any number of teens he'd pulled over in his years of service. He relished the stops he made on young kids that fought the law on wearing seatbelts. They often used the same excuse: "They're so stupid. I don't need to wear one." For those teens, he preferred to use his, "officer unfriendly," voice, but for Melissa, he only cracked up.

A boyish impulse wanted her to hit every zombie she could, so it would thin the herd, but he knew a body could get wrapped around an axle and take away their best asset. There would be no hot-dogging in the Zombie Apocalypse.

She only hit and crushed three others on the way to the exit, though many loitered in the grass. Most zombies seemed to part for the slow-moving truck as if they were going to open the side doors like good little victims. It was a curiosity as they crossed through center field toward the open gate on the outfield wall where their stadium nightmare began.

"Here we go." Her voice was calm, which steadied his nerves. His old Mel was back.

The truck hopped over the uneven pavement of the sidewalk and curb, and a moment later she had them pointed south on a wide, empty street, as promised.

"This is going to be easy," she chirped as she practically bounced in her seat. "Look. The zombies are gone."

He admired her zest and smiled when she looked over to him, but the zombies had to be somewhere. The entire downtown was practically a solid mass of infected earlier that same day and there was no way they could have all cleared out.

"I hope you're right," he replied.

A couple of minutes passed before they saw zombies in the lanes ahead.

Melissa pointed. "There they are. Some of them, at least."

There were zombies spread out across the four-lane roadway, like stragglers at the end of a marathon. They walked away from the MRAP until it got close, then they surged to it as if it had personally wronged them in their past lives. The inevitable collisions began before they made it a mile from the stadium.

It was a sound he'd never get used to. "Someday you and I are going to take a drive where we don't run over these things."

She turned to reply. "I'd like nothing better." He was reassured by her white teeth in the low illumination of the cockpit. "I know it helps us in the long term, but I'm tired of putting these things out of commission. Sooner or later we're going to run out of gas, and we need to be clear of them."

She'd gotten to the heart of the matter. He eyed the gas

gauge, finding temporary assurance it wasn't below the empty line, but it was on the lower half of the dial.

Ahead, there was no end to the stumbling creatures walking their way out of the night.

4

It took five minutes for them to decide they had to change their destination. The zombies moved south in what appeared to be one big pack, and the crowd got thicker as they drove the same way.

"It's like there's a dinner bell going off over the horizon," he reasoned. "What do you think is making them go that way?"

"We've seen them move in small groups. If those groups linked up, maybe this whole city is just one big blob of zombie goodness, now?" Her voice trailed off.

He waited for a few moments for her to continue, but the packed roadway took most of her attention. So far, she'd managed to avoid the explosive ramming of earlier in the day, but she came close a few times. She'd been turning left and right on side streets for the past few minutes, seeking a path through the ever-growing crowd of infected.

"I have an idea," she said matter-of-factly.

Melissa pulled into a small residential alleyway and shut off the lights, but left the engine running.

"Wait for it," she said while holding up her pointer finger.

Hands pounded on the steel doors in the cargo hold a few seconds later.

"There they are," she said with a heavy exhale.

Fences lined the back yards on both sides of the pavement, so there wasn't enough room for the zombies to get by them, but that wasn't enough security for her.

"Now to get rid of that knocking for a few minutes, so we can think," Melissa said.

She accelerated up the alley with her lights off. At the far end of the block she braked and put it back into park. She'd left a little space before the next street, so they couldn't easily be seen from ahead. The zombies behind them would probably follow, but it would take time to walk the length of the alleyway.

"That should do it," she whispered. The glow of the instruments inside the cab lit her up, but her smile was gone.

"We can't go south," he said, knowing it was obvious.

"We can't go east," she replied. "The bridges over the Mississippi are gone."

"If they're all going south," he said, "maybe we should go north?" It wasn't his first choice, since he lived to the south, but anywhere they could find less zombies would be worth a try.

She nodded, seemed about to say something, but went rigid. She keyed off the ignition which shut down the engine. She shushed him preemptively as he was about to ask what was happening.

She whispered. "Outside."

Without the streetlights of a normal city block, the tall trees on the main streets in this part of the city created valleys of darkness between them. The roadway ahead was broad and open but pitch black.

He did see something move for a second as his eyes adjusted.

The compact car-sized disc was jet black and hovered in the middle of the street. There was a faint hum as the floating shape maintained an even height of about ten feet. From the side, it could easily be mistaken for a sleek UFO, though he didn't believe in them.

"Don't move," Melissa croaked in her almost-whisper.

That wasn't a problem, because he was fascinated by the vehicle. As best he could tell, it was painted onto the windshield for how still it was. If he hadn't looked ahead to see it move and then stop, he would have thought it was there the whole time, almost drawn into the nighttime landscape.

"Nothing can touch us in here," he assured himself.

He got antsy the longer the standoff went on. The zombies behind them were almost certainly marching their way, but he couldn't guess how long they would take.

The black craft's only tell was its gentle hum. It remained perfectly stationary, minute after minute.

Finally, almost as a relief to him, a door opened from under the main airframe. A long blue beam flicked on, pointed somewhere out of their view. It held that for a few seconds, until the stealthy shape moved the beam in a semi-circle, toward them.

The light crawled over the MRAP and flickered a few times as it got near the glass of the front windshield. An unnerving tick in the back of his brain was yelling at him to crouch down, but another part of him told him to listen to Melissa and stay still.

He kept watch as the light changed from a solid blue beam to a strobe light. The effect mesmerized him, though his mental alarms were as loud as his squad car sirens now.

"Hide," he told himself.

But he couldn't. Instead, he broke the rules and turned to see Melissa. The strobing lights formed a grid on her face and she seemed just as captivated as he was.

"Mel, down," he hissed. He grabbed at her arm and

pulled. At first, she seemed upset and resisted, but then she allowed herself to duck beneath the level of the dashboard to be out of the direct line-of-sight of the craft.

"It painted your face with that laser. I think it wanted a mugshot." There was no evidence to back up his claim, but it was his first impression.

"Did it get me?" she asked, as if in a dream.

"Don't know. Maybe it got us both. We have to move." It was critical he not show the panic he felt bubbling around in his stomach. He was reassured by the armor around them, but he couldn't shake the notion the floating disc meant to do them harm, and the practical side of him knew nothing was impenetrable.

"Nothing good happens after midnight," his old police captain had assured him. In the Zombie Apocalypse, nothing good happened ... ever.

Hands banged on the back doors of the truck.

He and Melissa both lurched with surprise at the sound. She whipped her head around so fast, her ponytail slapped him across the brow.

"Damn!" he shouted without thinking.

"Oh, Phil, I'm sorry!"

He'd been waiting for the zombies to arrive, but the flying disc stole his attention. After taking a second to assure himself he didn't crap his drawers, he stood up and pulled her with him.

"Go, go, go!" he blurted.

She turned the key and the motor cranked over, to his relief.

"Ram that thing if you have to," he said as he hopped into his chair.

"But I'm dainty," she complained.

He felt no remorse about giving her the advice, even

though deep down he knew it had to be an alphabet agency or the military operating it. Some jerk wad down in Florida was probably having a good laugh, thinking he'd caught two twitterpated teens in a stolen military rig.

"Just do your best, young woman," he replied as if she was a student driver but knowing full well she would do whatever it took to get them away from there.

Melissa kept as low as possible while she gunned the engine and sped out of the alley. The flying machine moved a few feet higher, safe from any threat of collision. The blue light continued in its attempt to penetrate the front and side windows as they went by, but it couldn't have been a better view than painting them directly from the front.

Once they were into the street, and put the drone behind them, the blue light came through a rear window. The thick glass diluted and diffused the beam, but it didn't make him feel any safer.

They were a hundred yards down the street before she could finally turn to the left and get off that block. The maneuver broke them free of the blue beam and helped close the wide-open faucet of his adrenaline.

Melissa sat up straight in her seat, letting out a heaving breath. "Aliens. I freakin' knew it."

"What?" he replied with surprise. "I'm sure that was a drone."

She tilted her head in his direction, without a hint of humor. "No, aliens caused this. Think about how it makes perfect sense. Get us humans running from each other, then come in and clean up the mess. That little spaceship was primo proof, right sheriff?"

The MRAP rumbled down the four-lane street for many blocks while he caught his breath and considered her wild claim. It was nonsense, but something prevented him from telling her she was off base. In some ways, believing it was aliens was comforting. Up until that point, he'd pretty much assumed the whole zombie disaster was caused by fellow humans. It was kind of nice blaming someone else.

He rode that thought until the next flashpoint.

5

Melissa whipped them through the streets of the western part of downtown St. Louis as fast as the armored truck would go. Before the apocalypse, most streets were two lanes of traffic with a row of parked cars along each side. Now, without the order of parking police, the streets were mostly empty of cars, save a few abandoned or wrecked vehicles. Because they avoided the south and all the zombies in that direction, Melissa had more room to maneuver.

Ten minutes went by before she finally took her foot off the gas.

"Okay, you're right," she said with sadness. "I know it was crazy to suggest it was aliens. I'm not sure why I said that other than it made the most sense to me."

"I wanted to believe that, too," he replied.

"Seriously?"

He nodded and checked his rearview mirror. "It was safer to think of it as a little alien ship. Otherwise, it means some guy anticipated we'd be in that alleyway and he positioned the drone to wait for us to emerge. That's pretty frightening."

"I don't think they're still following us, unless it's hovering right over our heads." She punched the brakes and looked up through the uppermost part of the windshield.

He peered up, too, expecting the drone operator to make a mistake and continue in front of them, but the sky was empty as best he could tell.

"Hmm, did we get away?" she suggested with a voice full of doubt.

"Maybe it's high above?" he replied.

"Or is behind us, hovering in stealth mode, watching." She put her foot back on the gas as if to escape the thought.

"We're definitely on someone's radar," he said calmly. Each new flash of imagination made him less confident in the MRAP. They were in a fortress compared to the threat of the biting zombies, but a modern military could take them out with barely a button press. A bomb, missile, or the most primitive of IED's is all it would take. Whoever built the futuristic-looking drone probably had their own tools for prying them out of the truck.

They drove a few more minutes when he saw salvation.

"I have an IKEA," he said as if a light bulb had come on. He pointed where he wanted her to go.

"All right, I guess. What's that going to get us?"

His excitement was on his sleeve. "I'll show you."

She drove the MRAP onto the empty parking lot for the IKEA store. The big building sat alone in this part of the city. The blue color was partially lit up by the weak head-lights. A gaping rectangular hole stood where the front entrance had been. As they neared and saw the black stains above the doors, it was apparent a fire had consumed the inside.

"In there?" she asked, uncertain.

"Yeah, we can still go in. We don't need furniture. We need a safe place to park."

The crinkle of bent metal and falling glass squealed outside the hull of the truck as Melissa drove through the already-broken entryway. She barely avoided a pair of zombie women shambling near the front door, as if first in line for a sale that would never come.

"Head to the back," he suggested.

They were not the first vehicle through the doors. Several burnt car hulks sat near the exit, which Melissa deftly pushed aside. The tires had been burned away, and the metal wheels screamed as they shifted on the bare concrete.

"Wow, it smells like camping," he said. Once on the road they'd cracked their windows a tiny bit to help clear out the stale air inside the truck, but that hadn't done enough. The odor inside the store was pretty good by comparison.

She took a deep breath. "Must have been all that Swedish wood, or wherever they got it from."

The fire had long since burned itself out, and as best he could see, everything inside the store had been turned to ash. A few piles of junk might have been furniture or sales kiosks, but he couldn't make out anything for certain. Not in the pitch dark with two faulty headlights.

"There you go," he said. He pointed to the blackened EXIT sign over a pair of doors on the back wall.

He unlatched his seatbelt as Melissa pulled up to the doors and flicked off the ignition.

"Beth and I came here the day this store opened. I didn't see what the big deal was, but she was cuckoo over this stuff." He was hit with a wave of nostalgia every bit as potent as the wafting scent of the campfire. He forced himself not to tear up at her memory. As much as he complained about it at the time and joked about it with his brothers and sisters on the force, he did have fun that day. Darcy was there, and—

That made him forget the whole line of thinking.

"There's a stairwell to the roof. Right through there."

"You want us to get out?" she said with disbelief. "What's that get us?"

"Grab a shotty and follow me." He didn't wait for her.

Phil pulled his service pistol from its holster and moved quickly to the back door. He wiped a few tears from his cheek and berated himself for not holding it together. He wanted to be the strong police officer helping the cute girl in distress, but that wasn't the true dynamic.

He felt marginally better by the time she joined him.

"I'm sorry," he said. "I still can't talk about them."

"It's okay," she said softly. "We've got nothing but time." She flicked on her flashlight and kept it pointed at the floor of the truck. The glistening of sticky, dried blood couldn't be ignored.

He tapped on the back doors. "Once we open her, we'll search behind us for a minute, then run to the stairs and go up, if it's all clear."

"Do we lock the truck?" she asked.

He thought about the chances of someone coming along and stealing it from them. They only needed a few minutes, and the store appeared empty and left behind in all the chaos. Besides the two shoppers at the door, they hadn't seen any zombies on the inside.

"No, we'll be quick." He hesitated for a second before adding, "But still take the keys."

She unlatched the door, checked for anyone hanging on to the back or roof of the MRAP—it had happened before— and then hopped down the back steps with a flashlight and a shotgun. He followed her with his pistol pointed at the floor, ready for any possible attack.

They stood there and stared into the vast chamber for about thirty seconds. He fully expected the two zombie women to follow them, but he saw their profiles up by the destroyed front doors.

"I can't believe it's empty back here," he said.

"You think they are smart enough to move on when there is no one left alive?" She shined her flashlight over the ashy sales floor, but no zombies came out of the darkness.

He exhaled with relief.

"I guess they all got called somewhere else."

"Except those two at the front," Mel replied in a quiet voice. "I feel for their plight, and loved this store when it was whole, but let's be honest, how the hell are they going to assemble their furniture being like they are? If I turned zombie, I'd go somewhere else, like the North Face store. Even a zombie should be able to pull on some pants." She quietly let out a nervous laugh.

"You have expensive taste in clothing," he said as if to playfully provoke her.

"I like ... things that last," she replied with an impish smile.

He gulped loudly but didn't allow himself to be drawn into what she meant by that. They were exposed to the world and he had to stay focused on keeping them alive.

"Let's go," he said in a firm way.

After days of experience working as a team, they seamlessly covered each other as they went through the rear doors of the store. It was a little cleaner, as if there was nothing to burn in the bricked hallway. The steps were easy to find, and they went up three long flights before they reached the fire door to the roof. He ignored the stern warning not to use the door except in emergencies.

"Shut off your light," he said quietly. "We want to surprise them."

"Them?"

"The drone operators. If they tracked us from high in the sky, we'll see it looking for us, but we need our eyes to be prepared for near-total darkness out there." He spoke with police efficiency and calm, but instantly got nervous when he looked back to her.

She shuffled right up next to him before she clicked off her light.

"We need a couple of minutes for our eyes to adjust," he said casually. Between the campy fire smell and the powerful mix of perfume and sweat radiating from her body, he felt himself drawn hopelessly in her direction.

"Oh. Really?" she said with sarcasm in the total darkness. "How convenient."

He holstered his gun and heard the distinct sounds of her slinging her shotgun. Before he realized it was an option, she took both his hands while standing in front of him.

"We have to be sure no one is down below," he said, trying to sound sensible while ignoring how much his palms started to perspire.

They stood hand in hand while listening for signs they were followed from the stairwell. Each passing second felt like he was under the intense attraction of a powerful magnet and he seemed to get ever closer to what his steely heart really wanted. If a zombie showed up and ruined his moment, he was going to rip it in half with his bare hands.

"Everything is clear, Phil," she replied after they'd listened for a short time. He felt her voice on his face because she was so close.

"I think we're alone," he said in a whisper.

She let go of his hands and put hers around his waist. When he did the same, his hands slid over her exposed core and his heart reacted by shutting its eyes for a few seconds.

He'd never in his adult life felt shy around women, but Mel made him feel fifteen again.

When she got even closer, her nose bumped his lips.

"What should we do, now?" she said suggestively.

He separated from her a tiny bit, felt for her ponytail, and followed it to the back of her neck. He intended to guide her lips the last couple of inches, but there was no need because she was already on the way. All his fears and doubts temporarily evaporated as she met him with equal passion.

He kissed her like he'd never have another chance and ignored his conscience as it fretted over how much he enjoyed it. Soon, he was overcome with feelings for the woman in his arms, which confused him even further.

Was it wrong? Was it right?

When they finally came up for a breath, Melissa's fingers caressed his wet cheeks, exposing the lie of his tough-guy exterior. "Is this okay?" she asked with tender concern.

He still couldn't see her, which was a relief. Crying never came naturally to him, but the loss of Beth and Darcy had broken something in his soul. Giving himself to another woman so soon felt like a betrayal of his heart, but he knew in his brain his wife would approve of his choice.

"I need you, Mel, as much as I need my sidearm, my St. Michael, or even food. I couldn't be here standing in this nightmare darkness without you, but it's going to take me some time to square up my past, although I do think Beth would have loved you."

"You're sweet. I promise I'll make your wife proud, but I need you, too. We make a good team."

"That's undeniable," he replied with renewed optimism.

"So, sweet guy, did you plan this whole thing to get me

up here in the dark, so we could lock lips like two high schoolers in the A/V room?"

He chuckled. "I wish I was that smart. I was in police mode until I needed those two minutes. It just worked out." She couldn't see him shrug his shoulders.

"Well, police pursuit, you caught me. I don't know how you did it, honestly. Not after all the mean things I called you when we first met. But I'm glad you didn't give up on me back then, or today, in the truck."

"I guess I just like take-charge women," he joked.

She pulled back, as if trying to get a good look at his face. "You mean like the slobbering mess of a failure I was at the stadium?"

"Eh, don't sweat it. You got them all out. That's what counts. You're allowed a bad day." He reached up and ran a hand through her bangs. "Maybe that's when I knew I kinda liked you," he added.

"But you stayed with me when the plane took off. That was before you kinda liked me, right?" Even in the dark he could tell she was smiling as she said that last bit.

"Maybe I thought about you once or twice before today," he agreed. "When you didn't get out and run, I couldn't leave you. I wasn't looking for romance out here," he admitted, "but it found me. Who knows? I guess I had to see your bad side before I could appreciate your good side. I also sort of thought you were too strong-willed even for me."

"Now what do you think I am?"

"I think you're human. In a world full of zombies and endless zombie killing, I find that very attractive."

"Yeah, I like you, too," she replied.

"It's settled," he mused. "We're officially in like with each other."

They both laughed easily.

"Shall we seal this date by breaching the door?" she pecked him on the lips, then released him. He reluctantly let his fingers slide from her waist. They both got their weapons back out and in their hands.

"I thought you'd never ask," he replied while touching the emergency push bar.

"On three?"

"Yep," he said.

"One, two, three."

Together they pushed through the door and took a few tentative steps beyond.

Blue light went right into their faces.

"Well, shit," he said in a beat-down voice. "I guess they followed us, after all."

"Run or shoot?" she asked urgently.

The floating disc was thirty feet above, just far enough they couldn't hear the quiet whir of the fans. White running lights came on, like it was no longer afraid of being seen, and two black gun barrels projected from underneath. He might have chosen to fight it out if they weren't already zeroed in on them.

"Neither," he replied. "It has guns."

"We give up," he said in its direction, feeling exactly like he imagined all those teen kids he'd busted.

The drone descended until it was only a few feet above them. The wash of the blades felt like the beginnings of a strong storm.

They set down their guns at the same time, but he grabbed Melissa's hands instead of raising his arms in surrender.

"It was a great first date," he declared.

"I was looking forward to making you even more uncomfortable on our second," she said with a futile laugh.

"You might still get your chance," he replied. "At least we know they aren't aliens." He pointed to the faint words painted on the underside of the hull. "United States Air Force."

She squeezed his hand while they stood together to await their fate.

ABOUT E.E. ISHERWOOD

E.E. Isherwood is the New York Times and USA Today best-selling author of the Sirens of the Zombie Apocalypse series. He has designs for many other dystopian and post-apocalyptic science fiction and fantasy novels. His long-time fascination with the end of the world blossomed decades ago after reading the 1949 classic Earth Abides. Zombies are just a handy vehicle allowing him to observe how society breaks down in the face of such withering calamity.

Isherwood lives in St. Louis, Missouri with his wife and family. He stays deep in a bunker with steepled fingers, always awaiting the arrival of the first wave of zombies.

16

MORE FROM THE REANIMATED WRITERS

UNDEAD WORLDS 1

If you enjoyed Undead Worlds 2,
get Undead Worlds 1 Now!
www.reanimatedwriters.com/uw

THE REANIMATED RUMBLE

2 authors write a story based on the same theme,
you decide who wins!
Check out the first ever Reanimated Rumble!
www.reanimatedwriters.com/rumble/

REANIMATED WRITERS PODCAST

Join host RJ Spears as he interviews the authors you love
to read!
www.reanimatedwriters.com/podcast

FACEBOOK FAN GROUP

If you've enjoyed these stories and want to meet and
hangout with authors and fans, come find us on Facebook
and join the
Reanimated Writers Facebook Fan Group!

There is something happening just about everyday, games,
prizes, author takeovers, live events and more! Come
interact with your favorite authors and your fellow fans!

You can also find us on Instagram & Twitter!

REANIMATED MERCH

Get our latest designs and more at
www.reanimatedwriters.com/tees